BURNING SON

ALEX REED

Austin, Texas

PUBLISHER'S NOTE

Printed and published in the United States of America
Violet Crown Publishers

ISBN-13: 978-1-938749-08-7

ISBN-10: 1938749081

Also Available In Digital Format on Amazon.Com

ISBN-13: 978-1-938749-09-4

ISBN-10: 193874909X

This one is for the heroes, in their own way, at their own time.

BURNING SON

CHAPTER ONE

The Return

Jake Weathers pulled the truck from the barn to the house, still dripping wet. After opening the truck door, Jake slipped out of the seat and let his boots hit the ground. The brace on his left leg creaked familiarly, the same brace that had kept him home when others left for the war; the same brace he wore morning, noon, and night. He shut the door behind him and looked up. His father stood on the porch.

Sam Weathers had a young face for his years, but his dark eyes didn't have the fight they once did. The gray that peppered his hair was the only sign of his age. His medium build half-filled the doorway.

"It's ready." Jake pointed to the truck. "Good thing it rained last night, it'll keep the dust settled on our way into town."

His father looked him over once, his gaze stopping to stare at the brace on his leg once more, like always.

Jake took a step to the side.

"Is that what you're wearing?" his father said.

"Uh... no. I was just about to go put on something

nicer," said Jake. It wasn't true.

"Well, hurry up. We've got to get to town soon. It's not every day that your brother comes home from the second world war." His dad went inside.

Jake climbed the porch stairs and entered the house. The family home had a peaceful feel with walls colored in deep green and the floor covered in aged wood. Pictures of all the years of their family covered the wall. Couches sat facing a dormant fireplace.

He walked down the hall and up the stairs to his room. It was just a place he slept. A bed and dresser lined the bare walls. It could have been anybody's and nobody's room. A large window gave a view of the ranch that rolled away before him.

He glanced in the mirror. The dark hair and eyes were familiar, as was his slim build. Jake wiped some dirt from his cheek on a face worn beyond its years.

As he started to take off his shirt, he got the sensation up his spine that someone was watching him. "Is there a little monster in here?" A little grin came across his face.

Giggles from the closet confirmed his suspicion.

"Aha!" He yanked the door open and grabbed his kid sister Gracie from inside. He hoisted her up in his arms and softly dropped her on the mattress and began to tickle her. She laughed out loud, having all the fun in the world.

"Well, hey, kid, are you ready to go see Aaron?"

She stopped and looked at him. Then she clapped and laughed again, not in the way of a twelve-year-old, but as a two- or three-year-old would. No doctor had ever been able to tell what was wrong with her. They threw all sorts of fancy diagnoses at the family. Her body had grown, but her mind had not. But there she sat, her curly mess of short blonde hair fluffing in every direction. Her eyes were full of nothing but love.

Jake gave a little whistle and some soft tones to help her refocus. She looked at him. "Are you ready to go see Aaron?"

He asked again. She didn't respond. It occurred to him Gracie might not know who Aaron was. She was only eight when he left and could have forgotten him.

"Huh, well, you'll figure it out... hey, hey, go wait for me downstairs. I'll be right there."

She didn't move at first but Jake kept encouraging her until she did. Jake took off his work shirt and searched through all the garments in his closet. He reached for one, hesitated, then reached for another and another. He knew he'd never pick the right one so he settled on a shirt he wore to church.

The little girl waited at the big oak table. Rosalia poured little Gracie a glass of milk. The girl carefully held the big glass with both hands.

"You off to go pick up Aaron?" she said, her warm eyes meeting his, as gray strands framed her face.

"Yes, ma'am."

"Well, you hold on tight to that child. Don't let her fall out the truck."

"Finished!" Little Gracie announced as she put her glass down on the table. She brandished an obnoxious milk mustache.

"*Buena hija*, now you go with your brother." She patted Gracie on the back.

Gracie took Jake's hand and they turned to head out.

"Jake...," Rosalia called.

He looked back at her.

She held up his hat and smiled.

He took it from her. "Sorry."

Rosalia laughed to herself and began to hum as they walked out.

Sam Weathers waited in the car. Riding shotgun was Carl, who had worked for them so many years, he seemed more like family.

Carl had grown gray with many years of service. A little belly began to creep over his belt. Decades of work gave him a little bend when he walked.

"CARL!" Gracie screamed with a smile on her face.

"Hello, young lady," Carl said with a warm voice. They smiled at each other as the truck fired up.

"Take your sister and climb in," called Mr. Weathers.

"You know, boss, we could use a larger car. These pickups aren't enough for getting the family to town." Carl set his hand on the door handle.

Jake climbed into the back of the truck and, once Gracie got settled in his lap, took firm hold of her. Sam pulled away from the ranch house and onto the mile-long driveway. Only a few months ago, this part of the ranch looked like the scorched surface of the sun. Some of the lush now returned and the animals started to put on some home today."

"He is," Jake said.

"Are you excited?"

"It's been a long time."

"I know! I wonder if he'll even recognize me."

"I'm sure it won't be a problem," Jake said. Aaron never had a problem recognizing pretty girls.

While she gushed about his brother and high school, Jake managed to order Gracie a chocolate shake and asked for a piece of foil so Gracie could fold it into different shapes and entertain herself. It was impressive how long Mary-Lou could keep on talking. He remembered watching her laugh with Aaron during high school.

The shake and tin foil kept Gracie occupied for an hour, more than Jake could have hoped for. They only got out of the diner by promising Mary-Lou he would tell Aaron she said hello.

Jake took Gracie over to the elementary school, a school she could never attend, to let her play on the swing set. His limp-legged pace wasn't quite fast enough. She broke away and was waiting in her swing by the time he was ready to push her.

"Are you ready to fly?" he said.

"YEP!" she called.

"Let me see your pilot face!"

She furrowed her brow and clamped her mouth shut, trying to look discerning and serious. It must have been the way she pictured pilots.

Jake made engine noises as he pulled her back and

hoisted her into the air. The engine climaxed and he launched her into the blue. She rode that arch high into the air. He wondered what kind of plane she imagined herself in. He knew she left him far behind while he was at the playground and she was miles away on her imaginary adventure. She laughed like it was the first time a human had ever discovered laughter.

He looked at his watch and had to flag her down onto the runway for a landing. It was half past eleven. He figured they should get back to where the bus would arrive. Gracie wanted a piggy-back ride, so he knelt down and she climbed aboard. She rode into the parking lot on her limp horse.

The crowd had gathered in the parking lot. Scheduled to arrive on the bus were three young men, back home from Europe and the South Pacific. Between their families, friends, acquaintances and all folks just ready to be part of a crowd, it seemed half the town had showed up. Old Crane high school rolled out the marching band. Looking stately, Crane's veterinarian/mayor stood with his grandchildren. Half the shops had hung "closed" signs in the windows.

The carefree morning Gracie and Jake shared vanished in the buzz of the crowd. Jake lifted her off his shoulders and led her into the crowd by the hand. He took slow, deliberate movements so as not to limp too drastically. He hoped to pass through unnoticed. Carl and his father were ahead.

His dad waved him over. "Where have you been?" Mr. Weathers said. "You almost missed him. The sheriff already left to meet the bus at the county line."

Twenty minutes later the flashing lights came into view. The sheriff led the heroes' chariot into the borders of Crane. The crowd lit up and cheered.

Gracie pulled in tight to Jake. She covered her ears at the deafening noise.

The bus driver sounded the horn and the crowd got even louder. The driver pulled into the parking lot and stopped at the most prominent place.

The first few civilians looked lost as they got off the bus. Cheers faded as a preacher, an old woman, and a preteen boy arrived instead of soldiers. Just when the crowd began to lose hope, the trumpets sounded and the heavens opened as the first hometown hero appeared. He was clad in an olive drab uniform, square shouldered and iron jawed. The crowd erupted as if it was their first time to shout all day. The small marching band played like it was the Fourth of July.

Matthew Gibson, the grocery store owner's son, had escaped death from the Nazis only to be suffocated by his mother. His round-bellied father was close behind.

Then, there he was. The one who left Jake at the ranch so long ago to fight in the second great world war. The crowd cheered. Jake gazed at his brother's celebrity good looks and square chin. His barrel chest and square shoulders filled the bus door. Jake had watched Aaron be everyone's favorite kid his whole life. His brother charmed the gathering with his wave.

Jake sighed.

At last the moment no longer belonged to the crowd, but to the family. Jake stood back as his father broke through the gathered mass to throw his arms around his golden son, in a drawn-out but sincere embrace. Their smiles showed Jake the truth.

The crowd clapped for the hero and the father who raised him. Their embrace broke and Mr. Weathers opened toward the crowd and showed them his son. After the final cheers, the noise died down to a low rumble.

Aaron turned towards Carl. "Well hey, Carl." He shook the old man's hand. "You didn't take my room, did you?" They chuckled together.

Aaron made his way towards Jake. "Hello, gimpie!" Gracie raised her arms toward him, but he just patted her on the head. He pulled Jake into a hug. "You missed me," Aaron said. "Didn't you? I can tell!" He wouldn't release him. Then he reached down and tapped on Jake's brace.

Jake pulled his leg away like a snail dragging its head back into its shell.

"How bad did you mess up the ranch while I was gone?"

"Nothing you can't fix," Sam Weathers said. He and Aaron laughed. "You're probably tired, let's head home. Jake, grab his bag and load up." Their father walked back to the car with his arm around his son.

Jake stood watching the pair walk away, once again reminded he was an outsider. Aaron had their father and their father had Aaron. Jake was not part of their team. If there was ever anything he wanted, he would have to get it on his own.

And just when the crowd's energy seemed to be waning, Mr. Weathers climbed onto the hood of the truck and faced the people of Crane. "Everyone! And I mean **everyone** is invited tonight to the old Weathers Ranch for a welcome home party in honor of my son, Aaron!"

The crowd hooted and hollered like they were at a rodeo. With that, the Weathers family rolled out of town.

Sam and Aaron sat up front in the cab. Carl, Gracie, and Jake huddled in the pickup bed. Jake watched his father and brother laugh it up all the way home and it wasn't long before they turned down the Weathers' long driveway.

"There she is!" Aaron yelled and slapped the side of the truck when he saw the house. They pulled up and Rosalia came out onto the doorstep.

"Aaron!" she sang from the porch.

"Rosalia!" He ran up the steps and gave her a big hug. "Even all those French women couldn't make me forget you!" He released her, turned and burst through the door of the house, leaving it wide open. "Is my old room ready?"

As Carl pulled Aaron's luggage out of the back of the truck, their father turned to Jake. "You know that small twenty or so that stick to the north fence of the Mesa pasture?" Sam said. "There's a red heifer, the one that's got that sheen in the coat, you know the one?"

Jake nodded.

"Go get it from the herd for the party tonight. Get it on the spick and ready to go. Then help set up some of the tables in the barn."

"Yes, sir," Jake said as his father walked away. He took Gracie inside and, after changing out of his nice shirt, threw on his gun belt. Then he reached into the drawer and pulled out his 1911 Colt and slung it at his side. He patted it as it hung.

Jake left Gracie in the kitchen with Rosalia. The two of them would work on food for the party.

Jake left the house and limped over to a horse pen by the barn. He didn't have to wait long or whistle. He petted Rio's side and neck and led him into the barn. After throwing a saddle on the stallion, Jake climbed aboard and smiled for the first time all day. They headed away from the ranch house in no time.

On a horse, he was equal, not slower than everyone else. He would never come in last or watch people move away from him. When the horse's four legs replaced his leg-and-a-half, he could keep up. More than that, he spent enough time with the Mexican cowboys to learn a thing or two. He gave Rio a little nudge and the pair tore across their ranch.

After twenty-five minutes of hard riding, Jake eased Rio down the slope toward the Laurel River that split the land in two. A bridge waited a mile farther south for vehicles, but Jake crossed here. The water splashed around the horse as they made their way through to the other side. They came over the next hill and looked down on the Mesa pasture. The small herd grazed to the northeast. He rode down the ridge and followed the fence line over to the cattle.

He approached and pulled the rope from his saddle. He threw a loop around the red heifer's neck... it really was a good-looking animal. He pulled and led the animal back to the ranch house.

Jake tied the heifer in the barn and put Rio in the corral. He called over some of the ranch hands. They took wood from the burn pile and started a big fire in the spick pit. While the flames burned down, Jake and Carl brought picnic tables out of the barn and set them outside and straightened the inside of the barn. By now, the fire had settled and was ready to cook meat.

Jake limped over to the heifer and led it behind the barn. It stood there calmly, ignorant to the end. Jake jerked the Colt from his holster and took one last look around. Whenever he slaughtered animals, he always took care to make sure that Gracie wasn't present.

Jake and Carl skinned and gutted the animal. They put the spick through it. With help from some of the other ranch hands, they hoisted it up over the fire. Rosalia basted it and Carl threw some mesquite wood onto the coals to give the beef flavor. It was now late afternoon and the band arrived to set up.

When Mr. Gibson found out that Sam Weathers already asked the band to play, he decided to "combine" parties and have his family and friends celebrate the return of Matthew with the rest of the county.

Dusk came and the smell of that barbecue blanketed the air. Rosalia carried trays of cookies, cakes, and ribs. Someone set out the lemonade and beer. The ranch hands were ready to help guests park their cars. They lit a few fires here and there for ambiance.

Jake took a shower and washed away the dirt. He strapped on his brace and headed outside. Gracie came running from the house. She wanted him to marvel at the bow in her hair. He did, and she smiled.

Aaron joined them in the yard. "Is everyone ready for my party?"

Jake cringed.

Aaron snagged a cookie from the table and took a bite. "What? No champagne? All the way back from Europe and no champagne?" He slapped Jake on the back. "I'm just kidding, brother, it looks great."

Jake gave a half laugh.

"Jake, don't distract your brother," hollered Mr. Weathers as he arrived from the house. "He's got guests to entertain."

Before long, headlights showed down the road. The crowds poured in. Soon everyone was there. It seemed like the entire county came.

The band played and the tops of the beer bottles popped. The food was good and the dessert was sweet. The mayor managed to get control of the carving knife and took over trimming portions off the roasting cow and passing it to the crowd.

"Trying to keep the constituents well fed?" a county judge said.

"That's the trick to staying in office fifteen years." The mayor laughed.

Husbands took their chance on the dance floor, two-stepping with their wives. Mary-Lou found Aaron and got him out on the dance floor... so did Kate, Jenny, and Anne.

Gracie and Jake sat at a table on the outskirts most of the time. Gracie liked to watch big crowds but didn't like being trapped in the middle of them. Jake didn't even like watching them. To the town folks, he was either "the other Weathers boy" or "the cripple."

A few guests sat down at the lonely table to visit Jake. Most of them asked all the same questions. Was he excited about his brother's return? How was the herd? How was Gracie these days or had she improved in any way? He wanted to say there was nothing wrong with Gracie, but he just responded that she was the same as she had always been.

The preacher also came over. He talked about the weather and asked Jake how he was, all sorts of questions.

Jake always felt like the preacher must worry about his soul because he was so quiet in church. He just humored the man until he left to talk to other sheep of his flock.

While Aaron was busy dancing with Jenny, one of the girls who waited for him came over and asked Jake to dance. He said he needed to watch Gracie. She shrugged and walked away.

"Sorry," he called after her. He'd rather frustrate her than be exposed on the dance floor. He checked Gracie. The pie had gotten the better of her. She was wearing it, not eating it. His frown became a grin as he wiped off her face

When the song ended, Sam Weathers took the stage, a raised platform the roughnecks had erected that afternoon. He called to everyone. The noise died down and they turned to face him.

"Ladies and gentlemen," he began. "Friends and family! Thank y'all so much for being here to celebrate the return of my son!"

Everyone cheered.

"Five years ago, America called him and he responded. He bravely left home behind and went to a place far away. But he **had** to go. He **had** to let those Nazis know that they should never mess with America! And he **had** to represent Texas!"

Thunderous applause rose from the crowd.

"As a father, I couldn't be more proud... in fact, where is he?" His eyes searched the crowd. "Son?"

The guests around Aaron parted and encouraged him to the front. He stood before his father.

"Son, I am so proud of you. You've grown into more than I ever could have hoped for and I am so thankful you've found your way home and ready to take your place as my partner on the ranch!" He hugged his son.

Partner? Jake whipped his head up and stared wide-eyed.

Still more joyous chorus from the crowd arose. They demanded an appearance from Aaron. "Speech! Speech! Speech!"

Aaron took a weak step away but came back twice as fast. He waved away the crowd's applause, yet beamed in it. "Thanks, everyone, thanks. Thanks, Dad. You know, when I was over there it was hard, real hard. You never knew when a German bullet was going to hit you in the head."

Aaron glanced at Mary-Lou, who licked her lips. Jake wasn't sure anyone else had noticed.

Aaron continued. "But whenever I was tired and thought I had no more to give, I'd remember what I was fighting for. I'd think about Crane and Miss Nancy's Apple Pie. I'd think of the kids at the elementary and First Baptist. I'd think of walking down Main and waving at friends. Mr. Thompson opening his shop and all the teenagers gathered at the diner. And I knew I was fighting for y'all!"

He finished to the patriotic cheers of those who felt so touched at his words. After all, he had fought for them. Aaron left the stage and somehow managed, even with so many eyes watching him, to slip off with Mary-Lou, his first girl of the night.

Ricky Tremble, Aaron's best friend from high school, snagged the chair next to Jake. "How's it going there, Jakie Boy?" He tapped Jake's brace.

Jake pulled his leg under the table and looked into Ricky's bloodshot eyes. His brother's friend had a brewery on his breath. "Hi, Ricky."

"How come you never visit me down at the store?" he said.

"I don't know... I'm usually pretty busy here."

"You don't like me... you've never liked me," Ricky slurred his words.

"Of course I like you, I've known you forever." Jake leaned as far away from Ricky as he could without falling out of his chair. Ricky was a large person and he was drunk.

If he had some crazy impulse to flip over the table or push Jake, Gracie might get hurt.

"Ricky, how come you're not after a girl tonight?" Jake said.

Ricky just stared ahead, unable to make eye contact.

"Yeah, Ricky, all these girls want to dance and you're over here holding out on them," Jake continued. "Get out there."

Ricky got a little sick grin and headed off. Jake slipped away and put Gracie to bed. He didn't bother to return to the party. He was done for the night.

People stayed for hours. At last, the final beer had been drunk and the embers of the fire burned out. It was finally quiet on the Weathers' Ranch. Jake sat up in bed with his father's words echoing in his head... *Aaron, partner?* Jake never thought of this but was pretty sure he didn't like it.

Growing old on the ranch was all Jake figured he'd ever do. *What if Aaron changes all that?*

CHAPTER 2

The Wisdom of Carl

The alarm clock went off at 6:00 a.m. as it did every morning for years and years. Jake reached out and turned it off. Pulling the covers back, he felt the warm air trapped under his blanket escape and surrender him to the chilly morning air. As he reached over and turned on his lamp, his bare feet hit the wood floor.

He reached for his clothes. The snapping of the brace around his leg signaled he could stand. The peppermint of his toothpaste woke up his mouth. One of the perks of working on a ranch all day was that combing his hair got replaced by wearing a hat. Showering during the morning was in vain, as sweat was always soon to follow. He threw on his shirt and headed downstairs, taking the creaking floorboards past Aaron's room as quietly as possible.

Downstairs, Mr. Weathers and the ranch hands waited for breakfast. The crackle of frying bacon came from the kitchen.

Rosalia waved her spatula. *"Buenos días, mi hijo."*

"Morning," Jake said.

Rosalia wasn't quite finished so Jake went outside and crossed to the barn. Carl had already saddled up his horse, Duke. Jake whistled Rio over from the coral and took him into the barn. He put on the horse's tack.

"Jake, how'd you sleep?"

"Okay, you?"

"Real well. I like it when the air takes on a little chill. Helps the beard grow healthy." He stroked his clean-shaven face.

Some of the ranch hands milked cows in the barn. Everyone followed Jake and Carl into the house. Rosalia set the table for them.

Carl looked up from his meal. "Peter, Larry, you two head on to Big Feather pasture and open the east gate. Wait for the trucks to show up. Jim, Juan, head to the south side of the ranch. Between the river and Big Boulder, the fence needs mending. Carlos, Mitt, come with Jake and me to gather some mature heads for market."

"Keep an eye out for Aaron." Mr. Weathers set his coffee cup down. "He says he can't wait to get back in the saddle. I'm sure he'll join y'all today."

"Maybe, but he's been enjoying his bed a lot since he got home a week ago." Carl spread butter over a slice of toast.

"He just needs to catch up on his rest. He earned it."

"Of course."

"Well, I'm off to the office." Mr. Weathers swallowed the last of his coffee and left the cup at his place.

"Which trucks be coming this week?" Pete said.

Carl looked over. "Midland today, Tidwell Company tomorrow, J&R Slaughter house on Friday. We got good bids this time."

"I'd like to see an auction some day." Pete took another bite of eggs.

"You'd have to go to the stockyards for that," Larry said. "Carl, you gonna give us any time off so we can go into the big city?"

Carl grinned. "I wouldn't count on it."

"How many young'uns you figure we got growed up enough since last spring?" Mitt said.

"More than plenty. It's been a good year." Carl looked around the table. "Let's go to work."

The crew finished breakfast and headed off. Jake was on his way to the barn when two of the mutts at the ranch, Coyote and Axle, came out of the early morning. They looked guilty, like they had already been up to no good. Jake stopped to pet them.

Pete and Larry drove the truck down the driveway and turned onto the highway, taking the route on paved roads. Jim and Juan took a wagon with timber, tools, and fencing. They headed to the back of the ranch. The rest of the boys rode towards Big Feather.

The sunrise sent silky textures as orange chased the horizon, blanketing the view with warmth. The crew rode two men in front and two men in back at an easy pace. Thirty-six steers were needed for today's shipment. When they arrived, the cowboys found a small herd on the near side of Big Feather and started working them towards the gate on the far side. Carl led the way.

Carlos and Mitt rode on either side to keep them from spreading out and Jake pushed from behind. He spoke to them to get them moving. "Keep on, keep on."

Twenty minutes later, they got the steers to the gate Peter and Larry had opened for the trucks. After they backed the trucks in and opened the doors, the riders separated out the cattle that were big enough and funneled them onto the trailers. Steel ramps echoed and hooves clicked. A man stood on either side of the ramp so the animals wouldn't get too close to the edge until they loaded twenty-seven. They found nine more and got them on the truck.

"All right boys," Carl called from his horse. "Nice work."

"That's all?" Pete pulled his horse near the rest of the crew.

"Yeah, thirty-six," Carl said.

"We'll go check the tanks in the Back Forty, then."

With the transaction completed, the trucks left and Pete and Larry locked up the gate and drove to the front of the ranch. The rest made their way back as well. On the way, Jake noticed a tree had fallen into one off the irrigation canals they dug from the river, slowing the flow of water.

Carl looked the problem over. "Gonna need to take care of that."

At the barn, Jake and Carl loaded chains and drove the tractor back to the canal. Jake climbed down into the muddy creek bank. Muck swallowed his braced leg as he waded through the ditch. He looped chains around the trunk and connected them to the back of the tractor.

Carl waited for Jake to get out of the way and gave the John Deere a little gas and let it work. Deep treads in the tires dug into the West Texas soil and crawled away as it pulled on the trunk. And so the tug-of-war began. The old tree fought from where it rested.

The log lurched as the chains stretched taut, but the tree got caught on something and Jake watched it bend. He tried to holler at Carl but the trunk snapped in half. The chains whipped away with violent force, slapping a rock. Sparks flew.

Carl stopped the tractor. "Damn." He wiped his brow. "This just got harder."

The two dug the tree free and dragged the first half out. Then they replaced the chains on the other half and pulled it out. Now that the blockage was removed, the water flowed more freely. Jake climbed out of the ditch coated in mud.

They arrived back at the house and pulled the tractor into the barn. Jake crossed to the porch.

Aaron sat on the swing in his pajamas, sipping a beer. He held a second one in his other hand "Here you go, Gimpie." Aaron tossed Jake the bottle. "You're pretty dirty for before noon."

Jake took a seat and popped the cap on the bottle.

"You look as dirty as we did over in Europe when we dug in after we heard artillery coming." Aaron pointed his bottle towards the mud that covered Jake. "Yes, sir, brother, I envy you. Not having to go over there. Getting to stay safe here on the ranch, working."

Jake half nodded.

"You probably think I'm lazy, don't you? Not being up? Not helping on the ranch yet."

"Nah, Aaron, I know you're still tired from the war."

"Yeah, it was tiring. You never knew when you were going to get a German bullet in your head. But I would just think, *this is for Crane*! And you, too, brother, I fought for you."

"Thank you." Jake didn't know what else to say.

"Yeah, war makes lots of men scared," Aaron nodded. "But it's when the fireworks start that the real grit is tested. Something happens in you. A hero wakes up."

"A hero?"

"Yeah, you just react." Aaron nodded to himself and looked pensive.

The screen door opened. "What's going on out here, boys?" Mr. Weathers came out. "Is Aaron telling you about his adventures?"

"Yes, sir," Jake nodded.

"Yep, giving a taste of the exotic to this country boy here," Aaron said.

"Good, good, good... that's great... so... Aaron, are you going to be here tonight around six?" their father said.

"Sure."

"Perfect, I've got one last little treat for the big hero," their dad grinned.

Rosalia's voice calling them in for lunch interrupted the moment.

After lunch Jake got back in the saddle. He headed to

a lowland part of the ranch, found the gulley and worked north. Jake had set some traps for coyotes. The wild dogs often watered there in the gulley as even in dry months there was always some low lying water.

The first steel traps were empty. He left them alone, not wanting to contaminate the area with the scent of a human.

The third trap was a different story. Jake slid out of his saddle and used the crowbar he brought to pry open the trap. A small male had gotten his leg caught and died there. From the looks of it, the animal hadn't been dead for more than a day. Rigor mortis had not yet set in.

Jake reset the trap and hung the animal over the back of Rio. He got back in the saddle and kept working farther towards the rest of the traps.

He heard the hog before he saw it. As Jake came around the corner of the gulley, the beast shrieked the most haunting of sounds. He was a big one, almost 250 pounds.

The boar tried to charge the horse and rider. His forefoot was caught in the trap and pulled him off short.

Jake got off Rio and walked up to the monster. He stood close and stared hard into its hateful eyes. There were wild animals, and then there were monsters. This creature snapped its terrible jaws. Razor sharp cutters, a vicious weapon, stuck out past its nose.

Jake's nearness infuriated the animal more still. The beast looked at Jake as though it hated Jake with everything it had, yanking harder at the trap holding it back. By now, the chain had come loose under the strength of the beast, giving the foul-smelling animal a few more inches closer to

Jake.

Jake yanked the Colt 1911 from its holster and fired a round right between the devil creature's eyes. Even with lead through its skull, it took a moment for the hog to slow its thrashing. When enough blood shed, it lay down. Jake put another bullet in its lungs. After Jake pried open the trap and let its leg out, he reset the trap and hid it in the brush again.

"You ready to work?" He took a rope from Rio's saddle and looped it around the hind legs of the hog. He tied the other end of the rope to the horn on his saddle and led Rio up the side of the gulley, dragging the hog's corpse through the dust. Jake and Rio made their way about a quarter mile to the nearest dead pit, a big hole where they tossed carcasses.

After the gun went off, the vultures had circled. Jake tossed the coyote into the pit and cut the hog free. It slid down the side of the pit on top of skeletons. Jake wrapped up his rope and got back on Rio. The turkey vultures flew in and started to tear the carcass apart.

The rest of the afternoon bled away. Before long it was after five o'clock. Jake wondered how Gracie had spent her day, hoping she missed him. When he got home, she came running out of the house wearing one of her dad's old coats. It looked more like a cape on her. Jake tied Rio off at the fence just in time to catch his sister and sweep her up into the air.

"Swing!" she pleaded.

Jake took her to a tire swing they had set up in the

barn, tied to one of the crossbeams. Jake made sure she sat secure and gave her a good push. She laughed and laughed.

"I've got stuff to do." Jake helped her down.

Arms raised, Gracie looked at him with hopeful eyes.

"Okay, one more big push, then we've got to quit."

A while later he led Gracie out of the barn at the sound of a car pulling up. His father greeted a man in a nice suit.

"Jake, this is Mr. Woodland, all the way from Midland."

Jake and Mr. Woodland shook hands.

"He's here to measure your brother for a suit."

Jake thought even a stranger could guess the man's profession. He was out of place, walking a ranch in such fancy clothes. And it wasn't just a suit, but a really gaudy one, something from a magazine. "Really," said Jake. "All the way from Midland?"

"I was over measuring the mayor and your dad fetched me here to get one for your brother as well..." He studied Jake's clothes until Jake squirmed. "What about you, young man, do you need a suit as well?"

"No, no, no." Mr. Weathers grinned. "Jake doesn't need one. Never has call to dress up."

"Oh, hooked on the old ranch?" Mr. Woodland laughed. "I've met that type as well."

"Yes, sir," Jake pulled their eyes off him by pointing out the window. "Where is Aaron?"

Mr. Weathers looked around, "I'm not sure, I told him to be here at six... oh well, you know Aaron."

"Yeah," Jake said. "I know Aaron." He excused himself, saying that he had some work to do. He went inside and read Gracie a short story from Mother Goose.

Jake watched through the front window when Aaron finally came down the driveway at 6:45. He wasn't alone. In such a tiny town as Crane, he managed to find a girl Jake had never seen before. She leaned against the hood of the truck and rocked her hips slowly back and forth. Aaron sauntered inside to Mr. Woodland. Mr. Weathers instructed Rosalia to bring out a full-length mirror for the suit maker.

Their father grinned from ear to ear as he watched Mr. Woodland stretch the measuring tape across Aaron's shoulders and down the length of his arms. Aaron made predictable jokes when his inseam was taken. Mr. Woodland brought out samples of fabrics and colors. They talked about how to cut the cuffs around the ankles.

"You know, this pant cuff looks really good with these gorgeous loafers we order from New York... what size foot have you got there? Eleven?" Mr. Woodland was no rookie when it came to selling his products. "Yeah, these shoes would really complete the whole suit."

Aaron looked at his dad.

"Well then, get him a pair!" said Mr. Weathers, and just like that Mr. Woodland had sold a pair of very expensive shoes.

Jake looked through the window at the sun loitering considerably lower in the sky then when they started. The suit maker wound the measuring tape and barely got out the words "We're finished" when Aaron raced out the door and pulled the truck onto the highway.

Mr. Woodland stayed for dinner with the family and talked to Mr. Weathers long after. Jake and Gracie listened to the radio for a while. Gracie swayed to and fro with the rhythm, or bounced with the drums. Then Jake read her another story. A little while later he put her to bed. She, of course, needed a piggy-back ride to her bedroom.

After she was all tucked in, the porch was empty and Jake took a spot on the porch swing. A nice breeze offered him company. On the ranch the views were always beautiful and the aromas were constant, but only when he slowed down could Jake hear the land. He sat still and listened to steers lowing far in the distance. Horses neighed softly over in the corral. Crickets serenaded the night in. Wind wove between and out of the mesquite brush.

He rocked back and forth, lifting his leg to keep his brace out of the motion so it wouldn't creak. Carl came across the way from one of the back houses where the ranch hands lived. Jake nodded to him.

The old man climbed the porch steps. "Is this seat taken?"

Jake slid over and Carl sat down. The wood bent as he settled in.

"Just took a look under the tractor. There's a bad crack in the fuel tank. Have to replace it, nothing we can weld. Going to Odessa for the tank, maybe next week."

"Okay." Jake had more to say, a thought they had both entertained over the past few days, the same one that always came with this time of year. Even in the silence the conversation already played out in their heads.

Carl finally broke the trance. "Jake, next week is the day."

"I know."

"We'll have to start watching your dad."

"I think so."

"I've been wondering how your brother's return will effect your father. Maybe it'll be easy this year."

"I hope so," Jake said. But it was never easy.

Carl pulled out his pipe and filled the bowl with tobacco. He struck the match and, with slow, deliberate breaths, it blazed to life. The smoke was rich and curled away into the night. "Your dad has gotten worse over the last couple of years," Carl drew from his pipe. "A large part of it had to do with Aaron being away. I mean, you know how much your dad likes Aaron."

Jake didn't say anything. No one would guess that such a steady owner of a successful ranch would be brought down by a day that came once a year. Sam Weathers walked the streets of Crane as normal as the next person, but Jake knew what the man hid inside.

"Aaron is his favorite person on earth," Jake said.

"This is true... all the same, let's try and get the liquor out of the house in the next few days. We can hide it in the bunkhouse." Carl tasted the tobacco. "Have you talked to Aaron about it?"

"Not really, he's seems pretty busy."

"Maybe bring it up in a day or so." Carl blew a smoke ring that drifted out and dissolved. "We have to check the tanks in the high country. There won't be any rain up there for a while."

"What makes you say that?" Jake said.

"The spiders behind the bunkhouse took the time to build nests in those bushes. They wouldn't bother if it was gonna rain. Now, while that's not exactly scientific theory, it's always proved itself in my experience." Carl smiled, acting like the whole thing was a joke.

In Jake's experience, the old man was always right. "Hey, Carl?"

"Yes, sir?"

"How'd you know this place was for you? I mean, you've traveled. You could have lived anywhere. What brought you back here?"

Carl settled back in his seat. "I did travel, didn't I? Far and wide. Held all those different jobs, even fell in love. My soul was wild, looking for something, I suppose. I didn't know what." He exhaled a thick puff of smoke. "And then I figured it all out."

"What happened?" Jake said.

"When I lived in Chicago, I made friends with this little Polish man. His name was Marcin, owned a bakery on the south side. He came to the New World on the boat a few years before. I used to ask him about his experience and what it took him to get the bakery running. We talked about his family and what the journey had done to them... and then it happened.

"One day I was eating lunch there. It was just a Tuesday, no different from any other day, but some men came in," Carl said. "They planned to mess up the place, probably sent by someone uncomfortable with a Polish man's success. They frightened the customers and wrecked everything, flipping tables. It was chaos...

"But then that owner stood and looked them dead in the eye. I remember his voice was so very steady, 'My name is Marcin Grabowski. This is my shop, and I cannot let you do this here'."

Carl closed his eyes and shook his head. "Jake... you should have seen him. They told him to step aside. They struck him down, again and again, but he stood up every time. He told them they'd have to kill him. And he meant it. He wasn't going to let them do this.

"Before they could be stopped, one of those awful men pulled a pistol and shot Marcin. The blast scared the thugs as much as it did the rest of us who witnessed the terror. They ran off..."

Carl slowed his words. "I don't know why, but I bent down and held the dying baker. His eyes were swollen shut and blood poured from the bullet wound. It didn't take long for him to pass on, but the look on his face as he went... the only way I can describe it was a look of certainty, a calmness, like he knew something so sure he would fight the whole world if they said otherwise."

Carl stopped.

Jake waited for the old man to continue.

Carl shifted in his seat. "I thought long and hard about what happened. There was something about that old man... something in the look in his eye and the words he spoke. Now his shop wasn't big, or irreplaceable, but he was willing to die, *truly* to die for it. And then, I understood. I realized what it was about that old man that struck me, the thing I couldn't describe. That baker knew exactly *who* he was. Marcin knew Marcin. That man had lived and tested the limits of himself. He knew how strong, how brave he was, the hard work he was capable of doing in the nights he went without sleep. It was in the way he loved his wife. He knew it was Marcin Grabowski who had left everything to board a ship and head to the New World. He knew what he would die for, and what he would live for. You see, I was looking for an environment, an experience to define myself. Marcin Grabowski, defined the world around him. He knew himself to be a man and no one could stop him.

"I searched the world for the question while all the time possessing the answer. I caught my reflection in a window and stared at myself. I thought 'I'm Carl Jamison.' I too, knew what fears I had, and how I overcame them. I knew I was loyal to my friends. I experienced how much I could love a woman and the faith I had. Hard work didn't scare me. And I knew how long it took me to get up after being punched in the face. I knew enough about myself to look people in the eye—I mean *really* in the eye. No walls, nothing to hide because I was not ashamed." Carl nodded.

"And I knew that more than anything in the world, I liked waking up to a West Texas sunrise. There is something eternally pure about riding a horse over a ridge and something cleansing in seeing your own blood after hard labor. This ranch is my bakery, my passion. I came home to a circumstance I chose, not one that chose me." The aged face let some smoke slowly drift from his mouth. "There is nothing that makes a strong man stronger than knowing who he really is."

Truth filled the silence in which they sat. The air hung heavy with the words Carl had spoken. It was as though the two sat in the very pages of a book written by philosophers, though not of words but philosophers of deeds. Jake marveled at the man next to him.

Their moment did not last long. A horn honked and headlights came down the driveway, moving at a cautious pace, swerving back and forth. Then the beams gave up trying to stay on the driveway altogether. The clutch grinded roughly and the disaster finally came to rest somewhere near where the other trucks were parked.

The heavy truck door opened and Aaron's feet hit the ground. He steadied himself on the vehicle, leaving the headlights on and the door wide open. He staggered across the driveway in their direction, headed anywhere but the house.

The two on the porch swing stood up. Carl moved to care for the truck and Jake gave his brother something to lean on. Aaron smelled like an old sailor. He gave up on supporting his own weight and entrusted himself to Jake.

"Gimpy... I just... I want... I just want you to know that you're a brother," Aaron eyes were lazy. "A good brother... wish you legs..." The stairs up the porch might as well have been Everest. They took them one at a time.

"I can do this... do this... I was in the 51st," Aaron slurred.

"I know you can," Jake said.

Jake's number one goal in getting Aaron to bed was to not wake Gracie. Aaron wouldn't let go of Jake's neck when he tried to lay him on the bed. They both fell over. Aaron laughed.

"Be quiet!" Jake whispered. "You'll wake the house."

"Sure! Bring them all in here!" Aaron hollered.

Retreating to his own room, Jake left before his brother was inspired to make more noise. He tried to sleep, but Aaron sang some old bar tune. Jake tossed and turned in his bed, fighting the urge to tell his brother to shut up.

CHAPTER 3

Missing Heroes

"That doesn't look good." Carl pointed to the northwest. A black cyclone of vultures circled high above, like something dark and menacing. "We better check it out." He led the way.

Jake and Carl rode through a small patch of trees and up a rise. The smell hit before they could see it. They pulled out bandanas and tied them over their faces.

Jake coughed.

Sprawled on the ground before them, lay a dead cow, frozen in time. It was a pretty mature steer, brown in color and looked like it was sleeping. Except for its eyes that flared wide open as though it was terrified. The two dismounted and approached, walking around it a time or two, trying to see it from different angles.

Carl picked up a stick and used it to move the head from side to side. No blood or lacerations, no wounds or signs of attack by human or animal were on the beast. Its legs were not broken, which would have caused it to fall and starve to death.

"Damn." Carl tipped his hat back. "Looks like this one

got sick. We better burn it quick before the buzzards get to it and it reaches the rest of the herd." He turned to Jake. "You go get some gasoline while I keep the buzzards away. I'll put some brush around the carcass."

Jake rode Rio back to the barn for a canister of gasoline. When Jake returned, the dry wood was ready to burn. After taking the lid off the canister, he soaked the brush-covered animal until the fumes wreaked havoc on their noses. The pair stood back.

Carl tossed a match to it. The cleansing flames swept over the animal. The heat would kill the germs. The carcass sizzled and soon a dark plume of smoke replaced the towering crown of buzzards. The two waited upwind.

After an hour, Jake grabbed a shovel and threw some dirt on the embers, enough to stop the fire from spreading. Then they headed to the house.

"Hey, Gimpers! What was that fire burning over there?" Aaron lollygagged around in a bathrobe, carrying a large bowl of leftover mash potatoes. He dug into it with a wooden spoon.

"We found a dead cow that looked like disease might have taken it. We had to burn it because—"

"Hey, Carl," Aaron chimed in. "You're going into Odessa for tractor parts today, right?"

"Yes." Carl tilted his head.

"Good. Would you mind picking me up some typing paper? I'm going to write a book about my time in the war. I think I'll call it *My War*."

Carl nodded and took his horse back to the barn.

Just then little Gracie came running out the door. "Carry-Carry!"

"I'm busy right now," Aaron said. He scooted passed her and went inside.

Gracie scurried over to Jake and Rio. Jake pulled her up into the saddle in front of him. They rode down the driveway a little ways and back. She held onto Rio's mane and pretended she was leading him. Then she bent down and hugged his neck. As they approached the porch, Rosalia called them in for lunch.

A half-hour later Carl pushed his plate away and gave his stomach a satisfying pat. "You ready?"

Jake was caught off guard. "For what?"

"You're coming with me to Odessa for tractor parts."

"Actually, I was going to repair the windbreak in the back forty."

"No, come with me. Two reasons: one, I don't want to make the drive by myself. And, it's good for a young man to get into the city every once in a while." The old man stood and waited.

Jake knew there were no words he could muster that would change Carl's mind, so he followed him outside. They fetched the broken tractor piece from the barn and loaded it in the pick-up bed. Jake planned to climb in the passenger side, but Carl stopped him.

"You should drive. You spend more time in the saddle than in the driver seat." Carl smirked. "Yes, sir, I'm worried you'll forget which pedals do what."

It was probably a month or two since he had operated

the truck. Jake climbed into the driver's seat.

After Carl settled in, Jake started the engine and headed down the driveway. His brace didn't inhibit his driving. Coyote and Axle ran along side the whole length of the driveway, tormenting the truck with their barking. The driveway was long, however, and they gave up when the truck pulled onto the highway.

The first place they drove past was the McIntyre's ranch. Carl pointed out the big new barn the family had built. It wasn't even painted yet, just the fresh color of processed wood.

"They must be increasing their operation, running more heads," Carl said. "I'll have to ask John about that."

It was a good day for a drive, at the time of year when the temperature was perfect and no clouds in the sky. The wheels spun and they made pretty good time. Before long, they pulled into Odessa, which, along with Midland, had always seemed to Jake to be big towns. For someone who had never left west Texas, Odessa and Midland seemed to be the only urban areas in that part of the world. Indeed, sharing the road with so many other vehicles at once gave Jake a tiny thrill.

The first place they stopped was a little store that sold office supplies. When Jake didn't get out of the car, Carl said, "So I guess I'm getting Aaron's paper?"

Jake shrugged.

When he returned with a small package, Carl said, "That'll never get used." The old man set the paper on the seat between them.

Jake turned south for several blocks until they reached the tractor supply store on the edge of town. He pulled into the parking lot and turned off the engine. Staring straight ahead, he waited for Carl to get out of the truck.

"Come with me." Carl waved his hand.

Carl walked, while Jake hobbled behind him.

As they opened the door, a little chime informed the employees that someone had arrived. An old man sat at the counter talking to a burly fellow. Someone else thumbed through a parts catalogue. They looked up at Carl and Jake.

"What can I help y'all with?" said man behind the counter.

Carl approached him. Jake stayed farther away.

The old man squinted a little. "Wait... is that Carl?"

"Yes, sir, it is."

"Damn, brother, where you been!" Mr. Donner came from behind the counter to shake Carl's hand.

"Oh, you know, it never ends on a ranch," Carl joked. "Now I got a tractor that needs a new fuel tank. Think you can help me?"

"I reckon we can. We only have a few in stock. If we don't have it, we can go ahead and order it for y'all."

"Sounds good." Carl led Mr. Donner outside to take a look at the old fuel tank in the bed of the truck. Jake pretended to look at items inside the store. He wondered if the other men were staring at him. The little chime rang again.

"...ring it up at the counter and then you can pull

around and we'll load it," said the store owner as he came through the door with Carl.

Jake steered the truck around to the back and loaded the new tank, packed in a wood crate, lashed together with some old rope.

"Do y'all still want that one?" The man pointed to the old tank.

"There's always use for everything on a ranch." Carl patted the tank.

"Fair enough," the shop keep tipped his hat. "Take care, y'all."

They pulled out of the tractor dealer. Carl looked back to see if the new tank had slid around.

Carl said, "Go left."

"Aren't we going home?" Jake said.

"I feel like getting an ice cream." Carl pointed down the road. "There's a little place up here on the left."

Everything seemed a little bigger and a little nicer in Odessa to Jake. The road was four lanes wide, with ranch trucks and a few nice sedans passing by. The ice cream parlor looked like a big flashy carnival. A sign out front read, "Sweets." Jake stopped in a parking spot.

"So you don't want anything?" Carl said.

"I'm good." Jake sat still.

"All right." Carl got out of the car and walked over to the window of the parlor. The place had no seating indoors, but there were picnic tables set out for patrons. He looked over the menu.

"Hello there, young lady. I would like two scoops of—"

Carl stopped his order.

She didn't pick up her pen to write the order down or turn to the freezer.

Jake noticed her look of panic and couldn't figure out why she was afraid. She kept glancing at the people sitting at one of the outdoor tables.

A man stood up from the table. He wore a shirt with the name of the parlor on the lapel. He must have been a manager. With a stern scowl on his face, he approached Carl. "Boy, we don't serve niggers here. Now if you want to go around back, you can buy some ice cream, but you're not allowed to get anything up front," he said. He waved his finger in Carl's face and put his hands on his hips.

The air hung heavy. Jake watched the boney little prick try and boss around big, broad Carl. Some of those at the table looked as though they approved. Some looked horrified.

Jake wanted to say something, to say anything, to tell this man that Carl was one of the hardest workers he'd ever seen. He wanted to tell him he had no business calling a man twice his age "boy" and that he could take his damn ice cream and shove it. The manager would be lucky to be half the man Carl was. Jake wanted to tell him Carl worked Texas and *he* worked an ice cream parlor. He wanted to tell him the error of his ways and go to his friend's aide. The shotgun under the truck seat crossed his mind... but in the end, he remained silent. Jake didn't do or say anything at all, and sat with his shame.

Carl looked at the man and said, *"Abu no disce omnes."*

The manager's eyebrows shot up his face, as confusion clouded his face.

Carl got back in the passenger seat of the truck. The leather creaked under him as he faced forward.

Jake started the engine and pulled away. He wouldn't dare break the silence; he didn't feel he could say anything to Carl right now. If Carl hated him forever, he would deserve it. Jake feared he would loathe him for just sitting there and not standing up.

Carl broke the stillness. "I don't mind being hated by that kind of man."

Jake almost jumped out of his skin.

"A man like that can't really see. He can't really observe. He's crippled by what he's been taught. He doesn't know how to tell a good man, and so doesn't know how to tell a bad one. To be hated by him is like being hated by a wall or a tree... or a fool. But, to be hated by someone who can really tell a bad man from a good man, *that* is something to worry about." Carl rested his arm out the window.

Jake wanted to apologize. But in the back of his mind, a deeper question lingered. What if Carl asked him why he hadn't said anything? Jake wasn't sure he wanted to investigate that far. He didn't know what he would find. So he left it alone and looked for an opportunity to make small talk... small, shallow, talk.

During the drive home, Carl commented on other vehicles and on the weather. He talked about the ranches they passed and discussed all things with Jake as though nothing was wrong.

Yet Jake still feared the silence, because in the silence, Carl might decide to blame him.

When they arrived at the ranch, they set to work repairing the tractor tank. The pair reconnected the fuel line to the engine and the brackets that held the tank in place. A short while later they put fuel into the repaired tractor. After firing it up, Carl drove it around the barn once to check for leaks. Success.

After they cleaned up, Jake crossed to the house. Gracie held the book of children's stories in her hand. He sat and read, adding sound effects. She laughed and loved it. Jake imagined that in her own mind she was in the stories, living them. He read two of the short stories before Rosalia summoned her to the kitchen.

Jake leaned back and rested his eyes. The den was a quiet room in the front of the house, a more formal space for company. Heaviness plagued his eyelids. His left leg felt a little irritated so he took off his brace to let his leg breathe. Jake rubbed his leg where the straps choked his skin. It felt nice.

He opened his eyes when Aaron walked into the room, holding a magazine.

"Did you get me the paper I need?" He looked down at Jake.

"Carl did."

"How's this for a title of my book: *The Hero Comes Home*..." He paused for a moment. "Catchy, isn't it?"

"Very catchy."

"Did y'all get the part for the tractor, too?" Aaron got

a mischievous look in his eye.

Jake knew what was coming but his reaction wasn't quick enough. He reached from the chair as quickly as he could, but Aaron had already grabbed his leg brace.

His brother took it to the other side of the room, hooting. "You're in trouble now, aren't you, Gimpy!" Aaron cackled.

Jake tried to look like he was laughing. When Aaron left the room, Jake got down on all fours and crawled across the wood floors. He retrieved his brace, put it back on, and straightened himself up. He brushed the dust off his knees and headed from the room. His eyes drifted over the bookshelf, reading the titles of some of the leather-bound books.

The bottle of whisky sat hidden in the bookshelf. Jake pulled it down and looked around the corner. No one was in the hall. He made for the door and went out onto the porch.

He crossed over to the bunkhouse, where the employees slept, and stashed the bottle with the alcohol from the main house. Jake didn't want his father to find it as the anniversary of her death approached.

The next morning, the day was upon them. Perhaps God made the weather for them, cloudy, overcast, a rain seemed certain.

At breakfast, Carl did not include Jake in the work plan of the day. No one said anything about her. Jake looked at his companions, an expression somewhere between sadness and regret plagued each face. Some of them were there when it happened. She had meant something to many of them. The wound in the home had not healed and never would. The absence of her smile and warmth was given voice on this day. Missing her touch and generous heart caught up to them, try as they might to walk away from feeling her loss.

Jake didn't know why, but he put on a nicer shirt. After all, she wouldn't be able to tell. He stared at himself for a while in the mirror. He had a million thoughts and none at all. He left his room and passed Aaron's on the way. His brother lay on his bed starring at the ceiling.

Jake thought Aaron might have forgotten about the date. "Um... hey, Aaron?"

"What?"

"Have you been out there yet?"

"I'll go later."

That was good enough. Aaron must remember.

Everything was always different on this day, the anniversary of her death. Jake headed downstairs and found a dolled-up Gracie sitting in the kitchen. She remained unusually still. Rosalia had helped her with the little blue bow in her hair. Gracie looked up at Jake, not jumping into his arms. Instead she waited.

Jake looked at her, this beautiful mess of a little girl. This little angel whose handicaps made her so sincere, who lived a life of such wonderful bliss in a world built of her own imagination. He looked at her and saw his mother's eyes. He lost his breath as he thought about how much love his mother would have for her child.

"Gracie," he said slowly. "… you look wonderful."

Stillness gave way to her massive grin.

"Ready?"

She nodded and clapped.

In all the years he had taken Gracie out there, he never really knew if Gracie understood the situation. She might know what a mother was, though she never had one. Jake tried to explain that her mother died. Did she go out there every year thinking she was going to meet her mother for the first time? Was her disappointment countered by her inextinguishable hope? If only she understood.

She took Jake's hand and they crossed the driveway. One of the ranch hands had saddled Rio and left him tied up outside the barn. Jake climbed up onto his friend and reached down to lift Gracie. She giggled. Jake gave the horse a little nudge.

Gracie pointed out cattle and birds, chuckling without provocation. Jake was attentive to her murmurs. More than anyone else, Jake could understand Gracie's speech, about half what she said, but all her laughter.

Jake and Gracie rode down the west road about a mile and turned up a dirt two-track that led to the higher country of their ranch. The western side of these hills gave way to a rocky out-crop and cut back into a big gulley, making a ravine. This created a cathedral of the outdoors, hidden in a forgotten place. One end of the ravine sloped up to meet the rest of the hills, where they formed a barricade of earth.

The other end opened wide and looked over the entire

western part of the ranch, west Texas and the rest of the country, it seemed, all the way to the Pacific. It was a place separated from all things.

Right below dwelled one of the bigger watering ponds. The sun reflected against the water, sending simmering colors charging in all directions. No better view existed on all the ranch. The shades of the sun went on forever.

Mr. Weathers used to bring his wife up here to watch the day end. That is why he chose this spot to bury her.

Only one tree—one oak, old as time—stood eternal guardian. Her gravestone rested in its shade. Jake knew a gravestone would never be enough for such a woman. He lowered Gracie before dismounting. Gracie walked up slowly, almost reverently. Jake followed his sister to their mother's final resting place.

Chiseled in stone: *Margaret Anne Weathers, beloved wife and mother.* Then her favorite Bible verse: *Now faith is the substance of things hoped for, the evidence of things unseen. -Hebrews 11:1.*

Jake would never forget how it happened.

The weather was different that week, colder than anyone could remember for that time of year. The chill went to the bone. Young Aaron and Jake watched their breath steam and acted like big shots smoking cigars. They saw snow for the first time in their lives and it didn't last long, only a moment or two. Yet as they stood outside, the white flakes clung to their eyelashes and touched their hands.

The special doctor in Midland, who sized Jake for the

new braces as he grew, scheduled many patients that day.

"Thanks for taking us this late." Maggie said.

"Overbooked as usual, but wouldn't want you to go home without it," the doctor said.

Jake suspected it also had to do with the fact that his mother was beautiful.

"Now, young man, how old are you?" The doctor ruffled Jake's hair with his hand.

"Fourteen."

"On your way to becoming a man."

"Yes, he is." Maggie smiled.

The doctor measured Jake's inseam and the lengths of his thigh and calf. He asked Jake if he wanted brown or black leather straps. The manufacturer in Indiana gave all sorts of options, even what kind of buckles the patient might want.

"Oooooh, good choice!" his mom said. "That'll look handsome!" When the doctor opened a catalogue to show Jake a picture of what it would look like, his mother said, "If Wyatt Earp wore a leg brace, he'd have this one."

Maggie walked with her arm around Jake's shoulders as they made their way to the truck. She looked to the sky.

On the near horizon approached dark, soaked clouds, waiting to pour. The rain came down fast and hard. And it *came* down.

Jake's mother focused on the road, though they still laughed and joked. The windshield wipers struggled against the rain. The pair caught glimpses of the road.

Jake peered into the night from the passenger window

to see a land blanketed in darkness. They discussed his father's upcoming birthday.

"If Aaron and I put our money together, we can get him something good!" Jake rubbed his hands together to keep them warm but it didn't help.

"That would work." She played with the headlights. "But whatever you do, I'm sure your father will love it. Fathers are just happy to be dads."

"Are they?"

"Yes. The day you and Aaron were born, your father lost his mind." She smiled at Jake. "He didn't think he could ever love anybody that quickly."

His mother had the best smile ever. Her words made Jake feel good. He always thought his dad didn't know exactly what to do with him. A good father to an able athlete and charmer like Aaron, his dad seemed unsure how to approach Jake.

He liked the way his mother always encouraged him. She never gave Jake a moment to feel different by letting him sit out of the work, often making him carry bags for her, work the ranch, and giving him chores just like Aaron. She made a huge deal about how good he was on a horse, despite the brace. Whenever Aaron was on the athletic field, she always made Jake sit front row and cheer. Maggie never let her son pity himself. When she looked at him, he felt normal.

"Mom." Jake looked over at her. "I love you."

"I love you, too, sweetie…"

Their world ripped in two.

The force of the impact jarred their bodies sideways as glass shattered and surrounded them in a flurry of shards. His mother's side of the truck disintegrated and crushed inward. The steel shrieked as it crumpled. Tires screamed as they fought the soaking wet pavement. His mother's hair whipped around her face. He couldn't see her anymore... he reached out for her.

"Please," he whispered a prayer. "Please don't let anything happen to her..."

But then the tree came into view.

"God!" His mother screamed. The vehicle struck the tree with high-speed fury. Their bodies launched forward, but something, somewhere down there, held Jake where he was. His mother fell away from him. Her head plunged through the windshield; then her shoulders. Her body flew into the night. And Jake was left behind.

He drifted out for a moment. The engine revved and the wheels spun in the mud. The rain that poured through the broken window brought Jake back... *Mom*... his only thought. His vision blurred. He tried to get out of the truck but something kept hindering him, something from below. He looked down. His brace was caught on the door. Somehow it had become tangled and kept him in his seat.

Jake broke free and pushed the door until it fell off. He jumped from the truck and slipped in the mud, falling on his back. The car that hit them raced away.

Through the rain and mud that stung his eyes, he struggled and stood. He fought his way through the dark as he lost his footing again and again. He hit the earth. It wouldn't let go of him.

"MOM!" he screamed. "MOM!" He crawled, dragging that damned leg with him.

"MOM!" He made his way farther.

In the glow of the remaining headlight, she lay still, blanketed in rain, held by the cold, clutched by the mud. He pulled himself to her. He lifted her up into his arms and held her head. Her blood-soaked hair clung to her forehead. His cold breath brushed over her face. She wasn't breathing back.

Sometime later one of the county deputies drove by. Jake still clutched his mother. Again and again he asked Jake what happened. How long had they been there? But he got no answer.

Jake didn't know when he let go of her. He remembered the officers driving him to the house while he wondered where his mother was.

Jake sat still as his father came out the door, his face covered with dread. He looked them over as the officers lifted Jake out of the patrol car. As Mr. Weathers grabbed his chest, the boy realized she wasn't coming home.

Sam Weathers split the night with his screams. He screamed at them, he screamed at God, he screamed for his wife. He clutched his head and fell to his knees, beating the ground. The flesh on his knuckles tore against the earth. His father thrashed wildly as the deputies tried to calm him. Then he sprang up and put his fist against the barn.

Jake heard the crunch as his father's hand broke. Fear

overcame Jake.

Carl came from the bunkhouse and let quiet tears roll down his face as the deputies informed him of the accident. It took them a while to get Mr. Weathers back in the house. Jake tried to stay out of the way. Carl gave Rosalia some instructions and left Sam with the deputies, the last Jake saw before they took him to the doctor's house.

Many people came to the funeral, just as Jake knew they would, but no one talked to Sam Weathers. He didn't cry, only stared at the casket from his place in the corner, eyes darkened in a way Jake never thought possible. Rosalia wept and held Jake's baby sister. Their aunt comforted Aaron. Carl stood with his arm around Jake as a sea of people surrounded them.

It took Mr. Weathers months to come out of his room and even longer to talk to his son. It was seven months before he ever looked Jake in the eye again. The boy didn't know if his father blamed him for the accident or if he just reminded him of her. After a year, his father seemed to function again. Jake didn't enjoy how distant his father felt, but he was happy there seemed to be no animosity.

Afterwards, Jake felt like his father didn't know how to handle his crippled son and was numb to the fact his daughter was not progressing as a normal child should. His father placed all his hopes and dreams in Aaron.

Still there were nights. Nights that turned into days. Something would trigger Sam's memories of her and he would disappear into his room, emptying bottles of liquor.

Once or twice Carl had to talk a pistol out of Mr. Weathers' hand, a pistol with only one bullet.

These fits were often in the early days but later came only around the date of her death. Sometimes Jake was happy that Gracie didn't have to see her dad act like that.

"Butterfly, fly!" Gracie tugged Jake back to the present.

He smiled at her and stroked her head. He set down the flowers on the grave and gave some to Gracie. She took such care and notice as she chose her steps up to the grave stone and delicately laid the flowers in front of her mother's memorial. There were already flowers there. Carl must have come earlier.

Gracie pulled that little blue ribbon from her hair, the one she was so proud of, and set it on the resting flowers.

"Now Mama can look pretty," he said to her and took her hand. He let a tear go. They mounted Rio. He pulled the reins and headed Rio down the path, back to the road.

The house was quiet when they arrived home. Only Rosalia was working. Gracie ran off to her. Jake walked past his dad's room, the haunted aura radiating into the hallway. The door hung open a little. He looked in and held his breath. Mr. Weathers sat in a rocking chair staring at the floor. His hand clutched a bottle of whiskey. Jake climbed the stairs to Aaron's room.

"Aaron?" Jake knocked.

"What?"

Jake leaned in. His brother lay in the same place he was

earlier that day.

"You know, this day is pretty rough on Dad. I don't think he's doing well ..." Jake leaned back.

"I know, and?"

"...and, well, do you think maybe you could talk to him, or something? Try and cheer him up?"

"What makes you think I can do that?" Aaron looked at his brother.

"Because you... you know." Jake turned toward the door. "Forget about it." He hobbled back downstairs. He steadied himself as he pushed the door of his dad's room open. His father didn't turn around. Jake crossed the room slowly and stood next to him. Mr. Weathers never looked at him.

Jake was silent, not knowing what to say or do. He knew words would never come. He opened the drawer of the desk and retrieved the pistol stored there.

His father's eyes turned a little his way... they had no argument in them.

Jake took the gun and left his father alone in his room.

At eleven, the truck started up outside. Jake looked out his bedroom window and watched his father drive off towards the west end of the ranch, to where she lay.

CHAPTER 4

Chrome

Someone honked a car horn. Jake came out of the high brush in a near pasture. A vehicle he didn't recognize sat in the driveway. He couldn't really get a good look at it because the sun reflected off it. The thing was too clean and dust free for an automobile driving around west Texas. It was like some far off treasure.

The horn persisted.

Jake gave Rio a little tap and headed up the pasture towards the house. By the time he arrived, Rosalia, Gracie, some of the ranch hands, and Aaron had come out of the house. Jake now realized it was his father who had honked the horn.

"Well, what do you think?" Mr. Weathers patted the top of the car. "She's a peach, isn't she?"

The car looked like it was built yesterday, too pretty to be parked next to the barn, in the shadow the ranch house, all the while being sniffed by inquisitive mutts. Especially with the rest of the Weathers' fleet comprised of ranch trucks.

"It's a real nice car," Jake said as he slid off Rio.

"Whose is it?"

"Whose is it? It's ours, silly! I just thought that we needed something besides the trucks. Especially with Aaron and all the time he spends off the ranch. We need the Weathers driving in something respectable for a change."

Carl pulled up in one of the trucks. He had driven Mr. Weathers to the dealership in Odessa or Midland.

"45' Chevy Coupe! They just got it on the lot yesterday," their father said.

"Was that the only color they had?" Aaron scrutinized the red paint.

"Well... yes." Mr. Weathers turned to look at the vehicle.

"Hmmm. Well, it's good enough." Aaron strolled around the other side of the car.

"Want to take it for a ride?"

"Yeah!" Aaron caught the keys his dad tossed. He slid into the driver's seat and shut the door.

The leather seats seemed as painstakingly crafted as the finest boots Jake had ever seen. The inside was nicer than the Weathers' house. Every button and switch was a high gloss polish.

Aaron gazed at his reflection in the treated wood of the dashboard and gave the interior a quick inspection. Then he rolled down the window. "You coming, gimpy?"

Jake looked down at his dirty boots.

"Actually, you don't want to get dirt in here," his brother said. "You can drive it later."

"Uh... yeah," Jake nodded.

Gracie ran over and felt the car.

"Don't do that! We don't want to get handprints on it."
Aaron cranked the engine and it roared to life. It ran so
fresh and clean. It sounded like an approaching stampede.
Aaron revved her a few times. The heavy metal body shook
from the power of the massive V-8. Dust lifted into the air
in the wake of exhaust from the tailpipe.

Mr. Weathers climbed into the passenger seat.
Aaron pulled a u-turn on the grass. Once the front tires
straightened out, he shoved the gas and was gone. Between
the reflection of the sun and the trail of dust, the car looked
like a shooting star cruising down the driveway.

Jake headed back the way he came.

"Where you going, Jake?" said Carl from the porch.

"Neighbor called and said he saw one of our steers
stuck in the fence over in Lower Canyon, along the road.
Got to cut it loose."

"Want me to go with you?"

"I'm fine. I'll meet you back here and we can fix that
door." Jake moved away from the house on Rio.

In that moment, he realized he had the itch and looked
back to make sure no one from the house was watching.
He put some distance between them. Then he really kicked
Rio. He didn't know why but he decided to see how fast he
could make it to Lower Canyon.

They tore off across the front pasture, somewhere
between running and flying. The wind whipped through
Jake's shirt and over his face. The ground shred apart
under Rio's hooves.

Jake loved two things about Rio. The horse had a long

stride and moved his legs quickly. Across a flat, he was damn near uncatchable. The horse moved faster than a horse should move. Everyone said so.

The front pasture was soon behind them. When they hit the brush, they slowed stride a little, but Rio had a confident step and moved through brush with deliberate speed. Jake always figured Rio didn't want to take a spill any more than he did, so he let the horse do what he wanted. They plowed through, casting the still world into an explosion of motion and sound.

Next came Jake's very favorite thing to do. On the way to Lower Canyon, a creek cut a gulley in the earth. The gulley was deeper than wide and its sides were sheer.

They came upon it. Jake rubbed the horse's neck and said, "Do it." He didn't know what his horse thought of this. He liked to think he was letting Rio know that he was aware the horse was about cross the gulley. The rider was letting him know that he was ready to roll. This was the point when then they had to commit.

They didn't break stride. The world passing by slowed as his adrenaline pumped. Jake was aware of every step and stride. His own heart thundered in his ears. *Pound, pound, pound.* The heart in his chest and the hooves on the earth matched. Pound... pound... pound...

Rio left the earth behind. Jake looked down at the deep gulley below, convinced they could outrun gravity. They were so far from the ground. He was on top of the world.

They peaked and the horse lost its upward flight. They started to descend, pulled back down by a jealous earth.

Jake's stomach lifted inside him as the animal fell away from under him. Then once again, his momentum matched that of his horse and both came down on the far side. The hooves reconnecting with the earth. Pound, pound, pound...

Rio knew how to jump and not lose stride. The whole action was one fluid motion, smooth in a remarkable way. Jake was willing to be a little undignified and let out a holler of celebration and relief. The pair flew down the ridge. The heads of grazing cattle lifted to watch them pass.

They took one of the dirt roads and covered ground quickly. The trail of dust told the world where they had been. They splashed through a shallow creek bed and sent water exploding through the air.

Finally came the last obstacle to speed. To get back to Lower Canyon, the road cut wide around a row of mounds. The horse and rider's side was steep, made of loose dirt and rock.

Jake leaned forward in the saddle and Rio worked up the slope. Every step was sluggish as each stride sunk in. Rio kicked the dirt up and trudged forward, powering through the landscape. They made the top and headed down the much gentler far side towards Lower Canyon.

Fixing his eyes on the fence line, Jake traced the curve of the pasture. On the other end, just where their neighbor said, the trapped animal waited.

They rode over to it. Jake slowed Rio's gait. The steer struggled against the fence. Jake got off his horse and spoke to the steer in soft tones, but the animal panicked, kicking and yanking its neck in the fence and making the barbed wire dig deeper into its hide.

Jake stopped but the creature went crazy and tore its neck up, thrashing like it had mad cow disease. It would surely kill itself.

But today was not the steer's day to die. The animal's wild convulsions pulled its head free. The steer trotted over to some of the nearby cattle.

Jake checked the strength of the fence and then rode by the steer to check its wounds. It would live. It had settled in with the other animals. So Jake left them grazing and went to meet Carl and fix the door.

On his way down the slope, three coyotes bolted across the open ground. One was the largest coyote Jake had ever seen on their ranch. He knew it would pose a problem. Without a rifle, all Jake could do was hope the traps got that one later on so it didn't take money out of the Weathers' pockets.

Carl tinkered in the barn when Jake returned. He helped the old man with the re-finished door.

"There. That ought to last a few years." Carl put down his tool. "You want some water?"

"I'm good." Jake watched Carl disappear into the kitchen. The sun was getting low. Jake had no sooner thought Aaron and their father had been gone a while when the Chevy, slightly less dust-free now, cruised down the driveway. Aaron wasn't exactly all in the driveway when he came to a stop.

"Guess he'll just park anywhere," Carl said as he

returned to the barn.

Aaron and his father climbed out. "Whew, she's a beast," Aaron said as he headed inside. He tossed the keys to a dirt-covered Jake.

Jake looked at the keys and wondered what he was supposed to do with them. He gave the keys to his father as he climbed the steps to the porch.

"Don't want to get it dirty?" his father said, looking at Jake's muddy boots. "Well, you'll get plenty of chances to drive it."

But every day, Aaron left the ranch from early morning until late at night. Jake always wondered where Aaron would go because even he would run out of things to do in Midland, Odessa, and Crane in the middle of the day. It was as though he was back in high school, trying to see as many friends as he could. Aaron kept forgetting to clean it, too, because it wouldn't do much better in a beauty contest than any of their old ranch trucks.

On Friday, Jake returned to the house for lunch. Carl told him they needed to dig the foundation for the new smoke shack Rosalia decided they needed. It wouldn't be a very big one, just enough for a small shed out by the back house. They started digging. It wasn't long before Aaron came out with a shovel. He looked like he belonged somewhere else in his clean shirt and spotless jeans.

"Let a soldier show you boys how it's done." He twirled his shovel like a weapon before plunging it into the ground.

Jake thought his brother must really be bored if he wanted to help dig.

Aaron jumped in with cheerful enthusiasm at first. Then he split his time between digging and talking. He sat in the shade, chattering while they dug. Then he went back in the house. He had lasted half an hour.

Carl and Jake finished the hole, mixed cement, and poured the foundation. They inserted four uprights to serve as the four corners of the shed. Now they had to wait and let it dry overnight. They finished it the next day.

The first thing Rosalia smoked was a twenty-five pound turkey. It tasted good but her excitement resulted in smoked food at every supper for a few weeks.

Friday night, Jake fell victim to Gracie's request for stories once again. They sat together on the leather sofa. He tried to make it fun by giving the characters different voices, thinking this might help Gracie keep track.

"Let's go." Aaron came out of his room and headed toward the front door. His hair was greased and boots shined. A girl followed him into hallway.

Jake wasn't aware that anyone but family was in the house.

Jenny Dawson's hair appeared much shorter than in high school. She had rosy cheeks that always looked ready to smile. Ready for a night out, she was dressed in the latest trends.

"Hi!" Gracie waved at Jenny.

Jenny stopped. She hadn't noticed the two sitting in the den. "Oh... well, hello there," she smiled at Gracie. "Jake, how are you?"

"Uh... all right." He summoned something like a smile. "How are you?"

"Just great," she said. "What are y'all reading?"

Jake held up the book cover. "Just a... Mother Goose."

"How nice."

"Jenny, where'd you go?" Aaron came back into the house. "We're going to be late."

"Oh, I was just talking to Jake." Then her face lit up as though she had the most brilliant of thoughts. "Jake, would you like to come with us?"

"Oh... uh... no, thank you."

"Are you sure? It would be nice to have you along."

"No, I... have some things I need to do." Jake could just picture what she was thinking. "*Oh, invite Jake, he never gets to do anything.*" Besides, what would he do? Be the awkward third person?

"There's nothing that won't keep until tomorrow," Aaron winked at Jenny. "You can't refuse a lady's offer!"

Well, damn. There was no getting out of this, no excuses to be made. Jake surrendered. He left Gracie with Rosalia and followed the other two outside to an unknown fate.

They all shared the front bench seat in Aaron's car. Jake pressed himself against the door and stared straight ahead. Aaron drove, his arm around the girl's shoulder, pulling her in close. Jake tried not to take up space, shoved into his little corner.

"We didn't have cars like this to drive in the Army." Aaron patted the dashboard. "Just old Willy's Jeeps, and they sure as heck didn't have a smooth ride like this. Did I ever tell you about the time I had to drive one?" He didn't wait for either of them to reply.

Jake had heard this story twelve times.

"I was at the command post and the German offensive got a little too close for comfort. Then their planes appeared overhead. We figured we'd have to drive out of there while they dropped bombs on us. So we got the general in the back and took off!" He stopped, but it seemed like there should be more to the story.

"... and did they?" Jenny said.

"Did they what?"

"Drop bombs on you as you drove off?"

"Oh... well, no, but we thought they were going to!" He laughed.

They missed the turn for Crane.

"Um... aren't we supposed to go that way?" Jake pointed.

"That's not how you get to Odessa," Aaron said. "Gimps, you really got to get off the ranch more."

Jake sighed. He might be able to handle a quick swing through Crane but not Odessa. This was going to be a long night.

"Brother, you remind me of a guy I met in the spring of '42 when I was in Italy," Aaron started.

"I thought you said you were still getting special training in England in the spring of '42," Jake said.

"... No, no, I was in Italy." Aaron told them about a local Italian who asked directions from the visiting U.S.

troops.

Odessa came into view. Jake wanted to ask where they were going but the bright lights gave it away. They followed the trail of taillights to the Odessa Social Club, an old dance hall that was once part of the stockyards. And since this was the only thing for young people to do for fifty miles in any direction, it was packed.

Aaron found a parking spot and they went inside. People crowded everywhere. An old two-stepping band was up on stage. The guitarist on the lead microphone didn't look much older than Jake. He sweated in the heat of the moment and had the name "McGill" written on his guitar. Next to him bounced a fiddler, working his four-stringer with hands of fire, so fast that his motions disappeared.

In these few moments Jake was mesmerized by the band and lost sight of Aaron and Jenny. He spun around, lost in the crowd, confused in a sea of people. He wasn't going to yell Aaron's name. His voice couldn't be heard in the loud hall. So Jake wandered, searching the crowd for his brother.

Countless two-stepping boots had aged the wood dance floor. The lights were dim. Not the nicest of places, but it was enough for its patrons. Jake threaded his way among other cowboys around the outside of the room and found space to breathe. He walked past tables where they served pies and punches.

He navigated among the punch tables. Someone in a hurry brushed by and bumped him, knocking Jake off balance. He fell back toward the punch, but the tables were sturdy and didn't collapse as he caught himself.

He continued to move around while the crowd's energy hung heavy in the air. After a few minutes that seemed like forever, Jake spotted his bother and felt a little relief. Aaron sat with some of his old friends from Crane and waved Jake in. Everyone slid down to make room for him. Jake felt awkward as he swung his braced leg over the bench.

"Hey, slow poke!" said Ricky Tremble through eyes ever bloodshot.

"Hi, Rick," Jake said.

Aaron gave all his attention to Jenny so Jake surrendered. He couldn't believe his brother dragged him all the way to Midland and now wasn't talking to him. Jake ground his teeth and figured he had to make conversation with Ricky.

May, who seemed to be with Ricky, came up with two glasses of punch. The drink wasn't in front of Ricky for a second before he pulled out a flask and added his own special touch. May offered but Jake pleaded with her not to go get him a glass. Ricky turned all of his drunken concentration on her, and so spared Jake. She looked a little suffocated under the weight of the enormous arm he rested on her shoulders.

Then Jake made eye contact with Baker, one of Aaron's friends with a little more character. Baker had ginger hair and lively eyes. In high school, he was always up for anything. He turned around to face Jake. They greeted each other over the noise of the crowd.

"What are you doing now?" said Jake.

"I was just sworn in by my uncle. I'm going to become a

deputy in two weeks." He took a drink of punch.

"That's great," said Jake. "Of all the jobs in the world, being a deputy is a pretty good deal."

"I agree. Plus, it's a steady paycheck." He shifted his weight. "What about you?"

"Just working the ranch. Pushing horns and fighting coyotes."

"So are you part owner with your father now or a ranch hand, or land manager? You've been working out there long enough."

"No, I'm not part owner," Jake shrugged.

"Someday then." Baker toasted his glass to Jake and took a sip.

"Someday." Jake sat up a little straighter. "Are you married?

"Remember Amanda Jones? She was two years younger than us in school."

"Sort of."

"She's probably getting a ring from me here in the next couple of months. Once I save some money from the job." Baker smiled.

"Well done."

"Thanks." Baker noticed something over Jake's shoulder. "She just walked in," he nodded to Jake. "I'm off then."

After witnessing Baker's excitement, Jake considered himself an outcast for not bringing a girl. But who was he? What kind of girl would take an interest in him?

"I want to dance!"

Ricky's bellow made Jake whip his head around. Ricky dragged May off to the dance floor. Her smile looked a little forced. Pretty soon those Jake knew took to the dance floor. They spun and swung and dipped.

On the dance floor, Aaron soon captured the attention of the band, who dedicated a song to him.

As Jake watched, Aaron started with Jenny and worked his way through different girls as the songs changed. He even got a few married ladies. A pained May served as Ricky's crutch all over the dance floor. Jake caught a glimpse of an enamored Baker leading onto the floor a brown-eyed girl who glowed at the deputy.

Things were going fine until Jenny came up to Jake.

"Come dance with me!" She extended her hand, tilting her thoughtful eyes.

"Oh... uh... no, thank you," Jake squirmed.

"Please?"

Jake hated disappointing her, making the moment awkward, not being a gentleman. He hated everything about this situation, but he wasn't going out on that floor just to be the crippled boy trying to dance. She'd be disappointed, hopefully not hurt. And it would be terrible if she were insulted. She didn't understand and never would.

"I'm sorry... I... I'm sorry." He shoved her generosity back in her face.

"Oh... well," she gave him a little smile. "Maybe next time." She headed back to the floor.

Coming was a bad idea. He couldn't let Aaron talk him into stuff like this. Jake didn't belong here. Some people were just meant to live quietly, behind the curtain.

He felt a little better when Jenny found her way back into Aaron's arms. Whatever Aaron whispered in her ear made her laugh. Maybe she would forget the disappointment.

Eventually the music and the noise of the crowd grew wearisome. Jake swung his leg out from under the bench and moved to the exit, leaving the suffocating and packed dancehall. The parking lot was a relief.

He took a deep breath of the clean night air and headed to the car and only to sit on the ground next to it. Leaning against the door, he watched a few vehicles drive by. Jake found a good little stick where he sat and pulled out his knife. He shaved off its bark and carved words down the side. After getting as much entertainment out of that stick as he could, he tossed it.

He let his mind wander. A half hour passed, then another, and another. Before long he had been waiting by the car for two and a half hours. A couple he didn't know approached the car. He stood up, keeping his leg behind the fender, and tipped his hat. They headed down the street.

Jake started to worry his brother went back to Crane with someone else. He also worried Jenny might not get back home.

Shouting rowdy exclamations, Aaron, Jenny, Ricky, and May came walking from an alley behind the Social Club.

"What a night! We should come here every day! Every day!" Ricky's thick voice carried farther than he could possibly intend. The four walked as one, leaning on each other, swaying in every direction except toward the car.

"Brother!" Aaron pointed toward Jake standing by the car. "Where were you? We've been into it all sorts of ways!"

Ricky had a big cut on his forehead and dirt on his shirt.

"Aaron... what happened?" Jake said.

"I'll tell you what happened, I kicked the tar out of all of them!" Ricky said.

"You were in a fight?" Jake looked at Ricky's fat lip.

"Yes, we were!" Aaron said.

Jake studied his brother and annoyance took over. "I don't know, Aaron, you look like you're missing a few cuts and bruises. And there ain't an ounce of dirt on you."

"Well, Rickster got in a fight. I couldn't get there." He glared at his brother through his drunken haze. "But I would have! I would have taken some names! Right, Rickster?"

"Don't worry, Slow Pokes, they ain't coming my way ever again," Ricky drooled.

Jake loaded Aaron and Jenny into the car. Ricky slunk to his car with May. She took his arm, but he pushed her off, hard enough that she fell to the ground. Jake knew he should say something, even a drunk guy shouldn't do that to a girl. Instead he got into the car.

"So, back to Crane?" Jake said.

They never heard him. Their mouths were busy with each other's lips.

"Okay." He fired up the engine. He didn't mind them ignoring him. Jake was just happy the night was over.

As they neared Crane, he asked Jenny where he should

take her. Neither one responded.

Wondering what to do, Jake pulled the car up in front of the ranch house. He looked over at them and tried to say something but didn't know what. So he left them in the car. He put the keys on the dashboard and headed inside.

As he lay in bed, frustration robbed him of sleep. He couldn't get his brother's lies out of his head. Worry accompanied the frustration, as he was unsure of what Aaron had already misrepresented or would flat out lie about next.

CHAPTER 5

Tomorrow's Train

Jake came in the front door. As his father walked past with a death grip on a handle of bourbon, Sam's eyes were dead. He looked twenty years older.

Jake shoulders slumped. It was going to be a dark day. *What set my father off?*

Jake peered through the door of his father's room. Mr. Weathers sat in an old chair facing the corner, whiskey in hand. For now, breathing was good enough.

Jake slid the door shut.

It was easy to guess when his father would have a depression spell: his wife's birthday, their anniversary, Christmas. But something seemed different. His father had encountered rougher moments in the past and not experienced a set-back. Perhaps it was Aaron's return.

Jake retraced Sam's steps to find Gracie in the den. Gracie held up a photo of their mother she had pulled from where it hung on the wall and looked up at him with those big doe eyes, eyes she shared with their mother. "Mama!" She tapped on the photo.

Still though, something was different. Jake had seen

his father encounter rougher moments in the past and not experience a set back. Perhaps it was because the anniversary of their mother's death wasn't that long ago, or perhaps it was Aaron's being back for a few months.

Jake checked all the guns in the house. None was missing from the locked closet. Other ranchers in west Texas left guns sitting in every corner, but Gracie's condition made the family cautious. And Jake always kept his 1911 with him.

Mr. Weathers wouldn't pull any triggers today. Jake hoped his father would pass out before he could drink himself to death. He let Rosalia and Carl know so they could keep an eye on him.

He also told Aaron, His brother said he was busy and disappeared into his room

Despite the dim forecast, Jake resumed his chores. He and some ranch hands needed to break a filly. She was good bodied and long legged and would make a heck of a roping horse someday.

Around five o'clock, Jake and Carl leaned against the fence of the corral where they kept the filly. She withdrew to the far side of the enclosure to graze. They waited until she meandered closer to them, nibbling in oblivion to their presence. A handful of oats enticed her all the way to the pair. Jake slipped a gentle hand over the fence and stroked the palomino's side. She flinched, then came back to his reach.

Larry rode by on his horse. "Is it time?"

"Yes," Carl said. "Bring them all in."

A boyish grin stole across Larry's face as he rode off. Carl smiled and rolled his eyes at Jake. Before long, every wrangler and employee at the ranch gathered, vying for the best places to sit on the fence

Carl looked at them. "Don't y'all have work to do?"

"Come on, Carl. You know all work stops when a horse needs breaking," Pete said.

"Well maybe I'll just find me a few cowboys who don't stop working when a horse needs breaking."

"Are you saying you'll replace me if I stay here and watch instead of working?"

Carl raised his eyebrows and tilted his head.

Pete furrowed his brow like he was thinking, then looked up with a big smile. "Worth it!"

Carl snickered.

Soon Jake entered the pen. Animals acted like they trusted him. Jake guessed his crippled leg made him less intimidating. He took slow steps, giving the animal time to grow accustomed to his presence. Still, between the anxious crowd and the energetic horse, tension hung thick in the air.

"Don't let me down, Jake. I got twenty dollars says you get this horse handled first time around." Larry pointed to him from where he sat on the fence.

"I got twenty dollars against you!" Juan said. "So hit the dirt once for me!"

Jake got to the animal and spent a few minutes petting her and letting her get to know him. Her long and untamable mane drifted in the breeze. The look in her eye told him she was a wild one. With cautious movements he put all the tack on the horse. Then it was time. He moved to her side and got ready to climb aboard.

"What's going on here?" Aaron yelled as he approached from the house.

Everyone turned.

He arrived at the fence and surveyed the situation. "Old gimps, you gonna try and break that horse?"

"Yes."

"No, no, no." Aaron climbed over the fence and strode towards his brother and the filly. "If y'all want to see a real master, let me show you."

Jake sensed the horse tense up. "Aaron, I don't know if that's a good idea. She's a wild one." He stuck his hand up.

"Of course it is, but I can break any horse on earth." Aaron brushed Jake's hand out of the way and pushed passed his brother.

Jake stumbled on the clumpy dirt of the corral. He relinquished the reins.

Aaron threw his leg over the filly's back and settled in the saddle.

Jake scrambled out of the way as the bomb went off. She went a thousand directions at once, ripping the day apart like a hurricane. The horse kicked high and hard.

Aaron didn't last half a second. He flew far before his butt hit the ground with a thud. His eyes were wide with fear.

Everyone roared with laughter.

Jake approached to help Aaron up, but he pushed him away.

"Well, I'm sorry I had to go off and fight for our country and lost some of my horse breaking skills!" Aaron stormed off towards the house.

Jake took the saddle off the horse; the animal wouldn't be broke today. He spent a half hour calming her down.

Then it all changed.

A week later Jake rode in on Rio and entered the barn. He was not surprised to find Aaron and Ricky lounging on hay bales. Ricky smashed a bottle on the barn wall, then pulled another beer from the bucket.

Jake looked at his watch, six o'clock. Dinner hadn't been served, yet the two had burned through beer at a steady pace. Jake stepped over empty bottles scattered around the floor, evidence of their thirst.

"Well, look who it is!" Ricky nudged Aaron on the shoulder. "Old speedy here to visit!"

"Hello, Ricky." Jake tipped his hat.

Ricky stood up. "Been working hard today, eh?" He indicated the mud on Jake's boots.

"Something like that." Jake got off Rio and turned him loose into the corral. He didn't want Rio around a buzzed Ricky.

Aaron and Ricky made their way to the corral gate next to Jake. The filly that put Aaron in the dirt was out there.

"That's a fresh looking horse." Ricky pointed at her. "She's eyeing us suspiciously."

"Don't let her fool you. She's wild." Aaron rubbed his behind.

"She gave you a go, huh?" He laughed. "Too much woman to handle?"

"Look! I can handle any horse in Texas." Aaron narrowed his eyes. "She's just different."

"Yeah, I'll bet." Ricky looked back at the filly with menacing, almost evil eyes. "I'll break you." He tossed an empty beer bottle her way. It missed by a long shot, but it still sent Ricky and Aaron into a fit of laughter. Ricky eyed another empty bottle.

Jake tried to change the subject. "Did Rosalia ring for dinner yet?"

"I don't know, not like it's my job," Aaron said.

And then, as though it was rehearsed, Rosalia rang the dinner bell. The three headed over to the house together. Gracie ran from the house and gave Jake a big hug. She only got a half hug from Aaron, who shrugged it away, "Easy there, pip-squeak."

Jake held back frustration.

They sat down to dinner. Rosalia put on a spread as she always did. Carl came through the back door with some of the ranch hands. They all sat down and Mr. Weathers said grace, giving extra thanks for his son Aaron.

"Carl." Their father pulled a biscuit from the basket. "Did you reinforce the rain shelter in the Back Forty?"

"Yes, boss, yesterday," Carl responded. "It'll take a

hurricane to knock it down, now." Carl cut whatever was on Gracie's plate into bite-sized pieces; he could have been her grandfather.

"Jake, are you going to be ready for the trucks tomorrow? It's a big order, coming in from El Paso, Earnst Company, sixty head," his father said.

Jake looked over to answer. Just as he was about to speak, he was cut off.

"He can't, Dad. Jake's got to go pick up that girl from the train station tomorrow," Aaron said.

Jake stopped chewing. The words out of Aaron's mouth didn't make any sense. He thought Aaron was confused… or maybe he was confused.

"Excuse me?" Jake focused to interpret what Aaron had said.

"You've got to go pick up that girl tomorrow." He looked at Jake and everyone else like it was the most obvious thing in the world.

"Aaron," Jake said, "what are you talking about?"

"Jake, you're getting on my nerves." Then Aaron's expression softened. "Oh that's right, I forgot to tell you. Mary-Lou's cousin is coming to Crane for a while. I don't remember why, something about reading a book. She's staying with us."

The entire dinner party paused, halting their forks on their plates. Jake, his father, Carl, and Rosalia gave each other perplexed looks.

Has Aaron gone insane?

"Aaron," Carl said, "when did this all take place?"

"A couple of weeks ago." He put a fork full of okra into his mouth. "Yeah, Mary-Lou told me her cousin was coming out here for a while. She wanted her to stay here with us. Something about her house not having room because of an aunt or something... I don't know. Mary-Lou asked if we would let her stay here and I said yes ...I can't believe I forgot to tell you," Aaron laughed. He was the only one.

Their father smiled at Aaron as if they were alone at the table. "Well... wonderful! We'd be happy to have her!"

"And her train gets in tomorrow?" Rosalia said.

"Yeah, gets into the Midland station at noon." He turned to Jake. "Don't be late."

"Why don't you go and pick her up?" Jake gave away some of his anger.

"Because I've got to do that one thing," Aaron said.

"What *one thing*?" Jake said.

"You know, that one thing we were talking about. Anyways, it'll be good for you to get off the ranch."

"Carl?" Jake looked in desperation.

"Oh, I'm afraid I can't go. I've got to weld the hinges tomorrow," Carl said, smirking to Jake.

Jake knew the old man found his discomfort amusing.

"Now, Jake, it's really no trouble for you to go," his father said from the head of the table. "You should be happy to be able to help your brother out."

Jake tried to come up with something else to say. But in the end he kept his mouth shut.

How can my brother commit our family like that without asking? What is Aaron thinking?

Jake finished his dinner frustrated and remained so as he tried to fall asleep later that night. He was so annoyed his brother could get away with something like this, making a huge commitment for the whole family without consulting any of them. His father loved Aaron but this was ridiculous. Shaking his head, Jake wondered if his father would ever catch on to Aaron's tricks.

The next day he woke up early. He spent a long time trying to comb his hair. Truth was, it had been so long since he combed his hair he had forgotten it was time for a haircut. He was relieved when he gave up and just put on his hat.

Later that morning Jake found his brother still in bed. Aaron didn't remember the girl's name and acted annoyed Jake had asked. Jake went outside and made sure the inside of the pickup was clean, but the ranch had taken its toll and some of the mud would never be removed. Then he loaded up, swallowed hard, and headed off to find the girl whose name he never heard from a city he didn't know.

Carl down the way plowed the front pasture. The old man tipped his hat with a little smirk on his face as a frustrated Jake drove by. Then Jake pulled onto highway 385 and headed north. Why did he have to be the one to do this?

To get to Midland, he just had to turn right at Odessa. The sun was out and the sky was blue. It had been getting colder for a few weeks now so Jake kept the windows up.

It was amazing when he wanted to get somewhere, it seemed to take forever. And now that he didn't want to get somewhere, it seemed to take seconds. Jake hated how the mile count kept decreasing and how fast those white lines passed.

He pulled into the railroad station and parked in a convenient spot. He got out of the car and took the "Crane, Texas" sign he had made at home He had gone through multiples until he thought one looked nice enough.

The station sat lifeless. Looking at his watch, he realized it was only eleven-thirty. From his bench he watched the clock tick away and wondered what to say and thought of how rough the long, silent drive home would be.

As noon drew closer, people filled the station. The platform was wide, with rooms for offices on either end. Open to the weather, a breeze passed through. Jake pulled his jacket closed. Children asked whatever adult they were with, "When? When? When?" An older couple stood waiting. Pretty girls checked their reflections in the ticket window glass. A young suitor held flowers, waiting on his lover.

Flowers! I should have come with flowers for this girl! He would look so rude, but he didn't have time to worry. The train braked down the track, sending high-pitched shrieks through the air. Jake stood with his left leg behind a trashcan.

The engine passed the platform, vibrating the ground with its tremendous mass. It stopped and lined up the passenger cars perfectly with the platform. Jake could feel the excitement of those who waited. Those waving greetings at travelers seemed ready to burst. And then, the doors opened and the worlds of platforms and trains collided.

The pushy, loud people got off first. At absurd volume, they squealed the names of those picking them up and ran forward for their embrace. Children hugged parents, girls fell into the arms of their men, businessmen shook the hands of other businessmen.

Jake searched the crowd. He had no idea what she looked like. He stood there with his trusty sign. This girl could be anywhere. Maybe she would...

She stepped off the train. She *stepped* off the train ... She did not belong at all. Her dark hair drifted in the breeze, brushing against her face and neck, something foreign to the pinned up and restricted hairstyles of the day. Freely and rebelliously it flowed. The skirt she wore belonged in some exotic Mexican town, worn by a flamenco dancer.

This girl wasn't just in the wrong place, she was in the wrong time and space. She reminded him of gypsies or French maids. She was the wildflower breaking through the concrete in a city park, something pure and simply beautiful.

And though she dressed so freely, she carried herself like a queen. She stood there, Cleopatra of this moment in time, looking over that station as though she owned the place. Some of the formally dressed women gave her disapproving looks. They were perhaps jealous of how easily this girl had obtained beautiful.

Jake had never seen anything quite like her.

She looked his way; he froze. He couldn't move his

mouth to speak. He stood there trapped in the stare of her hazel eyes. Hazel eyes that didn't just glow, they burned. They were eyes that could kill a man, eyes that could give him life. She walked towards him in a way that hinted of dancing. Then before he knew it, she stood before him.

Somewhere in the back of his mind, something yelled at Jake to speak. So they faced each other, Jake and the princess. She was a burst of color splitting his existence.

She tilted her head, "I'm going to Crane, Texas."

Thank God. Jake came back to his senses. "Uh... uh... um... I'm, uh... Jake... um... Weathers." He cleared his throat and tried to pull himself together. "Are you Mary-Lou's cousin?"

"I am," she extended her hand. "My name is Ellie Peri."

He took her hand and shook it. "I guess I'm your ride." Touching her told him she was real.

"I *guess* you're also my host," she smiled.

"I've been told," he said.

One of the baggage handlers walked up to deliver two sizable suitcases. Ellie thanked him. She turned back to Jake. The silence got awkward for a moment. His mind had stopped.

"So, I guess we should get going?" She shrugged her shoulders.

"Oh yeah, right." Jake moved to pick up the suitcases.

Ellie noticed his brace. "Hey." She tapped it. "What happened there?"

Jake forgot about it because of the moment. She asked

with such forwardness that he didn't have time to worry about how to answer. "I hurt it when I was a kid."

"Can you still handle those?" She pointed to the suitcases.

"Yes."

"Then let's get moving." She clapped him on the back and led the way like one of Solomon's wives or Aphrodite preceding her servants.

Jake had known her three minutes and it didn't really bother him she had already asked about the brace. She knew he wasn't helpless; this was good enough for him.

He carried the bags to the back of the truck and put them in the bed. Ellie leaned casually against the truck, taking in the city of Midland that surrounded her. She pulled sunglasses from her handbag, like something Betty Grable or another one of those Hollywood stars would wear.

She looked as if she was waiting for something. He crossed in front of her and tried to act as though he had remembered to open the door.

"Thank you." She slid into the truck.

Jake went around to the driver's side and fired up the engine. They pulled out of the parking lot. Countless thoughts passed through his head.

"May we unroll the windows?" she said. "I've been cooped up on that train much too long."

"Sure." Jake unrolled his window as she unrolled hers. The cool air flooded the cab.

She stuck her face out the window and took in a deep breath. "How far is it to Crane?"

"About an hour." He tried to focus forward, afraid to look at her. What if he looked and she wasn't really there?

"And how did you get stuck with picking me up?" Her tone was teasing.

"I didn't have anything else urgent to do today," he said. His voice sounded mechanical.

"Isn't *Aaron* Mary-Lou's friend? I thought he would be coming and perhaps her as well."

"Aaron's pretty busy today. I'm not sure what Mary-Lou is doing."

"Are you upset you're having a stranger stay with you?" She pushed the hair out of her face.

Jake hesitated. He wanted to sound convincing. "Uh... no, not at all. The house is plenty big and there's more than enough room for all of us." He kind of even believed it himself.

"You're almost convincing me," she grinned. "And what do you do all day?"

He looked at her like it was the oddest question in the world.

"Are you a doctor, a butcher, a thief? I'm aware your family is in a comfortable situation. Do you simply exist?"

"Oh that. Well the ranch is a pretty big operation. I guess you could say I'm one of the head ranch hands. We run a lot of cattle so there's usually work from sunup to sundown." For a second, he took his eyes off the road to glance at her. He looked away immediately as though she were forbidden.

"Do you like it?" she said.

"Like what?"

"Like *it*. Do you enjoy what you do?"

Jake sat a moment. He definitely liked aspects of it, but *do I like it*? And why did this peculiar girl have so many questions for him?

"Well, yeah, I guess." This answer wasn't good enough for her so he tried to change the subject. "Where did you come in from today?"

"Dallas, but that was just for the night. I began in New Orleans."

"What's that like?"

"Like growing up in a play or a gaudy opera." Her eyes looked disapproving but her mouth grinned.

"Why was that?"

"I suppose the fact that my mother paid for my upbringing by singing at a gentleman's club. And the town always leaves the flavor of a gala in your mouth." She narrowed her eyes. "A sweet, endless gala."

"And what does your father do there?" Jake said.

"He gambles with his life and money, hoping to turn over the high card. I cannot condone him nor judge him. At times he is more religious than Saint Peter himself and at others more wayward than King Ahab!" She tossed her head in a dramatic fashion.

"Are they going to miss you while you're here?"

"Perhaps in the moments when they remember they are parents."

"So what exactly brings you out here?" Jake repositioned his hands on the steering wheel. This girl was like watching someone deliver lines from Shakespeare.

As he waited for an answer, Jake looked over at her, wondering if she had heard him.

She sat with her eyes closed as though searching. Ellie finally spoke, in tones so very theatric.

"I thank You, Lord, that I am placed so well,
That You have made my freedom so complete;
That I'm no slave of whistle, clock or bell,
Nor weak-eyed prisoner of wall and street..."

She flung open her arms and declared loudly to the roof of the truck,

"Make me as big and open as the plains!
As honest as the hawse between my knee!
Clean as the wind that blows behind the rains!
Free as the hawk that circles down the breeze!"

Jake didn't say a word. He didn't understand what she was doing. Sure, what she had said was beautiful, but she wasn't acting normal. Who is this person?

"Charles 'Badger' Clark," her voice hit him.

"Uh... what?"

"Charles 'Badger' Clark. He wrote the poem I just told you."

"Oh... okay."

"Jake, there are two things I love in life, poetry and painting. I even made them my focus of study at college."

"Your family let a girl go to college?" Jake tilted his head. "Where?"

"Saint Joseph College in Connecticut, but that's beside the point. You see, one day my studies shifted to American poets, some of whom are from the Southwest. I was given a poem to read, 'The Cowboy's Prayer.' A moment later and life was decided by a phrase and lyric. I felt something in me like I had never felt before. It was just so pure, so raw, so from the heart; it was so thankful. I started reading poetry of the Southwest more and more and have wanted... no needed, to come here and experience it for myself ever since." She gazed through the windshield with a look of fondness.

Jake was almost scared to ask, "Why?"

"Why? Why? To see the sun go down with nothing between us but the open sky. To be taken somewhere beautiful, somewhere endless. To experience Almighty God, not limited by the walls of a church, but in the limitless cathedral of His wide-open spaces. To hear, to listen, to myself. To see who I really am. To experience the sincerity that is in the simple. To let my bare feet touch, feel the earth. To sip water as it flows. For quiet nights, not just peaceful, but quiet..." she let out the rest of her breath.

Jake thought he understood. "...so you want a quiet vacation?"

"That, and of course to find my muse," she turned to him. "You are aware of what a muse is?"

"I remember something about that from school as a kid." He had read about it in one of Gracie's books. "And you need a muse to ...?"

"To write, and to paint, the Southwest." Her voice was commanding.

"And once you've written and painted the Southwest,

back to New Orleans?"

"Oh no! Onward to San Francisco. 'Tis the Renaissance Italy of our day!" She clasped her hands together and gazed toward the horizon.

"So San Francisco is the goal?"

"As it should be for any artisan of the modern era." She sounded certain.

"How will you know when you're ready?"

"Tears," she said. "When my own work brings me to tears."

Jake wasn't sure how to handle this girl. Oh well, he would encounter her rarely. She would be visiting her cousin, laughing at Aaron, or muse hunting most of the time. He wouldn't talk to her again. It surprised him that this thought gave him something like disappointment.

"I'm not exactly sure where to take you first," Jake said. "You're staying with us, but I don't know if Mary-Lou plans on being at our house or if we should stop by her place? What would you like to do?"

"We didn't really communicate that. I suppose we should stop by her house. I'd very much like to see Aunt Linda and her," she said. "Would you mind?"

Jake knew he'd have a very hard time saying no to this girl. "Sure."

They continued in the car for twenty more minutes. She spent the trip asking him questions about the ranches they passed. He told her anything she wanted to know.

"There it is." He pointed to Mary-Lou's house on the edge of town. A quiet little blue building with white trim sat on the lot. Dogs came running around from the back to jump up against the sides of the pickup. Their barking alerted Linda, Mary-Lou's mother. A screen door crashed.

"Is that my little niece? That grownup woman there?" she called from the front porch and came down the steps.

"Aunt Linda!" Ellie ran up with open arms. They embraced.

"Let me have a look at you," Aunt Linda said as she pulled back.

Jake watched from the background.

"Is that how they're dressing in New Orleans?" She looked her niece up and down with a cocked eyebrow.

Ellie laughed. "Is Mary-Lou here?"

"Oh no, darlin'." She nodded at Jake. "She went over to their house with Aaron to wait for y'all. How you doing, Jake?"

"Uh... just fine, ma'am." He tipped his hat.

"They can wait another hour or so, right?" Aunt Linda led the way to the house. "Come in and tell me about your life." They headed up the steps. Jake followed.

"Oh, darlin'," Aunt Linda said. "Can you handle those?"

"Yes, he can." Ellie went inside.

That was something new. Jake liked not having to explain that he had been climbing steps just fine his whole life. Aunt Linda had wondered, been told, and now she knew. That was the end of it.

Inside, Jake listened and drank lemonade as they talked. He continued sitting as their discussion evolved to girl talk and giggles. Aunt Linda seemed a little younger, healthier maybe, than when they arrived. There was something in the energy that her niece gave to her. Ellie, in her way, lit up the room.

An hour later, they said goodbye to Aunt Linda and her dogs and headed off.

"Do you want me to drive through town so you can see it, or take the highway to the ranch?" Jake said.

"Crane is pretty small, correct?"

"You could say that." He felt like he understated.

"Then I had better save it for some day when I need an adventure," she said.

Jake took the highway. It wasn't very far.

"There it is." He pointed out the entry gate, a wrought iron overhang stamped with a 'W' framed in a horseshoe. Jake got out and opened the gate, then he pulled the truck over the cattle grate.

Ellie looked around as though it was her last chance to see anything. She explored every inch with her eyes "Where's the house?"

"Up the driveway a mile."

"A mile? How big is this place?"

"About 4,500 acres."

"4,500 acres? What does anyone need with such a big ranch?" She looked at Jake.

"Oh, it's not for us." He pointed at some of the cattle grazing nearby. "It's for them."

When they arrived at the house, Mary-Lou rushed out, much the same as it had been with Aunt Linda. Close behind her was Gracie, who didn't know what was happening.

"And you must be Gracie." Ellie got down on one knee. "Very nice to meet you."

Gracie stood there, looking to her buddy, Jake, for guidance.

"It's okay, Gracie, she's nice."

Jake's reassurance was all it took. Gracie gave the biggest, warmest hug any visitor to west Texas could hope to find, holding the guest as though she had known Ellie her whole life.

Aaron was the next out the door. "What have you got there, Mary-Lou?"

"Aaron, this is my cousin, Ellie," Mary-Lou presented her.

"Ohm Shante, mademoiselle." He kissed her hand Aaron looked up at her and decided she hadn't enjoyed the greeting as much as she should have. He let her hand drop.

"Welcome to our home." Rosalia gave her a little embrace. "We're so glad to have you."

Finally the last two men came outside.

"Anything you need, Miss Ellie, just let me know." Carl extended his hand to her.

"It isn't much, but it's our home," Mr. Weathers said from the porch of his very large house. "You're welcome to stay as long as you like."

"You have such a lovely home," Ellie said as she entered.

"I'll show you to your room." Rosalia led the way to one of the guest rooms. She must have been excited to have another female in the house because she had made the guest room look like a palace. And wherever Ellie went, Gracie clung to her like a teddy bear. She insisted on sitting next to her at dinner. Ellie acted like she enjoyed Gracie, rather than pity her.

Dinner was a long affair. Mary-Lou and Ellie had to catch up from years apart. Rosalia served the meal with fine china and wine, a more formal fashion than usual. The feast came out in courses and ended with dessert.

After dinner, the family and their guest retired to the living room where they continued to talk and welcome Ellie for hours.

Afterwards, Aaron took Mary-Lou home. He was gone much longer than the time it took to drive to Mary-Lou's house and back. Rosalia put little Gracie to bed. Mr. Weathers headed to his room with a book. Ellie went to her room to start unpacking.

A while later, Carl lit his pipe up on the porch. Jake took a chair near the old man. When Ellie came out and asked to sit with him, Carl looked surprised.

Jake watched as Ellie went silent. He guessed that the west Texas sunset stole her away. She sat still like she was trying to paint the view on her soul. He assumed she endeavored to soak in every color, every detail as though she never wanted to forget it.

She looked entranced by all those reds and oranges, captivated by that gateway to eternity. "This is why people live here."

"Not the only reason," Carl smiled. "But it sure does help."

Only when a horse neighed in the corral was she brought back from her thoughts. "What was that?" she said.

"The horses." Carl pointed over in the direction of the barn. "I haven't fed them yet."

"You have horses?" Ellie hesitated, like a child in disbelief.

"We do," Carl grinned. "Didn't know you were getting yourself stuck in such a rustic environment, did you?"

"It's perfect!" She bounced up from her seat. "May I go see them?"

"Miss Ellie, you're family now. You don't have to ask permission to do anything." The old man turned and said to Jake, "Jake, take this young lady and feed those horses."

Jake didn't have time to protest. Ellie jumped off the porch towards the corral in an instant and Jake was after her. He managed to catch Carl laughing to himself. Ellie headed around the side of the barn.

"Hold up." Jake pointed to the barn doors. "In here. We've got to get their straw."

She walked behind Jake as he hoisted a hay bale into the wheelbarrow and two more on top of that.

"This way," he said.

She followed him out the back doors to the corral. As she passed through the doorway, her eyes went wide when she saw the horses. "I didn't realize there were so many!"

"There's twelve here, so Larry must still be out on one." He cut the cord holding the hay bale together. "See, what you want to do is break it apart into amounts about this big and drop it over the fence. Spread it out, too, so that everyone gets some."

She dived in. Jake watched her enjoy the simple, menial duty he had done thousands of times. Yet the almost dancelike, graceful way in which she made her movements seemed like Demeter the Greek goddess of the harvest, sprinkling seeds to feed the world.

"Is one of these yours?" she said.

Rio rubbed his face on Jake's shoulder.

"Oh, I see." She laughed. "What's his name?"

"Rio."

"Rio." She spoke as one speaks to a baby and stroked his face and neck. "Tell me all their names."

Jake recited them. A loud whine split the stillness. The wild, young filly reared up at the other side of the corral.

"What's that horse's name?" Ellie admired the beautiful animal.

"That horse?" Jake shrugged. "That horse doesn't have a name."

"Why not?"

"She's new. Hasn't been broken yet."

"Broken?"

"Means she isn't mature enough to let us get a saddle on her. She can't be trained to ride."

Ellie watched the animal and smiled with her eyes. "You were wild once here, don't let them tame you… maybe some things aren't meant to be broken…"

Jake didn't have a response.

"What is tomorrow going to be like?" She ran her hands down a horse named Alamo.

"The ranch hands get an early breakfast and then we head out and take care of the place. We were supposed to have trucks come pick up a load of cattle today, but they pushed it to tomorrow, so that's what we'll do first thing. Usually Rosalia is in the house with Gracie. And I don't know what Aaron is doing tomorrow."

"Does he not help on the ranch?"

"Aaron?" Jake thought he shouldn't demean his brother. "Uh ... he used to. He's still resting from the war."

"When did he get home?"

"A couple of months ago," Jake said, but their attention quickly turned when one of the horses decided to relieve itself. Jake was embarrassed but Ellie thought it was funny. They headed back to the house and said goodnight. Jake went to bed.

Hours came and hours went, but Jake didn't fall asleep. He kept thinking about this girl, Ellie. He rolled one question over and over in his head, the one she had asked him that afternoon. *Do I enjoy working on the ranch?*

Maybe it was hours, maybe it was minutes, but eventually he drifted off.

CHAPTER 6

The Gypsy

Jake woke up a little before his clock rang. The rooster crowed.

Ellie.

She was the first thought in his head. He was only half convinced yesterday happened, that he picked this girl up from the train station. He was even less convinced she had stayed in their guest room.

On crisps mornings, the brace was always cold to the touch at first. He strapped it around his leg and stood and put on his shirt. After putting on his holster and .45, he walked to the bathroom. Jake still wasn't sure that Ellie was in the guest bedroom, but in case she was and couldn't sleep through a tornado the way Aaron could, he didn't want to wake her.

He brushed his teeth, washed his face, and headed downstairs. Rosalia had prepared breakfast. Jake went outside and took a lungful of sweet, clean air. The sun illuminated the horizon in a warm glow, letting the world know it was coming. In the distance, steers lowed to each other.

His breath steamed in the cold. It wouldn't last long once the sun rose higher. Coyote and Axle, always a duo, came up to get petted before they took off to their mischief. Some of the ranch hands came from the bunkhouse with Carl and went in to sit down.

As Jake stepped into the kitchen, he froze. Something was off... there was an extra person waiting at the breakfast table. He looked at her. He didn't dream the girl up; Ellie was real. *What is she doing up this early with the rough necks?*

"Good morning, Jake," she smiled at him.

"Uh... morning, Ellie." He found a spot at the table and sat. "You know, Rosalia keeps the food warm for Aaron and Gracie. You don't have to get up this early for breakfast."

"Of course! But I don't want the work crew to leave without me."

Jake tilted his head. "Without you?"

"I didn't come this far to sit still all day," she said.

Jake raised his eyebrows.

Carl introduced Ellie to the ranch hands as they dug into the breakfast tacos Rosalia had made.

Mr. Weathers came into kitchen and ran through the plan for the day. "Carl, can we check the tanks in the highland?. We haven't had much rain and sometimes the herd gets stuck up there 'cause the brush is confusing."

While the men discussed their activities, Ellie sat among the weathered cowboys with the posture and etiquette of a duchess.

They made their way to the barn. She looked like someone from out East trying to fit in, someone who had learned what cowgirls wear from watching a Hollywood film. Her bright colors would soon fade in the sun. Her cowboy hat seemed like the most impractical thing ever to sit on a head.

Jake didn't see girls in pants very often and he thought it was a real pity that those shiny boots would get dirty. Jake made a mental note to try and keep Ellie out of the mud.

"Hey, Jake, why don't you put her on Puma," Carl called. "That mare is good for beginners."

"Puma, hey oh." Jake coaxed her in. "Here, get to know her." He left Ellie with Puma and returned from the barn with a saddle and tack.

The others were already saddled and headed out. Ellie patted the horse's side and talked softly to her. She stroked her face. "Where do we begin?"

"She hasn't been ridden in a while so we have to brush out her coat." He handed her the brush and showed her the motion.

"And why are we brushing her?"

"Horses will sometimes roll on the ground, getting dirt or grass in their coat. They can get saddle sores.," Jake watched her brush the animal. "Good job."

Ellie smiled. "Now what?"

Jake threw the saddle blanket on Puma and then hoisted the saddle. He showed Ellie how to strap it on. She struggled a little at getting enough leverage to fasten it tightly.

"Now you can go ahead and get on her if you want."

Ellie mounted the horse with incredible grace.

Jake shortened the stirrups just a little. "That feel all right?"

"I'm comfortable." Ellie sat on that horse like she was in a fashionable New York City parade. She held her shoulders back and her head high.

Jake handed her the reigns. "Just sit tight." He turned around to find his waiting horse, ready to work.

Within moments, he fixed up the gear for Rio, who moved when Jake needed him to. The worn leather saddle creaked between his legs.

As she watched how fast Jake and Rio got ready, Ellie joked, "I guess you've done this before."

Jake took the reigns from Ellie and led them outside. "So, first and foremost, when you want the horse to stop pull the reins straight back into your belly. Like this." Jake demonstrated.

Ellie copied his motions.

"Good, now right... left." Jake pulled the reigns to either side.

She mimicked him.

"Perfect. Now to go, kind of just nudge her and..." Jake clicked his tongue.

Ellie jerked her heels backward and Puma headed off. Jake gave Rio the go and they arrived along side them.

"May we take it easy for a while?" Ellie said. "I need to get more confident."

"Sure. Hold your reins a little lower."

Ellie obeyed. Instead of the pasture, they took the road, easier for a beginner.

"How long have you been riding horses?" she said.

"I remember my dad holding me in his lap and taking me for rides."

"It's so much quieter than a car." She patted Puma. "She's so precious."

"Yeah, I guess it is." He hadn't thought about that aspect, but it was kind of nice.

Ellie was getting more comfortable on the horse and started to look around. She noticed Jake's gun on his hip. "Do you get into a lot of gunfights out here?"

"Huh? Oh, that? No, but sometimes I have to put wounded animals down or dispose of varmints we've caught in traps."

"Is there something that can attack you on this ranch?"

"Nah, not really. Maybe a bigger hog."

"Could you not just use a rifle instead?" she smirked. "Or do you simply enjoy channeling Jessie James and Doc Holliday?"

"No, it's just that... it's lighter than... it's because ..." He was not sure why, but he admitted to her, a stranger, "... yeah. I guess that's really the heart of it."

"Feeling like you were born in the wrong century?"

"Sometimes."

How is she getting all these personal thoughts out of me?

"I'm often plagued by the same curse. I would have been better suited in a different time and place. Perhaps Colonial America. Think of it. Nothing before you but endless frontier to explore and wild new places to discover! Nothing behind you but routine and the Europe you had known, and turned from. No looking back. No fences, no bridges, no traffic. I would have been the first female explorer!"

"I'm sure you would have."

The two made conversation until at last they joined up with the crew, near the trucks. They turned off the road and headed across open country. The terrain got a little rough, between the brush and the broken ground.

As most first time riders do, Ellie gave Puma nervous, short commands, killing the fluid motion of riding.

"Easy there," Jake said. "The horse doesn't want to fall anymore than you do. Each horse has its own personality and way. You just have to let them do their thing. Right now, it doesn't matter what side of this bush Rio wants to go around. All I care about is he gets us to the bottom of this slope. Just trust your horse."

Ellie eased up until she and Puma began to get the feel of each other. The rider picked out the way and the horse picked the path. They were a team. Ellie grew more confident.

"There you go. Just get her down the slope, don't worry about where she wants to step. Unless there's something you don't think she can see. Your eyes are better than hers. And go ahead and lean back when you head downhill."

The group made the bottom.

Jake looked across the pasture. "We haven't taken cattle from this pasture in a long time. Plenty of steers here, but there's lots of brush so it's tricky. Just try and stay close."

She followed Jake into the brush as he started gathering cattle. After watching the boys work for a minute, Ellie turned to Jake. "May I try?"

"Yeah, I guess." Jake saw this girl really was serious about experiencing west Texas. "We'll start off slow then." He pointed at a lazy animal "Just get behind it and give a little holler to get it moving. It'll walk away from you."

She did so. The steer headed forward, but after a few paces it started to veer to the left towards thicker brush.

"Now get around on his left and push him back straight." Jake waved to the left.

Ellie obeyed and the animal moved ahead and out into where the pasture opened up.

"Nice work," Jake called. "Move him to where the rest of those heads are gathered."

She pushed it forward, timid at first but then she took charge. Ellie moved it to where the crew had collected the steers for shipment. She spun around with a huge smile on her face.

Jake smiled, too. "Good job."

Once the last of the strays rejoined the others, the crew had to move the herd across the pasture to the gate where the trucks waited. And Lower Canyon was a wider pasture, at a mile and a half.

"You and I will push the herd. All we do is ride behind and keep them moving. The others will ride along either side and try to keep the herd together." Jake pointed to their spot. "You ready?"

"Of course!" she said as though she were a child at her birthday party.

They started to move the group across the pasture. The ground thundered as all the hooves marched together at a steady pace. Dust turned up in their wake. The speed was slow enough to keep control while not losing the steers' attention. It was going smoothly and Ellie was doing a fine job. She laughed. Then the smoothness broke.

"GET HIM, JAKE!" Carl yelled to the rear.

One of the younger animals spooked and bolted away from the group, making its getaway. Jake jerked the reigns and pulled out. He searched where Carl pointed and spotted the young fugitive and the dust it was kicking up... the chase began.

Jake narrowed his eyes and pulled the brim of his hat low on his brow. And with a whisper, unleashed the stallion. Rio took off, as though hungry to run. He moved over the pasture like fierce wind.

While he pulled the roped loose from where it hung on the saddle, the pair closed in on the youngster. Jake hadn't found an animal in west Texas that could get the best of Rio, and certainly no steer. Jake swung the lasso, each motion slowed as his adrenaline pumped. Nothing existed in the world but him, the horse, and the steer.

Jake caught onto the pattern of the runaway and felt the rhythm of its run. He counted under his breath and waited for the perfect moment. Wait... wait... then he let the rope go. Rope met steer; the chase was done.

Jake tightened the rope around the animal's neck. Rio and the steer slowed down together.

"Easy there, fella'." Jake led the animal back in the direction of the trucks. They made way at a comfortable trot, running the fight out of the critter. Jake let him loose. He plunged into the center of the herd, as though ashamed at its pitiful flight attempt. Then Jake headed back to his spot in the rear and the drive continued.

"That was incredible!" Ellie's eyes were wide and her jaw had dropped.

"What was?"

"That! The way you caught up to him. And what are the odds of hitting him with your rope! That's not easy to do. That whole performance!" She looked annoyed that he wasn't as excited by it as she was.

For Jake, it was just another chore on the ranch. He had done this many times for many years. He had seen others do it almost as often, but her statements made him realize for the first time that maybe it wasn't the easiest thing in the world. Maybe he was pretty good at it. Even more so, maybe he was better than most. Yes, he finally admitted to himself, he was pretty good at that.

"Oh," he looked away. "That."

"Don't let him fool you, Miss Ellie. He's one of the best wranglers around," Carl called over and winked at her.

Being the focus of admiration felt odd to Jake. He helped with the loading and tried to avoid Ellie's attention. He pulled back a bit, hoping they would talk about someone else, anything else.

Forty-five minutes later they got all the trucks loaded. Someone south of Crane was sending cattle to the Hearst Company out of El Paso.

The owner, Dave Brandenburg, came to receive the animals in person. He walked over to where Jake waited on Rio. "You Sam Weathers' boy?"

"I am."

"I heard you just got back from the war."

"That was my brother," Jake said. He watched the man's disappointment.

"I guess you're the one in charge." He offered Jake the payment check.

Jake could easily have taken it, but something inside wouldn't let him. "He's the one you want." Jake pointed to Carl.

Dave Brandenburg gave him an odd look but didn't ask any questions. He headed over to Carl to finish business.

Jake reached down and patted Rio's neck. He wasn't in charge, it was all his dad's. And when Mr. Weathers wasn't there, Carl was in charge.

"That was so much fun," Ellie said. She looked confident enough to move the horse around on her own, with no one holding her hand. She rode over to Jake.

"Good," he said. "You can help us any day you like."

The thought seemed to please her.

"Hey, Jake, take that girl up to the highland and check the tanks," Carl said.

"All right," Jake nodded.

"What are 'the tanks'?" Ellie said.

"I'll show you."

They crossed back the way they came and took the road. Ellie decided she could use more speed. She got Puma moving at a trot. Jake caught up next to her.

"Okay, nice. Now let your body move with the horse and it'll feel smoother."

She did as she was told and enjoyed a more fluid and less jarring ride. The miles passed and they arrived at the highland twenty minutes later. Jake led her up a little lost trail. Thorn bushes sticking out on all sides grabbed at them as they made the short ascent. Grapefruit sized rocks covered the ground.

"Will the cattle even come up here? It seems like too much effort."

"Oh yeah, they'll go anywhere and everywhere," Jake nodded. "I've found steer in the most random of places. Places even hard for a person to get. One got through the house fence one time and we found him standing on the porch by our front door."

The thought made Ellie laugh out loud, a sweet, honey-covered laugh.

The pair got up top. Jake took a look around. The ground opened to a little grazing pasture. A rain shelter for the cattle sat along the side.

Probably twenty-five or thirty head of cattle grazed there. They were skittish and moved away from the pair, and lowed their warnings to others.

"That's the tank." Jake pointed at something that appeared to be nothing more than a wide, shallow crater in the ground. It glistened with moisture but no pool of water stood at its center.

"What do you think is the problem? Where's the water?" Ellie watched him survey the situation.

"I'm not sure…" he looked around. "Oh, the windmill pump isn't working." The tall windmill that pumped water from the depths of the earth to fill the pond remained motionless, despite the steady breeze.

They rode around the pond to the contraption. Jake slid off his horse. He helped Ellie down before investigating the problem.

"Don't we need to tie up the horses?" Ellie watched him leave Rio unattended.

"Not these horses."

She cautiously dropped the reins. "I guess I've see too many cowboy movies at the cinema." She joined Jake under the windmill.

"That's the well where the water comes from, and that shaft drives the pump." Jake pointed out other various parts. "So why isn't it working?" He checked the mill over and pulled on a few of the parts.

"Does that have something to do with it?" Ellie pointed to the top.

Jake looked. Something green grew where the propeller was attached to the gear. He moved over to the ladder built into the side of the windmill. He started climbing, expecting Ellie to ask him if he could… she never did.

At the top he examined it. Weeds tangled around the mechanism. He jerked some of them loose. "Tumbleweed," he called down. "Enough of them blow across the ranch to hit the exact area and tangle up the gears." He yanked the rest out.

Almost instantly the propeller started to spin. The gears rotated and the pump far beneath the ground started to work.

"You did it!" Ellie applauded as he made his way down.

The ground gave forth. She watched the life giving water pour from the pipe to the edge of the tank and flow down to the center. "With a twist of your hand, water to the creatures of the Earth." Ellie spoke as though reading the Bible or speaking to an audience.

"It wouldn't do us much good to let them die of thirst."

She looked like she might enjoy a more theatrical response. Jake went to help Ellie get onto her horse.

"No," she waved him away. "I've got to learn to do this on my own." She listened to Jake's pointers as she got in the saddle all by herself. As the day progressed, she put her own graceful flair into getting into the saddle, almost as though she were performing a ballet.

They came down a ridge after taking care of some more chores around the ranch. The day waned and soon it was time to head back to the house. Jake took them on the road home.

Ellie asked if they might go cross-country. "I so love horseback riding. It's wonderful not being held to the confines of the road." Ellie bounced along on Puma.

They headed through the pastures and soon the house came into view. Its white siding was painted the color of the sky in the light of the low sun. Its porches called and seats beckoned. Smoke poured from the chimney of the smokehouse .

Gracie leaned off the porch, searching the horizon. The little girl jumped and raced towards them. Gracie glowed with excitement as she came nearer to her Jake and this new person, Ellie.

Jake stopped Rio and bent down, as he had done thousands of times, and pulled Gracie up into the saddle with him but she insisted on riding next to Ellie. They sauntered all the way around the barn three times.

Gracie clapped for the show. Jake showed Ellie how to take off and store a saddle. Then Jake, Ellie, and Gracie let the horses loose into the corral.

They crossed from the barn to the house. They found a waiting Rosalia.

She looked Ellie over. "Miss Ellie, now you've gone and got your pretty little New Orleans self all covered in this west Texas dirt." Rosalia tried to dust her off. "They'd never even believe it was you."

"That's the plan!" Ellie said.

They headed inside to dinner. Aaron and Mary-Lou waited in the back room for her cousin. They sat close together on a couch, looking through a magazine. Mary-Lou stood to greet them while Aaron remained seated.

"You really went out and worked cattle all day?" Mary-Lou listened to the cousin she viewed as the pinnacle of elegance as she told them about her day pushing horns.

Ellie exclaimed so vehemently that she enjoyed herself,

Jake was inclined to believe her. Mary-Lou doubted that she too could do such things. Ellie encouraged her.

"I don't know," Aaron said. "It seems pretty backward to me to have a girl out working the herd."

"Miss Ellie was a natural out there." Carl winked at her. "I'd take her for my crew any day."

She smiled and Aaron shrugged. The group sat down to dinner.

"So what are you kids planning on doing tonight?" Mr. Weathers put a hand on Aaron's shoulder and gave it a light squeeze.

"We haven't thought of that yet, Mr. Weathers," Mary-Lou said.

"Just take care of him. I'll want my war hero back when tomorrow comes," Mr. Weathers chuckled.

"Yes, sir."

After dinner, Mary-Lou and Ellie continued their conversation in the den. Aaron stayed to grace them with his wit and charm.

Bill Clemson, who lived down the road, telephoned and informed the Weathers that one of their steers got out and was making a break for it. Jake went with Carl down to the highway and found her a quarter mile to the east. They started pushing her back.

"Miss Ellie sure is something lovely," Carl said.

"Something lovely... and something odd."

Carl chuckled,. "I'll give it to you. She's certainly nothing like what they've got here in west Texas. Truth is, I bet she's nothing like they've got anywhere. She's really her own breed. You should take her dancing."

"Heat of the sun has made you crazy."

Once they got the heifer back to the ranch, Jake searched for vegetables in Rosalia's garden. He stood off to the side of the corral, away from where the horses gathered. Rio didn't need to be called over. The horse's lips brushed across his hand. Jake stroked his face and combed the mane out of his eyes.

"That a boy," Jake said in a soft voice. He pulled some horse vitamins from his pocket and fed them to Rio before he headed back to the barn.

"Still pumping your horse with that doctor's wonderjuice?" Carl tweaked the tractor.

"As long as he'll eat it," Jake said. "That doctor in the magazine said it'd make him fast."

"Adding sugar cubes to it, I don't think the end is coming anytime soon. I think I need some of that stuff." The two laughed.

Jake figured it was about time to head into the house and wondered where Gracie had been. She wasn't calling for him to come and read to her or give her a piggyback ride. He climbed the front steps.

And where did the others go? Aaron's car wasn't in the driveway. His brother and those girls must have headed out. In the den, Jake picked up the used drinking glasses and carried them into the kitchen. Then he went to check on his little sister.

That's odd.

He could hear her giggling before he got there... and

another voice. The door stood ajar. He pushed it open.

The two of them sat on the bed. Ellie ran the brush through Gracie's hair with extended, thoughtful strokes. Gracie looked like a princess. Jake had never seen her hair look so long. Their faces glowed in the light of the little girl's lamp. They laughed together as though they had been doing this for years.

Ellie's hair was different, a mess of barrettes and bows, like she had let a child with a special condition have her way. The chaos of her locks whispered of a little girl having fun.

Ellie told Gracie a story about a princess named Gracie. It was now that they noticed him. Gracie calmly stood up and walked over.

"No boys," she said. She pushed Jake back into the hallway. Ellie gave him a wink and grin as Gracie shut the door behind him.

Jake figured the little girl was getting to experience what it was like to have a sister. He chuckled as returned to his room.

CHAPTER 7

Secret Wounds

Jake grew fond of seeing Ellie at breakfast in the morning. At first, he thought she would be a one-day wonder. She'd get over her initial excitement while growing tired of the early days.

Ranch work wasn't easy. He was used to it, but it took grit to get up everyday, fighting the sun, rain, and cold, and to go out to mend those fences and push those horns. Holes didn't dig themselves. Always dust or mud and fingernails that were never clean. Blood and bruises, a constant. Bad things always become worse things in the unending struggle, but the roughnecks get up everyday and do battle with a harsh land.

And here she sat at another breakfast, weeks since she sat down to the first one. She was ready to go, a smile on her face. "Good morning, Jake." She pushed out the chair next to her.

He took it.

She had gotten pretty decent at taking care of ranch business. She could saddle her own horse in no time. If Jake left her by herself in the barn for anytime at all, she would saddle Jake's horse as well. Every part of her was always ready to go. Her eyes didn't look tired. If there were anything she couldn't do, she'd try until she convinced herself she couldn't do it on her own.

She was as confident on a horse as one born in the saddle and made good time getting around the ranch now. She loved riding through the backcountry. And those Hollywood cowgirl outfits started to look like they'd been around the west a time or two, while Ellie vocally celebrated every dirt stain.

"Today, we're going to check for unbranded animals in the back of the ranch." Jake said.

"But don't all the animals receive brands when they arrive?" Ellie said.

"They do, but Dad has always liked the ranch to have a wild feel to it. We have some bulls that roam wild and father calves all the time. No one really knows how many animals we have out here."

They found a good spot near the center of one of the pastures. Jake started a fire and waited until it burned strong. Then he stuck the brand in it to heat up and left Ellie there to make certain the fire didn't burn down all of west Texas. He mounted Rio again and went off in search of the young ones.

He found a young calf in a group of nine and tossed the rope around its neck. He led it back to Ellie. It took issue with staying still. Jake had to give Ellie the lead rope to keep the calf from getting away.

Then Jake got off Rio and wrestled the animal to the

ground. He gave it a quick hog tie and asked Ellie to fetch the iron. Smoke sizzled off the hide as the brand left its touch forever. On its back quarters, the animal would bare the proud Weathers' Ranch mark: the 'W' inside a horseshoe.

"It is as though we were giving them tattoos," Ellie said.

"Yeah," Jake said. "I guess it kind of is."

"Oh Jake, I wish you could have been there! Once, when I was traveling about, we encountered some Tahitians who were such an interesting people, caught in a lost time. The tribe still practiced many of their old culture's ancient traditions. They had such tattoos!" She lit up as she reminisced. "Their warriors were painted for battle. All those women paraded beautifully adorned in stunning patterns! They had them down their backs and on their faces, every inch of their bodies."

"I'll bet that was something to see." He forced himself to sound calm, perplexed by the girl still more.

"It surely was." She looked down. "I only had the nerve to have them paint a tiny one."

"Just a tiny one... " It took Jake a moment to realize what she said. "Wait... you have a tattoo?" Only sailors and dark foreigners had tattoos, certainly not pretty American girls.

"Yes, of course, why wouldn't I? I'd miss out on a local tradition. Haven't you ever met a girl with a tattoo before?"

Jake shrugged.

She pulled back her sleeve and took off her glove. She wore a rather large bracelet, Jake had noticed it before.

She removed it.

"See?" On her wrist, maybe an inch long, she had a little Chi-Rho tattoo.

"I get tired of having to wear bracelets all the time. Most people probably think I'm a heathen or a harlot." She let Jake touch it. "I chose this because they all had marks of their religions, and I certainly wasn't looking for luck in war or fertility."

Jake felt he should be shocked and offended, but those feelings never came. Ellie was a fine person who simply had her eccentricities. He found himself not caring she had a tattoo. In fact, he thought the tattoo looked almost nice.

Jake smirked at how easily Ellie transitioned from wild tales to cattle work, but as adventurous as she was, it took Jake a little longer to get Ellie to brand her first animal. The odor of burning hide and hair made her cringe, but she did it. And every time after, it was easier.

They only found a few to brand. Unmarked, wild grown animals weren't a common occurrence, but Jake actually found a mature cow with no brand. That's the way his dad wanted it: an animal to be conceived, birthed, grown, and matured on their ranch without ever having been noticed. The ranch was so large, it wasn't crazy to think there were a couple of animals that the Weathers had never seen.

This one was going to be tricky to brand. Jake couldn't knock down, much less hold down, a fully mature cow. He laughed as the idea came to him, but Ellie didn't call him crazy when he told her what he was about to try. He made sure the animal was out on open ground.

"Ready, kid?" Jake said to Rio and took to the saddle.

Ellie handed him the glowing iron. He kicked Rio and was off. He had to cross the ground, chase down the animal, and try and stick it on the rump all from the back of a horse. Jake knew Ellie watched him. He made his moves as crisp as possible.

Rio's hooves pounded the ground as he tore the pasture apart. They moved so fast that the animal didn't notice them at first. Then it jumped and took off, startled into a run. Jake looked down at the iron. It had lost some glow. Rio was upon the animal in no time. He had one shot. Jake reached out and gave the steer a good, steady tag. It was perfect because the other cattle kept this one from turning.

The fur singed until Jake caught that unmistakable whiff. He pulled away to let the animal settle down. It lowed in pain, warning the other animals to stay away. Jake checked to see how the brand came out. It wasn't as clean as he hoped but was still unmistakably the Weathers' mark.

He felt satisfied and rode back to Ellie. Jake didn't need to mark that animal, but it was fun to try. He threw the brand on the ground to cool off. Then he and Ellie kicked dirt on the fire.

"Jake," Ellie turned to him. "You *need* to teach me to rope."

"Well, I guess if I *need* to." Jake handed her one of the ropes. "*Come on.*" He caught himself feeling comfortable around her.

They headed back to the barn and found some posts set at various distances.

"Hitting a calf in midstride *has* to be harder than this," Ellie said.

"Different than throwing a rope from your horse, but we got to teach you to throw from the ground first."

"Indeed, for if man had not learned to lasso from the ground first, how then would we have first captured the horse that later we would mount?"

"...Right." Jake thought he had said the correct thing. "You hold it like this, with your fingers around the knot."

She mastered it quickly. He demonstrated how to hold the rest and give it enough slack so it would fly through the air, how to swing it above her head.

"All right, since you want the line to wrap around this part, you aim here." Jake pointed to the spot. "And remember to end with your hand aimed where you want it to go."

"If you really want to learn how to throw that thing, sugar, you better let me teach you how it's done." Aaron walked by.

Jake frowned and looked away.

Aaron paused, but Ellie just kept tossing the line.

"I say there, sweet peach, why don't you have me teach you that?"

She still did not acknowledge him.

This time he squared off, making sure he would project loudly, "Hey, Ellie! Why don't you let me teach you that?"

Ellie looked over at him. "Oh, I'm sorry, were you

talking to me? This whole time I thought you were looking for someone named 'Sugar Sweet Peach'." She smiled. "Anyways, I already have a teacher. Jake's quite the cowboy."

Aaron stood there with his mouth hanging open for a second. Then he muttered to himself and headed for his car.

Ellie went right back to tossing the rope. "Like this, Jake?"

"Yeah, that's perfect." Jake let himself grin a little, but didn't say a thing. He couldn't recall a time when someone had chosen him over his brother.

Two days later, Jake went out with Carl to push horns. It felt a little odd to ride back alone. He had spent so much of the last couple of weeks with Ellie in tow. Call her his student, call her his sidekick, the point was that she was always there.

Jake pulled the collar of his jacket up a little higher against the cold. He made sure to lead Rio around standing water. Rio's hooves on the cold, compacted ground sounded different than they did in the warmer days.

He left Rio outside and went into the barn. He searched around the bench and through a few of the boxes. His fingers closed around the tool he needed.

"Hey, cowboy."

Jake whipped around and searched the barn. His eyes took a moment to adjust to the dark interior, but then she came into focus. Ellie smiled and gave him a wave from her perch in one of the lofts overhead.

Before he climbed the ladder he unbuttoned his coat so he could ascend more easily. First he came to a lower loft and then from there took another ladder to the next one. As he came over those last rungs of the latter he stepped into Ellie's domain.

She had built quite a little nest for herself, sitting wrapped in a heavy blanket, nestled in straw The girl had brought something warm to drink from the house and a few books to keep her company.

Jake grinned as he noticed that her wrist was bare, as though she had to come here to get away from the world and be herself.

"What are you reading?" Jake smiled.

Ellie looked up from her book and held it up to him. "Emily Dickenson. Do you like poetry?"

"No."

"Have you ever really tried it?"

"Not really." He contemplated his words. "I guess I just don't understand what's so great about it... I mean, why do you like it?"

"Why do I like it?" Her eyes lit, as though she were pursued by a lover. "For so many reasons, describable and indescribable. Because words are thought incarnate; and thought is what makes us human. It is in the enchantment around a baby's first words and the power in a dying breath."

She touched Jake's forearm. "Somewhere in 'I love you' can make one invincible, and 'I hate you' can break the unbreakable. Words topple nations as easily as an army of thousands. Men strive their whole lives to build empires only to hear their fathers say, 'well done'." She closed her eyes as though dreaming.

"And poetry? Poetry is the ballet of words. Poetry takes the ordinary and makes it extraordinary. It is a symphony of common instruments, brought together in an orchestra incomparable. Poets are the ones who really live so connected to their emotions and passions, squeezing from their days every drop of life. And we read their words to learn to find the beauty, and to live, really live. To taste, touch, and feel fully. In their eccentric phrases we read something we have buried in ourselves. And we take it back."

She inhaled deeply as though awakening from a dream and looked so very rested, speaking in such sweet terms as the Jake had never heard. And her books, once dead to Jake, suddenly had fire.

"How could you have never tried poetry before?" Her tone sounded like a doctor seeking to diagnose a patient.

He knew why, that in the land of the living, in west Texas, the work of Frost takes a second seat to a plow. Also the high school English teacher had about as much appreciation as a tractor for the arts.

"I don't know." Jake shrugged "I don't understand how poems can say a lot more than they... well, than they say."

"That's the fun though, is it not?" she reached for a book. "Decoding what the poets meant to say is half the challenge." She read:

> *"We never know how high we are*
> *Till we are called to rise;*
> *And then, if we are true to plan,*
> *Our Statures touch the skies-*
> *The heroism we recite*
> *Would be a daily thing,*
> *Did not ourselves the Cubits warp*
> *For fear to be a King."*

Ellie closed her eyes as though digesting the poem. He thought she let it sit on her tongue while every taste bud had their way with it. She opened her eyes. "What does this mean?"

Jake took the book from her and gave a serious look at the text. He tried and tried, and he came up with, "We are on top of tall statures of kings?"

Jake thought he sounded stupid and waited for Ellie to laugh, but she did not.

"Look at the first two lines. We learn that the subject of the poem is us: *'we never know how high we are'*."

Jake looked at the lines again and nodded.

"Then when we read *'true to plan'*. What could true to plan be with regards to a human? More specifically with regards to a planner?" She waited for him to respond.

Jake thought that if there were a planner for human lives, it was God. What God plans for the lives of men is who they were meant to be.

"So *'true to plan'* means we are who we were meant to be? Maybe? Our destiny or our character?" Jake hoped that this was something like correct.

"Yes! Very good." She touched his hand. "Now having said that, I look at the next four lines. Take the mention of 'heroism' tied to something we recite to mean the bravery we preach or sing of. Then to look at *'for fear to be a King'*. This poem seems to praise courage, and a king, being the highest level of praise, must mean the highest level of the courage... " She trailed off for him to fill in the gaps.

"... It means we're afraid of the courage in ourselves, or maybe, the greatness in ourselves?" Jake determined it must be right by the smile in Ellie's eyes.

"And the beautiful thing is the poem could mean something completely different to someone else," Ellie said.

Jake was still thinking about her hand on his.

She handed Jake a book. "Try it out."

Jake read the cover: *Edgar Allan Poe*. Ellie gave him an encouraging nod. He sat down in the loft with her and cracked open the book. He read pages and pages. The guy who wrote this stuff was obviously a troubled character. Yet Jake was impressed when the words put images in his head, vivid images. They made his heart move in odd ways. They made him feel a chill, but why should they do that? He had a coat on and the loft wasn't that cold.

Somewhere in the bewitchment of the words he felt the power of the work. And for one brief moment, in the slightest of ways, he understood Ellie's passion. "I used to think the stuff was frivolous." Jake said.

Ellie winked at him. "Don't worry, nobody is perfect."

He switched to another book and read pages and pages

of that author's work. Every so many pages, he looked up to watch Ellie read. He started to understand her thoughts on the words of poets and how they made the experiences of readers so much more.

In their beautiful lyrics Jake saw her motions as he compared her to other lovely things. Even the cold barn became an endless library of praise and condemnation. One could sing in glorious detail of the life the barn gave or the cold and dark it could just as easily cast. Jake lost sense of time. He just read and read, enjoying the company of this very odd girl from New Orleans and who knew where else.

He read Poe, Dickenson, and Shakespeare, making note of the way language evolved. In turn, the audience must have as well. These people could find so much about something so small and yet dismiss things as grand as existence itself. Poets were a different breed.

Hours passed until the dinner bell rang. Jake was brought back in a thunderous crash to the present as his thoughts were pulled from the pages. He looked at the wake of havoc he left on the ground: a pile of small books. Before he had not read them and now he had. They were his forever. He caught his thoughts now having a hint of the melodious as he reviewed the situation that made his current condition.

"We better go." He broke silence that seemed as invincible as eternity.

"I know," Ellie smiled at him. She had tied a bucket to a rope with which she lowered the books down to the floor of the barn.

"You've done this before." Jake said.

"Of course." Ellie climbed down first. Jake offered to lower to the rest of the books to her.

At dinner, Gracie insisting on sitting between them. Afterwards Mary-Lou, who came to dinner probably four nights out of the week, swept Ellie away to visit Aunt Linda again.

Gracie came up to Jake, her request written all over her big blue eyes Jake sat down in the den. She found his lap. He reached for the book of her stories kept on the table, but then he paused. Instead, he reached into his pocket and pulled out something from earlier that day: a collection of poems from different authors.

"Hey, Gracie?"

She perked up.

"Would you like to read Ellie's book?"

She nodded.

He opened it and read to Gracie, trying to get lost in it the way Ellie would. Gracie listened and Jake read her into the night, then he put her to bed.

When he tried to fall asleep, he couldn't wait for morning, knowing Ellie would be there, and wondered what else he would learn from her.

Sometime later that week Jake and Ellie saddled up by the corral and waited to head off into the morning. The neigh of the un-ridden filly split the crisp morning air. Her wild mane, highlighted in the rising sun, looked majestic, like she was queen of her world. The young horse trotted in circles at the far end of the corral her breath blazing from her nostrils in the cold.

Ellie sat there, admiring the wild horse in the corral. "She's too guiltless and free... have you named her yet?"

It didn't occur to Jake she was still nameless. "Not yet."

"Can I name her?" Ellie looked at him with hope in her eyes.

"Absolutely," he said, anxious to give her something unique. He watched Ellie search her imagination.

She seemed to thumb through all the pages she had ever read and replay every story she ever heard. The girl studied the horse's movements and mannerisms as the filly moved through the cold morning. Ellie ran her hand across the wood fence and stroked its textures. She waited. "I'm going to need more time."

"Not a problem."

They headed out of the barn, taking the road at a slow pace to a part of the ranch far away. It was one of the trouble spots for varmints, especially coyote.

"Teach me something." Ellie twisted in her saddle towards him.

Jake looked around for inspiration, something useful, something from the ranch. He searched the road and the landscape.

"You see those buzzards?"

Several vultures posed in an old dead tree, like something straight from Edgar Allen Poe. "Something died here last night. They ate recently."

"How can you tell?"

"Because their backs are to the wind. If they need to eat, they sit the other way so they'll have an easier time leaving the tree. When they've already eaten, their backs are to the wind."

Ellie stuck her hand in the air to test the wind. "Where do you learn something like that?"

"It gets passed down. Someone told me and someone told them. Sometimes the 'facts' we operate under seem to have no scientific backing whatsoever. We follow them, I guess, just because we always have."

Ellie smirked. "So they pass the tradition test but not the truth test?"

"That's a good way to put it. Where'd you hear that?"

"I once heard a preacher in Africa speak to the natives that same idea as a measure for judging the witnesses sent to them," Ellie told him.

She visited Africa, too? When she had first arrived, she was a mystery to Jake, and remained so. Jake wondered how she found anything of interest in dry, west Texas.

As her hair drifted in the breeze off the land, she seemed at home. She was the kind of girl who belonged in boots on a ranch as much as she did dressed in an evening gown, in the passenger seat of a hot rod and in the backseat of a chauffeured limousine. She could sit at the table of presidents or a picnic table behind a country church. She belonged everywhere and nowhere at all.

Jake broke his stare and patted Rio. The two horses matched pace down the dirt road.

"Jake?" She said his name without looking at him.

"Yes?"

"I've been out here for a while and... perhaps out of simple curiosity..." she paused. "What happened to your leg?"

Jake didn't squirm or flinch. The fact was he had a brace and she knew it. She hadn't pitied him and he didn't believe she ever would. He ran his hand across the steel joint. "This thing?"

She nodded.

"I guess I was ten or eleven years old. It was Christmas Day. And it was cold, real cold. We had something sort of like snow falling. Truth is, we had really great Christmases when Aaron and I were kids. The moment we heard our parent's door open in the morning, the floodgates broke. They always made us read the Christmas story out of Luke first to get our minds right, but that didn't help too much. The moment the wise men were done visiting the baby Jesus, we would tense up. Then we'd get the 'go ahead' nod from our father and we destroyed those packages."

Jake let himself smile at the memory. "It was a good day. Our parents got so excited about the things we had bought them from the dime store. They were such pathetic gifts, but Aaron and I were so proud. We had to save our allowance so long. Carl's the one that drove us."

"We spent all morning together, content to play with our things, but then our father started acting goofy. He went outside for a long time and got us to come outside. Mom made us put our coats on first but we got out there as fast as we could. I remember he was so excited. He told us to wait on the porch and to cover our eyes. And we didn't peek because we had learned our mother had eyes in the back of her head…"

He looked over at Ellie. "…We heard them before we saw them, the steady approach of hooves across the gravel."

"'Open your eyes!' our dad told us. I remember Aaron screamed with excitement. My dad laughed at us. He stood there with a pair of new white quarter horses. He had gotten us each our very own horse. Our skin was the only thing holding us together. He always said we had to wait until we were thirteen but he broke his own rule." Jake felt the moment all over again.

"How perfect," Ellie said.

"Yeah, it was… it really was," Jake said. "We each ran to one of the horses and started petting them. I named mine Ranger… I don't remember what Aaron called his." He stroked Rio's neck.

"We led them to the barn and threw saddles on them right away. Our dad got his horse ready to go as well. We waved to our mother as we headed out for a ride. Dad stayed out with us all day. The three of us rode and rode and rode. Our hands almost froze to the reins. My parent's couldn't get us off them. They bargained with Aaron and me to get us to come in for dinner, then we were out again. Our father didn't want to give in, but he took us for one last ride across the ranch… he took us for one last ride… just one more…"

Jake slowed his words, his voice cracking. "We were riding down a ridge and… it was wet. There was a lot of mud... that horse wasn't real confident and I didn't really have a feel for it... uh, him yet. He was real young... sort of wild still."

Jake hesitated. "The horse lost its footing. We tumbled... we fell... we fell far and long." He took a breath. "His weight went into my knee. Something popped. I felt it echo through my whole body. It filled my ears. It stopped my heart. My dad screamed, Aaron cried, and when they got the horse off me, I couldn't stand without my knee slipping. It just couldn't take my weight any more. It's such an odd feeling when your knee gives out, it just sort of quits on you. It's not there anymore."

Jake rubbed his knee. He couldn't remember how it was supposed to feel.

He looked at Ellie. "My dad had fear in his eyes. I remember his eyes so well. He scooped me up and carried me back to the house. Between the cold, the pain, and the tears from my mom, I don't remember what happened after that. I sort of recall my mom drove me to Odessa or Midland, some hospital. I woke up the next day and I couldn't walk on it. My mother came in first. She watched me on the crutches and tried to be calm. The doctors came in and asked what feeling I had. They tested my motion. In the end they figured I tore up all sorts of stuff in my knee, ligaments and tendons or such things."

Jake flexed his knee. "That next day they strapped on the first brace. I took those initial steps with crutches, then without." Jake swallowed hard. "And it's not walking with the brace that gets to you. It's that first time you try to walk without it. That first time you can't."

She didn't push further.

Jake continued. "My father looked at me that first time like I was something foreign. He didn't know how to look at me. I wondered about the horse. Later I got out of the house by myself. It wasn't in the corral. On the ground, only blood. All Carl said was we wouldn't be seeing that horse again." Jake looked down the road. "And my father was never the same around me. I guess he blamed himself."

He looked over at his friend. "I've never really talked about this with anyone."

"It's all right, Jake." She touched his braced leg with a loving hand. "I don't think you're broken."

"Maybe I'm not." He looked to the horizon. "Maybe I'm not." But he wasn't convinced.

CHAPTER 8

Boots and Belles

In Friday's mail, the Weathers received an invitation to a party in Midland celebrating the military heroes of the region, called "Gratitude in Western Latitudes."

A week later, the family loaded into two vehicles for the trip to town. When Ellie appeared on the porch, Jake forgot what he was doing and where he was going. He just gazed at her. She looked like a sunset.

He offered a feeble compliment, knowing his words would never be good enough, realizing his silence spoke volumes his words never could. She offered to ride with Jake in the pickup.

The moment they arrived at the school, the party patrons swept Aaron away and shoved him into a seat on stage. The committee led the family to their place at the table reserved for them. So excited was their father for Aaron, the Weathers arrived first.

"...and we are so honored to have them here tonight."

"Since the time our Founding Fathers boldly signed the Declaration of Independence in defiance of tyranny, this nation, this idea has been in a constant war. No, not an active war at all times with a tangible enemy, but a war nonetheless. From the moment those signatures hit that piece of parchment we were letting the world know—letting eternity know—we would stand for freedom. And with our guns or our bare hands we would challenge anyone who would try and take that from us! Our brave heroes, rise!"

The speaker paused for the audience's applause.

"Some have walked off the boats that brought them home, others have been carried... but their legacy shall not be forgotten nor shall it be erased. This generation and the generations of Americans to come shall look to their glorious example and remember that we shall not fear evil. And we shall bear the burden of being light in a dark world of tyranny. We shall be more! We shall hold ourselves and our heads high, always willing to fight and ready to die! We shall stand at our borders and shores and look out into the mist and fog with our fists clenched and looks ablaze, and yell out 'WE ARE AMERICA!'"

Some in the crowd yelled this phrase back as they cheered.

"Tonight we have the honor to show our gratitude to some of these brave young men. They've fought and bled for every one of us here and for all the dreams we hope someday to chase! Please join me in the best show of gratitude we can muster!"

The speaker, a Texas senator from Austin who had traveled all the way from Washington, D.C., led the applause like rolls of thunder across the plains.

A large group of people had gathered, perhaps two

thousand, and filled the gym at Midland High School. Red, white, and blue banners draped the walls. The band played the few patriotic songs they knew over and over; everything from the "National Anthem" to "Hail to the Chief," even though the President was not there. The committee of housewives who had planned and hosted the event at first decided the theme should be *Navy Ship*. Perhaps because of a stretched budget, *4th of July Hospital* seemed to be a more available theme.

Jake thought between the men who dressed as the Founding Fathers and Civil War generals, the clashing cymbals, and a few children who dressed like Indians, the theme could be *4th of July Mental Hospital*.

Aaron sat up on stage in full dress uniform behind the speaker, in the company of seventy-five other G.I.'s.

"This is so wonderful!" Sam turn to his family "Aaron is getting the recognition he deserves!"

"Does anyone else think Aaron looks like he's trying to hide?" Ellie pointed to where the soldiers sat.

Jake also noticed that Aaron was keeping an unusually low profile on stage.

Mr. Weathers laughed. "He's probably just tired."

Jake thought it looked like more than that.

The Weathers sat at a table together. Gracie sat between Ellie and Jake. The little girl seemed obsessed with all the bright lights and colors. Her eyes were big and bright. Uncomfortable in the crowd, she sat rather still as she surveyed the unnerving masses.

Jake looked over at Ellie. She was already a beautiful

girl; and the dress she wore only reminded the world of that fact. He noticed every pair of eyes thrown her way. All his senses fired as though he were roping a bull. He positioned himself in between obvious gawkers and her.

A principal, a mayor, a colonel and finally a state senator took turns speaking. A local music teacher sang the National Anthem and led those attending in "America the Beautiful."

Next a tiny woman of the committee took the stage and approached the microphone. "Thank you, thank you, thank you, Senator." She waved her hand in his direction. "Thank you, families of the men up here who supported them and fought the war from home while they were away."

She turned to the uniformed men behind her. "Thank you for your valiant defense of our country." The crowd agreed with her and showed their support.

"And now, ladies and gentlemen," she continued when they had settled. "Please, there is more food than we could ever know what to do with. Eat! In a few moments the band is going to open the dance floor. Other than that, enjoy yourselves!"

Soldiers blended into the crowd as the audience dispersed. Some ventured to the food tables, some to the dance floor. Mr. Weathers engaged people as the proud father of a hero. The music started and soldiers escorted ladies onto the floor.

Mr. Weathers stood up in his seat. "Young lady, would you make this old man's night and give him a dance?" He bowed slightly and stuck out his hand

Ellie smiled from ear to ear. "Of course!" She took his hand.

He escorted her as a father leads his daughter to dance at her wedding.

Jake helped Gracie get some food and made a plate for Ellie as well. Local wives and mothers had made the same spread at funerals, picnics, and church potlucks. He tried to convince Gracie she didn't want as a big a piece of cake as she thought she did. Jake glanced over at the dance floor. Mr. Weathers made Ellie laugh as he moved her across the floor.

Jake looked down at his body not in uniform. *They must be thinking, didn't get to go to war? You probably would have been too scared anyway.*

He led Gracie where the crowd was smallest and allowed everyone the right of way. The brother and sister sat down. Ellie and his father returned to the table.

"Not as young as you act, eh?" Rosalia teased him.

"Just an old bear in his last season," he winked. The patriarch headed off into the crowd.

Ellie sat in her usual proper manner as she relaxed after the dance. She looked at the plate of food in front of her. "Is this for me?"

"Uh… yeah." Jake didn't want to meet her eyes at first. "I was already up there with Gracie."

Ellie smiled.

Sometime later Mr. Weathers found his way back to the table. "Isn't this party wonderful!" he said. "Carl, have you seen Aaron?"

Carl shook his head. "I wonder where he is, Boss."

He turned to the rest of them. "Have any of y'all seen Aaron?" His father furrowed his brow, but just then the very same senator who spoke earlier visited their table with the woman on the event committee.

"Mr. Weathers?" The woman nodded at him.

Everyone at the table stood up.

"Senator, this is Samuel Weathers. He is a proud father of one of the soldiers here tonight."

The senator took his hand. "Very nice to meet you, Samuel. Now wait, Weathers? Don't y'all own a fair piece out by Crane?"

"Yes, sir, we do," Mr. Weathers grinned.

"And y'all have owned your fair share of rail lines out this way as well?"

"Well, you know, here and there." Mr. Weathers tried to turn the conversation from the family's finances. "It sure is our honor to have you all the way out here this evening."

"You should be very proud of your boy," the senator said. "I'd love to meet..." He glanced over Mr. Weathers's shoulder at the table. "I'd love to meet your wife... is she here?"

Knots turned in Jake's stomach. His family's faces cringed.

"She... passed away," his father said.

The senator raised his eyebrows and tilted his head. "Oh, I'm so sorry."

"It was a long time ago." Mr. Weathers' gaze dropped to the floor.

Jake held his breath, waiting for someone to bring the awkward pause to an end.

At last the senator said, "Please enjoy your evening and be safe in your travels home."

"We certainly will," Carl said in a loud voice.

The senator excused himself with his companion.

The table was dead silent and motionless except for Gracie, who explored her plate.

Jake sat and watched his father as clouds rolled over his demeanor. For a moment, it looked like he would recover, but then he pushed away from the table and left the gym. Jake stood to follow him, not sure what he would do.

"Hold on, Jake," Carl stood. "I'll take him this time. Parties belong to young men." He flashed his eyes towards Ellie, then followed Mr. Weathers out of the room.

Jake sat back down and turned to face Ellie. "Sometimes Dad has a really hard time with mom's death."

Ellie's eyes went soft as her gaze followed Mr. Weathers.

"Miss?" A square-jawed, handsome young G.I. stood before her offering his hand. "Would you care to dance?"

"I... " She turned to Jake who tried to seem unaffected by the G.I.'s offer. She turned back to the bold young suitor. "I would love to." She accepted his extended hand. The soldier led her off into an open area on the dance floor and found the rhythm.

Rosalia smacked Jake up the side of the head.

"Ouch!" He rubbed the spot "What was that for!?"

"Can't you tell who she really wants to take her out there and dance with her?"

"But I can't…"

"Don't give me that! You can take her around just as easy as anyone else." Rosalia flared her nostrils.

"Well… maybe, but…"

"But nothing! A young man should jump at the chance to take a girl like that around the floor!" She folded her arms and leaned back in her chair like a mother waiting for her child to make his bed.

She was right. Ellie looked every bit of breathtaking. By now, she was dancing with someone new. Her beauty escaped no one. All night long men, young and old, had not been able to take their eyes off her, not just her beauty, but also her foreign sense of style, not like the way the other girls dressed.

Jake sat there. He knew his place even if Rosalia didn't. He wasn't the one meant to be out on the dance floor. Fate dealt him a different hand. He was forever the one to watch from the table. He was the background, an afterthought, someone to fill the space. How could Ellie be displeased with her current situation? She had plenty of soldiers waiting to dance with her.

But something Rosalia said echoed in his head. Jake did not like the thought of ever making Ellie unhappy. Maybe these were the thoughts that lifted him from his chair. And maybe these were the reasons he crossed the gym to the dance floor.

If he took care to walk at a steady pace, no one would notice him or his brace. He crossed the open area. A mother chased two children past him while toasts and congratulations resounded in the air. And *she* was on the other side of it all.

Jake stood at the edge of the dance floor, on the outside looking in. His gaze rolled over those dancing. Maybe he would find her. He might even go out on that dance floor. He could take her by the hand and ask for a dance, but what would he do once he was out there?

Then in a moment, Ellie looked over the shoulder of her dance partner. She lit up and smiled. They were so close. Jake had taken so many steps. He only had a few more to take.

But the gathering was large and the rhythm fast. He took his eyes off her. Seconds later he stepped away and whipped his head in both directions to make sure he was in no one's way.

Somehow the crowd got between them. He was drowned in a sea of strangers. He thought about finding her again, but that was for the guys meant to dance. And he was one meant to sit. He found his way back to the table, back to Rosalia and his sister instead. And Jake faded into the dark.

"Now that wasn't so bad." Rosalia helped Gracie wipe frosting off her mouth.

"No," Jake let slip out. "I guess it wasn't." But he felt something, like someone staring at him. A little boy at the next table had locked his eyes on Jake's brace.

It would have been stupid of him to go out there. The chair was his, the background was his, and the silence was his.

"Hey, gimpy, are you ready to leave?" Aaron approached the table.

"Whenever," Jake said.

"Have you seen Sam?"

It took Jake a second to realize Aaron meant their father. "No, I haven't."

Aaron disappeared into the party in search of their father. Gracie began to squirm.

"I'm taking Gracie outside," Jake told Rosalia. After he helped his sister put on her coat., he put on his own. She squeezed his hand as they made their way to the exit. She only wanted to watch the crowd.

The stillness of the cool night air provided a welcome relief from the crowded gymnasium. Jake took a deep breath. They crossed the parking lot and the street that separated the elementary school from the high school. The staccato of Jake's boot and metal brace echoed off the pavement into dark skies.

Halfway there Gracie caught sight of the playground. She laughed.

Jake helped Gracie pull her sleeves over her hands to protect them from the cold chains. He hoisted her high in the brisk night air and let her fly. The silent playground grew full of life at the little girl's laughter.

"Higher!" she said.

"Higher?"

"Higher!"

"All right then!" He gave her a little extra boost that took her to the sky. She loved it.

"Straight to the moon!" came a warm voice from the other end of the playground.

Jake jerked his head to see who it was.

"Hahahaha!" Gracie laughed all the harder.

"Oh," Jake missed a push on the swing. "Hey, Ellie."

Ellie stood there, wrapped in her coat. The same shoes that carried her over the dance floor carried her across the playground.

"What have we got here?" Ellie said. "It's Gracie, the girl eagle!"

"We've got ourselves, Gracie, the flying squirrel!" Jake said.

"We've got Gracie, the human cannonball!"

Gracie laughed like it was her first time.

"We've got Gracie, the human tornado!" Jake shouted.

"We've got Gracie, the shooting star!"

Gracie laughed so hard she coughed.

Ellie's heels crunched as she crossed the gravel. "Got a little tired of the party?"

"I thought Gracie could use a break." Jake pushed in rhythm.

"Yes, one can dance only so much." Ellie pulled her coat tighter.

Jake thought maybe she was trying to lead the conversation to his missed opportunity.

"Done!" Gracie wanted to walk towards the lights from Main Street, not far away.

Jake held her one hand and Ellie her other. Gracie pulled each of their hands to her chest until they touched.

They moseyed down the sidewalk and into the streetlights.

A few cars rolled down the quiet road under the welcome banners that hung across the street. The shop lights were off for the night and the doors locked. Down a ways, a lone dog crossed the street avoiding a couple strolling hand in hand.

The stoplight at the corner replaced its green, yellow, red pattern with a simple blinking red. From one of the apartments above the shops came the sound of a record playing, a lady singing in a language Jake didn't know. Her voice filled the streets with its whisper, accentuating every thought and word.

One of the shops remained lit in its front window. On various shelves were little trinkets and other decorative items.

Ellie placed her hand on the glass and gasped. Cradled in the display lighting's warm glow, protected from the chill and the night, rested a painting of a field at sunset. The sun's shades of rich orange and yellows seemed to project themselves from the work and pull the viewer in.

Slightly off center was the silhouette of a woman. Her details were set askew by the sun behind her. It was something anyone in Texas could see any given day, but in an older Texas.

"Isn't it beautiful?" Ellie's rich hazel eyes looked hard at the painting.

"I guess so." Jake tried to sound convincing.

Ellie turned to him. "Jake, that's a beautiful piece of art."

"I believe you?" Jake hadn't convinced himself.

"Look at all the artist created." She touched her hand to the window glass. "See the woman in the painting? She's broken by the work of the day. Yet at any moment could deliver the most magnificent grace! The reach of the sun makes her all but invisible to us. Yet we are fully aware that she is beautiful. Her beauty and the sun's warmth radiates off the canvas. We can almost feel it. Then there's the mystery of the artist. Is this from his memory? Someone he once knew? Did he know her or just admire her from afar? Or is she no one, just a blank slate for him to convince his mind it is the woman he is meant to love. Think of what it does to us. Who do our minds tell us it is? This painting tells an entire story in a moment, a story that we can determine for ourselves. This painting is *perfect*."

Jake studied the painting. He let all those ideas run through his head. He started to understand, not fully, not completely. Yet through Ellie's words and passion, he was not only looking but also experiencing.

The light of the display warmed her face and illuminated her eyes. And her grin betrayed her, the grin that told the world the painting had gotten to her heart. Then a tear, a single tear glistened down the curve of her cheek. She would make a good painting.

They moved past more banners set up for the evening, old recruitment posters set up to gather troops from years before. It was odd to be in the moment-the war won, the fight over, and remembering when it all started. Had all that fear, excitement, and moments that stole breath, really been that long ago?

"Seems like yesterday that we waved goodbye to my brother. That day on the porch I kept waiting for Dad to break down. And now these years have passed. The moment we all hoped for has come. Victory…a sweet, slow victory." Jake said.

One poster offered a chance to be heroic and promised adventure waited. It said, "Be Part of the Story!" and featured troops walking through some exotic land carrying *Old Glory.*

"If you were in the war, what would you have done?" Ellie said.

Jake paused. She didn't ask if he would have gone, or if he felt sad he couldn't go. There was no question of *whether* he would have volunteered.

They continued up the street. In his heart, he had spent 1,467 days wishing he could have gone, damning the brace that held him down.

"I don't know," Jake said.

"I'm not fooled, Jake. You know exactly what you would have done."

Jake was very near telling her something he had never told anyone, something he thought about often, a truth that was with him during the war and still now. "Well…"

"Yes?" Ellie nudged him.

He looked at the sky, that boundless, never-ending pasture. "…I really wanted to fly."

"Fly what, a bomber or a fighter?"

"I wanted to be a fighter pilot, a P-51 Mustang..." Jake shrugged. "I don't know, I kind of wanted to fly one of those."

"And to walk around in those pilot sunglasses and leather coats?" Ellie smiled.

"Something like that..." Jake's shrugged.

"What made you want to fly?" she said as Gracie pulled them along the sidewalk.

"I like the thought of the open skies." Jake was willing to give a little more. "It's just you up there."

"It sounds nice, doesn't it?"

"Yes, it does... it does." Jake could not remember the last time he had he told someone so much. *I might be falling for this girl.*

A question came to him, one *he* was excited to ask. He didn't know where it came from, but it was just the sort he thought Ellie would like. "What about you? What would you want to do? You know, if women could be in the war?"

A huge smile found its way across Ellie's face as she looked to the sky with big, dreamy eyes. "I think I'd like to be a Navy diver. Yes, wouldn't it be something? To see as the fish see! Beneath the waves, the one realm we have not mastered."

"I bet you'd be the best," Jake said. "And there'd be so much to see."

Ellie put her hand on her chest. "So much!"

The clock standing guard over the street informed them it had gotten late. Gracie found a can and kicked it all the way back to the school gym.

When they arrived, Rosalia, Carl, and Jake's father were gathered at the table. Mr. Weathers seemed better as he spoke with Carl. The crowd had died down and the band no longer played. Jake wondered where Aaron was.

As soon as he asked, Aaron's head poked out of a side room. Jake expected him to open the door and let some new girl escape into the crowd, but no girl came. Instead he seemed to search the room. When he saw his entire family assembled at the table, he crept through the crowd and made his way over to them.

"Boy, this was fun!" Then he seemed to fake a yawn. "Whew, I am tired! Let's go."

Mr. Weather studied his son, then agreed.

They found their coats and made their way to the parking lot. Aaron already paced by the car. Sam got in the car with him and the engine roared.

On the way home Gracie fell asleep on Ellie's shoulder and Ellie dozed off leaning back on Gracie. And Jake drove carefully so he wouldn't wake them. In his mind it wasn't a pickup. It was a P-51 and he had a long way to go before he made it back to base.

CHAPTER 9

And Still It Poured

"Give it another crank," Carl called from under the hood.

Mr. Johnson gave it another go, but the starter just kept grinding. The engine wouldn't catch. He gave it a couple of tries. "Nothing," called Mr. Johnson.

"All right now, I think I know what's wrong." Carl stood up straight. "Jake, hand me that wrench."

"Why don't you replace this damn thing?" Jim Byron remarked from where he leaned against the workbench. "I swear it's acting up every time I'm here."

"What's that tell you?" called Mr. Johnson from inside the truck.

"That this thing never works," Jim said.

"It tells me you're over here too much!" Mr. Johnson said.

Everyone in the barn laughed.

"Besides, I don't need a new one. I've got Carl here." Mr. Johnson pointed to the front of the truck. The truck was old and weathered just like its owner. Its paint was peeled and had more than a few dents.

Carl dragged Jake along with him to the Johnson's place a few hours before. Every time Jake came here, the same crew gathered.

Jake surveyed them. Mr. Johnson, the owner of the ranch, was an older man, short and stocky; his best friend and greatest critic, Jim Byron, tall and lanky. In the corner stood Eugene Bakke who sold off everything he owned and downsized to live out his days. Sitting on a barrel was Wes Trevis. The man who wasn't homeless though no one knew where he lived; he just showed up. Older than Texas and still refusing to trust cars, Old Man O'Malli with glasses so thick they made his eyes appear rather large.

Jake always saw these five in their same places scattered about Mr. Johnson's barn. They were having the same conversation they always had. Maybe they never finished it or maybe they finished and decided to try it again and again, he didn't know. These men had little interest in anything out of eyeshot. The barn was the extent of their existence. They had their routine that went from after lunch every day until before dinnertime. Except of course on Sunday, the day their wives dragged them away from each other and off to church.

The problem became more complicated than Carl expected. He had to pull the alternator out of the engine. The old man didn't mind the work or the extra time it took and enjoyed coming over here to fix things because those good old boys were entertaining.

Between their commentary and the beer they drank, it took Carl a while to get the alternator fixed. When Carl slid the piece in under the hood, the sun was done for the day. "Give it another try," he called.

Mr. Johnson got back into the cab of the truck and turned the key. It choked once but turned. After it cleared out some carbon buildup, it sounded more or less smooth for how old it was.

A jolly group cheer rose from all the boys. They congratulated Carl and complimented his sixth-sense with engines. Of course, they toasted their beer in success.

"You hear that, Jim?" Mr. Johnson called from inside the truck. "Sounds like she's got another fifty years in her!"

"Try fifty miles," Jim hollered back.

Mr. Johnson chuckled as he climbed out of the truck on his short stumpy legs. He walked over and shook Carl's hand. "Thank you, my good man. Y'all should stay for dinner."

"That sounds great," said Jim.

"Not you, you old drugstore cowboy!" Mr. Johnson grinned, "I want to enjoy my dinner."

Jake didn't really feel comfortable doing it, but Carl said, "Of course, we'd love your wife's cooking."

"That makes one of us!" Mr. Johnson got them all laughing again. He shut the massive barn doors after they were outside.

"That don't look too good." Eugene Bakke nodded toward the sky.

An enemy approached dark and swift, the most evil-looking of cloud fronts. Its bulbous and menacing face loomed over them, like a bully threatening to unleash a barrage of fists. It extended from one end of the sky to the other. Just then a moisture heavy gust of wind touched their cheeks.

"It's gonna be a big one," Wes Trevis said. "I ain't seen one like that in years."

"On second thought there, I think we're going to have to take dinner another time," Carl turned to Mr. Johnson. "Jake and I had better get home and batten down the hatches."

Mr. Johnson nodded. "I don't blame you, I'd take any excuse to get away from Martha's roast," more laughter, "y'all just be careful on the ride home."

"Yes, sir." Carl and Jake climbed into the truck.

"Oh, my Lord." Carl looked out the window at the wet mess when they were miles away.

They continued for a few miles until they had to stop and wait for the rain to soften.

"This is a bad one," Carl said.

"Yeah," Jake said. "I hope everything's all right at home."

"If it continues like this very long, the river will flood in the lowland. I hope those steers will get it in their dumb heads to high-tail out of there." Carl tapped on the wheel.

Jake had never heard Carl sound nervous in his life so he shifted in his seat. "But maybe Dad took care... " Jake remembered that his father left town today.

"I know," Carl said.

"Well, maybe Aaron..."

Carl gave him an "in your dreams" look.

They were stuck for twenty minutes before it let up, just enough to allow them to drive slowly. They passed a car that had hydroplaned into a ditch.

They came around a curb and arrived at the bridge, already covered in an inch of water.

"We're going for it." Carl gritted his teeth.

They crept across the bridge and held their breath. Jake winced. Once they reached the other side, Carl let out a sigh of relief

They pressed on as the rain intensified. Pellets beat down on the roof of the cab in deafening rhythm. Their breath fogged up the windows. They had to roll them down a little to help clear the windshield. And the whole time, it was cold. They were soaked.

Jake looked at his watch when they turned onto their driveway. Two and a half hours had passed since they left Mr. Johnson's. Jake surveyed the storm wrecking their ranch.

Rain pounded the earth. Huge amounts of water gathered in the depressions of the front pastures. New temporary ponds sprang up. Some of the cattle huddled under the rain shelter for protection and warmth. The wind blew fiercely and abused the few trees in the pasture. The downpour broke up the dirt roads so much the truck sank down as they drove, but if Carl just kept it moving, they wouldn't get stuck.

Finally they closed in on the house. Their driveway never seemed so long. The closed barn doors trapped the horses outside. Jake felt like hitting himself when he remembered he didn't take off Rio's saddle before he left with Carl to go to Mr. Johnson's. He would have to dry it and treat it with leather care.

They pulled up and stopped in front of the barn.

Carl turned towards him. "All right, Jake, get the horses in the barn and I'll..."

Rosalia sprinted into the rain from the house with wide eyes and clenched teeth. Hair on the back of Jake's neck stood up. He felt sick.

Carl opened the door so fast, he almost ripped it off its hinges. The woman fell weeping into his arms. Jake climbed out next. He could barely hear her above to the rain.

"She's gone!" Rosalia cried out.

"Who's gone?" Carl said.

"I don't know where she is!" Rosalia yelled through her tears.

"Slow down! Who? Who's gone?"

"She hasn't come back! I don't know where she went!"

Jake could not understand her desperate ramblings that followed.

"Rosalia!" Carl shook her by the shoulders.

She slowed down just enough to get out the words: "Ellie! A walk! Never came back!"

Jake's heartbeat was all he could hear, not Rosalia's cry or Carl calling out for him to wait. He tore wide the corral gate and flew inside. He was on Rio in moments.

He grabbed the reins and kicked the horse hard. They charged into the rain, into the night... into the tempest.

Water beat his face like a thousand bees. The storm

licked its lips for another victim. Jake looked at the sky and whispered, "Bring it on."

The ground was slick with mud, while every stride ran the risk of taking a spill. Jake squinted hard to see through the pouring hordes. His skin ached in the cold. His face, his hands, his neck burned. His every breath had the edge of frost on it. It bit his lungs, but he didn't care. Ellie was lost in the storm. And he wasn't going to stop.

He tore across the front pastures, lost in the night. A layer of water flooded the ground everywhere. Rio's every step splashed in the air and sprayed a trail behind them. They raced passed a cluster of cattle. The animals fled him and his crazy horse.

They approached a rise that was soft earth, even in dry weather. Mud buried Rio's ankles as they trudged up it. One step forward, three steps back. His steps slipped as they lost ground.

Jake jumped off Rio to lead him to the top, but he slid all over the place as well and finally just let Rio go. The horse used what momentum it could, and disappeared into the dark up the ridge.

And still it poured.

Jake fell to his hands and knees and crawled through the muck. Every fistful of mud got him one step closer. And he felt angry for trying to take this rise in these awful conditions. He would crawl up so far and then seemed to lose it all on a slick spot. He went face first into the mud more than once, but he kept moving forward. It was all he could do.

Jake made the top and felt grateful his old friend waited for him. Rio shook his mane. Jake pulled himself off the ground and into the saddle. Once again they went flying across the land when flying shouldn't be attempted. Jake rode for the lean-to cattle shelters set up in this pasture. The cattle packed the shelters to the brim. Some of the steer stood clumped nearby, just hoping to get a turn.

Jake and Rio raced up to the shelter. He yanked the reins hard. The two slid to a halt. Jake ran into the shelter, scattering the cattle, who pushed hard to get out of his way. He cleared them out of there.

"Ellie! ELLIE?"

No answer. He was gone in seconds. Jake and Rio crossed the rest of the pasture. Jake yelled out her name as though she could hear him.

Then the ground shook with a rumble of thunder as the rain became a winter storm. Lightning split the sky and illuminated a whole pasture, letting Jake see through the dark for a moment.

The dark and speed didn't give the horse his best trip through the menacing branches that reached out for him. He plowed through and ran over whatever he could. One branch grazed Jake across the face, sending blood down his check. He tasted it. The next branch tore the sleeve of his jacket. He couldn't stop the nightmare.

And still it poured.

"Come on, kid!" Jake whispered to Rio.

They came out the other side as a few bursts of lightning allowed Jake to search the next pasture... no Ellie. They had to travel down a rise now. As he and Rio tried to take it too fast, the horse started to slip. They would have tumbled if Rio had not rested on his hindquarters. The pair slid down the rest of the slope.

Rio neighed high into the dark. When the ground leveled out, Rio stood on all fours once more. Jake checked Rio's stride before he kicked him again.

Jake could tell that the dam way up river fractured, and badly, forming a temporary second river. Jake guessed the river was three and a half or four feet deep in the middle. Runoff rolled down from the higher parts of the ranch.

And still it poured. The sky was so black.

With powerful strides, the horse fought his way through to the other side. They made the far bank. Jake looked back for just a moment. The swirling current had washed the legs out from under a small calf, now carrying it toward disaster, unless Jake went for it. He only had one purpose. The calf would die.

He headed across the next pasture. An old broken cabin used a century before sat abandoned in the pasture. They arrived and Jake fell off Rio. He shoved the door open.

"ELLIE!" he yelled. "ELLIE!" He punched the wall. If she was in trouble, he was running out of time. He got back on the horse.

Where the hell is she? Where does she like to go? Maybe she is by that tree she sometimes reads under. Yeah, by that tree... the one in the lowlands... where the flood would be the worst... then his heart stopped, "*...oh no.*"

He kicked Rio harder than he meant to. The beast

reared back, screaming as his front legs lashed the air. Jake didn't apologize. They took the road to the ridge over the lowland, the longest two miles of Jake's life. He rode as if the devil chased him. The storm made thunder, so did Rio. The rain beat at him like it wanted his soul.

"Come on, God," Jake thought. "Give me something."

The sky lit up with God's answer when lightning streaked long and bright, illuminating the whole of the lowlands, just for half a heartbeat, but it was enough. The whole area looked like a damn lake with a dark figure alone amid the chaos.

They headed down the two switchbacks that took them below. Ankle deep in water, Rio's every stride splashed as they crossed the pasture toward the figure.

A slight incline dominated the far side, leaving a patch of ground uncovered with water. Puma, the mare, stood on top, by herself.

"WHERE IS SHE?" Jake called as though the horse could answer him. He headed off the incline into the water and farther into the chaos. It wasn't too deep. They dominated the building tide and went from water to ground every other stride.

And still it poured.

Jake looked across the river at the lean-to they constructed, now surrounded by the flood. "She couldn't be in there, that'd be the worse possible thing."

"JAKE!"

The cowboy stopped the horse.

"ELLIE?" He cried out.

"JAKE!" She came out of the little rain shelter and screamed at the top of her lungs.

Jake's heart sank. She was trapped on a little patch of ground, surrounded by rushing water. He stopped for a moment, his momentum lost. She seemed a world away.

The rain beat down in the cold dark.

"Oh, this is as bad as it could be," Jake said to his horse.

Rio followed him a little farther up river from her and Jake slid down from his horse, taking off his hat. It was so wet it had lost its shape. He tossed it on the ground.

"All right, boy," he said into Rio's ear as he pulled the rope from the saddle. "You're already the best horse. Now, I'm counting on you."

He tied one end off on the horn of the saddle and wrapped the other end around himself. "Stay right there, kid," he told his horse. Jake stood on the edge of the tempest and looked into the rushing water. "Here goes nothing..."

He took the first step and the force of the current struck his foot. Jake took another step and the force grew as he sank up to his knee. He couldn't stop. He wouldn't stop.

Another step, more force beat at his leg. He was up to his waist now, the flow wrapped around him, trying to take him. He took slow, shaky steps and inched his way across. With every step he let out a little more rope. Step, step, step...

Gone.

The ground gave out beneath and the river swallowed him. The air he breathed abandoned him. The water filled his mouth and nose. He lost his sense as he was shoved below the cold and dark current, into the hard bottom. He couldn't swim against it while his lungs begged for air. He was drowning in panic.

No! Focus! Keep going!

Jake rolled on the bottom and held tight to the rope. Jake angled his body upwards and pushed to the surface, breaking through but barely able to tell, so horrendously poured the rain. Air filled his lungs. He rolled over and got close to Ellie's side until his leg hit bottom. While the water rushed around his knees, he stood and took two big steps to higher ground. He still felt a little disoriented when Ellie's arms wrapped around his neck.

"Oh Jake!" she whispered in his ear. She held on so tight.

He escaped drowning in the water only to be suffocated by Ellie. As he caught his breath, something in her hug made the night less terrible.

She shivered, soaked to the bone, and tightened her grip on his shoulders.

But they were only halfway home. The water was rising and their little patch of ground conceded to the intruding tides. Their island would soon disappear.

"Stay still!" Jake yelled over the rain. He wrapped the line around himself and Ellie and tied it off. He checked the other end to make sure it was still fastened to Rio. That river would get another go at him.

"Hold tight!" he said.

She clutched him hard and buried her face in his chest. He thought he heard her pray.

"ALL RIGHT, KID!" he yelled at Rio. "MAKE IT HAPPEN!" Then Jake closed his eyes and fell back into the water, and Ellie followed him into the dark. The depths waited for the pair as they found the bottom again, but Jake couldn't worry. All he could do was hold her and not let go. The line was taut.

Jake waited for forever. *Hold her... hold her... hold her.*

Something hit his right shoulder. He felt down... ground! They pushed off and broke the surface. The two were in knee-deep water on the Rio's side of the river. Rio had pulled them across.

"Ellie?" Jake lifted her face.

"I'm still here."

He helped her up higher on the bank. They were out of the water, but that wouldn't last long. Jake took off his soaking wet coat and put it around her shoulders. He picked his hat off the ground and put it on her head.

He patted Rio's neck. "Thank you." After he lifted Ellie up on Rio, Jake climbed on behind her. "Let's move."

Rio made his way through shallow water and headed for higher ground. They fought for every step until they reached one of the depressions on the rising side of the pasture. Rio took his first steps down and trudged through the water. His big, muscular legs worked against the weight of the riders and force of the current.

They were too far to turn back when Jake felt Rio's hooves get heavy. His horse sank in the newly formed mud underwater. His legs fought the ground that consumed them.

Jake knew Rio couldn't make it with the extra weight of two people on his back. He examined the flow of water. A fence passed through the river's path downstream. The water flowed through.

"Hold these!" He handed the reins to Ellie.

She hesitated, then took them. Jake took a breath and slipped off the back of the horse. He was shocked by how quickly the current swept him away. Ellie screamed.

Jake hit the submerged part of the fence with his side, knocking the wind out of him. The current pinned him hard against the barrier. He forced his hand up out of the water to grab the top of the fence and pulled hard.

When his face broke the surface, he gulped air and managed to get his other hand up there and pulled some more. The rest of his body rose out of the water. Jake found his footing. The water rose up to his torso but he supported himself on the fence and pulled his way across.

He crawled through a few inches of water until he could stand up. Ellie and Rio waited for him at the top of the riverbank. He hobbled over to the two of them.

She shivered; the cold trying to take her away. Jake climbed on and pulled her into his chest and tried to warm her. The cold shut him down, too, so he gave Rio a nudge and left it in the horse's control, only vaguely noticing passing Puma and grabbing her reins.

He breathed and he felt Ellie breathe. The rain punished them the whole time. It screamed at them never to forget this night.

He knew the way back as well as he ever knew anything

in his life. Still, the landmarks seemed so out of place. *Why are they so far apart?*

The house came into view at last. The lights inside split the night like a lighthouse calling in wearied sailors after they fought a merciless ocean. The moment they were near enough to be cast in the light of the house, Rosalia and Carl charged out the door.

"Take her!" Jake hollered. He let Ellie fall down into Carl's arms.

Carl carried her into the house, moving swiftly like a much younger man. Rosalia ran after them. "Put her in a hot bath and give her a glass of brandy!"

Jake took both horses to the barn and led Puma to her stall. As he turned to stroke Rio's neck, he said, "You don't understand what I'm saying, but you're the best horse that ever walked Texas."

Rio trudged over to where Jake kept the sugar cubes stashed and waited. Jake laughed and followed him. With achy hands, he pulled a fistful out and spread open his palm. As Rio licked and crunched his treat, Carl walked into the barn.

"Hell of a horse," said Jake.

"Hell of a man," said Carl.

Jake was too tired to protest. Carl hadn't been there and didn't see Jake falling or getting swept away by the rivers or how pathetic the rescue attempt was. The old man didn't see Jake had failed time and time again.

"Let's go inside," Carl said.

Jake followed him through the pouring rain one last

time. He took the stairs up to the porch, opened the door, and walked inside to the warmth. The cup of coffee warmed his insides. Upstairs he found dry clothes.

In the hallway stood Gracie with a big smile on her face. She latched onto Jake with a big hug before he could point out that he was a soaking mess.

An hour later they gathered around Ellie's bed as she told them how she got stuck. She had taken Puma out in the later afternoon. She wanted to do some reading and sat under the tree out there in the lowlands. The breeze picked up and proved a little chill. It kept blowing her pages around. She surrendered to the conditions but wanted to stay outside. So she sat inside that little cattle lean-to to get out of the wind. The book she read failed to keep her interested and she soon fell asleep. When she finally woke up from her deep sleep, she was under assault. The flooding river had driven Puma away and left Ellie trapped.

"I thought it was my end." She looked into the light of a lamp.

"That's enough questions now, y'all," Rosalia told them. "She needs her rest." Rosalia led the way and Carl followed. Jake trailed them.

"Jake," Ellie whispered.

He turned to her.

"Jake, I ..." Tears glistened at the edge of her eyes. She opened her mouth a few times, but no words came out.

When she tilted her head in silence, Jake understood she didn't know what to say. He drew near to her side and brushed a stray lock of hair from her face. "I'm happy you're all right."

She grabbed his hand and rested it on her cheek.

With a gentle motion, he pulled her blankets over her shoulders. Then he left her there to her dreams.

Later as he lay in bed, he didn't know what to do with all he felt. All he knew was that his skin still burned from the fire in his hands, ignited the moment he touched her face.

CHAPTER 10

Cowboy's Poem

The minute Jake stepped out into the sun the day after the rain, he knew it would be a mess. Dark clouds of buzzards circled high in the sky over the lowlands.

Carl and Jake loaded up with some of the ranch hands. They all headed out to the lowlands to see the damage. Carcasses dotted the field.

"Those buzzards' bellies are going to burst." The old man wiped his brow.

The ground was by no means dry, but it grew much firmer in just an hour or two of sun. All the floodwaters dried up or flowed away. The horses sank in only enough to leave hoofprints.

The boys set to work and dragged the steer carcasses to the center of the pasture. The crew couldn't get a truck back to this part of the ranch, so they hitched up a two-wheel wagon to some plow horses.

The group chopped down two trees to get enough wood and packed it in all around the animals. The wood was still wet from the night before. They even chopped up the two-wheeled wagon and spread its dry splinters around.

A rider approached. Jake raised his eyebrows.

"How many did we lose, Carl?" Mr. Weathers said.

"Twenty-four, boss. We got lucky."

"In a way. I suppose."

Carl nodded and struck a match to the box. It grabbed life and burst into flame. He lit the rest of the box and dropped it to the ground. The fire hit the tail of gasoline they poured and sent sparks dashing across the ground. The inferno ignited the huge pyre and sent the blaze high into the air.

Jake pulled his bandana over his face as the putrid odor of burning carcasses rose.

The heat intensified quickly. Everyone backed their horses off and took another position to watch. Deep black smoke swelled high into the sky, echoing the plumes from other ranches.

"I'm sorry I wasn't here Carl," Mr. Weathers said. "It must have been a real circus here last night for you and the boys."

"Actually it was Jake here who really got a taste of the storm."

His father turned to him. "What happened?"

"Oh nothing, I just had a heck of a time getting all those horses out of the corral and into the barn." Jake hoped Carl wouldn't elaborate.

Carl shook his head.

Mr. Weathers said. "I may order in some excavators and see if we can't dig some relief channels back here so this won't happen again. It'll be a big investment, but it should be worth it over the next couple of years."

"That should do fine, boss," Carl said.

Back at the house, Jake had just pulled off his boots when the phone rang. By the third ring, he realized no one else would answer. He had trouble recognizing Aaron's voice over the music from the jukebox in the background.

"Aaron, the ranch is wrecked after the storm the other night. Where are you? We need you here!"

"Uh, I can't come home right now. Too busy."

"With what? Get home now."

The line clicked as his brother hung up on him. Jake slammed the receiver down. He found his father later and informed him Aaron wasn't coming back to the ranch to help.

"Aaron deserves a little fun. You'll just have to take up the slack for him." Sam walked away.

Jake left the house and tried to shake his frustration.

Two days later he held Rio's reins while the visiting blacksmith tacked the horseshoe in place.

"I ain't never seen legs and a neck like that," Bob said between spits of his tobacco juice. "What did you tell me he's got in him?" Every time Bob came they had this same conversation.

"His sire was a Morgan horse and his mother was an Arabian," Jake said.

"Arabian? That's one of them fancy-boy horses, ain't it?"

"Sort of." Jake felt bad for not defending the animal. He figured that Bob wouldn't realize that the Arabs bred Arabians for endurance and speed in hot climates, more intense than west Texas summers. The man had also probably never heard of a Morgan horse.

Bob continued shoeing the other horses and returned them to their stalls, but Jake took Rio for a quick walk around the barn to make sure the shoes were on correctly. Later, Jake stood by as Bob got paid at the house and loaded all his equipment into his truck. He jawed with Mr. Weathers a while longer before he left. Rosalia gave him one of the cookies she had made.

Jake let Rio loose in the corral and headed back to the house. He investigated the empty kitchen, found some fixings for a sandwich, and ate it over the sink.

Rosalia came in from the back. "You insult me," she winked. "I'm paid to cook you good food and you go for a sandwich?" She took Jake's glass from him and cleaned it and put it back in the cupboard.

"So," Jake said. "How is Ellie doing?"

"You know where she is." Rosalia nodded toward the hall. "Go ask her yourself."

Jake didn't move. He just worried that the experience of the storm three nights ago would have made things odd between them.

Eventually he walked down the hallway and put his ear to the door of Ellie's room. Ellie and Gracie's voices crept through the wall. He knocked on the door and waited for an answer. Gracie opened the door and giggled out loud.

"Jake!" Ellie smiled.

Gracie pulled him into the room and shut the door behind him. She pushed him into a chair and returned to sit on the bed where she and Ellie looked through books.

"It's about time you came walking through my door." Ellie sat up straighter.

"Yeah, I know... things have just been real busy out there." He cleared his throat. "How are you feeling?"

"As healthy as anyone ever was." She waved her hand. "I'm staying in here because I promised Rosalia I wouldn't move until tomorrow. Boredom and not the flu is going to be the death of me. But how are you feeling?"

Jake touched the cuts on his face. Only the one he got from the tree branch had stitches. "Just fine," he said. "What are y'all reading?"

She held up the book. "Photos a guy named Ray Wever took on his travels to China." She put the book in Gracie's hands. "Go show him."

His little sister crossed the room and jumped into his lap. She flipped through the pages and pointed to stuff. The photos she really liked made her giggle.

Jake studied pictures of rural China, where the cattle seemed lean and small. Other photos from a train and still shots of kids. One of them had his leg in a brace of sorts.

"Funny. Other side of the world and they live just like us." Jake brushed Gracie's hair out of her face.

"It makes me want to travel to China and see the Great Wall and the other marks of such an old culture," Ellie said.

"I guess there would be things to see."

"You sound tired. Isn't Aaron helping you yet? I haven't heard him thumping around lately."

"I don't know. He won't be back for a few days, took off right in the middle of a crisis like this." Jake shook his head. "But is there anything I can get you or something you need?"

Ellie closed the book with a mischievous look on her face.

Jake perked up.

"Can you bring my notebooks?"

He grabbed some notebooks off the table.

She chuckled as she patted Gracie's head. "Not those. Remember where you found me in the barn? There is a loose board under where you were sitting."

"Of course," he shrugged and turned. "Don't go anywhere."

He walked outside the house and crossed to the barn. He checked to make sure no one was looking before he climbed to her spot. It might be a secret and he wasn't going to ruin it for her.

Climbing to the first loft, then to the second, he made the landing. Jake tapped the loose boards under the straw with his knuckles and pried them up with his knife. Dust covered the leather pouch.

He put the board back. For good measure pushed some straw back over it. Then he stood and made to climb down the ladder to the lower loft, but as he did the pouch slipped and fell. "Idiot."

A few of the papers were scattered over the floor. He knelt to gather them.

But these papers were odd, not like her other poetry, the ones from a book. A person's own handwriting filled the pages. Elegant and soft cursive wound its way across the lines like water down a fountain. And where the writer had failed and made an error, a simple line crossed through the word and the word re-written.

As he straightened the stack of papers, one title, larger and bolder than the rest, drew his notice. "My West" was very much Ellie's private work, but he let his eyes invade her words as he searched the poem.

"This place is the soul of calm,
knowing that an end, a change comes,
fighting a sentence of death,
seeking to be constant as it always was... ,"
He skipped a few lines.
"This place, the most deceptive of existences,
an island, surrounded by land,
an ocean of today, waves of quiet,
this place, seeking only for times before,"
He skimmed still further down.
"why here to be so safe,
so secure, at rest, a home?"
He forced himself to put it down. He had no business doing this. Yet his resolve hushed itself to non-existence as his eyes read the title of another of her works, "Broken Cowboy." He read.

"The cowboy's burning eyes,

don't know the sight of me,
they know the sky, the work, the land
the cowboy's weathered hands,
don't know the feel of me,
they know the whip, the rein, the fight
the cowboy's bent legs,
don't know the walk with me,
they know the ride, the earth, the dust,
the cowboy's boundless hearts,
don't know the love of me,
they know the wild, the eternal, they know forever,
and there was nothing immortal ever,
as the mounted son…,"

The hair on the back of his neck stood up. He felt warm and cold at the same time. All things were good and bad, happy and sad. He felt enough to breathe but these words had taken him. Caught off guard, he smiled.

The words could have been about anyone he had ever worked with, about him, about anyone who ever pushed horns. All that mattered in this moment in time was that these words were his to experience, his to remember.

Jake stuffed the pouch under his arm and climbed down the ladder and left the barn. *What if that poem was about him?* Jake went back into Ellie's room.

"We were about to send a search party," Ellie said.

"I got a little distracted." He sat down on the edge of her bed again.

Ellie took her pouch and tucked it into a drawer. "Jake, can I ask you another question?"

"Yes." But then he regretted it, as Ellie's demeanor became far more serious.

"Your mother... what happened to her?"

He studied her face. He had never told the story to anyone. Jake wondered if the pain he kept hidden inside would make his voice quiver. Maybe the words Ellie wanted to hear wouldn't come, so deep had he buried them. Yet Ellie asked, and Jake knew he would share this part of his life with her.

When he didn't say anything right away, Ellie patted his arm. "Jake, I'm sorry, it was not my place..."

"No, that's... that's fine. I want to tell you." He wanted her to be happy by knowing. Someone like her would appreciate the beauty of his mother. He pulled his hat off and ran his hand through his hair, taking a deep breath. After he felt confident no one besides Ellie was there to hear him, he settled in.

He looked at Ellie; those big hazels gazed back at him. He squared himself off and started the tale. He told her of the doctor's office and of the rain, describing the laughter and tears. He recited the crash and the end.

"...then life around here all changed after that and now she's buried up in the high country," Jake said. "Probably at the most beautiful spot on the ranch."

"I'd like to go up there sometime. Such a dark fairytale." Ellie wiped a tear away. "And your dad still has a hard time with it."

"*Real* hard, probably the hardest..." Jake reached for his hat and stood up. "Well, I'm off."

"Could you tell me how they met? Your mother and father, I mean."

He sat back down. "Well, at first they met growing up here in Crane. They were in the same class in school since they were nothing. Mom used to tell me that the other boys our dad's age made fun of him for trying to sit by a girl all the time. I guess he was pretty nuts about her all along. Dad would climb a tree outside her bedroom window and get her to sneak out with him."

Jake pictured it. "They would take horses across the pastures on nights when there was enough moonlight. My Grandpa was the sheriff back then, so they might as well have branded my dad a fugitive. It didn't do for the son of the biggest land owner in the county to be a wild child, but they couldn't keep him away from her."

"And they fell in love?" Ellie squirmed and leaned forward.

"Mom kept turning him down," Jake said. "She said she wanted to see the world."

"What happened?" Ellie sat up straight.

"World War I," Jake said. "Dad ran off after adventure, just a crazy cowboy. Before he left he said to my mom, 'Maggie, I'm going to think about you everyday. If I don't die, I'm coming back and I'm going to marry you.' She told him she hoped he wouldn't die but that she wouldn't be there when he got back. That didn't bother him.

"He was in Europe over a year, took a bullet once. Then the war ended and the soldiers came home."

"And your father came back and married your mother?"

"Actually, Dad got back here and she was gone," Jake said. "She had left just like she said she was."

"How did your father find her?"

"He went straight to her house, ring in his pocket and flowers in his hand. After a lot of convincing, Grandpa told Dad she was in New York, working in a little shop. Dad got right back on a bus east, with just a few dollars and a ring."

"Your mother was swept off her feet when he showed up in the city, wasn't she?" Ellie clasped her hands.

"Nope," Jake said. "She told him she was staying and he should head back."

"Oh no! What did your father do?"

"He sent a letter home saying he didn't know when he'd be back from New York. He got a job, a room to sleep in, and visited Mom every single day. Took her flowers and begged her for each date," Jake grinned.

"How long did it take?"

"One night my mom got real sick and there was only Dad to take care of her. He looked after her with every ounce of energy he had. No one could get him to leave her hospital room. Mom saw how reckless his love was. She fell into the love already there. Dad didn't even wait for her to get better and sent for the preacher the next day to come to the hospital, marrying her right there as she lay in her bed."

Jake examined the lines of his palm. "Mr. Samuel Noah Weathers and Mrs. Margaret Anne Weathers."

"And they came back?"

"They stayed in New York for a while because Mom wanted to. Dad just wanted Mom. After a few years, she longed to be somewhere beautiful, beyond those dark skies and filthy streets. And they came back."

"What a beautiful story. How much he must have loved her."

"Loved... loves, yeah he did," Jake said.

"Now I see why your dad has such a hard time with her memory," Ellie said. "It still gets him pretty badly?"

"Yeah... yeah, I think so." Jake looked out the window. "And it'll always be that way until the end, I guess."

"Must be quite a thing to love someone that much." Ellie moved herself closer.

"Yeah." Jake could feel her breath on his face. "Quite a thing..."

The door flew open. Jake's hand instinctively landed on the pistol at his side.

"What are you clowns doing?" Aaron stood in the doorway.

"Where have you been all these days? We've got loads to do around here and you're off God knows where! All this stuff involves you, too!" Jake furrowed his brow.

"Don't you worry about it." Aaron winked at him. "Have you seen Sam?"

"*Dad?* No."

"Let me know if you do." Aaron disappeared.

Jake left the room, too, and went back to chores, regretting every step he took away from Ellie.

CHAPTER 11

Moonlight Adventure

"**O**pen it!" Ellie slid a package across the table to Jake, small enough to hold with one hand. The box was covered in postage. And over all the postal markings Ellie had taken a paintbrush and written, "To you, from me," in large purple letters.

Jake closed his hand around the package and lifted it from the table. He didn't know whether to be exited or worried, but that's the way it was with Ellie, always guessing. He tore away the brown paper wrapping.

Inside was a tin case, shaped in an oval. He shook the package and the case dropped into the palm of his hand, cool metal against his flesh. He opened the case.

"So!?" Ellie clapped her hands.

Jake looked down. It was a pair of aviator sunglasses, the same kind that World War II pilots wore in all the pictures. Dark lenses held in place by gold frames, and tucked in the corner of the lens was the legendary name 'Ray-Ban.'

"But," he raised his eyebrows. "What are they for?"

She looked at him like he was crazy. "They're for you!"

"For me?"

"Remember you told me you wished you could be a pilot." She nodded at the glasses. "Everyone has to start somewhere."

How on earth did she remember what I said about being a pilot?

"Well?"

He let himself smile and be as honest as he could be. "They're probably the best gift I've ever gotten."

The *next* best gift he ever got was the look on her face. It told him how pleased she was. He liked the look on her face even more than the glasses.

"Try them on!" She tapped on the table.

Putting the glasses on, he followed Ellie to the mirror that hung in the hallway. He had to look twice at himself and let his mind pretend. In just the slightest way, he was one of those pilots on the recruitment posters.

"Captain Weathers!" Ellie said over his shoulder. She saluted and stood at attention, chin up, eyes forward.

"At ease, Lt. Peri." He played along because he knew she would enjoy it. "To the horses, on the double!"

She headed outside double-time. He joined her and mounted up.

"Just like the cockpit," she said as Jake got on Rio.

"Absolutely," he laughed.

The next morning, Jake wore the sunglasses, expecting the catcalls and humor coming from the crew.

"Hey, what's Cary Grant doing out here with us?" Larry said. "Shouldn't you be in L.A.?"

On the front porch that afternoon, Aaron tried to take the glasses as he joked around. Jake tucked them in his pocket.

Two weeks later Jake and Ellie came across torn up ground on the range; the overturned earth sprawled about in clumps. A nearby heifer limped. Jake figured it must have rolled its ankle.

"Hogs." Jake pointed to some tracks. "They like to do this, but it creates a hazard for the animals."

Jake got down and kicked the lumps around in a pathetic effort to level the ground. Ellie got down and joined him.

Finally Ellie looked up at him. "We're just rearranging the chaos, aren't we?"

Jake turned to her. "Just seems like a shame to do nothing... unless you know how to hunt."

"That I do not," she gave him a graceful bow.

"I half expected you've already bagged a tiger in some wild jungle or took the kill shot on a whaling ship in Antarctica."

"Not yet!" She laughed.

Jake examined the sky. "I'll tell you what. If it's clear tonight, we'll sit out and see if we can't put a few hogs in the ground."

"I'd love to aid you in sending hogs to the boatman, but... ," She closed her eyes in dramatic defeat, "I have never used a gun before."

"I can fix that."

They headed back to the house where Jake showed her the family gun closet. He pulled the key from a hidden spot only he and Carl knew. The door creaked as it opened.

"When did Napoleon move in?" she joked as Jake started to shuffle through the collection. "So much steel."

"We're going to need this one." He passed her a light, small rifle. "And these two," he handed her two heavier guns. Then he pulled some ammunition boxes from the shelf.

"Wait, don't I need one of these?" She put one hand up and made a trigger pulling motion with her index finger. A little gun noise came from her mouth.

"You mean a pistol?" Jake grinned at her gung ho. "You don't really need one."

"But you have one." She pointed at the .45 on his hip. "Doesn't every western legend need one?"

He reached into a box and pulled out one that looked like something Pat Garrett carried. "How's this one?"

"Perfect," she nodded.

"Here we go." He slipped the belt around her hips and tied the strap to her leg. Too late he realized how bluntly he approached her hips and leg. Best to act like he hadn't noticed and he hurried to retrieve some empty cans from the kitchen.

Rosalia came into the room. She caught sight of the beautiful, graceful gypsy girl with a pistol at her side and a rifle in each hand. "Just when I finally have another woman in the house, you go and put her in boots and guns!"

Ellie laughed. "Texas changes you!"

"Yeah, well, don't lose sight of that dress yet." Rosalia

turned to Jake. "Your father would like the family to be presentable tonight for dinner. We're having company, some prim and proper folks from Dallas, seven o'clock."

The two of them headed outside to the horses. Jake tucked the guns in the saddle and they rode away from the house about half a mile west to a clump of trees. They slid off the horses and unpacked the guns. Jake leaned them all up against a tree. Then he set up the can on a stump twenty-five paces away.

"All right, kid, grab that gun there." He pointed at the smallest rifle.

She picked it up and held it in front of her.

"A .22 rifle isn't very big, so it'll be easy for you to learn." He pulled a box of bullets from his coat pocket and showed her how to put them in the weapon and handle it safely. "Always keep the business end down range."

Ellie nodded. They each put in earplugs.

"You're going to shoot that can over there." He pointed at the stump.

She raised the gun.

"When this safety is back like this, the gun can't fire." He flicked it for her. "Okay, now aim and shoot."

There was a burst of dust as the bullet connected low with the side of the stump.

"Not bad for your first shot ever. Now try taking a deep breath, then let out half. Pull the trigger while you exhale slowly."

She hit the stump in same area.

Jake checked her form. "Pull the gun tighter into your

shoulder and slide your hand closer on the stock."

After several misses, he put his arms around her and showed her how to hold the gun, placing his hands on hers. The wind blew a strand of her hair across his cheek, and he brushed it towards the nape of her neck, letting his hand linger in soft, dark tresses. He wanted to bury his face there and get lost forever.

"Yeah, like that," he whispered as she had good form at last. "Now squeeze the trigger."

The can leaped from the stump. Ellie squealed in delight.

"Nice work" he said.

She turned to him and her eyes met his. This moment sneaked up on him. They were so close... so very close. And she didn't draw back.

Jake tried to look away, but Ellie pulled her left hand free and laid it on his chest. The warmth of her palm passed through his shirt. He could feel her breath on his face. When she tilted her head back and closed her eyes, he imagined himself pressing his lips against hers. She seemed so kissable.

His heartbeat slowed to a crawl; it teetered on the decisions to follow. Maybe he could... maybe he should...

But something in the back of Jake's mind reminded him this wasn't something he would do. He was the back row, the workhorse. The girl was never his to kiss.

"Try it again." Jake couldn't tell if it was disappointment on her face or simply nervous concentration as she put down the rest of the cans, one by one.

"Well done." He set her up with the bigger gun, the 30-30 Winchester.

She seemed to enjoy the bigger challenge and distance, pounding cans over. "I'm channeling Annie Oakley."

Jake waved his hand. "You're probably better than she was."

"So are we going hog hunting tomorrow?"

"We're going tonight."

"But your father is having company over." she cocked an eyebrow.

"Don't you worry," Jake said. "They'll be long gone before we head out. We'll be hunting in the middle of the night."

"Oh! Quite the adventure!" She smiled.

Jake wondered if the moonlight adventure would count as a real date.

Jake would never think fondly of Chandler James, much less his wife. The tall, gray-bearded businessman from Dallas had tried for years to convince Sam Weathers to sell the ranch and join him in business.

Mrs. James was not a pretty woman, even if she never seemed to age. She cast a haughty eye upon Ellie. Ellie, as usual, looked beautiful, just in a way that was some other place's beautiful.

The group sat down at the long oak table in the formal dining room, which Rosalia had set with elegant china and table linens. Mr. Weather's made them wait for Aaron. The conversation ran dry and so did the cocktail glasses by the time his son arrived.

"There's my boy!" He stood up.

By that point, the smell of beef from the kitchen distracted Jake from the late hour. Their father sat at the head of the table, with Mr. and Mrs. James at his right and left. Ellie sat at Mr. James's far side next to Carl, while Gracie sat between Jake and Mrs. James. Aaron sat at the other end of the table from his father.

"I'm telling you, Samuel, the cattle industry wont last forever," Chandler James said. "The government will find new regulations to set, that have only been partially thought through. Ends that don't justify means. It's just the government, not understanding the issues they're ruling over. It'll drive the cost of raising cattle up so high, there'll be no profit left."

"Perhaps, but politicians will always prefer steak to fish," Mr. Weathers said. "There'll always be need for cattle."

Mr. James nodded. "But you'll find yourself waking up trapped in a game you cannot win."

"And on that day, I'll let you say, 'I told you so.'" Mr. Weathers smiled.

"And don't think I won't," Chandler James laughed. He turned to Aaron. "And what are you up to these days, young man?"

"Oh, just working around here," Aaron said.

"No better place to recuperate from the war, eh?" his father said.

"I guess." Aaron yawned.

"Are you expecting you'll stay on? Ready to take over the old Weathers' Ranch. Or will you do something intelligent, unlike your father, and invest in something that will last?" said Mr. James.

"Don't know."

"Will you listen to him? *Doesn't know*?" Mr. Weathers chuckled. "Thinking of more adventures to take him away, this one is. Of course you'll take the ranch."

"Sure, Dad," Aaron said, his eyes half-lidded. "Whatever."

Jake bit down hard on his food. After dinner they retired to the den, as Mrs. James went on about her garden and her grown up children. Aaron slipped out, leaving Ellie and Jake to nod and smile at their pompous, boring guest.

"… but it's the soil that does the trick. I have topsoil shipped in from up north. Good, dark soil that can compensate for the hard ground around our house."

"Really?" Mr. Weathers said. "Where is it shipped in from?"

"Oh, Michigan. The soil there—"

Gracie reached for a vase and tipped it off the end table. Pieces of the porcelain were scattered everywhere. Mr. James and Sam jumped to their feet. As Gracie began to sob, Ellie reached for her. Jake bent down to clean up the mess.

"It's okay, baby," Ellie stroked the little girl's head. She put her arm around her shoulders, hushing her. Ellie stood her up and took her to her room.

Jake continued gathering pieces while his father apologized and the Jameses insisted everything was fine. After a while the energy settled. They continued drinking their coffee. Jake returned to the couch.

"Do you never worry for her? A girl in her condition?" Mrs. James sipped her coffee. "…A ranch can be such a dangerous place."

"It can be indeed," Mr. Weathers said.

"Have you never considered the Whaley Home?"

Goosebumps covered Jake's arm. His hearing intensified. He waited for every word.

"It provides a safe environment for children with special conditions." Mrs. Chandler set down her coffee cup.

"I'm not sure that's necessary for her," Jake said.

"But they have such lovely facilities."

"She doesn't need it."

Mrs. James wasn't the only one who gasped at Jake's brazen tone.

Jake drew in his breath and waited for criticism, but his father said nothing. Jake sat up straighter in his chair, not daring to glance at Ellie, who had returned to her seat. After a moment, he blinked twice, as the realization sank in. He had stood up to someone.

"She's not going anywhere right now," Mr. Weathers said.

Unlike his father, Jake didn't accompany their guests to the front porch when they left. He checked on Gracie instead.

She lay in her bed, held in its blankets, resting her head

in Ellie's lap. Ellie winked at him as he peeked through the door to let him know that everything was fine. He whispered to let her know that if she still wanted to try her hand at nighttime hog hunting she would need to be ready at midnight.

The house grew quiet and dark, as its inhabitants slept. Jake readied the rifles. He spent the next few hours reading one of Ellie's books in the living room. The pages were rich and spellbinding.

At midnight he silently slipped to Ellie's room and gave the door a tap. Nothing happened. He knocked again. Ellie must have fallen asleep.

Jake didn't want to disturb her. He crept away as quietly as he could, but her door opened that moment and Ellie emerged. In the dim light her eyes looked dark and sunken. Her warm coloration had receded to a pale complexion. Someone might even guess she had given in to the flu. Her motions were slow. She coughed.

"Are you feeling okay?"

Her hand shook. "I just took a nap so I'll be wide awake."

"We can always go tomorrow."

"Nonsense! I'm fine and adventure waits!"

He wanted to let her do whatever she wished. She took the front porch stairs one at a time. Jake followed her outside. She headed to the barn.

"No horses tonight, we need the spotlight mounted on the truck so we can see the hogs in the dark." Jake opened the door for Ellie.

"So what is our plan?"

"It's a pretty full moon, so they'll be moving," Jake said. "This is good for us. We're going to bait this one place I'll think they'll be. Then we'll park up on the ridge above and wait."

"That truly works?"

"Hogs aren't the most intelligent of God's creatures."

When they had gone several miles, Jake stopped the vehicle and climbed out. He retrieved a heavy sack from the bed of the truck. Jake hoisted it onto the bench of the truck and slid it between them in the cab.

"Is this our bait?" Ellie ran her fingers through it.

"They love that stuff." Jake continued farther up to the area they had seen the hogs tear up the ground. This area was broad and barren. He crept along the road and poured scoops of the corn out the window, baiting a thirty-yard stretch. The corn hit the hard ground with a crackle. Then he pulled a beer out from the back and popped the lid. He retraced their path and poured the liquid over the corn.

"Are they alcoholics?" Ellie chuckled.

Jake laughed. "This gets the aroma into the air and draws them in."

He dropped the empty beer bottle in the backseat. They continued up the hill. Then Jake turned the truck around and faced down the hill, angled so Ellie's window faced the direction of the trap. They tested the spotlight to make sure it was pointed at the corn. Then Jake turned it and the truck off. And there was silence.

"Now we wait," he whispered. "When we think we see them, you're going to stick your gun out the window, quiet as you can. Then when you give the go-ahead, I'll flick on the light. Just try to hit what you can."

"Our own back woods Texas safari!" Ellie laughed.

The light of the moon cascaded over them. She had lost her sunken eyes and the color came back to her face. She was probably right when she told him it was nothing. Now the truck had taken on the scent of something pretty, either the soap Ellie used or the perfume she sometimes wore.

They sat in silence for a while. Nothing stirred. It would take an hour or so, but he didn't want Ellie to get bored.

Then in a moment of excitement she grabbed his hand and whispered, "Oh, Jake, is that one?"

"Just a shadow from some brush." Jake whispered back. "Don't worry, I always think the wrong things are hogs."

Ellie settled back in her seat, and never let go of Jake's hand. She sat there looking out the window and holding his hand. She seemed like she didn't notice what she was doing.

He didn't want to make an awkward scene by pulling it away. So he didn't move... her hand was very soft. He considered never letting it go.

A while later he still concentrated so much on her hand that it was Ellie who first saw movement down on the road.

"That moved! That moved!" She whispered loudly enough for Arizona to hear her.

Jake peered through the darkness. "Those are deer."

"Wow!"

But then, in a dash the deer disappeared in the night.

Something big and black waddled into the moonlight. It moved like a clumsy bulldozer. The creature clambered onto the road and started to consume on the corn. Soon other bulky, broad beasts emerged from the brush.

"Here we go," Jake whispered. "Ellie, just pick the biggest one and aim dead center at its side."

Ellie slid her gun through the window and took aim in the general direction. Her breathing came short and quick.

"All right, pull the hammer back."

She did so.

"Okay, on three I'm going to turn the spotlight on. Line up and shoot. One, two, three!" He flicked the switch and daylight poured down on the road beneath them, illuminating the hogs. They didn't run, jerking their heads in every direction.

Ellie centered on one. She aimed. She held her breath. And then... nothing.

"Quick!" Jake said.

But still nothing happened. At last the hogs ran away.

Jake worried the gun had jammed. "Ellie?" he waited... then he knew what had happened.

Ellie turned to him and in the moonlight he saw embarrassment in her eyes. Her lower lip pouted like a child who knows she's in trouble. "I just couldn't do it."

Jake couldn't help himself. He threw his head back and laughed out loud. "That's fine! Don't worry about it; lots of people have trouble their first time." He kept chuckling.

"Some adventurer I turned out to be," she said.

"Whoa, whoa, whoa." Jake held up his palm. "I guarantee you no other women in West Texas are out at two in the morning hunting hogs."

A smile crept across her face.

"Let's go home," Jake said. He turned on the truck and drove them home. He kept telling Ellie how proud he was of her.

At home she ascended the steps of the porch in front of him, then stopped to turn around and face him. "Thanks, Jake." She gave him a hug and a little kiss on his cheek. "I had a lot of fun."

She went inside and left him there, on top of the world.

CHAPTER 12

Hell's Nest

"**D**o they make these in red?" Ellie pointed to the chaps she wore.

"I guess, if you were in the circus." Jake chuckled. "You'll be glad you've got them on when we ride through Hell's Nest. The brush'll reach out and try to pull you off your horse. Every once in a while we hire a crop duster from the next town east to fly over and see how many steers we have back in Hell's Nest. The pilot flies low to give the animals a little scare, driving them out."

A unanimous moan rose up from the ranch hands when Carl informed them the pilot couldn't scare the steers out. The riders wore thick coats to avoid cuts from the violent plant life.

"Ellie, maybe you should sit this one out," Jake said.

She narrowed her eyes.

"All right, here take this jacket." He held the jacket open for her and waited until her arms slid down the sleeves before he settled it on her shoulders and noticed the softness of her hair as it passed across his knuckles.

The brush was so thick that Jake couldn't see the

ground from his perch atop Rio's back.

"The steers moving through the brush look like hippopotamuses negotiating the Nile." Ellie pointed.

Jake and Ellie pushed through. They hollered and forced the cattle onto open ground. The cowboys covered the area.

It took an hour or so to push out enough cattle to make their effort worthwhile. They drove them far away so they wouldn't find their way back into the brush and pushed them a couple of pastures over. The herd didn't take long to get settled in.

"So Jake, have you decided on whether or not you are going to Ricky's birthday party?" Ellie said.

Jake shrugged. "I don't really enjoy parties."

"I'll be there if you decide you want to go. Mary-Lou made me promise to come." Ellie's tone turned suspicious. "What's that?"

Jake looked where she pointed. "That's a bull. There's five or six of them that run on the ranch. Dad likes the wild feel. If we just keep our distance we'll be fine. Weird seeing it so close to the house though. This is a little dangerous."

Jake led them away.

Later that day the two of them headed back to the house. When they arrived Mary-Lou sat on the porch with Aaron. She wore a yellow taffeta dress, and her long blonde hair had been pinned up.

"Oh dear, cousin," she held her hand to her mouth. "What would the high society of New Orleans think?"

"They would probably be content to have something new to gossip about."

"Come inside, let's get you ready." Mary-Lou extended her hand.

Ellie gave a bored look to Jake and handed him her reins. She followed Mary-Lou inside. The door shut behind them, leaving Jake and Aaron alone.

"I don't understand why girls make such a big deal about getting dressed up." Aaron looked at his brother. "They even have to do it in teams."

Jake nudged Rio toward the barn. He took Puma inside and removed her saddle. As Jake hung the saddle, something rattled inside the saddlebags. Jake opened the bag and pulled out sheets of parchment.

Black and white sketches done in charcoal or chalk, something grainy, drawings of cacti and fence posts, steer and saddles. One of the larger drawings silhouetted a cowboy on his horse up a ridge with the setting sun behind them. The rider and his horse looked tired and worn, his shoulders slumped with toil and labor. The horse's legs seemed played out. Maybe the pair had beaten the day or maybe the day had beaten them. The point was that it was over. Victory or defeat, the two headed home.

Jake was intrigued by Ellie's ability to draw an emotion from what he had experienced. Then something solid hit his toe. A very small, empty brown bottle had fallen from the bags. He picked it up and looked it over. No label covered it. Jake gave it a sniff, no lingering aroma. He set the empty bottle on a shelf and put Puma out into the corral. She joined the other horses at the watering trough.

For a while, Jake worked on one of the latches to the barn door, tightening the screws. Now was as good a time as any to tighten all of them. He finished just in time to hear the engine of the car fire up outside. Someone honked the horn. Jake pictured the scene before he got out there.

Aaron slouched in the driver seat waiting for the ladies to come out. He hollered for them. After a moment or two, the front door swung wide and Mary-Lou led Ellie out.

She looked just like Jake hoped she would. He tried not to get caught staring. She bounced down the front steps, ready to go. All he could wish for her was a nice evening. Her happiness gave him happiness.

All three hopped into the car. Ellie gave Jake a little wave. He managed a smile and waved in return. Aaron drove on the lawn and sent grass flying as he peeled out and away.

Jake watched the group disappear down the driveway. He limped inside and found Gracie. She had touches of makeup on. He read her a chapter and then sat down for dinner.

After dinner, Jake sat out on the front porch with Gracie. Carl joined them. True to his routine, the old man lit his pipe and let out deeps puffs of smoke. Gracie abandoned her toys and chased the smoke as it floated up and away. Jake gave his jackknife a work over with a sharpening stone.

"Hey, Carl?" called Pete. The ranch hand walked up from the bunkhouses in the back.

"What's going on, Pete?" Carl waved him up onto the

porch.

"I'm not sure, but Larry hasn't come back yet," he said. "His horse ain't in the corral."

"Where was he last?"

"He was over in Big Rock, north end," Pete said. "Want me to go check?"

"No go, you had a long day." Carl put his pipe out. "I'll go see what that fool is up to."

"Probably thought he saw a girl," Pete said. He turned and ambled back to the bunkhouse.

Carl stood and put his pipe in his coat pocket. "Never ends, does it?"

Jake stood to join him. "Never."

"There's no need for you to come," Carl said.

"I don't mind."

"Feeling restless?"

"Maybe a little."

"Something to do with Miss Ellie's absence?"

Jake shrugged.

Just then, Sam stepped out onto the porch.

"Can you watch Gracie for a while, sir?" said Jake.

"Where are you going?"

"Larry hasn't come in from Big Rock."

"By all means." His father waved them on.

Jake and Carl left the barn on their horses and took the road towards Big Rock. It was probably nothing serious. Larry might have simply fallen asleep under a tree. However, his absence might be due to a rattlesnake bite.

"So, Jake." Carl tapped his pipe bowl empty. "Why are

you out looking for a lost cowboy with an old man? There's a pretty girl somewhere else who wanted you to follow her."

"I don't know. I guess I just don't enjoy that kind of thing."

"Tell me this, young man. When you're out on the ranch, and she's with you, do you enjoy it more than being by yourself?"

"More, I guess."

"So don't you think you could find some enjoyment in a situation like that party, as long as she was there?"

"Maybe."

As they rode, the night air grew chilly. They kept a slower pace so their eyes wouldn't water.

"Jake, you are content where you are, but it's okay to want a little more out of life." Carl's tone was warm.

"Like what?"

"Oh, I don't know. Maybe more of a partnership with your father in the ranch. You know this land as well as anyone. Sure, your dad hasn't known how to handle you for a long time. The death of your mom didn't help, but that's your father's problem. Not yours," Carl patted him on the back. "Maybe you could even use a pretty girl."

This forced a little smile from Jake. "Oh, yeah?"

"Yes. It doesn't take a scholar to notice the way that girl looks at you or the way you look at her. And now, she's all dressed up, waiting on you." Carl said. "Now I know I'm just an old fool but…"

"Carl, you're the smartest man I know."

"'Pride goeth before a fall'," Carl said. "But I have

managed to learn a thing or two in my tenure." He looked up towards the rising stars. "Did I ever tell you about that girl, the one I met in Chicago?"

Jake shook his head.

"Years and years ago, when I was out on my sojourn, finding all sorts of things including myself, I lived in Chicago a while. There was a woman I loved, but I lost her because of my own damn self," Carl said. "I kept making excuses about why it wouldn't work. And they were good reasons, too, every last one of them. But you know what the damnedest part of it was? I never got to experience those reasons. I never tried to handle the hard parts. Life could have been rough, but with her, it could have been beautiful too."

"Why are you telling me all this?"

"Because, you're a better man than you believe. You don't want to be out here someday on a horse thinking back about the chances you didn't take." Then Carl grinned. "And because even if there is no other success in growing old besides warning the young, then that makes growing old worthwhile."

They rode along in silence for a few minutes, the only sound was eight hooves pushing dirt.

"Carl, what do you think love is?"

Carl closed his eyes as though searching through annals and records of experiences. "You know, love is thinking about her first and last in your day. Love is when your self-sacrifice to make her happy isn't self-sacrifice because you want her happiness more than you could ever want anything for yourself. Love is her asking you to leave everything behind and your only question being when does the journey begin. Love is purpose, it makes you more invincible and more fragile than you've ever been in your life. Love is blindness. Love is... that fool losing his horse."

Carl pointed to an animal materializing out of the darkness. "What's he got himself into now? Out there somewhere on foot." Carl reached over and grabbed the horse's reins. He led the horse along behind them as they made their way back to Big Rock.

They continued for another mile or so. At last a figure appeared, walking on the road towards them.

"Lose something?" Carl called out.

"No! I just felt like walking back!" Larry hollered.

Carl chuckled.

"Damn rattlesnake spooked her and sent her sprinting. I hate those things," Larry said as they met up. "Don't do that to me," he told the horse, patting her neck. He climbed on. "I thought those things were supposed to be hibernating this time of year."

"Sometimes they don't." Carl gave him a slap on the back. "Did you kill it?"

"Yeah, and I'd have done it slow if I knew how far I'd have to walk," Larry said. "It's a big ranch. I'm starving."

"We're all out of food, guess you'll have to wait until morning," Carl said.

"I think I'll shoot this horse and eat it."

"She'd probably just get you one more time and give

you indigestion."

The three of them turned around and headed back. They had gone about a mile when Jake pulled his horse up short. "I'll be back in a little while."

Carl grinned and tipped his hat to the young man.

Jake turned Rio and gave him a kick. They rode off in the direction of the fence they shared with Ricky's ranch.

"Where's he going?" Larry said.

"Where else would a young man be foolish enough to ride on a cold night?" Carl laughed. "To see a girl."

"This is crazy," Jake said aloud. Why was he doing this? Well, Ellie was his friend and she *did* want him to come. *What if it makes her happy? Maybe it would.*

She'd probably get a kick out of the fact he rode there on a horse, but what would he say when she asked him *why* he came? Guess that was just something he would have to figure out when he got there... there would be others there, but she would be there too. Jake figured that was enough.

He let Rio run and lost Carl and Larry behind him. He knew this part of the ranch and the moon was bright enough for him to navigate the property line without risk. Jake grew more excited with each stride of his horse. They cleared the fence at full speed. Rio's hooves hit Ricky's land. Jake slowed now, not knowing his neighbor's acres.

The moonlight bounced off the dirt road, illuminating Jake's passage. Ricky's homestead sat along the northern property line by the main road so he kept heading north, following Polaris.

He rounded a bend and caught the faint sound of voices in the air, soon followed by the delicate scent of fire. He was heading in the right direction.

When he neared the house he surveyed the party, watched the people, and lost a tiny bit of his resolve. But he kept going forward.

The gathering surprised him. Looking around, he realized the party was well past its peak. Only now did he consider it had been hours since Ellie left with his brother. He tied off Rio and walked toward a dozen picnic tables.

Trash covered the ground and the remains of a cake sat ravaged on a table. Empty beer and whiskey bottles lay scattered around like confetti. A few guests napped any and everywhere.

Jake laughed at himself. He was so nervous and uncertain about coming here, and now there was no one left. Disappointment followed his resolve as he concluded he might not see Ellie. He sighed.

Jake ventured toward the parked cars. At the sight of Aaron's hot rod, he grew hopeful, but when he approached the car, muffled noises made him hesitate. Aaron wasn't alone.

Jake didn't care if he embarrassed the girl or his brother. He yanked the car door open.

Aaron whipped around in his seat. His expression began with fear and soon became confusion. "What the... Jake? What the hell do you want?"

"Where's Ellie?" Jake remained calm.

"Ellie? What? Still here, how should I know?" Aaron tried to shield the girl who had joined him.

Jake shut the door, getting no aswers from Aaron. He turned and headed for the few remaining guests seated at one of the picnic tables.

"Good evening, friend." One of those sitting waved him over.

Jake recognized him as Otis Watley.

Otis' eyes were lazy and half closed. "Would you like to sit down?"

"I'm looking for Ellie."

"Who's Ellie?"

Another guest lifted his head from the table. "You know Ellie, she's that new girl. Came with Aaron."

"Oh yeah, the dish. I saw her walking that way." Otis lifted a heavy hand in the direction of the barn. "Didn't Ricky go that way?"

Jake didn't hear the rest of the conversation; he didn't wait to hear the rest of the conversation.

The barn was hundreds of yards away from the house, beyond the reach of the lights. Jake walked into the darkness. Soon, only the moon lit his path.

As Jake neared the structure, something inside crashed. He paused, held his breath listened, closer. He waited for a sound...

A scream banished the quiet night to its death. He ran. Another scream. His eyes narrowed.

The barn door stood open. A table and chairs lay in pieces upon the floor. A lantern now existed as shards.

Ricky's big frame straddled over his sweet Ellie. She lay pinned on the ground. Blood ran from her mouth and nose. Her dress was torn away down the front. And she wept.

Anger burned in Jake until it hurt. He clenched his fists so tight his knuckles popped as intense hate exploded through his forehead.

Jake grabbed Ricky's shoulder and spun him around. Jake pistol-whipped him across the face with all the viciousness he could summon. The noise of his cracking jaw snapped in the air.

Ricky hit the floor hard, spitting out teeth and a river of blood. He looked up through the haze of pain. "You?... you piece of shit!" he cried. "I'm going to cripple your other leg!" He tried to stand up.

The Colt .45 shined in the moonlight. Jake pointed the gun right between Ricky's eyes. "Go on," Jake said in a cold voice. "Let's see if you're bulletproof."

Ricky lay there, shaking.

Jake looked up from his enemy. A whimper caught his attention so he shifted his eyes sideways, leaving the gun pointed at Ricky. His Ellie struggled to sit up and pull the front of her dress closed.

How dare he touch something so sacred. How dare he even look at her.

The heat passed over Jake once more. He turned his attention back to Ricky, whose eyes went wide. Jake swung his leg over Ricky and straddled him, tucking his pistol into the holster. He grabbed Ricky's collar with one hand and unleashed a whirlwind of fists with the other. Jake pulled the wretch into every punch, putting the effort of his whole torso into it. Ricky's facial bones cracked, but that wasn't enough. It would never be enough.

Finally, when he pulled back for a breath, he let an unconscious Ricky fall away. He stood and turned toward the injured girl.

Jake lifted Ellie off the ground. The girl fell into his arms as she let herself be held, gasping. He put his heavy coat around her shoulders and covered her tattered dress.

"Thank you, Jake," she whispered. "Take me home."

Jake led her outside the barn, leaving Ricky unconscious behind them. Jake slowed his steps to match Ellie's, wincing at her pain. Her face looked like she had taken hard hits. Jake lifted her into the saddle and climbed in behind her. He didn't have to nudge Rio. The horse headed back the way they had come.

Ellie shivered. Jake wrapped his arms around her and handled the reins. She fell back into his chest and closed her eyes. She breathed deeply.

The gypsy girl grabbed his hand on the rein and held it. Rio's hooves working the ground was the only sound.

Jake couldn't grasp what had happened. He was with Carl and for some reason decided to go to the party he knew he would hate. He went. He heard a scream. Something told him who it was. He beheld Ricky's atrocious act and acted. Sure Ricky deserved it, to be shot even, but had Jake really done it?

Why am I not being like myself? Why am I acting so

strange?

But now, he knew the truth. He loved Ellie. Because of her, he was strong. And he would never let anything happen to her. "We're almost there," Jake whispered.

Ellie rubbed her face against his chest. "I know you'll always get me home."

The house came into view. That warm, safe place waited for them.

Jake gently lifted her down from the horse. He helped her up every step and opened the door for her. After they passed through the entrance, he led her through the quiet home into her bedroom. She sat down on her bed.

"Wait here." He went into the kitchen and filled a basin with warm water. He found bandages in the cabinet. All these he put on a tray and brought them back into her room. She had climbed into her blankets.

He sat down on the edge of her bed. Dipping a washcloth in warm water, he dabbed her cut cheek and the wound on her forehead.

Ellie watched his face as he tended to her.

"That should feel better," he said as he worked her wound. "It doesn't look that deep. You're not going to need stitches." He put a bandage on it. "What happened, kid?"

"The party had grown old, so I went for a walk. I turned around in the barn and... he was there." Ellie's eyes grew tearful. "He was so drunk. I fought him as best I could. It was an awful feeling, being powerless." She shook her head. "I don't want to think about what would have happened if you hadn't come."

Her hand found its way to his face. She ran it down his cheek. For a long moment, their eyes met, staring into each other. The lamp cast a warm glow on her face.

The hazel fire stole him away. He swept her dark hair from her neck and shoulders, twining it around his fingers. He could think of all the reasons he shouldn't do this, but then he thought of the one reason he should… it was her.

Her lips were warm and soft and her mouth was intoxicating. Every inch of him caught fire. Her fingers brushed the back of his neck. One kiss turned to many, until they both fell asleep.

CHAPTER 13

The Gypsy and the Cowboy

Jake was happy. He had been happy before but this was a different kind of happy. There were things he knew made him happy. He loved being on his horse at sunset and roping steers at dawn. He loved the smell of oil when he cleaned his gun and enjoyed hearing Carl's thoughts on life. Gracie's laugh was wonderful.

But for the first time, his happiness didn't come in moments, rather it was constant. It flavored everything he did and stayed in the back of his mind. It spread to the tip of his tongue. The dullest of tasks and duties were accented by the thought of it. It wove itself through the fiber of his being.

In the morning when he woke up, he was in love. When he closed his eyes to sleep, he was in love. When he held down a steer to brand it, he was in love. And when the weather dampened the day, he was still in love. When he was by himself in the farthest reaches of his father's ranch, he knew that on the other side his girl waited. He was in love all the time. It was constant feeling that never tired and never grew old.

He was a novice at it and wanted to do it right. If he let himself go, he'd never give Ellie a moment alone. No work would ever get done. So Jake tried to balance it all, but then the moments came when he could unleash the flood and let go.

Jake and Ellie took a break from pushing cattle and sat under a tree halfway up a rise looking over the cattle below. The sky was crystal blue. He leaned up against the tree and cradled her in his arms. She showed him some of her artwork, a sketch of Gracie running with a smile on her face. In mid-stride, her hair bounced like it had a life of its own.

Ellie had also drawn Carl smoking his pipe. The lines on his face made him seem real. If a stranger saw this picture, they would assume Carl to be a fountain of wisdom.

"And this is one of the ones I did of you." She pulled out a larger work.

On the page he stood over a hogtied calf on the ground, his sleeves rolled up and his hat pulled low. The flow of the drawing gave him the feeling he had just finished with the calf and stood up to catch his breath. The shading told him it was sunset.

"You know," Jake said "This picture makes me feel all the things I feel when I'm actually doing that. I have to catch my breath right now."

"Wonderful!" She kissed his cheek. "That's what it should do." She found another page. "You're going to be under the impression I'm a silly girl."

"I already think that."

She laughed. "When you read this one," Ellie handed him the page, "remember it's from the day after you came and got me in that rain storm. I never told you about it. Then I added to it the day after you came and got me from Ricky's party."

Jake didn't like hearing his name. He took the page and started to read.

The storm is coming, a horizon beast,
It would take my soul far and away,
So I need you to pick me off this ground,
Where the shame covers my face,
I'm all out of tears,
Here at the end of all fears,
To give up, a last whimper,
Then there you whisper:
I'll find you in the night,
When the darkness overwhelms you,
I'll stretch out my hand,
And pull you from the dark,
I'll take you away,
But if the darkness is too deep,
Then I'll follow you into the night,
And we'll fade, but fade together,

"You know, Ellie, I'm not exactly an expert on poetry," Jake said. "But this is really good."

"I still have to polish it a bit," she said. "How does the ending make you feel? Be honest."

"Kind of sad, I guess," Jake said.

"Why?"

"The fading into the dark part. Isn't that a sad ending?"

"All things end. Surely there can be only happiness at the thought of having it end with someone you care about."

"Yeah. That sounds good."

They sat for a long while. She read from a book and he listened. She told him what she liked about the work or how it could be better. He didn't want to look at his watch. It would tell him to keep moving and get back to work.

Ellie saw his glance. "We need to get going, don't we?"

"It's about that time. The boys will be over there soon and we've got to go help."

"Why is your father trying to work more cattle?" she said.

"That's just what we do. The operation has gotten both bigger and smaller over the years. This is just the season for it to get bigger."

"Has it?"

"Sure. Back turn of the century we were probably twice as big. It seems like it follows how big the family gets. That was back when all the boys wanted to be ranchers. Then not so many of the next generation wanted in. It just sort of happened that the operation shrunk. My dad has two brothers. One is a pastor in San Antonio and the other we never hear from. Dad was the only one who wanted in. We're smaller right now."

"And there's you and Aaron."

"I think Dad just has hope for Aaron."

She held his hand. "I suppose you want to do this, too."

"It's all I know how to do," he said.

"I don't want to speak ill of your brother," she said. "But he doesn't seem to take much interest in all this."

"He still recuperating from all he went through."

"All the same, would you like to be more of a partner in the ranch? You're obviously dedicated."

"I don't know, I guess my father will let me know."

"Do what you will, but maybe you could talk to him about it some time," Ellie said.

"I'll think about it."

As they stood up, they dusted the grass off their pants.

"Ready?" Jake turned to her.

He gave in to her desire for a kiss right then. And he wasn't going to object. They got on their horses and headed out.

"Race you there!" Ellie kicked Puma and raced off.

She had really grown as a rider. The two of them were fast.

Of course, Rio was extra fast for a horse and Jake had worn his saddle in. For Ellie's fun, he caught up in an instant but held Rio a few lengths back as they raced down the dirt trail. Jake really tugged at the reins because the instinct in Rio's legs told him to pass everything in front of him. If horses can be annoyed, Rio definitely was.

Carl laughed as Ellie came flying up and shot past him. Puma's hooves slipped until she managed to slow to a trot. In the end it was remarkable to him how in a second she could show up crazy like that, whip her wind blown hair into place, then posture herself like Queen Victoria.

"I see you're making that horse earn its dinner," Carl

chuckled.

Ellie smiled "I just don't want her to forget she is a horse."

The three of them waited. Some of the others rode up a few minutes later, right before Mr. Weathers arrived. "This is a huge push of cattle so it will take everyone we can pull."

Jake looked around at excited faces. This would be the drive of his lifetime.

A caravan of twenty or more trucks came rolling down the highway. Ellie stared at the vehicles.

Jake turned to her. "Dad bought out a cattleman, Kip Jones, from a few counties over. He's old and tired, got no sons to take over the business. This'll ensure him a comfortable retirement.

When the delivery pulled up, Mr. Jones parked and got out of his vehicle. He took slow, bent steps, the kind years on a horse will give a cowboy if he lasts to old age. The trucks fought for position, forward and reverse in chaotic fashion. Mr. Weathers and Carl slid off their horses to greet him.

Jake studied him. Mr. Jones had old eyes, weathered by years on the range, one slightly lazy. They were strong, though sad. Jake wondered if this transaction would break the old man's heart.

On the one hand, this good old cowboy who'd worked hard his whole life would be taken care of for the rest of his days. On the other hand, he was giving away a part of himself. This herd was his life's work. He wouldn't be getting up in the morning to see those animals scattered across his pasture anymore. His saddle would get dusty and his spurs, rusty. That herd was his mission and his mission would now be gone.

In a handshake and the stroke of a pen he had sold his part of Texas. Not only that, but the clients he had sold to for years would now have the Weathers' name instead.

"I just wanted to come myself and thank y'all for taking these off my hands," Mr. Jones said.

"They're good animals," Mr. Weathers said. "We're lucky to have them."

"We're honored to have the Jones name backing us as a provider," Carl said. "Your reputation is as fine as they come."

"Sometimes you just get tired," Mr. Jones looked towards the trucks. "I'm fixing to do this."

"You heard the man," Mr. Weathers said to Carl.

"Yes, boss." Carl waved to the men. "Everyone good?"

All the cowboys returned his wave. Each rider had positioned himself to form a giant semi-circle when the waves of cattle were unloaded, so they didn't take off in every direction.

"All right," he turned to Mr. Jones. "Let them go, captain."

Mr. Jones waved to the first truck driver. He let the doors fall away. Then he climbed in at the front of the trailer and pushed the animals ahead.

That first new steer's hooves hit the Weathers' ranch. One by one, they exited.

As soon as the first truck was empty, it pulled away

from the gate and made room for the next load. Animal by animal, truck by truck, the herd grew before them. And when the last truck driver closed his doors, the largest gathered herd Jake ever saw waited before him. The sound of the countless steers lowing was deafening.

Mr. Weathers looked past Jake to Mr. Jones. "Thank you so much."

"Push them hard," Kip Jones said with misty eyes. He gave one last look. Then he turned to his truck and left his existence with the Weathers.

"You heard the man!" Carl yelled to the crew. "Take it nice and easy! Pete and Larry push the rear. Juan , Ellie, you work the left. The rest of you on the right. Jake, chase the runners!" He looked at Mr. Weathers. "Lead the way, boss."

Mr. Weathers kicked his horse. The others funneled the cattle in the direction they needed to go. Larry and Pete whooped and hollered to get them rolling.

The ground rumbled beneath Rio. After a minute, the mass got moving in the right direction. It was as though the landscape flowed.

Jake showed Ellie a good spot to push a large herd. As she positioned herself, she looked confident. So he left her there. He pulled way behind so he could see either side of the herd and catch any steer that tried to break away from the group. He was grateful the late winter soil still had some moisture in it, holding down the dust. Soon, circling the whole herd seemed much more fun.

It was odd being on one side of the massive herd and

seeing the great distance between the riders on the other side. Communication was much easier over the backs of the animals in a small herd, but between the size of the herd and the noise they made, even shouting wasn't a guarantee. It had been a long time since Jake had to focus so much in a push, and they still had a way to go. This pasture was no good.

When they reached where they needed to go, they still had to break the group up and spread them around. Over 400 animals grazing in one pasture is a good way to strip all the foliage. If the family spread them out, with smaller numbers of animals in any given pasture, the land would have a fighting chance at growing something.

"JAKE!" yelled Larry, pointing right. "RUNNER!"

Jake whipped his head around. "Yee-haw," he said under his breath. "Well, kid, let's get him." He let his horse run. They closed the distance in seconds.

"Easy cow, easy," Jake spoke to the animal. He didn't need to rope it, just get it turned around and pushed it back to the herd. The escapee wove itself into the fabric of the rest of the animals and, in the rhythmic flow of the herd, was lost in its tide.

Jake had gotten the steer back within minutes.

Carl grinned. "You feeling tired today or something? A little slow."

Jake circled over to Ellie. She smiled at him and showed him how she got Puma to sidestep. Jake gave her an approving thumbs up.

The cattle were so thick, Jake was sure he could walk

on their backs right across to the far side. Their lowing chorus was a song for Texas. They trod their way on at a still, steady pace. He looked behind him. All the trucks had rolled off.

"You've never pushed a herd this large." Jake rode up next to Carl. "Have you?"

"Once when I was a younger man," Carl told him. "We pushed a herd a little larger than this…" He reined in his horse and looked beyond Jake's shoulder. "You're up, slugger."

Jake spun in his saddle. Another reckless animal had decided it was better off elsewhere. Jake jerked Rio's reins and the horse reared as he spun around. Rio held nothing back and went after the getaway like a mad locomotive.

The steer kept charging on and away. Jake pulled the rope from his saddle and set to swinging it around its head. He got up next to the rogue and whipped it in there. The lasso fit itself around the animal's neck and tightened down.

Jake yanked the line and was in charge. He tied it off to the horn of his saddle and dragged the steer back towards the herd, using the other end of the rope like a whip to strike the troublesome steer's rear. The steer cooperated as they moved a little quicker to catch up, but before long, Jake let the animal loose in the crowd.

It was a good day to be a cowboy.

After two hours they got the cattle where they wanted them. They split the herd and pushed half of them to another pasture over. Then they pushed other steers elsewhere still. Then it was up to the animals to find the water troughs.

"I think I'm a real cowboy now," Ellie said to Jake when they had finished.

"I reckon you are." Jake watched his girl ride away.

Yes, sir, it was an excellent day to be a cowboy.

A few days later, Jake searched the barn for the lid to a never-used oil drum where they stored oats for the horses, not wanting mice or raccoons to get in. The shelves and back towards the corral were the first places he looked, among the tools and horse tack. He finally found it on the floor of the barn. One of the tractor attachments was on top of it. His choice was either go and get someone to help him or hook it up to the tractor.

He contemplated his next move. If there were any fuel in the tractor, Carl would know. Jake waffled between starting up the tractor and trying to move the machinery by himself. Why not? After bending down, he got a good grip and shoved hard.

It was heavy, real heavy, and didn't move, but he pushed through the uncertainty and got the encouragement of that first nudge. A few heaves later the lid was free.

He looked at what he had done. Hard to believe he had moved something so heavy, but he spent a considerable amount of time carrying fence posts and hoisting hay bails. It made sense he had some strength to spend.

Jake put the lid back on the drum but not before sneaking some oats with the special concoction for Rio. Rio made short work of the stuff. Jake took care of a few more chores in the barn. Then he headed over to the house.

"I don't know, boss," Carl said to Sam as Jake walked in. "I'm not sure this move is in our best interest."

"It isn't as though it's some obscure workshop. Mexibeef has been in business for years." Mr. Weathers leaned back in his chair. "Lots of ranches in Texas are having success in their dealings with places south of the border."

"I would feel better about this if I knew the man we're dealing with. You should insist on their payment first before we send the cattle. I don't care if we insult them. Obviously this ranch comes first." Carl scratched his head "But if it's a good deal, we shouldn't miss out on anything."

Jake had overheard his father talking with Carl over the past few months. They wanted to open up trade with some beef distributors in Mexico. He didn't realize his father was that serious until now.

"I'm just saying, I agree, boss. Rushing into business deals can have dire consequences. Of course, there are the occasional Louisiana Purchases," Carl said. "You could always go down there and deal with them."

"I don't have time to go down there. All sorts of legislation is going to the capitol. I need to go over things with Raleigh. You should go."

Carl chuckled, "Oh, boss, I'm too old to make a trip like that."

"That's fine. I've got a better idea." Mr. Weathers turned his head towards the door. "Aaron!"

Moments later Aaron walked in, still dressed in

pajamas. "What?" He didn't try to hide the annoyed look on his face.

"Son, someone needs to go to negotiate the deal in Mexico. Carl and I cannot. That leaves you, and who better to represent us?" He winked and smiled.

"All the way to Mexico?" He first looked dismayed by the errand, but mischief soon took over his expression. "Sure, I'll go."

His brother pictured señoritas and tequila. Jake cringed, but he also remembered Ellie's encouragement.

"I should go, too." Jake felt surprised at his own words.

"I'm not sure that's necessary." Sam looked at him, eyebrows raised.

"Yeah, I don't need you," Aaron yawned.

"Really, Aaron? How many heads do we run in a typical year?"

Aaron scowled at his brother.

"How many acres do we own?" Jake tapped his foot. "What type of cattle do we produce?"

Aaron looked down in silence.

"Aaron, how many *employees* do we have?"

Sam drew back at his son's lack of answers.

Carl grinned from ear to ear. "Jake should go, too. He knows the ranch best."

"Well, to a degree."

"He can push heads like anyone. He knows this herd."

"But he's still so young, Carl." Mr. Weathers leaned over his desk.

"Actually, boss, he's a year older than you were when

you took over the ranch as a young man," Carl said. "And from knowing the both of you, I can tell you he's just as ready for his moment."

Mr. Weathers turned to Aaron. "Well, what do you think?"

"Boss," Carl said. "Trust me, Jake can do it. It's not like this is hard anyways. If he goes down there and it doesn't work out, we'll chalk it up to providence."

Mr. Weathers stern face softened.

"I can do it," Jake said in a low voice.

His dad studied him the way he would a new employee. Jake resisted the urge to squirm.

"All right," his father said. "But you should go over the aspects of the deal with Carl. Check our side of the paperwork. You boys are leaving tomorrow morning."

"He will, boss," Carl said. "He will."

Sam left the room. Aaron followed, looking more excited about Mexico than disappointed he wouldn't be alone.

Jake and his friend Carl had their moment. "You're going to Chihuahua."

"That's a really long drive." Jake rubbed his brow.

"Y'all better leave early. Which means we better go over the deal tonight."

"Just let me go tell Ellie." As he left the room, the resolve of the moment passed. *What the heck was I thinking? I'm not ready for this.*

"BOOOOO!" Gracie jumped out of the closet with her hands held up like tiger's claws. Her smile was wide.

"Oh!" Jake grabbed his chest. "You got me!"

Then she rushed in for a hug so fast it pushed him back

into the wall. He gave her a good squeeze.

"Hey! Want to go see Ellie?" he said matching Gracie's energy.

"Yea!" She grabbed his hand and yanked him down the hall. She knocked Ellie's bedroom door wide open like a conqueror entering her opponent's palace. Jake grinned, but Ellie was not there.

"Let's go look somewhere else!" He stopped short, turned the light back on, and walked over to the bedside table. On the floor between the table and the bed lay something familiar. He bent down and picked it up. Another of those tiny brown bottles fit in the palm of his hand. He raised his eyebrows.

Gracie tugged on his shirt so he'd follow her. He set the bottle on the table. His sister led him from the room. They found Ellie in the swing on the back porch, bundled up in warm clothes and reading a book.

"Gracie! Where have you been all my life?" Ellie flung her arms wide open and caught Gracie in their embrace.

Gracie drowned herself in Ellie's hug. Then she forced her way onto the swing next to her so she could play with Ellie's hair.

"Oh Gracie! Where did you find this guy?" She nodded at Jake. "What are you up to?"

"Here's the deal... my dad is looking into doing business with a new company and um, I'm... he wants to send me to meet the men we're going to do business with... sort of a representative." He felt like a nervous boy asking a popular girl to the dance. "It's in Mexico. He was going to send Aaron, who knows nothing about any of this. I thought about what you said and… sort of volunteered. So now I'm going, too."

"Wonderful!" Her face lit up. The only thing keeping her in her seat was Gracie leaning up against her.

"It's short notice…" Jake touched the back of his head. "It's tomorrow."

"Tomorrow!" She untwined herself from Gracie. "Let's get you packed!"

Jake admitted to himself he felt excited. He took Gracie inside with him.

Carl waited at the table with numerous papers spread out and grinned at Jake. The old man shoved out a chair. "Sit down, my apprentice."

The two of them spent hours going over the ranch's position on the venture, various questions the folks at Mexibeef might have, and how Jake should answer. Numbers needed to be calculated. Carl took a guess at which items in the deal would please them and which they would be against. He discussed what Jake could bend on and what he had to insist upon. After running over the information again and again and, Jake could more or less quote it verbatim.

Carl rubbed his eyes. "Well, kid, I think you've got it."

At one in the morning, Jake scratched his head. He went upstairs and lay down. Years had passed, almost a decade since he slept anywhere else. And now he'd be gone for a week. He thought about what he needed until he thought himself right out of bed. He worried himself into enough energy to pack.

The suitcase under his bed had been gathering dust for years. Jake opened it and found an old shirt he hadn't seen since he was in high school.

He felt it over and smelled the musty scent it had accumulated. He went through his drawers and tried to decide what he needed for this journey and ended up packing something for every conceivable situation.

Jake stared at his full suitcase. He gave in and tossed the .45 in. After all, who knew what could happen?

Nothing else could fit. The thought of failing the first time his father trusted him gave him a sick feeling. And now there was Ellie. He *definitely* didn't want to look foolish in front of her.

After a while he took a second try at sleeping. When sunlight hit his eyes, he wasn't sure if he'd ever achieved it.

CHAPTER 14

Hermanos Go South

Jake rose early. He showered, finished packing, and took his bag downstairs. From the front porch he watched the dawn chase night away.

Carl laughed when he came around from the bunkhouse. "Trouble sleeping?"

"You could say that." Jake rubbed tired eyes.

"Where's that brother of yours?"

"Still sleeping."

"Better wake him up."

Jake's shoulders slumped. "Fine." He stood and walked into the house, passing through the hallway. He knocked on his brother's door. "Aaron?"

No answer. He knocked again. Still no answer. "Aaron?" Still nothing. He pushed the door open and looked at the pile of blankets, waited as he considered his options. The lateness of the hour overcame his hesitation. Jake pulled the curtains wide open and let the rays flood the room, cascading its warmth into every nook.

A moan rose from his brother.

"Aaron, get up." Jake tapped his brother's shoulder.

Nothing. He jerked the covers away and exposed a sleeping Aaron bare before the world.

"Stop," Aaron murmured.

"We have to go. Get up!"

"Fine. I'm up. I'm up." His brother's eyelids opened. "What time is it?"

"Time to go." Jake headed downstairs again, and there she was, his breath of fresh air.

Ellie kissed him on the cheek, his favorite greeting. "Ready?" she said.

"Probably not."

She laughed. "You'll be fine."

"We'll see."

Jake sat down to breakfast. Hunger plagued after a night of anxiety. Hot coffee warmed his gullet. Halfway through the meal Aaron stumbled to the table, un-showered and un-dressed. Rosalia force-fed him coffee.

Jake didn't wait for him but marched outside and pulled the hot rod around. He loaded his suitcase in the back, along with his brother's. From the looks of the flashy clothes and party ware, Aaron was expecting a very different experience.

Mr. Weathers appeared on the front doorstep. He embraced his drowsy son while expressing confidence in his ability. Their father loaded Aaron in the front seat, who pulled his hat low over his eyes, scrunched down in the seat, and propped his head in his hand. "Jake, assist your brother any way you can."

Jake nodded. As he shook Carl's hand, the old man

winked at him. Rosalia handed him a bag of biscuits and cookies for the road. He knelt low and scooped his sister up in a huge hug, then stood up.

In the crisp dawn air, he wrapped his arms around Ellie. Mesmerized by her warmth, Jake got lost in the embrace. "I don't like the thought of being apart from you."

"Don't worry. I'm not going anywhere." Her hand touched his side and slipped something into his pocket.

He looked down at the yellow parcel. "What's this for?"

"Don't open it until tomorrow morning." She grinned at him.

"Yes, ma'am." He smiled. Jake stepped back and beheld her once more, knowing he wouldn't see her face for a few days.

The family waved as he pulled down the driveway. He returned their gesture, as his brother was lost in sleep.

Jake turned left on Highway 67 and made the engine work. He watched the sun in the early morning through the windshield. The clouds shone deep purple outlined in blazing orange. While his brother slept, they covered miles.

Alone with his thoughts, he savored the serene moments. The quiet was meditative. In the silence he recited to himself all that he and Carl went over the night before. He took the envelope Ellie gave him and inhaled deeply. It smelled of her, roses and infinity.

Aaron still slept when they turned west on I-10. With every white stripe, the hours and miles passed. Jake wasn't thrilled with the road, hating its parameters and missing his horse. Horses didn't have to obey the boundaries cars did.

When Jake drove through Fort Stockton, Aaron awoke. "Well, good morning, partner," Jake said with a hint of sarcasm.

"I don't even remember leaving home." Aaron laughed. "Go figure."

"Yeah. Go figure."

"I'm hungry."

Jake reached in the backseat and pulled the bag Rosalia gave them. "There's food in here."

"I need something hot." Aaron said.

Jake drove until he spotted a roadside stand. He parked the car and the two of them walked through the brisk air to a woman selling hot breakfast food of eggs, beans, and tortillas.

Seated at the roadside picnic table with their food, they lazed in the morning sun and watched the occasional truck pass by on the highway and as he looked at his brother, he realized there was no one he knew more and less at the same time than Aaron.

"So, ready for the meeting?" Jake took a bite of the migas.

"I'm ready for Mexico," Aaron said.

Rolling his eyes, Jake watched his brother inhale food and feared the tranquil ride was over, but his brother returned to the vehicle and fell asleep once more. Jake smiled. He burned as many miles as he could before his brother awoke again.

They blew through Fort Stockton and took 194 southwest out of town. Eventually, they merged with 67 and headed for the Mexican border. Disappointment flooded Jake's thoughts as his brother fully roused.

"Let me drive," Aaron said.

"Fine." Jake pulled over and took the passenger's seat.

"Let's see if I can't make up time for your slow driving."

Jake didn't mind the passenger seat as long as his brother was going to set a quick pace.

Before long, they arrived in Alpine, taking 67-90 through Marfa and then south once more, on 67. Hours of silent riding later they utilized the bridge from Presidio to Manuel Ojinaga arriving in Mexico.

Highway 16 was their final road. The day grew long and there was still over 200 miles to go. They stopped for a mid-afternoon meal at a roadside eatery.

Jake was miles farther from home than he had been in his entire life. Aaron was his only companion, someone he was more and less comfortable with than any one else in the world. He wished Ellie was with him because with her, he knew he'd savor the view and cherish the moments more.

He and his brother said little to each other for the duration of their journey. Jake didn't mind, since he valued so little the things Aaron had to say.

A few hours more and they closed in on Ciudad Chihuahua. They passed through the town bombarded with looks from the locals. Jake guessed it wasn't often that the citizens saw two white gringos in such a spectacle of a vehicle.

"We need to find a hotel." Jake said. "How about that place?" He pointed to an old building with a clumsy sign.

"No way I'm staying in a flea bag motel like that!" Aaron gave the car gas and pulled away from the spot towards bright lights across the plaza. The vehicle rumbled over the brick streets.

The two arrived at what Jake assumed was the nicest hotel in the area. Aaron panted like a dog when he saw the girls walking about the place. "Here. You check on accommodations while I make sure the staff is adequate."

Jake walked inside to the front desk as his brother romped around wide-eyed. Jake pulled an envelope of money their father gave them for the journey and retrieved the cash required for a room. After hearing the price of the room, his eyes bulged.

The hotel, a two-story adobe structure, was laid out like a "U" with a courtyard and pool in the center. No sooner had the brothers arrived in their room than Aaron insisted upon leaving.

"I found this perfect place to eat to dinner," Aaron said.

"Let's go someplace quiet so we can discuss the meeting tomorrow."

"Yeah, yeah. This place'll be fine."

Jake and his brother passed through the lobby. Jake stopped for a moment at the front desk to inquire the best way to the Mexibeef headquarters the next day.

Jake looked up. Aaron wasn't in the lobby. He went

outside and didn't see him in the streets either. He huffed as he limped the few blocks immediately around the hotel. His brother was nowhere.

Jake sat down in a cantina alone and ordered food. As he ate his meal, many people meandered by, but never his brother. After he paid the bill, he clenched his fists and left the restaurant. He made another pass through the neighborhood streets, checking his watch every few minutes.

Jake tossed up his hands. He couldn't spend all night looking for his brother. Aaron was on his own. Jake knew his father wouldn't approve, but he needed his wits for the meeting in the morning.

He left a key for Aaron at the front desk then climbed the narrow tiled stairwell to the second floor and walked through the arches to their room. He laid out the suit he borrowed from his father for the next day and frowned. Soon he was in bed but anxiety once again robbed him of sleep.

Hours later, as the night waned, the door handle banged against the wall when Aaron spilled through the entrance and flopped onto the other bed.

"Aaron? Where have you been?"

But the snores rumbling from Aaron told Jake there would be no explanation. Jake fought his racing heartbeat and tried to fall asleep.

The alarm clock rang loud and true. Jake's eyes flew

open. He silenced the bell and rolled towards the open window. Warm cascades of orange and yellow, emanating from a rising sun, brushed across his cheek as he wiped sleep from his eyes. The rooftops to the horizon existed as nothing more than silhouettes in the dawn. Jake pulled the letter Ellie gave him from under the pillow.

The envelope wasn't sealed and the letter inside, hand written. He read it slowly.

My Jake,

I'm so proud of you. There are such wonderful things you can accomplish today. You can do it, I know you can. But win or lose, triumph or fail, I'll be here for you.

Love,

Ellie

He traced his fingers over the signature, a small piece of her. He smiled and sat up. "Get up, it's time for the meeting," Jake said.

When Aaron didn't budge, Jake headed for the shower, grooming himself all the while yelling reminders to his brother.

His brace didn't sit well over the pants nor with these shoes. He tightened it a notch, aware of the change. Now, he too would notice the brace as much as anyone else. He polished the thing anyway with metal and leather treatment until it shined like new. Jake wished he could tarnish it again so it wouldn't reflect the light, drawing eyes to it.

His father's large shirt felt foreign, the suspenders like a straight jacket. The tie was a noose. Jake attempted the knot multiple times. He almost reached for his jackknife to shred the whole thing when his final try worked.

Finally, he stood in the mirror and examined the cowboy turned businessman. A few dark bangs spilled across his forehead. He fought them away.

"Aaron! Get up!" Jake kicked his brother's bed. "We need to leave!"

Aaron didn't stir.

Jake yanked the covers off him and articulated in his brother's ear. "We have to go!" He pulled back at his brother's sour odor.

"Shut up," his brother yawned. "I'm not going."

"Dad is not going to like this!"

"I don't care, I'm tired."

"We gave our word we'd handle this!"

"Go away." Aaron rolled over.

"Fine." Jake went downstairs, uneasy he would be on his own. The taxi he had ordered from the hotel staff the night before awaited him at the curb. Before long they passed through the streets, part of the morning commute. They entered the industrial area of the city before arriving at their destination.

Jake paid the driver and turned away from the vehicle. He studied the building before him. Lastly, he reached into his pocket closed his fingers around the note Ellie gave him.

"Here we go." He exhaled deeply and took his first steps forward.

"Mr. Weathers?" A secretary greeted him in the lobby. "Mr. Aaron Weathers?"

"Sort of. You can call me Jake."

She gave him a confused smile; he guessed she dismissed it as a language barrier. Searching around, he made a note of the marble floors and mahogany paneling of the building the company was headquartered in.

The secretary led Jake to an elevator. Jake counted and guessed this was the eleventh time he rode in an elevator. Only on the rare occasion when visiting relatives in bigger cities did he get the opportunity.

Jake followed the secretary down a long hallway, past the windows overlooking the city. His eyes focused on the heavy wooden doors waiting for him at the far end. Before Jake was mentally prepared, he arrived and stepped through the threshhold. He felt like he had jumped off a cliff.

Inside, he drowned in a whirlwind of handshakes and greetings. Seven men from the long table arose. "Señor Weathers, so nice to meet you!"

Señor Gomez, president of the company sat at the head of the table. "May I offer you something? Coffee? Champagne? Water? Cigar, perhaps?"

"I'd take coffee." After one sip, Jake set it aside.

"Señor Weathers, we are very excited to discuss things with you. I was just telling these gentlemen about your family's business."

"Oh..." Jake worked to form a sentence. "Were you?"

"You see, Señor Weathers, my country has a long past of struggle and hardship," Señor Gomez said. "But every so often, something good comes our way."

"And has something good come your way?" Jake perked

up.

"Americans, my friend," Señor Gomez took a long draw from his cigar. "They are coming by plane, car, and bus. Tourism has found its way here. Europe has long been the destination of the elite traveler, but war has changed that. And as for Caribbean playgrounds, Cuba calls. Americans, they love their travel. The beaches of the world have always drawn crowds. America has her beaches, but few of them have... how you say, the palm trees, the coconuts-things one desires on a trip to the seaside."

"I suppose the arctic waters of Maine don't fulfill this," Jake said.

Men at the table laughed and Jake struggled to not express pleasure at successfully cracking a business joke.

"This is exactly what I speak of. And while Mexico may lack in many things, beaches is not one of them. The people come and come. They come for the warmth, the mountains, the sea." Señor Gomez raised a glass to his lips. "And we have learned our lessons. American tourists want American hotels and American bars... this is where you come in. You see, our economy will thrive if we can compete with Cuba and even Europe for the American tourist dollar. Hotels along the playas have redecorated to American standards and booked your entertainers, such as Cab Calloway. Then our guests return to your country and tell their friends. We are on the brink of a... how would you say it?"

"Sounds like quite a boom," Jake said. He caught himself sitting more comfortably, almost settled.

"Quite a boom. Yes. We have succeeded in hotels,

entertainment and so forth, but one area of complaint is food. Most notably, the beef. The cattle down here graze differently and we don't have the steer infrastructure as does America, yet. But for now, we would love to advertise American beef in our hotels. Just one more feature for those Americans to discuss back at home during their golf games." The man leaned back in his chair.

Jake grinned. He could talk beef. "This is where our ranch comes in?"

"We have been searching for suppliers. They've mostly been in Texas, to fulfill this need," another one of the men chimed in. "We've been shopping around, discussing prices and options all over the southwest."

Then the discussion turned to Jake and the ranch. They asked how big the ranch was and what kind of cattle they ran. The men wondered how far the ranch currently shipped cattle and how prices and pounds related. They asked how steady a supply they could be guaranteed.

Jake's answers came slow at first, but more and more correct answers kept coming out of his mouth. At this point he realized; he knew his business. He had been observant and paid attention for years. Before he was even aware of his own transformation, Jake began to rattle off answers like an expert. Once the questions ceased, Jake realized he had enjoyed speaking with authority, being a professional they couldn't stump.

With every answer and bit of information, the board members nodded to each other. Jake discussed the cost of the cattle and getting them south of the border. Their order would be large, so Jake calculated a generous deal for them.

The secretary brought lunch. Jake found himself enjoying the company. They went from business to leisure over the course of sentences.

One of their lawyers wrote up a contract, drafted in English and in Spanish, but it truly came down to everyone's word and handshake.

"If you send the order," Jake looked Señor Gomez in the eye, "I give you my word, the cattle will come."

"What a prosperous day!" Señor Gomez put his arm around Jake. "Let us sign the contract and I will take you to one my restaurants."

"Actually, I'm not the primary name on the business. I can't sign anything. I'll have to take it back to my father."

"Good enough!" Jake's new partner chimed in. "This boardroom tires me. Let's see what else we can find in Chihuahua."

The group ushered him out the doors and down the elevator. Upon entering the lobby, Jake felt the eyes of every employee fall on the men.

"Bring the car around!" Señor Gomez called.

A minute later the Rolls Royce waited for them out front. Jake, his host, and some of the other men climbed in the back.

"I want to show you my city! Drive us around!"

The group passed down the streets and roads of Chihuahua, through some passages that seemed far too narrow for the massive car.

It amused Jake to hear his host's take on the city. Gomez was born there and seemed to know everyone. Every street corner was where he got his first kiss, or the café where he won a dice game when he was young.

He related to Jake the history of the city. The man spoke of Blas Cano de los Rios and Antonio Deza y Ulloa, Spanish conquistadors who founded the city. They discussed the city's involvement in the Mexican-American War as well as the French invasion.

Señor Gomez kept making the driver pull over so he could visit with people he claimed were cousins or other relations. The group also stopped every hour at a different cantina, arguing which establishment had the best tequila.

Jake excused himself from the beverages but enjoyed the company.

As they laughed in boisterous conversation at one of these bars, a little boy raced around the corner towards their table. *"Señor Gomez! Señor Gomez!"*

The man waved the child away and said something in Spanish. The boys responded and Gomez raised his eyebrows. He stood and found a telephone behind the counter. Jake couldn't understand this conversation either.

"Gentlemen, it seems my white bird is here!"

"It's arrived?" One of the companions stood.

"Yes! We're going for a ride!"

Jake did not understand but was caught up in the merry spirit that swept over the crowd. He followed them to the car and fifteen minutes later they reached outskirts of town. Parked near a hanger, Señor Gomez's plane glistened in the sun, his *white bird*.

"It just arrived from the factory." The owner ran his hand along the wing. "Care to go for a flight?" The host welcomed them onto his plane.

It was more luxurious than most of the nice houses Jake had been in. He tried to remain poised, despite the fact he was extremely excited to fly. He had never been on a plane before. Right away he did a gut check. Jake had to remind himself that most people flew in planes that didn't resemble palaces.

No sooner had they sat than Señor Gomez offered them champagne. A young señorita rubbed the man's shoulders.

Jake settled into the soft wide seat and wondered what to expect. The thunder of the engines roared as they choked to life and shook the aircraft. The cylinders were hungry animals, begging to be set free and take this plane from the ground.

Jake's attention split between talking with Señor Gomez as he bragged about his plane and watching liftoff from inside the cabin. The pilot revved the engine and let loose the brake. The force pushed Jake back into his seat as he grabbed the armrest, never experiencing speed like this before.

Jake's heart skipped a beat, not in fear or terror, but in absolute wonderment as the ground drifted away beneath them. They climbed higher and higher. Who knew that buildings and cars could look so small?

Señor Gomez had more comforts on his plane than one could imagine.

"My brother was in the war. He told me about the craft they flew in." Jake looked at his host. "I never thought a plane could be as extravagant as this."

"I'm glad you like my new toy."

The craft powered through the skies as sunset began. Instead of watching the painted sky, Jake felt part of it. There were no boundaries, not even the clouds. He tried to tune in to his host's conversation but spent most of his time mesmerized. Flight seemed so incredible a thing. They lapped the desert for an hour before the owner gave the command to land.

Jake watched the ground pull them down as they descended. Then he held his breath and waited for the thud of the wheels to make contact with the earth. As he disembarked, he decided he needed a plane someday as well.

The group drove to one of Gomez's restaurants and enjoyed a rowdy meal. A dozen young ladies joined them, all of whom the Señor introduced them as his nieces.

Thoughts of Ellie led Jake to dismiss himself, informing his gracious host that he must rise early the next day for the trip home.

Señor Gomez opened a briefcase and pulled out the contract, which contained the Weathers' and his terms of agreement. "I'll patiently await the mail."

"I'll send them off just as soon as they're signed," Jake promised. He stood there and looked this businessman in the eye. Jake summed up all the sincerity he had and stuck out his hand. "I can't possibly thank you enough."

"Cowboy," Señor Gomez threw his arms out and squeezed Jake in a big hug. "You come back and see me again."

"Yes, sir!" Jake waved good-bye and caught a ride in his host's chauffeured car. He couldn't sit still, he was so excited about the future and his new friend. Someday soon he would bring Ellie to see this place.

When he arrived at the hotel, Aaron wasn't in the room. He sighed and contemplated leaving his brother in Mexico if he wasn't back in time to leave in the morning

CHAPTER 15

The Cowboy's Desires

Jake experienced another sleepless night. This time anxiety didn't plague him, but excitement. He was so proud of the business he conducted and looked forward to the future. Mr. Weathers would *have* to respect him now. Jake had done this and shown he was ready for anything the ranch threw his way. Surely his father would accept him as partner soon.

Not only the long-term, but the short-term future excited him as well. Jake would get to see the gypsy girl today.

To Jake's relief, Aaron had found his way back to the hotel during the night. Jake packed both suitcases and gave the bags to a bellman. He bent down and scooped Aaron up and carried him over his shoulder. The sleeper never woke as Jake hauled him downstairs and threw him in the passenger seat of the car. Jake smirked when he pictured Aaron's face waking up miles from here, possibly back in Texas.

They returned the way they came and Jake was generous with the gas, ready to showcase his triumph back at the ranch.

Aaron roused far past the border. "Jake?"

Jake stared at the highway.

Aaron shuffled in his seat. "Are we back in Texas?"

"Yes." Jake's eyes were invisible behind the aviator lenses, according to the rear view mirror.

"Did it go good?"

"Yeah."

Then Aaron fell silent again for miles. When he became fully awake, he complained of a headache and dry heaved. He begged to Jake to pull over.

Jake drove the whole way; Aaron never touched the wheel.

The wild child Gracie came tearing out of the house when the pair pulled up. Her eyes full of blind love looked brighter than a flash of lightning in a heat storm. She didn't waste time hugging Jake.

When Jake stood from his sister's embrace, *she* was waiting for him. *Oh good, the dream continues.*

"Hey there, cowboy!" Ellie ran over to him. Her arms felt like silk as they wrapped around his neck. She kissed him with lips soft as bluebonnet pedals. "How'd it go?"

Jake raised his eyebrows and grinned.

"I knew you could do it."

"So Jake," Carl said. "How did everything go?"

"Carl," Jake pulled away from Ellie. "I've got a lot to tell you."

Ellie whispered to Carl under her breath, "He's finally realizing the man he is."

Jake caught a very satisfied grin from Carl.

Mr. Weathers came out of the house. "Jake." He nodded and smiled. His attention turned as Aaron climbed out of the vehicle. "Aaron! How'd it go?"

Aaron nodded and gave a little wave.

"You've got something to sign," Jake said.

"Why don't y'all rest for an hour or so then meet in my office?"

Jake arrived to the office before his father or Carl did. He listened for footsteps coming and quickly inspected his father's drawers for any liquor. Out of curiosity he looked over some papers his father had been reading earlier that day. Jake meant what he said about being involved in the business end of things.

The office, the symbol of the paperwork and business part of the ranch's operations, now meant more to him than when all he wanted was to herd steer. The rich mahogany desk from Philadelphia made it like an office on Wall Street. He father's ranching awards from across the years covered the wall.

Alongside them, the last family portrait hung, the one before his mother died. There were old pictures, too. Jake looked at his grandfather and his children. Mr. Weathers was only a boy in the photograph, and could have passed for Aaron.

The office was full of interesting things. The first deed to the ranch hung framed on the wall. An old saddle sat in the corner that supposedly belonged to a famous Texas

Ranger. And an old Cherokee hatchet someone found or won rested on the wall.

Jake's favorite piece was a musket pistol, passed down from the American Revolution. Someone related to Jake fought in the war. Although kept in good condition, it probably couldn't fire anymore. And along the side, carved into the gun's wood stock, the word that stole the soldier's heart: "Freedom."

Jake referred to the gun as the "freedom pistol". After hearing his father and Carl approach, he replaced the gun. He stood to the side, leaning against the wall. He didn't know how to appear. He didn't worry and took a seat.

Aaron was on time. This perplexed Jake but he understood shortly. For the first time in his life, his brother must be worried about his father's approval. After all, he had slept through the meeting.

The room did not have the air of a father and son chatting but more like a professional interview. While Carl took another chair, Mr. Weathers sat formally behind his desk. "So, how'd the meeting go?"

"Well sir—" Jake said.

"It went wonderfully! Couldn't have gone better," Aaron said.

Jake turned his eyes on his brother. "Aaron, I was talking."

"Don't worry." Sam waved his hand. "Your brother's just excited." He turned to Aaron. "What happened, son?"

Jake had enough. "Yeah, Aaron, *what happened*?"

His older brother shot a dark look his way.

Jake flared his eyes. "Go on, tell him how it went."

Their father looked hopeful.

"Think maybe you have something else to tell him?" Jake had rarely experienced confidence in his life, and now he guessed this new feeling was cockiness.

Aaron at last bowed his head. "So I may have missed the meeting."

"Missed the meeting?"

"Yeah, your son was too busy going wild in Mexico to wake up for the meeting."

"Is this true?" Sam's frowned.

"So what?" Aaron said. "I wanted to experience Mexico a little. It's Jake's fault for not waking me up!"

"I tried to! Besides, you're a grown-ass man. You can get yourself up!"

"You really missed the meeting?" Mr. Weathers said. "It was pretty important."

"Whatever! I don't need this!" Aaron stormed from the room.

"I don't know if he's cut out for this work," Carl said.

Awkward silence followed.

"That's too bad your brother didn't join you. So," Mr. Weathers began the inquisition. "They want American beef for their hotels? They really think that's going to drive up sales?"

"Yes," Jake said. "And I wouldn't have believed something that seems so insignificant would ever sway business, one way or another. After being down there, it does seem like they try to market any gimmick they can figure."

"So it's jazz music, the finest French Champagne, *and* Weathers Ranch Beef?"

"That's what it looks like. You know, sir..." It was odd addressing his father as sir, but nothing felt natural. "They're trying to develop trade with a few different places stateside. They must recognize our efficiency."

"They must." Mr. Weathers motioned for the envelope. "Let's take a look at the contract."

"He and I discussed the terms." Jake retrieved the envelope with the hefty contract and passed them to his father. "I looked them over, they seem fine, but of course we don't want our signatures on anything until we run these by our lawyer. Things could get even harrier because the deal is international. I'll be interested to hear what Mr. Clint has to say."

"You're right about that." His father thumbed through the pages. "Looks pretty straight forward. Guess I'll take this into the post office tomorrow and get them in the mail." He looked up at Jake. "Good job."

The "good job" was meant to end the business meeting, but Jake wasn't quite done. Maybe he felt tired, maybe he felt bold, or maybe it was the girl outside and the victory in Mexico "There's... one more thing," he said.

"What's that?" Mr. Weathers said.

"I've been pushing horns and working the ranch for a while now. Being in the business meeting in Mexico made me realize I know this ranch inside and out. How the cattle behave in certain weather and how to get a good deal shipping them. I plan on doing this the rest of my life and...

well..." Jake caught the astonished look on Carl's face. "I'd like to be made partner. I'm near twenty-six years old and... well, yes, I'd like to be partner."

"Why? I was just a ranch hand until the day my father died and my name got on the deed," Mr. Weathers said.

"I know," Jake said. "But not only can I do the saddle work, but I've also got some ideas about the business that I'd really like to try and make work." Then he said straight to his father's face. "I want this."

His father stared at him hard with blank eyes as though considering Jake's words.

"You know, boss," Carl said. "Jake does know this ranch better than anyone. And he did get us one of the most profitable deals we've ever closed. If you couldn't run this ranch yourself anymore, Jake's the only one other person I'd ever trust. The timing makes no difference. If these boys, or I should say, these men are going to get the place someday, it doesn't matter if it's now or years from now. Jake isn't going to learn anything more about the cattle side of things. He knows it through and through. And he's plenty fine with the business end, it would seem. He's ready."

"I'm ready." Jake nodded.

"Biggest deal ever," Carl said.

"Yes..." his father said "Yes, he did, but Jake, you're so young. Maybe you should read some texts on running a business, or start taking part in the books first."

"I think I have earned this." Jake looked his father in the eye, man to man.

Mr. Weathers leaned back in his chair and rubbed his brow. "All right."

Jake fought to act reserved and reached out his hand. "Thank you." He made polite talk for a few more minutes before excusing himself. He just needed to exhale and let out a grin, then journeyed to tell Ellie, but the light in her room was off. She must have gone to sleep a while ago.

He strolled back down the hallway, but this time, for the first time he could remember, he stopped in front of the mirror. He liked the person who returned his gaze, excited about being himself. After a moment, he joined Carl out onto the front porch. Jake enjoyed watching his friend light up his pipe. "Anything important happen while I was away?"

Carl exhaled. "That mare went ahead and had her colt. He looks like he'll be a decent enough horse." He shifted in his seat. "And old Pete swears on his life he saw something big out there in the back country, said it was a mountain lion." Carl grinned. "I told him he needs glasses."

Jake laughed. "So business as usual."

Carl's demeanor changed. "Jake, there's one more thing. It's your father... he had another one of his spells."

"He did?"

"Yes, and I can't figure it out. He's been doing so much better since your brother came back. I can't figure out why he's declining." Carl furrowed his brow.

"Have you checked his room for... you know, anything he could hurt himself with?"

"The other day I went in there when he was gone. Unless

he's got a real clever hiding spot, he's just in for a few dark hours whenever this happens," Carl said. "But Jake, I'm proud of you." Carl said, only sincerity in his voice.

"Thank you. That means a lot to me."

"Ellie really missed you."

"I really missed her."

"She's all kinds of special," Carl said. "I've noticed a lot has changed since she showed up around here."

"Yeah, it has." Jake leaned back. "It sure would have been nice if she could have met my mother. They would have loved each other."

"I *know* they would have loved each other." Carl exhaled his tobacco smoke.

Jake glanced towards the barn. Just then the horses neighed from across the way, one horse in particular.

"He's wondering why you haven't come see him yet." Carl nodded in the direction of the corral.

"Truth is, I was trying to wait until I could get over there by myself," Jake said. "I hope he's not mad at me."

"The morning you left, we noticed that mare, Aurora, was acting a little ill. We tried to put Larry on Rio." Carl chuckled. "He wasn't letting anyone near him with a saddle. Kept looking for you."

Jake slapped Carl on the knee. "Guess I better go mend this relationship."

"Please do. That horse can be a real snob."

Jake crossed the driveway to the corral, opened the gate, and walked in. Most of the horses plodded over expecting treats. Jake patted them, but his pet stood at a distance.

Jake wasn't sure if horses could give a cold shoulder but that's how Rio acted. Jake smiled.

"Hey, come on now kid," Jake said as he walked up.

The horse didn't move. Jake stroked his face and neck and patted his side. He worked on Rio's coat with a brush. "I just had to take care of some business. Don't worry, boy. That car didn't have anything on you."

After more affection, Rio seemed to forgive and responded to Jake. They spent a good half hour together. Jake took him for a bareback lap around the corral before he said goodnight.

The next morning Ellie wasn't at breakfast.

"Where's the girl?" Jake said.

"Must be sleeping." Rosalia shrugged.

Jake hit the range with the boys and went to work. When he slid into the saddle, it felt so right. The sight of the land, the feel of the rein, the smell of leather seeped deep inside him.

They returned to the house for lunch. Jake climbed the stairs and shuffled down the hallway to Ellie's room. A new painting she had started rested on her easel unfinished. Maybe that's what she intended.

Jake looked at it fondly for a moment then continued his search, but when he took a step, something crunched under his foot. He bent and ran his finger across the floor. Tiny shards of dark brown glass stuck to the end of his finger. Jake still had not asked about those little brown bottles.

He went out the back and found Ellie and Gracie sitting

on the back porch. Ellie braided Gracie's hair.

"Hey, Ellie, were you pretty tired this morning?" Jake said.

"Yes, I slept in a bit," she offered him a half smile. But something wasn't quite right. She was missing her glow. Her eyes looked tired.

He wanted to prod but not be pushy because he assumed it was just girl issues. "So, I talked to my dad last night like you suggested. And, well, he's going to make me partner."

Some of her glow came back. "Jake, that's wonderful. I'm so proud of you. I knew he would!" She hugged his leg from where she sat on the floor with Gracie.

He appreciated her effort to congratulate him and knew she meant it. In truth, he was more concerned about her at the moment. "Yes, I'm real excited," he slowed a bit. "But uh, Ellie, are you sure you're fine?"

"Yes. Just tired." But crimson glistened below her nose.

"Ellie, your nose is bleeding."

"My what?" She touched her upper lip.

"Let me get you something."

"No, no, I'm fine." She stood. "Must be the dry air." She disappeared into the house.

He tried to follow her, but Gracie tugged at his arm. Jake picked up a storybook nearby and, despite his concern, he read Gracie a few pages.

When he had finished more pages than he intended, he took Gracie back inside the house and got her interested in helping Rosalia. Then he checked on Ellie. Now she seemed much better and made a bigger deal than she had earlier about Jake and his father's negotiation.

Jake walked past his father's office, his father called his name. He stepped in. "Yes, sir?"

"Here's the contract." His father handed him a stamped envelope. "Put them in the mailbox so they get picked up tomorrow."

"Actually, I think I might drive into to town so they get out before tonight." Jake held that package like he was holding the baby Jesus Himself. He walked tall out of his father's study. He passed Aaron outside in the driveway.

"Hey, gimpie," Aaron said. "What have you got there?"

Jake didn't care much when his brother called him that name, but it had never thrilled him either. "Hey, Aaron? Do me a favor?"

"What's that?"

He looked his brother in the eye. "Don't call me 'gimpie'."

Aaron gave him a huge blank stare. "Oh, Mr. Big Man, thinks he's a big shot."

"I don't have time for this right now." He left his brother behind him.

Jake drove into town to the post office. All that waited for him was a sign that read, "out for lunch." Jake sat and waited for a while.

Then finally, the postman came back. "That's a fancy looking package. Must be important."

Jake tipped his cowboy hat. "Be sure and take care of it."

The clerk nodded. "Should be out of here by this

evening."

"Perfect," Jake said.

The sun was shining bright and this day made the future look bright. Still a little chilly but Jake let the windows down anyway. He enjoyed the drive through his part of the world. Jake felt right in the role he now played.

Then it hit him. Something he had been thinking about for a very long time. *Sure, why not?* He made a turn that wouldn't take him home. This had been a long time coming, but better late than never. This was his day and he would take it.

The aging man on the porch of the house stood as Jake pulled up in the truck. He put down his beer and met Jake as he approached. The character was bent with age and decided he didn't need to wear a shirt with the overalls. The tired dog at his feet stayed where he lay.

"Hi there, Mr. Longer." He took the old man's hand.

"Jake Weathers, what brings you here?" Mr. Longer tipped his hat.

Jake pointed at the bi-plane resting inside the Longer's barn. "I want to learn to fly that."

CHAPTER 16

Flying Son

Jake visited Mr. Longer's house every couple of days to learn to fly, growing closer to his dream of being a pilot. The training started out simple: the mechanics of the plane and its basic science. He gave Jake a few books on aviation to read. They looked as though Mr. Longer had never touched them.

After a few days, Mr. Longer pulled out a mock cockpit, a huge barrel hollowed out with a seat inside. He threw Jake in it and ran him through the steps of flying. Mr. Longer shoved the barrel from the outside to make it swing around like a real plane while narrating Jake's flight. The scenarios would often end with Jake dead in a fiery crash.

As the only resident crop duster and cattle-surveying pilot for a few counties around Mr. Longer kept busy. The old man had to go up daily.

Flying was a world different than the plane he flew with Señor Gomez. That plane felt like a comfortable room with an occasional vibration and noise. This biplane was something else. His experience was rocky at first but Jake grew confident.

In fact, the only element that made Jake uneasy was Mr. Longer's careless training approach. Sometimes Jake felt he didn't understand a principle enough or he missed something important.

Mr. Longer told Jake he was worrying too much, but not enough had happened between the day he approached Mr. Longer about learning to fly and today. Now it was Jake's turn to fly.

The plane is not going to get off the ground in time. The airstrip is too short, even for a bicycle to get up to full speed.

Jake swallowed hard and let his grip slip over the joystick. He looked to either wing and tested the flaps. Everything seemed to be working. Jake examined the gauges. All the knobs were turned to where they needed to be. He checked his seatbelt and his goggles, making sure both were snug. The pedals did what they should.

Jake sat in the pilot's seat, as ready as he'd ever be to fly the plane all on his own, and started the engine.

Mr. Longer sat in the other seat, hand on a beverage. "WHAT ARE YOU WAITING FOR, NANCY? GET THIS BUCKET OFF THE GROUND!"

Jake licked his lips and cleared his throat. It was now or never. He pushed forward on the throttle and the engine revved. He eased and eased until the propeller pulled at the air enough to get them rolling down the airstrip.

"PUNCH IT!" Mr. Longer hollered.

Jake gave it everything. The wind whipped past, the tail wheel lifted. He felt jarring bounces as the plane struggled with gravity. They gained speed and Jake pulled back on the joystick. And into the air they soared.

He cleared the trees by several feet, got to altitude and leveled off, just like Mr. Longer had told him. Then Jake relaxed his shoulders, exhaled, and looked around.

"Woooo Boy!" Mr. Longer celebrated. "You're flying now, son!"

The air tasted so crisp this high. Jake surveyed the vast West Texas kingdom this plane carried him over. He had dreamed of flying in the war and believed he'd always be too far from that dream. Now he had decided to learn to fly. Here he was. He did it.

Jake knew every house and ranch on the two-dimensional ground below. The cattle scurried like ants on dirt roads.

"Hey!" Mr. Longer yelled. The old man waved and twisted his hand back and forth indicating a maneuver he wanted Jake to execute.

Jake thought that Mr. Longer was out of his damn mind but went for it anyway. He tilted the plane sideways and pulled up on the stick, veering right. Then he swung around and pulled the other way. Jake repeated this a few times, performing it fairly smoothly. Mr. Longer stuck out both hands and gave him double thumbs up.

Then the old man seemed to tune out. He cracked a beer and toasted the highest party in Texas.

Jake gathered that Mr. Longer's mind was somewhere else, so he just did as he pleased. His confidence in his ability grew and he felt more at ease. He could definitely get used to this. In his mind though, and he didn't tell Mr. Longer, it didn't quite beat riding a horse across the range. But flying was definitely a close second.

Jake turned the nose of the aircraft south. He had told Ellie when to be outside so she could see him fly over.

Ellie had shrieked when he told her he was learning to fly. Carl had laughed heartily when he heard. He thought planes were a fool's errand and voiced it. When Rosalia found out, she crossed herself and rattled off some panicked Spanish. Jake tried to describe to Gracie what he was doing. He never really knew if she understood.

He told his father and Aaron but they seemed uninterested. These days Jake didn't care.

He flew over their pastures and couldn't find a spot of ground without any steers nearby. When he was above it all, their ranch seemed larger.

The house came into view along with the barn, the trucks, and the car. He could pick out the corral and which horse was Rio, a good-looking horse even from this high up. He kept looking and... there she was. Ellie stood behind the house craning her neck toward the sky and waving at him. Little Gracie stood next to her. Ellie pointed the plane out to Gracie, who waited for a moment before she jumped up and down. Ellie wrapped a blanket around her shoulders.

Over the last few weeks it got worse. She kept having spells that left her pale and tired. She often locked herself in her room for hours. Sometimes when they would be on the ranch, her nose would start bleeding without explanation.

Jake wanted to take care of her, but he also wanted to believe her when she said it was nothing. At first he suggested she see a doctor. She said it wasn't necessary. When it didn't seem to get any better, he begged her. As it grew worse, he forced her. Her fiery soul wouldn't go down without a fight. Somehow Jake got her to go.

Jake never heard the doctor's diagnosis; Ellie told him the doctor said she needed rest, but Jake didn't think that was good enough. Ellie already had a thin frame but she seemed to be losing weight. Her sunken eyes lingered. To Jake, the worst of it was her glow; it grew dim and faded. Yet the moments she smiled changed everything, every time.

As Jake circled above, Carl came out of the house. He waved his hand in the direction of the plane in a dismissive way. Jake laughed. After all, planes were a "fool's errand."

He didn't want to make Ellie stand outside any longer so he headed away from the ranch he turned the plane parallel to old 329.

Mr. Longer signaled for Jake to head back to the hanger. Jake's comfort died immediately when he realized he had to land, but he calmed down. "We can't stay up here forever. I've got to do this sometime."

He lined up with the airstrip dropping altitude gradually, almost too soon. Jake eased the stick down. Then those old lovers, the runway and the landing gear, reunited with a peck. They pulled apart for a moment, and then embraced wholeheartedly. The tail wheel joined the party.

Jake pulled back the throttle and applied the brakes "Whew." He guided the plane in front of the hangar. Jake removed the goggles he wore and massaged the chill from his wind-thrashed face. The plane sat still and lifeless. He took in a deep breath.

Mr. Longer climbed out of the plane without a second look.

Jake preferred a different ritual. As one touches the rocks at the top of a mountain or stores a sail after surviving a storm at sea, Jake ran his hand down the body of the biplane. He spit in a hanky and spot spot-shined the instrument gauges and took satisfied steps back and looked her over.

Now was the time to pay the piper. For every two hours of plane time, Jake had to dedicate one hour to talk time on the old man's porch. Mr. Longer told him the story of his life and then started over. Fortunately, now that Jake had flown, he could steer the conversation towards the topic of the pilot's license.

Mr. Longer was a certified instructor and could sign off on his license after Jake had spent a couple more hours in flight. He would have to execute numerous landings and takeoffs.

When Jake finally got away, he headed home. Gracie gave him a wave like he was a long ways off, then ran inside. He chuckled then headed to his dad's office.

Weeks passed since Mr. Weathers had promised to make him a partner and yet had not acted upon it. Jake felt the need to say something. He walked in and his father set down a very thick book.

"Can we talk a moment?" Jake closed the door behind him.

His dad looked as though he had to decide between words with his son and the book. He leaned back in his chair. "What is it?"

"Well," Jake tried to be delicate. "I was just wondering. I mean, we had that discussion a couple of weeks ago about my becoming partner in the ranch."

"Yes," Mr. Weathers raised his eyebrows. "I remember."

"It's been a while. When can we actually make it happen?" Jake sat up straight and did his best to look his father in the eye.

His father broke eye contact and looked to the side. "These things take time. There's all sort of paper work to accomplish and our estate lawyer has to write you in."

Jake swallowed hard to keep himself from saying anything.

"But don't worry. I'm working on it and it's progressing as it should," Mr. Weathers said. "Who knows? Maybe we'll have to cut your brother in as well."

Jake gave a less-than-courteous half laugh. The thought of Aaron owning part of this dear ranch made him grind his teeth, but Jake decided that was enough for now and left his father to his book. He went down the hall to Ellie's room and tapped on the door.

"Is that you, Jake? Please come in."

He entered and closed the door. She lay in bed reading by lamplight. Her sunken eyes held deep shadows. Her skin voided its rich color for pasty white.

He sat on the edge of her bed and brushed her hair behind her ear. "How you feeling, kid?"

"Oh, not bad." She gave a little smile. "Just trying to do what the doctor said."

"Good," Jake said. He looked around the room. Art filled every inch of the walls. She had increased the amount of work she was doing.

"Is that a new one?" He pointed to a painting of a lonely horse in the wind. "You're getting extremely good!"

"I finished it earlier today,"

"We're going to have to hang these up around the house or you won't have room to sleep in here," he said. "Or you could send them to a gallery. I'd drive them to a gallery in Dallas or Paris if you need me to. Would you like that?"

"Hmmm." She threw her head back in theatric fashion. "Alas, I shall have to consider my options."

He told her about his flight that day, straining to be animated, the way she liked stories to be. She laughed a little and smiled when he told her of Mr. Longer's antics. Eventually, Jake kissed her good night and tucked her in. He headed for the door.

What is wrong with her? Why is she in such bad shape?

"Hey, Jake," she said as he was leaving.

"Yes." He turned.

Her words came out slowly. "You'd love me no matter what, right?"

He looked into her endless eyes and summoned every truth in him. "No matter what," he promised.

"Even if I lost my hair and my youth?"

"Even if you lost your hair and your youth."

"If I got and stayed sick?"

"If you got and stayed sick."

"If I died young and left you behind?"

"That wouldn't happen. I'd follow you." He winked. "Broken heart."

For the briefest of moments, her face looked healthy. She gave him a warm smile and blew him a kiss. He closed the door.

Over the next week, Jake flew the plane every day. Better to do it for a solid week and pass the requirements rather than space it out over a few months. Jake did so many takeoffs and landings, they were no longer a thrill. He and his instructor went up in clouds and in the clear.

Towards the end of the week, Mr. Longer received a large envelope in the mail containing a written test from an aviation accreditation bureau. Jake took it. More prepared than he needed to be, he finished in sixty hours.

On Friday all Mr. Longer told him, "Take me to Abilene." Mr. Longer didn't say anything else and refrained from giving Jake any instructions or reminders.

On his own, Jake checked the plane out beforehand, fueled up the rig and measured the fluids. They took off and he headed northeast to Abilene. He found the runway and set her down.

The pair took a break, then headed home again.

When they touched down back in Crane, Mr. Longer

looked at Jake and said, "Well done, pilot."

They filled out all the paperwork and sent it off. Mr. Longer dug out some old pilot medallion to commemorate the occasion but couldn't remember where he got it from or for what. Jake didn't mind the old man's long twist of tales. It seemed fitting for the last day between the master and the apprentice.

At home Ellie congratulated him over and over. Carl continued with his entertaining disapproval of being off the ground. Jake figured he should mention it to his dad.

Overhearing him, Aaron shook his head. "You should have seen the stuff some of the pilots I knew had to fly through. And they got to be above the battlefield! We had to walk right through."

"Where were you?" Mr. Weathers looked with big eyes at his son.

"Outside Brive-la-Gaillarde."

"Really?" Jake said. "I didn't think your division went that far south."

"Uh... you know, French towns all sound the same." He looked out the window. "Didn't know if we'd make it out, but we handled it. I saved the lives of eight men that day."

"What a hero." His father smiled.

"I didn't always feel like a hero, but yeah, I guess I was."

Sam beamed at Aaron and seemed to forget Jake's accomplishment.

Jake sighed, stood up, and walked out of the room.

But Jake didn't care, he didn't do this for them. He did this for himself. His father and Aaron were going to be presences in his life, but that was all. They could do as they pleased as far as he was concerned. Once his dad made him partner, he could give serious thought to his future with Ellie. Nothing on the ranch proved more than he could handle.

He bounced into Ellie's room and together they read a story to Gracie.

The next day his father announced he was leaving on a business trip to Brownwood and would be gone for a few days. Aaron let everyone know that he too would be away. He claimed a colonel, who later became a general, wanted to meet with him in Dallas. He said they were old army buddies. Yet for some reason, it seemed necessary for him to take three of his friends with him.

And the ranch would be lighter still because Carl planned a personal trip. His nephew in El Paso had had a second child.

The family remaining in the ranch house came down to just Rosalia, Gracie, Ellie, and Jake.

As Jake waved Carl down the driveway, a chill went up his spine.

CHAPTER 17

Broken Gypsy

Jake's boots hit his bedroom floor. He looked out his bedroom window at the sun just peeking over the horizon. "Welp, here we go."

In the kitchen, Rosalia and some of the boys waited for him. Jake made sure to sit still and act dignified. Between the trip to Mexico and jumping right into flying, he hadn't hit the ranch in a while. His legs itched for the saddle and his hands ached for the rope.

Fresh Texas morning air called. The crew took down their bacon and eggs with a fresh pot of coffee.

The absence of Carl and his father left Jake in charge. He found his way to the chair at the head of the table, where the boss sat. A feeling of weight, but good weight, touched his shoulders. The crew waited for orders from him.

"It's the third Thursday of the month. Let's handle it like we always have," Jake told the crew. "This is nothing we haven't done before." After reciting a few specific orders, he left for the corral.

Rio looked ready and almost excited to get to work, shaking his mane and grunting. He hadn't been worked hard in too long. Jake brushed him down and got his saddle on him. The moment his legs wrapped around Rio's sides, the horse was out the doors of the barn.

Rio misbehaved a bit, not waiting long enough for the other ranch hands to get on their horses. Jake really had to yank on the reins but didn't punish Rio's enthusiasm.

The riders headed off to Lower Canyon to get the shipment for the army base in San Antonio. The family had managed to get the profitable contract years ago because Jake's grandfather became friends with the commanding supply officer.

Dew from the night before coated the herd in enough moisture to make their coats shimmer. Jake had done every one of the necessary steps many times before, but today it was so sweet. He matured a decade in the six months since Ellie arrived. Today it seemed as though he could visualize the result, nearly part owner of the ranch. He had fulfilled a lifelong dream to be a pilot all the while leading the crew. And he had Ellie.

"All right, Larry, Pete, come split up through there and push that way." Jake pointed to the left side of the mass of animals. "Then just sit tight and make sure the bunch doesn't split. We've got to sort the ones to go. Let's pinch them off and get them to the trucks."

They moved like a well-oiled machine, splitting off eighty head, and pushed them to the edge of the pasture where the military's own shipping trucks waited. Jake sat back ready to chase down rogue steers. When none bolted, he let out a sigh.

A stout and jolly uniformed man showed up, the same officer for the last five years, to get this load. He didn't quite fulfill the image of the iron-piece military man. "Hey there, Jake." He gave a little wave. "Where's Carl?"

"Hello, Captain Miller," Jake called. "Visiting family. But don't worry. Even without him, the cattle still taste like beef."

"I know it's last minute, Jake, but could we get ten more head?"

Jake looked back at the pasture and counted over some steers. "Sure, and I'll even cut you ten cents on the pound discount." Jake had seen his father offer the same courtesy before. He spun to the rest of the boys. "Get them on the trucks. I'll be right back."

He kicked his horse and headed toward a cluster of steers. Jake got behind them and hollered at them to move, zipping his horse back and forth to keep the mass uniform and moving together.

The Captain paid the rancher with a check from the United States Military. He thanked Jake and all the others. Once he got his drivers to their trucks and fired up the old diesels, Jake and his riders separated to go do other work.

When it was time to head in for dinner, Jake realized doing the work well gave him particular satisfaction today. The day was a good day.

The family's seats at the table were empty. In such a small community the absence of a few is much louder than it is elsewhere.

"Chicken with mole sauce?" Jake looked up from his

plate. "Is this because Carl's not here?"

Rosalia winked at him.

After dinner, Jake and Gracie listened with childlike joy as Ellie read with dramatic inflexion, channeling the characters in a way that made them come alive.

Later Ellie retreated into her room and returned with her artist's satchel and headed for the door of the house.

"Hey, kid?" Jake cocked an eyebrow. "Where are you off to?"

"I just wanted to get some fresh air," she said. "I think I'll go for a drive, see if I get inspired."

"It'll be dark soon, hard to paint."

She looked out the window. "There's an hour at least."

"Sure but you feeling good enough for this?"

"Absolutely!" She smiled.

He hesitated. "Want me to go with you?"

Ellie patted her satchel. "Actually, I'm feeling a bit of the creative. I believe a masterpiece is on its way," she smiled. "But I'll need to focus."

Jake didn't like the thought of her off by herself. What if she got sick? But he knew that sometimes Ellie needed to have an adventure to herself. *Roses don't grow when they're smothered.*

"I want to see it when it's done." He nodded at her.

"You'll have to wait your turn to bid on it like everyone else," she laughed. "Maybe I'll give you a discount." She headed across the driveway and climbed into one of the trucks. She drove off down the driveway.

Jake watched as the truck disappeared around the

bend in the road. He played with Gracie until the phone rang.

"Jake," Rosalia called from the kitchen. "There is a call for you."

He put the receiver up to his ear. "This is Jake Weathers."

"Jake?" came a voice on the other end. "Hello, this is Mr. Holland. We got a package for you today and it looks kind of important. It's from a machine shop in Dallas."

"It's a piece for one of our plow trailers."

"Yeah, well, I thought it was important so I brought it home. I figured I'd give y'all a call so y'all could come get it here since the office is closed," he said. "But if you don't need it, I'll take it back and you can get it from me tomorrow morning."

Jake thought about this for a second and decided a responsible rancher would go and get the part now. "No, Mr. Holland. I'll come get it now if that's fine."

He drove to Mr. Holland's house and hoped to slip out just as quickly, but Mrs. Holland would have none of that. She offered Jake three different kinds of pie. He sat upright on the edge of his chair fighting off the realization that this would be a long visit. It was well into darkness by the time he made his getaway.

After he arrived at the ranch, he unwrapped the package in the barn. Installing the part took the better part of an hour. As he wiped the grease from his hands, he wondered what Ellie had painted. Then Jake went to the house and crept up to Ellie's door, gently pushing it open. The door creaked on its hinges and he quietly slipped inside.

She was sound asleep, a deep breathing mass of pillows. Relieved, he tiptoed out.

In his own bed, he savored the hours of rest before his second day without his father or Carl. There would not be much to do, and the crew had the day off. He could give his whole tomorrow to Ellie. Maybe he could even get her to talk about how she was feeling. Jake wasn't convinced it was merely a sickness. He tossed and turned as he drifted to sleep.

The next morning he woke up with a bad feeling. Uneasiness crept up his spine, the same uneasiness he felt the day Carl left. He got out of bed and put his clothes on.

In the kitchen he started the coffee With the ranch hands absent, Rosalia had slept late. Jake sipped it slowly and poured the second half of the cup down the drain.

For a long time he fought the urge to check on Ellie. He tried to sit but after a few moments, he paced the length of the kitchen three times. Jake felt stupid wanting to see for himself that she was well, then even more stupid for trying to talk himself out of it.

He walked the hall to her room and pushed opened the door. His heart rested. There she still lay as he listened to her steady breathing and finally breathed himself.

Then, without warning, she stirred.

If he crept away she could sleep longer, but he caught himself wanting to see her eyes. The covers came away and she rolled over. The biggest smile in creation came with the face…

… but the face wasn't Ellie.

"Gracie!"

"HELLO!" Gracie yelled.

Where is Ellie?

His own pounding heart drowned his sister's laughter. He rushed to the bed and dug for Ellie in the sea of blankets. She wasn't there. Jake ran to Gracie's room and looked for Ellie there; the room was empty. He ran through every other room of the house and searched for her.

"Oh, God." Was Ellie lost? Hurt? Then the panic took over. He ran outside to the barn, she wasn't there. The truck she had driven wasn't parked where it should be. Ellie hadn't come home last night. Worry overcame Jake as he threw up in the grass.

He ran back inside the house as the phone rang. "Ellie?"

"Uh… no? This is Officer Wellers with the Odessa Police Department. Is this the Weathers' household?"

"Yes!"

"Sir, we found an abandoned vehicle with papers from your ranch in it."

"Where?"

"Bavarian Inn, southwest side of town."

"I'm on my way." Jake missed when he tried to put the phone on the receiver. He hit the screen door so hard it blew off its hinges. The engine of the only remaining truck roared as he blasted down the driveway and onto the road.

Odessa! What the hell is she doing in Odessa?

Jake's mind raced as he drove in a mad panic, nearly blowing the truck's top end. The thought of a big city conjured the nausea Jake always felt when he neared urban realms. He made a fist and pounded the dashboard.

It seemed as though centuries and eons passed before he arrived in Odessa. He aimed for the southwest side of town but realized the hopelessness of finding the Bavarian Inn in the large area. He needed to know where it was.

The pickup slid to a halt, then he threw it in park. People filled every chair in the diner.

Jake stormed in. "EXCUSE ME!"

The crowd fell silent as every person froze and gaped wide-eyed. The sizzle of the grill was the only sound.

"Can anyone tell me where the Bavarian Inn is?" He waited.

No one answered, still with dumbfounded looks on their faces.

"The Bavarian Inn!" He turned in a circle.

An old man raised a pointed finger through the window. "Go down a mile and turn right on Moss—"

Jake didn't take the time to thank him. He powered through that mile and took a right. After another mile, his target came into view.

The missing Weathers vehicle sat in front of the filthiest motel Jake had ever seen. The dilapidated sign let him know it was the right spot. Jake searched the vehicle and found nothing. In his way, he ran to the office. He approached an empty front desk.

"Um, hello?" He called.

Sounds of a radio convinced him someone was down the hallway. Jake let himself through the counter then advanced down the hall. After rounding a corner, he startled an unshaven man, half-dressed who smelled like stale meat.

"What the hell are you doing back here?" The man stood from his chair.

"Did a girl check in here last night? Dark hair? Hazel eyes?"

"I'm calling the cops." The man tried to push past Jake.

Jake shoved him down on a couch. "Dark hair! Hazel eyes! Is she here?"

"Yeah, room twelve." The man scrunched his eyebrows.

Jake ran across the parking lot, but just as he was about to charge in, he slowed. Ellie had every right to come stay at a motel if she wanted. She probably had a good reason. He would look like an overbearing worrier.

So he took a moment to calm himself, and rapped on the door. "Ellie?" He tried to look through the window but the curtains were closed.

"Ellie?" he knocked again a little louder.

No response. He gave the door a try. It was locked.

"Ellie!" he shouted.

Nothing. He shouted a few more times. As his voice grew louder, so did his anguish. He pounded on the door. "ELLIE!"

Any regular sleeping person would have heard him. He kicked the door with everything he had. It splintered as the hinges trembled and gave way before his wrath. The heart in his chest broke in two as he saw her on the floor.

The girl's beautiful figure was sprawled as though she had spent the night thrashing in agony. Blood left its mark from her nose and mouth. Her face showed no peace as she lay motionless on the floor.

As he fell to the floor next to her, his knees hit hard. "Ellie!" Jake grabbed her and shook her. He fought to pull her from whatever evil held her.

She made no response.

Something crushed beneath him. The floor was covered in brown bottles. Her own hand clutched them. He pulled one from the ground. Its label was a curse. "Medicate Opium."

"Ellie!" He held her head and opened one of her eyelids. "Oh shit." Her eyes were rolled back in her head.

"Oh God! Please!" He slapped her face but she refused to come. He put his ear to her chest, but her lovely heart beat so weak. *If only it would fight, if only it would pull her from the dark. She would come.*

"Ellie! Please!" So many things came together, every shadow in her face, every piece of brightness stolen from her eyes. Now they had a reason: the drug.

But the victim wasn't coming back. That face he loved, that face that made him a man, was lifeless and broken.

A tear stole its way down his face. He did not fight it.

"Don't leave me," he whispered. "Come back."

She lay limp in his arms. He brushed the hair from her forehead and stroked her face. "Ellie, wake up!" he yelled.

Why didn't I ask her?

And now the pills were taking her. It was them and what they contained, the very worst thing on earth. Hatred for them filled the depths of his soul in an instant. They were his personal enemy.

He blamed them for stealing the soul from his beautiful girl. They had stolen his whole world. Jake wept.

With one hand, he grabbed one off the floor in front of him. Closer and closer, he pulled it in, and through tears read and reread every last letter of that damned label. He pulled it in, until it was tight against his forehead, but his anger did not stop. The rage in his hand pressed it until it shattered into a million pieces against his skin. Crimson flowed into his eyes and ran down his face. He tasted the blood.

Jake held her broken body and knew he was now done with all things. She was everything and she was gone. He was left alone. Now he didn't know what to do, he didn't know what to think, paralyzed in the moment and crippled in a way far beyond all he had ever experienced. The breath escaped from his lungs. Jake swore he would sit there for eternity holding her, cradling the lifeless shell she left behind.

Her delicate hand still clenched the bottle that killed her. *How can it end like this? Why hadn't I seen it before?* ... And how dare that bottle still rest in her hand? He despised every one of those bottles framing the scene of her death, but the one in her hand he hated the most.

Jake tried to pull it from her fingers, but Ellie's fragile fingers closed around it. The fight meeting his grip sent his heart into a frenzy. He froze, she moaned. He pulled the bottle some more, she fought even more... she wasn't dead.

"Oh, Lord." Maybe it was a long awaited prayer, maybe it was relief. He pulled on the bottle harder; her hand resisted more.

"... No," she whimpered.

The forces collided as the bottle caved into their tug of war and cracked.

"No!" he cried in panic. "Ellie!" He held her close and hoped. Jake felt hope as one of her perfect eyes half opened. He caught a glimpse of hazel... she could come back.

Energy rushed through every muscle in his body. He became ten men in an instant. He shifted her body to his left side and shoved both arms under her and stood with the fury of a storm.

She moaned louder.

And it was that same moan, and every delicate breath that came from her nose transformed Jake into a hurricane. Nothing would stop him. He had hope. *What to do?* Jake called Dr. McKinney's office from the motel phone.

The nurse answered.

"Where's Dr. McKinney? I need him right now!"

"At the Sand's place, not too far from your ranch."

"I *need* him to meet me at my place immediately!" Jake scribbled the Sand's number in his palm and called the doctor. At least half an hour, maybe longer, before he could be at the Weathers' ranch. If he sped, Jake could get Ellie home by then.

He dropped the receiver. He carried Ellie across the

parking lot to his truck and slid her into the passenger seat. Then he jumped around the hood and climbed into the driver side.

"What's going on?" The manager yelled across the parking lot.

Forty miles and thirty-two minutes passed and they arrived at the ranch.

"ROSALIA!" Jake lifted Ellie from the passenger seat. He climbed the stairs of the front porch and took her though the door. "ROSALIA!" Jake carried Ellie down the hall and set her gently on her bed, covering her in blankets.

But he had no time to breathe.

Rosalia came in. "My God! What happened?"

He didn't think the world needed to know Ellie's secret. "I just found her like this!"

"Get cold water and a washcloth now!" Rosalia yelled.

Jake ran to the kitchen and back.

"Dab her forehead, keep her cool!"

Jake watched sweat gather on Ellie's brow. Her breaths were short and hard.

They wrapped her hand in bandages, but it wouldn't stop bleeding. And still more, her nose ran with more blood.

"Why isn't this working?" Jake said and ground his teeth in frustration.

"I don't know! I don't know!"

It seemed like eternity and a half for the doctor to arrive. The pair let him into the room. He examined Ellie and asked Jake questions.

"I found Ellie like this when I came into to wake her."

Jake looked down at her.

The next hour was nails down a chalkboard for Jake. The doctor checked her vitals and administered medicines to revive Ellie, but her breaths grew shorter and harder until she stopped breathing completely. He compressed her chest and breathed into her mouth.

The physician fought with every bit of knowledge he had, yanking a syringe from his bag and sticking it in her arm and waited… nothing… nothing… nothing.

Jake couldn't keep his body still. He crashed through the back door of the house into the wide, open existence. Jake fell to his knees in the grass, lingering there for what seemed like a moment and hours.

Time was all the same. Eternity sprawled in every direction. His mind's eye tracked the rising sun and how it burned in an endless sky. The cattle grazed in the distance and a fly landed on his arm. If days could have emotion, this day couldn't care less about what was happening. He had nothing to give.

"God?" Jake winced. "God… I don't know what to say. I don't really expect anything from You. I don't deserve to ask. There's no promise I can make… but God, please…" Jake grabbed the locks of his hair. "Please, God, please, God, please, God!"

He knelt and let the breeze brush his face. He waited, out of words for the Master of all things. Tired and as the terror had taken its toll, he only breathed as his eyelids grew heavy and fell. His shoulders loosened. And Jake felt a moment, though only one, of rest.

"Jake!"

Rosalia's call brought him back from the dreamlike state. He climbed to his feet, limbs tight and sore. Jake limped inside.

"She's going to pull through," the doctor said.

Jake closed his eyes and exhaled. He brushed his hair off his forehead as his soul restored.

Ellie appeared to be sleeping, peaceful and calm.

The doctor tried to get more information out of Jake but received the same answers, answers that led nowhere. Then the doctor gave Jake and Rosalia instructions on taking care of the patient for the next few hours and insisted they call if they needed him.

Dr. Walter asked Jake to walk him to his car. As they stood outside, their roles changed, no longer a doctor and a nervous bystander or even an elder and a youth, they were just two men.

"Jake, I know there's something you're not telling me."

"But—"

The doctor raised his palm. "And that's fine if you don't want to tell me. But just know that whatever happened cannot happen again. She was inches from the edge in there, and probably couldn't survive another trip." He looked Jake hard in the eyes. "You need to deal with whatever is going on."

Jake narrowed his eyes. "I'll take care of it."

"Do that, Jake," the doctor said. "It doesn't take someone brilliant to see what that girl means to you. So take my word for it, the best thing you can do for her is change whatever it is that needs to be changed."

"Yes, sir." Jake shook his hand firmly.

After the doctor's car disappeared down the driveway, Jake went inside to check on the sleeping Ellie. She didn't stir but rested comfortably. Jake and Rosalia watched her throughout the day.

After midnight, Rosalia offered to take the morning shift if she could manage a few hours sleep now. Jake encouraged her to get some rest.

Alone with the sleeping Ellie, he held her hand and waited... just waited.

CHAPTER 18

Last Ridge

It was the morning after. Ellie survived.

Jake had been waiting for Ellie to come out of her room. Hours before, he sat down at the table. Even after watching her come so close to the brink of her life, he still wished he didn't have to do this. He didn't know what he would say and didn't want Ellie to feel cornered. That's why he had sat down when he did. He knew that was the first step. So in a moment of commitment, he forced himself to sit down and wait.

She would come to him. She would surely come.

As he sat there in the hours of dawn he ran over every moment, every clue he witnessed. All those empty bottles insulted him with their bravado. Every nosebleed Ellie suffered and the times she snuck away to do things she was ashamed of. He had watched her deteriorate for months; his Ellie, for ages.

She was sick and suffering and he did nothing. All the days in the sun she had missed, all the times she should have been free to run, this curse imprisoned her

Seeing his Ellie brought to her knees shook him to the

core. The girl he built so much of his confidence upon had made so much of him, and now she was broken. He let her down. It was his fault.

She came down the hallway. The wood floors creaked beneath her. She sat down across from him and waited with him in the quiet. The air was thick with tension. And the lack of words made it worse.

After a few minutes Jake stood and started making coffee. He had never done so with such detail. It was the most carefully brewed cup ever at the Weathers' house, made in his procrastination to avoid the conversation. He had elongated every step of the process.

But they were both committed. Jake knew Rosalia would rise at some point. Gracie could come out of her room any minute. And this was a conversation for the two of them alone. It was now or never.

The coffee had long since lost its steam. They never touched it. Jake sat at the table in the kitchen waiting for her to speak.

The kitchen remained eerily silent. Yet the little brown bottle on the table between them screamed and echoed its presence; it was the reason he was here. Her little secret— what Jake had feared so long—had almost been the end of her. And it seemed ridiculous that a thing so small could cause so much hurt. How strange that so simple a thing was both Jake's nemesis and Ellie's master.

He looked up at her. "How did you sleep?"

"It's a form of liquid opiate."

"But how... when?" he stammered.

Ellie shuffled the coffee mug closer. "I've tried to figure that out. I guess there was really no first, no first choice. No first time. It was going to happen long before it ever did. If I were honest, I'd have to say that." She gave him a moment of eye contact. "My college friends and I were so young, in a whole new world, a bubble of existence. We lost ourselves in the wonderment of art. We learned about these geniuses of creation, these artists. With every page of rhyme turned, and every canvas we consumed, we were romanced by these artists and the lifestyles they led."

"You've told me some rough stuff about the artists." Jake said.

"Rough indeed," Ellie nodded. "But slowly, the more we exposed ourselves, the more our disapproval became indifference. Then, somehow indifference became tolerance. We found ourselves being understanding of the things they did. And not just the ones we read about in history books but the ones we encountered on the boardwalk and in the darker places in town. Curiosities became first sips and nibbles."

She grimaced. "Then we decided we would be smart about the things we were partaking in. We knew how to control them. We were in charge."

"What happened?"

"The same thing that always happens to individuals 'in control': denial, on the way down and we didn't even know it. After too much red wine or an extra glass of champagne and marvel at the projects we created while we were under."

Ellie took her first sip of cold coffee. "And that's how it was for a long time. We played out the characters we wanted to be. We wanted to be artists so we followed their example."

Jake indicated the bottle. "So when did this happen?"

"A local artist, his work didn't seem real. Then we learned his secret." Her first tear fell.

Judging by the look on her face, Jake knew he didn't have the words. He tilted his head.

"I don't remember what it felt like... I just remember it felt. We believed the hallucinations unlocked our talent, gave us ability to produce masterpieces. Our minds ran wild."

Jake gave her a look that said it would be okay. He stood and walked around the table, sat down, and put his arm around her. "Did you know what it was?"

"We thought we did. Our minds played tricks on us, convincing us we got the edge we needed." She buried her face in her hands. "We didn't understand the price." She turned to him and pleaded. "We didn't know, Jake! We just didn't know!"

"That it was dangerous?"

"We didn't understand it was addictive. After a few days without it, it steals your thoughts. We played it off as craving to paint or write something, but it wasn't the ends we craved, it was the means." A sob burst from Ellie. "And then she died."

"She?" Jake handed her his handkerchief.

"My friend, she used it far more than the rest of us. She didn't survive…" Ellie sniveled. "We found her on a Sunday… who ever dies on a Sunday? She was alone in her last moments, locked in a closet."

"I'm so sorry, Ellie."

"We thought her death saved us. I believed it saved me at least. Afterwards our guilt and loyalty to our friend drove us to abstain. We were in a struggle for our own souls. That was… well, that was around two years ago. Then college ended and we parted ways and I headed to New Orleans, proud of myself. I thought I had won, thought I was free, but soon enough it whispered in my quiet thoughts. Somewhere, somehow, I found a man, a worm who knew how to find me more opium, or something similar."

Jake ground his teeth. "What's his name?"

"No Jake," Ellie smiled through the tears for first time today. "You're not going to shoot him." She took another sip of cold coffee. "And when I headed for San Francisco I brought some with me."

"And then you stopped here," Jake said. "Why has it gotten worse? You've been getting sicker for months."

"I've been using it more and more," Ellie rubbed her eyes. "I've been doing a lot more artwork out here, but I know I'm just using that as an excuse."

"How much do you have left?"

"Enough." Ellie's shoulders sagged. "Enough."

"Why did you go to Odessa?"

"The same vile fiend I knew in New Orleans sent me a letter that he was passing through on his way west. He told me he had more for me." She shook her head. "I tried so hard not to go."

There it was before them both. The choices of the past were exposed to light.

"So that's everything?" Jake grabbed the edge of the table.

"It is."

"So where do you want to go from here?" Jake stared into her eyes. "I believe you would change the past if you could. And I'd do anything for you, even bend heaven and earth. If I needed, I'd chase you down eternity and back again. I want you to be happy... I want you to be free." Jake narrowed his eyes. "So now is the time to act."

"Save me." She looked up. "Help me. Carry me. Because deep down, I don't want the drug to go." She put her hand on the table. "Where should we start?"

"Well, I..." Jake hadn't thought through things this far, "...I guess we could see a doctor. Or maybe we could get rid of the stuff you have left."

Ellie winced and in a flurry she stood and raced down the hallway.

Jake stood and followed her. "Where are you going?"

She led him to her room and bent over her bedside table. She pulled the drawer open. It was empty, but she continued to pull the drawer out and off its glides. Then she reached her hand into the space the drawer occupied. Ellie pulled out a leather pouch and hesitated before she handed it to Jake.

Before she could pull it away, he grabbed it. "Where

else?"

"This way." Ellie led him back into the hallway and to the den. She reached for a vase in the corner with a fake plant hanging out of its top. She moved the plant away and pulled another stash from inside the porcelain hiding place. This time she nearly threw the package at Jake.

He looked up from the pouch in his hand. "Good job, kid."

She smiled at him. While still looking physically sick, in that moment some of the hazel fire came back to her eyes. She looked ready. She looked burning. Today would be her first day.

"Ellie? What on earth are you doing up this early?" Rosalia called from the kitchen. "She should be recuperating!" She turned to Jake. "And you should be getting ready for work!"

Rosalia moved like a whirlwind. She put Ellie back in bed where she belonged and forced Jake upstairs to get the rest of his gear for ranch work today.

On his way out, Jake stopped by Ellie's room. He stuck his head in. "Ellie. I'm really proud of you." He left her with a smile as he headed to the kitchen.

Before long, the men sat down to breakfast. After their day off they were ready to get busy. Jake wanted to spend the day with Ellie, but he didn't have an excuse to tell them to take another day off. Also, he wanted to prove to his father that he was more than capable to run the ranch. After all, this was what he would be doing for a very long time.

Now he knew the sad and ugly truth. No more wondering about her or worrying about a phantom. Yes, it would take work, but he could help her on the long journey ahead. This morning was the first step.

Jake walked out on the porch and scanned the horizon from one end to the other. Something in his chest jerked, not painful or even physical, but more of a feeling, a sense. The ranch had another big shipment headed out later today. For now they had smaller tasks to accomplish.

Hours passed before Jake gave the order for the boys to head off for Last Ridge, a lower pasture where they would select the cattle. Jake liked it when they all packed up and headed somewhere in unison, like a posse in the Old West. They kicked up their fair share of dust.

They planned to move the herd from a lower pasture called Last Ridge. On its far side the land sloped up to the highway. Vegetation only grew there once a year so it remained uninhabited. It was steep and a hard cattle drive.

But that's what it was going to take today. And that's what the boys would do.

Jake looked, then looked again. On this particular day, the Last Ridge was absolutely packed with cattle, instead of only the few he needed. They would have no trouble rounding up enough for the shipment. Hundreds gathered.

Jake wondered how the animals were comfortable being so close together. There was so much room on this property why would they choose to be confined in such a way? From his vantage point Jake saw more backs of cattle than they saw open ground.

The only thing Jake could figure was that the thunderstorm a few nights back drove the cattle there. The moon had been unusually orange, perhaps that had something do with it. All sorts of tiny weather related reasons that affected cattle, but this situation troubled him. So much of the family's holdings grouped into one spot seemed risky. There were loads and loads of animals here. What if the ground opened and swallowed them up? The family ranch business might very well be ruined.

"Hey, Carl?" Jake turned to his friend. "You ever see anything like that?"

"Not often, but it happens," he said. "At least we won't have to wear ourselves out getting enough beef together."

"This is weird," Larry said.

"Yeah, what the hell are they doing?" Pete said.

"They never make sense," Carl said. "But quit gawking and let's get to work. You're gonna dry up in this sun."

Everyone laughed. At that moment trucks came down the road. The lead one sounded his horn.

"Couldn't have timed that statement better!" Jake called, "Let's roll."

They pushed their way down the rise. They couldn't race across the pasture through the crowd of steers. The boys made a rough estimate of how much of the herd had to be cut off to fill the shipment.

Jake and Carl rode to meet the man in charge, a tall, confident looking man, standing on the embankment. The suit he wore belonged on someone in a city, not receiving a cattle shipment.

"Good afternoon," Carl called to the man as they approached. He and Jake both reached down from their horses and took turns shaking the man's hand.

"Hello, the name's Kelly Thomas," he said to Jake. "Are you Mr. Weathers?"

"Might as well be," Jake said. "I'm his son, Jake. And this is Carl Jamison, best cattle worker in these United States."

"He's only saying that 'cause it's true." Carl tipped his cowboy hat.

Kelly Thomas smiled. "Well, y'all got some beef for me?"

"As we understand it, y'all are in need of around eighty head." Jake looked the trucks over.

Kelly Thomas looked to the herd gathered before them. "Doesn't look like it should be a problem."

"Nope. It'll probably only take a few minutes and we should have everything you need." Jake said.

The three of them made conversation after that. By leaving the round-up to the posse, Jake made sure Kelly Thomas would come to him to handle transactions from now on. Kelly Thomas would have no doubt Jake was the boss.

Carl went silent as a shocked look came across his face. And all he could spit out was, "Oh, shit."

Five tons of truck plowed down the slope into the overcrowded pasture. The trailer slid sideways off the road pulling the cab with it.

"GET OUT OF THERE!" Jake yelled at two of his riders in that direction.

But the coming disaster forced everyone to partake. The truck rolled over and twisted metal shrieked as a rock punctured the gas tank as metal sparked on metal.

The ball of fire unrolled high into the sky. Hell opened and spat forth its evil on the earth, captivating Jake's eyes. The roll of heat and eruption of noise greeted him. The feeling of sound waves impacting his chest felt sickening and the temperature smacked him in the face. Everything went up in an eruption of chaos as all fury ripped loose. Jake fell from Rio.

Kelly Thomas dived for cover. Every horse within two hundred yards reared up in fear and threw their riders. All the cowboys landed on their backs hard against the earth. Some of their animals bolted off, driven in terror by the enormous explosion. The ground itself shook and the sky split with the blast. Everything went up in an eruption of chaos. All fury ripped loose.

Hundreds of panicked steers took off in a run that rumbled the earth.

"In all my years...," Carl said, staring wide-eyed at the creatures. He looked over to Jake who was fighting to stand from the ground. He found his legs and tried to pull himself together. Carl stood as well and headed for his escaped horse. "Well!" He yelled at a dazed Jake. "Go get em'!"

Go get em'? Yes.

Jake shook the dizziness from his thoughts. He definitely

needed to go do something about that herd. Jake never saw a stampede before. *So what do I need?* He couldn't catch them. He needed a horse. *Rio.*

"Rio!" He searched.

Waiting a few yards away, the horse looked ashamed he had panicked. Jake scrambled over and got into the saddle. "We'll talk about that later." He set the horse off into the dust the herd had kicked up.

The herd had already charged up a ridge and were halfway across the next pasture over, sweeping other grazing animals into their madness. The steer advanced toward a pasture division fence and plowed it over.

In the dust Jake couldn't tell if anyone else found their horses yet or if they followed him. Jake waved his arm to clear the air, but the thick dust choked his lungs and blanketed his eyes. Pulling his bandana over his mouth and nose, he urged Rio toward the front of the herd. He tried riding wide around the side, but they spread out so much that pathways were few and far between.

Jake and Rio were loose in the mayhem, lost in a hurricane of cattle. If Jake fell or if Rio tripped, the two would be crushed.

In the thundering chorus and the dust that made his eyes water harshly, Jake's stomach turned as he realized this path led over a cliff less than a few miles away.

Jake pulled up on the reins and let the herd whip past him. He jerked the horse right and gave him a kick. They raced south out of the dust and bolted through some dense brush bordering the edge of that pasture.

Rio leaped and dodged and made his way through. Jake ducked to avoid getting a tree branch in the face. They dropped down into an empty creek bed and followed its bend around and up to another pasture.

Jake slid his butt back in the saddle and got low on the horse, giving Rio the signal to run. He would make him fly. Jake wanted to catch the wind.

From the brush the pair exploded onto the flat, wide-open ground. In seconds, his hat blew off his head. When the dust rose over the trees to the side and behind them, Jake knew Rio had passed the stampede.

The upcoming ridge took them down to the next pasture ahead of the cattle. Jake and Rio raced alongside the cliff he feared, as he looked over the stones below. Just in time, he spun Rio around as the lead steer charged up the far edge of the pasture. They had maybe a mile... now or never.

Jake and his horse blasted toward the raging animals. They confronted the thundering mass, a pair so small compared to all of them.

Ahead of the main herd, a few lead steers charged in the direction of the cliff. Focusing on them, Jake pulled Rio to the left and came hard across their path. He hollered, trying to crowd the animals and nudge them toward the tree boundary to the North, but they paid him no attention.

He drew his gun and fired it into the air. They pulled to their left a little.

Jake fired more shots and got in real close to the leaders. "COME ON! YOU STUPID ANIMALS!"

The drop off loomed closer. He pushed harder. He stuck out his leg and kicked the lead animal in the side.

The stampede veered its course. Jake pushed them until they listed left. He pushed them some more. The lead steers charged ahead at a left angle. The rest of the herd followed, sweeping towards the tree line.

At last, they had nowhere to go. The confused leaders slowed their pace and the tired followers gave up the pursuit.

Jake swept wide. Sweaty, covered in dust, but satisfied, he finally exhaled.

Later Jake sat on his horse watching the herd graze. He held up his hand but his racing heart wouldn't let him hold it still. He should have been relieved, but all he could think about was how much damn fun he had had. He had never felt more like a cowboy.

"Decent at best," called a voice from behind.

Jake turned and laughed with Carl. "That's enough adventure for today."

The crew spent the rest of the day and early evening splitting the gathered number up. They didn't want to risk so many animals in one place again. Thomas Kelly and his crew took over cleaning up the mess of the burning wreckage.

By the time he returned to the house, Jake's back hurt in a good way. He unsaddled Rio and turned him loose in the corral. He wanted to get inside and see Ellie.

He came out of the barn and smiled. She waited for him on the steps to the house. Jake pulled off his retrieved hat.

"Howdy, lady."

"Hello, Jake."

The voice was not the one he expected. Jake peered harder through the dark. "Oh, hello Jenny."

The girl before Jake kept shifting her weight, looking up at him and then back at the ground.

"Can I help you?" he said.

"No... um, yes... uh, I don't know." She held her hand to her mouth and gnawed on her thumbnail. "It's just... is your brother here?"

"No, I don't think he is."

Her voiced quivered. "Well, okay. Could you just... can you tell him I need to see him whenever he gets back? Or you see him... yes." Tears shimmered down her cheeks. As she got in her car and pulled away, she screamed.

Jake shook his head and spit on the ground. He really hated the things that happened to girls whenever they were around his brother.

CHAPTER 19

Sky Rodeo

Jake got to thinking. Since he had graduated high school, he earned a paycheck as a ranch hand every week. And every week, he faithfully deposited those checks in Crane's one and only bank. And since he never went anywhere or did anything that wasn't a business expense, his savings added up.

His jaw dropped a little when he checked to see how much he saved. By no means an independent millionaire, Jake could choose never to move another muscle and probably could sustain himself in some fashion for years and years.

Wednesday, Jake and Ellie lounged beside the pond enjoying the sun. Her eyes were no longer sunken with pain and her skeleton frame gained some healthy weight. And now her complexion had bronzed after a few days in the constant sun.

"You've gotten back your glow." He said.

"It hasn't been easy."

"I know, but you took a first step. And then another. Now here you are, the longest you've gone without that chemical in four years!"

"An art critic would point out that my work has suffered," Ellie said.

But this is the sacrifice you have chosen."

"It's true. Now it's deep breaths over short painful ones, strong strides instead of struggling steps. Yes, the art has suffered, but I realize a masterpiece on canvas isn't worth the cost of a masterpiece of a life." She smiled.

Later that day as Carl and Jake climbed into the truck, Ellie asked them where they were going.

"Just stick around a while," Jake grinned. "And you'll probably catch a glimpse of something."

"Oh, will I?" She smiled back in the morning light. "What about you, Carl? Are you going to continue with this intrigue?"

Carl made a motion indicating his lips were sealed. Jake gave her a mischievous smile. He blew her a kiss and got in the truck. The pair drove off.

The old man drove Jake to an aged biplane he'd found for sale. He made the purchase and told Carl they'd meet back at home.

Soon, Jake flew low over the house, amusing himself with the racket he caused. He brought the airplane down with a decent landing and pulled her near the barn in front of his spectators. Swapping the flight goggles for his cowboy hat, he heaved himself out and slipped down from the cockpit.

The eyes of his whole household met him as he turned around.

"What in the world is that?" His father's face twisted.

"That, sir, is a Douglas O2 M." Jake ran his hand down the side of the craft.

"What's it doing here?"

"I bought it."

"What do you mean, you bought it?" Mr. Weathers tilted his head.

"A man in the next county sold it to me. He gave me a really great deal, on account it looks a little rough."

His father studied the ugly duck. "Is it even safe to fly?"

"She handles just fine. We only have to make her complexion a little prettier."

His father cocked an eyebrow. "I knew you got your license but I never thought... it seems like an odd purchase. Not really something your brother would do." Mr. Weathers straightened up, "Well, um, just make sure everything else on the ranch gets taken care of as well." He turned and walked back into the house.

The others looked the O2 over and took turns sitting in the cockpit. Ellie came up behind Jake and wrapped her arms around his waist. "You've been up to no good."

"Just making up for too many quiet years," he smiled. "But there's just one problem."

She looked over his shoulder. "And what's that?"

"She's not as pretty as she should be. I might even go as far to say she's a mess. I'm gonna need a painter."

"Oh, are you?" She grinned.

"Yeah." He turned so he could put his arm around her shoulder and kissed her rosy cheek. "Know where I can find one?"

Ellie pressed up against him. "I'm quite sure there's one around here somewhere."

"Good. Tell her to get ready because the paint I ordered should be here next week."

"Don't worry," Ellie said. "Her schedule is pretty open."

Jake didn't sleep much for the next couple of days. He kept staying up late into the night to work on his toy. First, he and Carl took the engine apart and cleaned every single piece. A few days later they gave the engine a test start. The coughing and sputtering changed to a steady and confident hum.

"Carl," Jake slapped him on the back. "You're simply a wizard."

Carl looked at him. "I'll get it running for you, but you ain't ever getting me to ride in this damn thing. You want to kill yourself, I won't stop you."

Jake laughed.

A few nights later, they sanded the body down, to get it ready for new paint. Gracie helped. Working that sand paper held her interest. She acted ready to rub a hole right through the side of that plane.

Jake also took some of the leather oil they used on their boots and worked the pilot and the passenger seats over. The old leather soaked up the moisture and got some of its gloss back. The smaller cracks closed up.

Aaron walked passed the barn and saw the crowd gathered around the plane. "Looks like a death trap. Probably could have put your money to better use."

"Yep! Probably!" Jake said.

Aaron had no response.

A few days later, Ellie shrieked when the paint order arrived. Jake caught her putting the primer on by herself. She and the plane were covered in it.

"What is this primed for?" Jake pointed to a piece of scrap.

"That's the same material as the plane. I'll put a coat on it first to see how the paint acts on it."

"Brilliant!" He winked at her.

Next, she showed Jake the design scheme, twenty or so different sketches, including the one she liked best.

Saturday, Ellie climbed atop a hay bale in the barn to address her work crew. Jake, Carl and Pete listened with grins as she instructed them on the specifics of the paint. She taught them how to apply it so it would come out perfectly. Rosalia and Gracie came out to watch the show. Rosalia had made a plate of cookies for everyone. She set the plate by Gracie and soon the cookies were gone.

The painters set to work. Jake and Pete started from the tail. Ellie and Carl started at the front. After a few hours, they all met in the middle. The crew stepped back to take in their work.

An entirely new plane sat before them. Jake barely believed it was the same rig he bought a few weeks before. Ellie's helpers had colored the body a rich brown close to a lighter, dark chocolate with hints of rust, like a western brown. The group painted the wings and the tail rudders white, a nice glossy finish in it.

"It's incredible," Carl said.

"I'm by no means done! There are all sorts of finishing touches I have to do." Ellie turned to Jake. "Swear you won't sneak a peak!"

He laughed. "I swear."

Over the next couple of days, as Ellie worked furiously away on the plane, Jake went out of his way to avoid going into the barn. Even when he did, he kept his eyes down and never looked at the plane. He laughed at his ridiculous maneuvers to fulfill her wish.

Jake couldn't park the plane in the barn forever. So some of the boys helped him put a dozen uprights in the ground and built a roof over it farther down the driveway. Eventually they had a hanger with no walls to protect the plane from the rain- a simple but sturdy structure.

Four days later, Ellie rushed into the kitchen. "Come quick! Come quick!"

What's wrong?" Rosalia charged into the room.

"It's done! It's done!" She grabbed Jake's hand and yanked him from where he sat. The procession followed her from the house to the closed barn doors. Then she whirled around with her back to the doors and faced them like a ringmaster at the circus.

"Ladies and Gentlemen! Girls and Boys! With no further ado, it gives me great pleasure to introduce to you today, the one! The only: *Sky Rodeo!*" Ellie spooled her tongue, making a sound like a drum roll. She shoved the doors wide open. "Ta-da!"

Together they moved as a crowded mass towards Ellie's creation. Every detail was to the utmost level of perfection. And it was the coolest thing Jake had ever seen.

Ellie had painted the Weathers' Ranch brand on both ends of the wings, top and bottom. She painted the propeller white as well and really made it pop. On the sides of the engine cowl at the front of the plane, she traced shadowy figures of horses, but only their upper portions. They were only slightly defined, just the suggestion of horses. They were charging and strong, like a chariot team of wild stallions pulling the plane through the sky.

Behind the horses, along the body on either side of the plane, painted in big white letters, highlighted in black Ellie had written: *The Sky Rodeo.* Under the rim of the pilot's cockpit she painted in beautiful calligraphy, *Capt. Jake Weathers.*

Beneath his name on either side of the plane she drew Jake's favorite detail, a large skull and crossbones. Instead of a human skull and crossbones, she had painted a steer's skull and crossed six shooters.

On the right side of the plane, just below the passenger cockpit she included seventeen tally marks, similar to the ones fighter pilots sketch on their planes for every enemy shot down. Down towards the rear of the aircraft she wrote "Crane, Texas." Lastly, she had painted a strand of barbed wire on the tail rudder of the plane and wrote its original registration number, barely distinguishable when it first arrived.

Carl traced the lines of Ellie's artwork with his hands.

"Ellie," Jake faced her. "I'm absolutely amazed by what you've done. This is surely the best looking plane that ever flew. It puts all other planes to shame." He gave her a hug, lifting her off the ground.

Aaron sauntered around the corner. He viewed at the plane then at his hot rod in the driveway.

"Pretty cool, ain't it?" Carl looked at Aaron.

"Wouldn't catch me dead in it."

Jake grinned. "Wanna race?"

Aaron stormed away.

"Well, what are you waiting for, flyboy?" Ellie said. "Get off the ground."

He grinned. "Yes, ma'am." He turned to everyone else. "Help me get it outside."

Together they wheeled the plane outside. *The Sky Rodeo* then first emerged from the darkness and shadow of the barn and broke out into the sunlight. The gloss finish gleamed in the cloudless sky.

Jake stepped back. It looked too pretty to fly... almost.

Jake fueled her up and topped off her tanks, ready to roll. He performed all the preflight checks and everything seemed to be in working order.

"All right," Jake told them. "I'll take her up and make sure she can still fly. If I make it back fine, I can take y'all up if any of you would like to try it."

No sooner had he finished saying this than someone shuffled into the passenger cockpit.

"Ellie," he looked up at her. "Just wait until I make

sure it's safe. I'll come back and get you."

"No, sir!" She laughed. "If this thing goes down on the test flight, I'm going with it. I spent too much time painting it."

Jake looked at Carl for support.

Carl shrugged his shoulders. "That ain't the kind of girl whose mind you can change." The old man laughed as Jake's shoulders fell in defeat.

Jake climbed into the cockpit in his own unique way because of the brace. Carl held his hat as Jake slipped on the pilot goggles, checking that Ellie wore hers as well. Then he kissed his fingers and touched them to the body of the plane. "Here goes nothing."

"Stand clear!" he yelled out and hit the ignition. The engine turned over and the heart of the plane roared to life. She ran clean and true. The *Sky Rodeo* vibrated with the motion of the propeller.

One step down.

He pushed the throttle stick in a little and rolled away from the barn and headed down the long driveway. For about a mile there were no nearby trees and the compacted road would make it easier to get up to speed. The wind also blew in a favorable position to help them take off and land.

Jake experienced a single moment of surreal euphoria. This was *his* plane. And right there was *his* house. He was taking off in his plane in front of his house. He, Jake Weathers, could fly planes. The excitement made him want to go everywhere at once, and up was as good a direction as any. This plane was his horse in the open range of sky, no boundaries.

He punched it. The wind from the tremendous energy of the propeller sent up a cloud of dust around them in every direction. They surfaced from it on the far side as they raced down the driveway faster than Aaron's car had ever gone.

Then came the thrill of the bobble. The wheels left the earth for the shortest second, then fell back. It bounced once or twice but the final time, it didn't come back. The force pushed Jake and Ellie into their seats as they climbed into the endless blue wilderness.

"WOO-HOO!" Ellie threw her arms into the air.

Jake could barely hear her over the wind. They ascended rapidly. He gave it too much throttle. The plane had more power than Jake was used to since Carl had worked the engine over. Jake leveled off and got his bearings. He would take things slow, the mature thing to do.

"HIGHER!" Ellie hollered over the wind as she pointed up into forever.

Jake had just enough teenage boy left in him to try to impress the girl. The pair continued up. Even in the Texas heat, the air changed to cold. How miserable it would be to fly over Europe in winter during the war.

The pasture appeared tiny below them and although the engine roared. Jake sensed a stillness. He stayed up a while, paying attention to where they were heading so he could find his way back.

Ellie pulled off the cap intended to keep her hair under

control, tilting her head back and forth, letting the frigid wind whip through her locks. Jake headed down again.

He didn't want to go too far and not be able to recognize landmarks anymore. When they dropped a few thousand feet, he was ready to give Ellie a simple steady ride.

Instead she looped her hand in a circle and then waved it all over the place. Half of Jake didn't want to put them in danger; the other half was tempted to see what this plane could do.

He jerked back on the stick and throttled up to face the sky vertically. The engine raced to pull the body up without the aid of lift from the wings. Their stomachs rose up into their throats when the nose of the plane tipped backwards. They fell towards the ground.

The rush came as they went tail over nose and found themselves in a dive. They continued to pull up, not knowing for sure the plane would level off, but it did. Jake was completely satisfied on adrenaline for now. It wasn't wise to test his luck and continue with fool hardy maneuvers, but Ellie seemed intent on breaking the plane, begging for stunts. So he jerked that aircraft every which way.

He kept his eye on the driveway as he came in. Though it was unlikely, he checked for cars. When the wheels made contact with the dirt road, the first successful flight of *The Sky Rodeo* ended.

As the engine stopped and Ellie climbed out and into the dust she looked back and said, "I'm going to have to thank you later." She grinned and gave him a naughty little wink.

Gracie ran up and latched onto the plane. Her puppy eyes pleaded for a ride, looking as though she would never find happiness again.

"You know, Carl," Jake looked over at him. "She could probably ride if you—"

"Don't even think about it," Carl snapped. "I would sooner sleep with a snake in my bed."

The group hesitated, and Gracie's face fell to sadness. Tears ran down her cheeks.

"The tears of those who never cry are always more painful." Ellie smiled.

Then Carl, the oak, bent. He peered at Jake. "Slow and steady."

Jake laughed. "Sure, slow and steady."

"I mean it, Jake," Carl said. "If you do anything crazy, I'm going to turn you into boots."

"Fair enough." Jake bowed and waved his hand like a concierge and led Carl to the plane. Minutes later Gracie sat in his lap. Even after Jake wrapped the seatbelt around both of them, everything made Carl jump.

But Jake wasn't cruel. He leveled off and held the stick as tight as he could. He flew over things he thought Gracie would be interested in seeing. She loved school buses and Jake pointed one out. She bounced up and down as much as she could in her belted restraint. Carl held her tight. Jake kept her up for twenty minutes, figuring Carl probably rode with his eyes shut the whole time. Jake turned and maneuvered like he carried a load of china dolls.

When Jake landed the plane, Gracie climbed out and took off running. She looked energized from the thrill ride, as she scampered around the yard.

Jake turned back at his passenger. "So? What'd you think?"

Carl looked up with a grin. "As they say, 'if God wanted us to fly He would have given us wings.'"

"Oh don't worry. I'm sure it'll grow on you."

Carl walked away like he wasn't sure he was really back on the ground. He blew a kiss to the ground and laughed.

Jake's figured his father wouldn't ask for a ride but surely curiosity would bring him outside before dark.

Later Jake walked by his father's room as Carl tried to lift his father off the rug. The empty whiskey bottles spoke for themselves. Mr. Weathers was still breathing. Jake entered the room and shut the door behind him to save his father's dignity.

"Help me," Carl whispered.

Jake got under the other arm and helped Carl lifted Mr. Weathers into his bed.

"What set him off?" Jake bent to pick the empty bottles and a picture of his mother his father must have kept to himself. Jake smiled at the lovely bride in the photo, as she peeked over her bouquet at the camera.

His father always made a big deal about their anniversary. Still though, these outbursts happened too often. Things could get real dangerous, real fast. Why now?

"Oh, no." Carl lifted a loaded pistol from the desk.

"How did he—" Jake left the room and went to the gun closet only to find the lock broken. "He must've done it while we were outside flying."

Jake returned to the room. "What should we do, talk to a pastor or doctor or something? Or what about writing a letter to a psychiatrist in Dallas or something?"

"I've never known what to do. We just have to watch him closer."

The two didn't talk about it again, even though Mr. Weathers depression lingered. He stayed in his room for a week. And when he came out, he looked like a dead man walking, so frail.

Sam, Carl, and Jake never discussed the new industrial strength lock on the gun closet.

It was a long day. Whenever his father came out of a slump, he gave everyone extra work. Jake wondered how long he'd have to wait before he could mention becoming a partner again.

CHAPTER 20

Mañana

Then it all fell apart.

Over the next several weeks, Jake labored on the ranch with his crew, moving cattle, repairing fences, unloading feed. Sam showed up at the work sites less frequently and seemed to trust Jake with day-to-day decisions, but hadn't made him a partner yet. For now, Jake was content to wait a couple of weeks longer, then press the issue of partnership.

Despite the fact he still had to work out some things with his father, Jake sorted out his relationship with Aaron. They didn't talk much but Aaron no longer acted obnoxious. He stayed out of Jake's way and that suited Jake just fine.

Ellie made him wish nights would go away so he could rise the next day and see her. The ghost of her old habit never surfaced and she breathed deeply. Gracie was a joy as ever.

Jake had almost settled into the rest of his life. Working the ranch, falling more in love with Ellie, watching the sunset every night. His next fifty years called to him.

On Tuesday, Larry returned with the mail and handed Jake a large envelope with strange markings and odd stamps, all in Spanish. Jake knew what it was before he opened it.

Months had passed since they sealed the agreement and Jake fretted that Señor Gomez might never request a shipment. It was months since they made the arrangement, but with the letter's arrival, those thoughts were far away. In fluid motion he drew his jackknife and slit the envelope open.

Carl stood by as Jake slipped out the fine letterhead note. Over his own typewritten name was the crest for Mexibeef and title of president for Señor Gomez. His Mexican host had penned the perfect balance between a professional business transaction and personal correspondence.

The man opened with a cordial greeting, Jake could almost hear Señor Gomez and his trilled R's, as well as the man's thoughts in every inflection of grandeur, giving the letter texture. Señor Gomez expressed his hopes that Jake was doing well. The sender lamented how bored he was without him. He joked how tired his "nieces" made him feel, and how much he disliked the drabness of everyday business matters.

In the next paragraph came the request. Señor Gomez's first cattle shipment from the Weathers' Ranch would be a large order, as though he hoped to feed everyone in Chihuahua a steak. He closed his letter expressing his hopes for all the best things for the Weathers and their ranch. His postscript was an open invitation for a visit anytime they chose.

He stopped to let Ellie read it.

"That old playboy," she laughed.

Jake took the letter inside. It was his trophy, the next step in a deal conducted fully by him, without his father or anyone else. He had taken control of this one.

He marched into his father's office, trying to remain calm and casual. The letter landed on the desk with thunder. Jake wouldn't show how much he felt was on the line.

Mr. Weathers examined some bank statements. "Yes? What is it?"

"Here's the first order from our new Mexican clients." Jake pointed to the papers, endeavoring to sound professional. "This proves something, doesn't it?"

His father's eyes follow the lines across the page as he took the time to read the letter in its entirety. "Is he a client or a friend?" Mr. Weathers stared at him over the top of the paper.

"A client."

"This is quite an order he's calling in for. Obviously we can do it…" His father took a sip of his tea. "There's just one problem."

Jake forced his demeanor to remain steady. "What's that?"

"He didn't include a check with the letter or any form of payment." Mr. Weathers scratched his chin.

Jake hadn't noticed that detail. "The money will probably come with the trucks he's sending to pick up the animals. Obviously the man can be trusted."

"Perhaps." His father leaned back in his chair. "You can never send the cattle before you get the cash."

"I know." Jake crossed his arms and shifted his weight as his father gave him this juvenile lesson. He fought off rolling his eyes over his father's suggestion that Señor Gomez was anything but an upright businessman.

"But like you said, he's probably just sending the money with the trucks." His father set the letter aside and picked up the bank statements again. "I'm sure there's nothing to worry about."

"I'm sure," Jake said.

Aaron walked in. "What are you clowns up to?"

"Your brother's business deal came through for the first order. It's a big one."

Aaron lost his smile. He looked at his father and then to Jake. "Well, Jake, good job." Jake didn't believe his brother's compliment.

It became Jake's mission to make sure the shipment would be perfect, since this was his real baptism into the business side of things at the ranch. If he executed it without a hitch, he would have a final ace card. He could twist his father's arm until his name was down on paper.

Neither the title nor the money gave Jake his desire for part ownership. It mattered more how far he had come. Being made partner was the last step of a long journey. He wanted to be that man: Jake Weathers, part owner, for the memory of his mother and for Ellie. And also, because he loved the hell out of West Texas.

The day of the shipment, his father left the ranch for a meeting in El Paso.

Jake wanted to execute the entire deal by himself from start to finish. He received a call telling him the trucks had crossed into the U.S., and would arrive at the ranch in the morning.

"He'll finally respect me more when I handle all this, you know?" Jake said. He sat with his arm around Ellie, watching the sunset.

Her face was cast in warm shades. "I'm sure he notices all you do around here. He's got more confidence in you than you're aware."

"Maybe, but he still hasn't made me partner like he said he would. I'll really have something to show him after I do this. And, not only him, but I gave Mr. Gomez my word; when he called for steer I'd deliver." Jake cracked his knuckles. "I just want to come through."

"No one questions that you keep your promises," Ellie rubbed his back. "You come through more than anyone I've ever met."

"This is me for the rest of my life," Jake said. "I want to start it off right."

"Now Jake, don't put that kind of pressure on yourself. There will always be rough spots. Things will happen that you didn't count on," she added. "But it'll all still be here for you... we'll all be here for you."

He kissed her forehead. "So you think you could do the rest of your life here?"

"I told you, this is home. I've always been here, I just didn't know it. In all those years, it's always been here... all of this," Ellie looked around. "It's like getting to shore after treading water for a very long time."

Jake thought about her words as he lay awake that night. He liked the idea of Ellie here with him forever, living a lifetime of evenings spent on the porch swing with her. Building her a little art studio in the lofts of the barn would be his first act. Since she enjoyed transforming the plane into something astounding so much he would unleash her on anything she wanted; the trucks, the tractors, the house. It didn't matter as long as she was happy. In his heart, he knew it was love.

As he lay there, he made up his mind. He would ask Ellie Perri to be his wife. He would take the money he made on the sale tomorrow and buy her a ring. It should be a unique ring, maybe antique. She'd like that.

Maybe the two of them would live here in the house, or maybe they would build a little cabin on the other side of the property. He wondered if they would have kids. After watching her with Gracie, Jake had no doubt Ellie would be a wonderful mother. Jake grinned in the dark as he pictured funny little versions of Ellie running around the house. The world needed more Ellies.

In the dark and silence, Jake thought about many things. He rehearsed the conversation he would have with the men who came for the order. How many different things could go wrong? He considered solutions. Jake would ask Carl to take a backseat and let him do the talking. Then sleep took him.

Jake was up before the roosters and alarm clocks. He put on a nice shirt, nicer than a cowboy should wear on the range. He gave his brace a little polish, fully aware of the futility. It would get dusty again on the ride to the pasture.

He went into the barn and treated his saddle. He brushed Rio three times, deep and thoroughly. By the end, the horse looked a different color.

The crew gathered in the kitchen.

"How did y'all sleep?" Jake reached for coffee.

The crew shot each other perplexed looks. "Fine?"

"Everyone feeling good?"

"…yeah?"

"All your horses healthy?"

"Yes?"

"All right, eat up. The trucks don't arrive until noon, so take care of whatever you need to, but we're meeting at eleven-thirty." Jake bit into the bacon.

"A half hour before?" Larry spread butter on his biscuits.

"Yeah," Jake said.

Jake went over the sales receipt many times. He had drawn up paperwork before using the former receipts as a model for today's transfer. Giving them to Carl, he asked him to read it over. Later he had Ellie do the same. His only mental reprieve that morning was when Gracie found him and managed to take his mind off things with those big, joyful eyes.

Jake left for the pasture at eleven. He stopped on a hill to inspect the cattle, determining how much grade A stock the crew would have to push from another pasture. He reviewed the crew's various strengths and weaknesses and considered how he should place them. From his mounted spot he played chess with men, horses, and steers.

When a truck passed on the road, Jake got a sickening feeling he had the time wrong and the trucks were arriving now. Sweet relief followed when the vehicle kept on its way.

But soon the men and trucks rolled in. The crew pushed the cattle into the pasture. Carl kept back, just like Jake had asked him to. Jake felt in charge.

After his experience in Mexico and because of the workforce of Señor Gomez, it surprised Jake that the individual sent to gather the shipment was a white man. He introduced himself as Garth Owens.

"So that's all of it?" Garth said to Jake.

"Should be around three hundred fifty head."

"Each of these trucks will divide up across the border and head to several different locations." Garth stuck out his hand. "So, I guess we're done here."

Jake took his hand. "Just one more thing."

"What's that?" Garth said.

"The payment." Jake laughed.

But a twisted look crossed Garth's face. "Oh, haven't you gotten the check in the mail?"

"No, we haven't," Jake let go of the handshake. "Only his order, never a check."

"Gomez mailed it before we left, so I'm surprised we beat it here." Garth scratched his head. "It's hard the way you can't trust the mail these days." He stood straighter. "Tell you what, that check should be here any day, probably got here today. I'll take these steers and if y'all don't get the check in the next few days, contact us and we'll send you another one right away."

The plan wasn't ideal, but Jake felt it would do. Besides, he'd given his word to Señor Gomez. Plus, Jake was happy not to have his father come home to three hundred fifty unshipped animals. Garth was right, the check would probably arrive today or tomorrow.

Jake nodded. "Deal. Y'all be safe on your drive back to Mexico." Then he waved them off over the horizon and sat there feeling pleased. He told everyone what a good job they had done.

On the way back to the house with Carl, Jake relived the success of the order and delivery. As soon as he had that check in his hands, he could present the completed job and the money to his father and get the ball rolling on all his plans. Things were coming together.

Jake drove to the post office that day. Nothing from Mexico, not even any check-shaped envelopes, but worry had no part of Jake's thoughts. *The payment will come tomorrow.*

Jake came back to Crane next day and received the same report: no payment from Mexico. He remained calm. His father wouldn't be back for two days. Without a doubt, the money would be there tomorrow. But Jake finally began to worry when he returned on the following day and found no word from Mexico.

The only thing that arrived in Crane the next day was Sam Weathers. Jake raced by the post office early in the day before his father could ask about the payment. Nothing. For the rest of the day and over dinner Jake hoped his father would not remember the matter. Jake's luck held out for the rest of that night and even lasted long enough for one more visit to the post office the next day. Still nothing.

"So how did that shipment to Mexico go last week?" Sam put his coffee down.

The hair on the back of Jake's neck stood up. "Oh, fine. They came in at noon and we loaded them up."

"No issues? Nothing went wrong?"

"Nope," Jake said. "The crew moved well. The animals got into the trailers, and the trucks headed off." Jake hoped his racing heart wouldn't betray him. "For such a large load, things went surprisingly quick."

"Good, good." His father went back to the paperwork on his desk.

Jake thought he might have bought more time.

"What did you do with the payment?"

His father's words caught him like a noose around his neck, pulling him back and forcing the air out of him. "The payment?"

Jake knew he was caught and could not get away from it. He thought it best to say it like a man, but also with optimism the money would arrive soon. "You know, apparently Señor Gomez sent a check in the mail, even though his crew arrived first. I figured it would be here soon, so I sent them off with the cattle... and..well ..." He looked at his watch. "The check is probably here now. I bet the mail truck just got into town."

"So, you sent the beef off without getting payment?" His father raised an eyebrow.

"Not without payment. We're getting payment. It's just not here yet," Jake said, looking him in the eye. "In fact, I'll drive into town right now and check the post office."

"Yeah, why don't you do that?" The tone in his father's voice pointed toward the suspicion in his mind.

The words, "No, nothing," from the lips of the postal worker echoed in Jake's ears, ricocheted off his bones, and tore up his guts. He wanted to demand that the clerk look again, surely he made an error, but at the core of him, Jake knew. The money wasn't coming. How could he have been so stupid?

He imagined what would follow. The Weathers would assume in good faith that Señor Gomez simply forgot to send the payment. They would send a letter and make a phone call, but neither inquiry would expedite payment. Then one of the family members, or perhaps a lawyer would make the journey south. And then, the final realization would be carved in stone: Jake had been an idiot.

Losing a ton of the ranch's resources and putting the business in jeopardy was never part of his plan. Feeling like he had blown everything, his stomach turned sour and

Jake started to hate himself.

The courts did not transcend enough to protect the ranch from fraudulent international deals. Jake had given his word—everything he had—to convince Sam to invest in Jake's deal. And now Jake's promises fell apart. They were broke.

Jake went home from the post office with his head held low. He turned his eyes away as he informed his father that no letter from Mexico arrived at the post office.

His father handed him a letter. "This is a message reminding Señor Gomez about the payment, in case, he forgot. Go mail it," Mr. Weathers said. "I'm going to try to call him as well."

Jake felt like such a boy, needing his daddy to save the day.

The next two weeks dragged on with letters of inquiry and unreturned phone calls. No answer signed the death sentence to the transaction Jake authored.

When his father left with his lawyer for Mexico, Jake walked off in the night to throw up behind the barn. His hands wouldn't stop shaking.

His pursuit of the ranch he loved was thwarted by his awe at the foreign businessman's glamour. He knew what his father would say when he returned: no cash for the cattle.

Jake felt like a fool's fool and a terrible employee as well. Not only did he hurt the ranch, his actions threatened all that his family had built. He no longer looked in the mirror.

Nothing could settle Jake. He was absolutely hateful with himself, avoiding Ellie and Carl while not realizing it.

"Jake, you couldn't have known." Ellie found him in the barn. "You made one little mistake."

"I guess we were both wrong about me. I'm not ready for this, never was." He turned away from her.

"All men make mistakes—"

"I'm not a man," Jake said. "Just a boy pretending to be one. A ranch hand playing the part of a boss."

"Now that's not fair."

Sighing, he walked away.

The day his father arrived home from Mexico, Jake hid out on the ranch, doing chores. Carl found him in a lower pasture. "Your dad—"

"I know." Jake walked his horse back to the ranch. His feet felt heavy as he plodded through the house on the way to his father's study. Arriving at the door terrified him.

Aaron stood in the corner with a little grin as his father waited at the desk.

Jake felt very alone.

"I've just returned from Mexico. The news is grim…" Sam rubbed his hands together.

Jake stared at his boots.

"I know you were excited to execute a business deal, but that's no excuse to have been so cavalier. *Never* send off the animals without payment." He looked down at his papers. "I suppose it was my fault. I gave you more than you can handle. You just weren't ready."

Aaron stepped up. "Guess you're not ready to run the place—"

Jake threw a rear elbow into Aaron's face. His brother's chin popped upward as he fell back in a daze. Blood poured from his nose. Jake dived on top of him and hammered him with fists.

Aaron screamed. Mr. Weathers' hand came around Jake and shoved him off his brother. Jake rolled across the floor.

"Jake! What the hell are you doing?" Sam bent down beside his elder son and cradled him.

Aaron touched his thrashed face.

As Jake looked up, he could feel their resentment all the way across the room. They were feet apart but it might as well have been miles.

He slammed his fist into the floor and stood. The hinges on the front door creaked as he pushed through and ran out into the driveway. Jake needed to get away.

Jake rushed the pre-flight check. He just wanted to get up in the air. This plane couldn't pity him; it was just a machine. The engine started the first try and offered him his escape. He gave it throttle and pulled out of the hangar.

As he left the ground behind, his worries kept up with him. He hoped gravity would hold them down as he soared over the ranch he crucified. Jake flew over a pasture and considered what it would look like not missing three hundred fifty unpaid-for steers.

He swung the plane south. Maybe he would just go ahead and fly straight to Mexico and plant the plane right in the heart of one Gomez's hotels. Then he turned east. Maybe he would fly until he was over the Gulf and try to see how far he could go before he ran out of gas. After all, he wasn't a very good swimmer.

The colder altitude made him feel a little better. He took deep breaths. The plane didn't have the fuel to make Mexico or the Gulf. He couldn't run and instead needed to be at the ranch to face the consequences. It wasn't right that his family would have to look for him if he went missing. So he turned back.

As Jake maneuvered he realized he hadn't flown as far as he thought. He held the joystick and looked down the wing. Learning to fly was a dumb choice as well. He spent too much money and time getting this dumb bucket off the ground, money he could have used to pay his father back, time he could have spent improving the ranch.

When did I lose all sense? What the hell is my problem?

He came in low from the south to line up for a landing; a landing he performed a hundred times before without a hitch. And like each time before, he turned every knob, lowered the throttle, and worked the stick. What seemed different was the awful clanking noise from the right wing. It sent a shock through the entire frame of the plane and rattled Jake to the bone.

"Oh, shit."

The plane rolled right and wouldn't correct. Jake tugged at the stick and pressed the pedals as hard as he could but plane wouldn't level back. The ground approached. The aircraft flew sideways towards it.

The landing came fast, just so fast. Jake ground his teeth. As the earth raced past, he looked to his right and cringed.

The plane came in sideways and the right wings caught dirt, crumbling away against hard earth. As the wings ground shorter and shorter, they caught and jerked the front of the plane forward. The propeller plowed into the dust. The engine crunched as it slammed down. Flames erupted as the plane flipped over itself again and again and again.

Jake waited for death. He looked up from the cockpit as flames filled his view. Blood poured over his eyes; his hands covered in the crimson flow. He choked on the thick smoke. Paint peeled away from the cockpit frame, melting in the heat of the inferno. And somewhere, up there, the sky sat over the crippled boy who tried to fly.

He couldn't hear over the roar of fire as all was consumed by a world of incineration. He couldn't feel his leg or his arm… he couldn't feel. Flesh burned as he walked a line somewhere between consciousness and eternity.

He fell from heaven with Lucifer into damnation and the lake of fire. No hope, no second chance, no morning; this was it, standing on the surface of the sun and fighting for breath. No room for him in this place, in this existence. It would do away with him.

His thoughts were weak and hazy. Pain invaded him; it owned him. No talk of regret, just talk of the end. He had nothing left to do. He would die in the searing heat. This was his end; no glory, no guts, just flames.

In the haze two powerful hands reached through the flames and grabbed him. A knife came with them, making quick, decisive cuts, freeing Jake from the grip of his seat belt. The cockpit fell away behind him as he was pulled across the ground. Jake felt weightless as he was hoisted and thrown over the shoulder of a giant of a man. Something like the sound of crying.

And then... the black.

CHAPTER 21

Cold Remains

Fierce white replaced the black. At first it came in fuzz and haze before it slid into focus. The color narrowed itself and existed within the confines of light above. The bulbs hanging from the hospital ceiling beat down, assaulting Jake's fragile pupils. His gaze raced everywhere, struggling to recognize his surroundings.

He lay on a stiff hospital mattress unfriendly to his body. As his eyes began to focus, he realized he was alone. He tried to turn his head but his neck fought back, stiff and taut. Pain shot down his core as he tried to shift his position.

What's wrong with me?

Jake couldn't move his arm. He turned his eyes downward. A cage of white cast held his arm in position.

Then the flooding memory of the plane crash swept him away. At first, it felt like trying to recall a nightmare. Soon the vivid details intensified, as the plane failed and the ground swallowed him. The bang and the flames tried to pull him away. He remembered his concession to death.

Crane had no hospital. He rolled to his side to try and

get out of the bed, trying to swing his right leg over, but the leg didn't come as quickly as it should. He looked down.

"No." he said in disbelief. His right leg also was entombed in a cast. Alone and powerless, Jake started to cry. Warm tears dripped down his face while their saltiness flavored his lips.

He cried for a while; out of anguish, out of fear, out of hate for himself and actions that brought him here, until he ran out of tears.

Steps in the hallway outside his door interrupted the steady drone of the hospital machinery. A nurse pushed the door to his room open. "Oh, good, you're awake." She put her clipboard at her side. "You gave us all a scare. I'll go get your friend now." She left the room.

Friend? Jake didn't want to see anyone. He wanted to wallow alone.

Moments later a steady pace come down the hallway. Jake closed his eyes.

"Glad you're not dead, Jake," Carl said, with total and utter pity in his eyes.

Jake looked away.

"After the crash…" Carl began relaying the events of the past thirty-six hours. "We brought you here quick as we could. You're in Odessa General, by the way. After the doctors patched you up, we've all just been waiting for you wake up. Miss Ellie wouldn't leave your side for the life of her. Nearly fist fought the staff when they tried to force her out of here," he chuckled.

He looked at Jake for a response. "I finally got her and

Rosalia to go home and get some rest. Two days is long for anyone to wait in the hospital, but she swore up and down she'd be back here first thing in the morning."

Jake looked at Carl. Silence was more painful than speaking. "What happened to me?"

"You've broken your right leg and arm. You also got a nasty gash in your side. That took a while for the doctors to stop the bleeding and you've..." His face darkened. "You've got a pretty nasty burn on your upper back and up the side of your neck."

Jake reached up with his left arm, his only working limb, and touched his neck. Thick bandages covered the burn. Even with his soft touch, thousands of nerve endings fired and made him wince. He jerked his hand away.

"Do you need anything?" Carl tilted his head.

Jake closed his eyes, hoping to drift away.

After a few minutes of silence, Carl said, "I'll let you get your rest. It is the middle of the night after all." He flipped the light switch and shut the door, and Jake waited in a grave that wasn't six feet under.

Jake tried to deceive himself into believing he would wake up and find this all a dream. But he wasn't a good liar.

Morning came like a violent storm of smiles and consolations. Ellie arrived at the crack of dawn, just as she promised. She brought things to hang up on the walls to make Jake's room feel more like home. Rosalia fetched pots and trays filled with his favorite food.

Jake never smiled at their attempts to make him happy

and never responded to their efforts to make conversation. He hoped his silence would be deafening. The guests filled the void by commenting on the hospital care or the weather. He barely responded to Ellie and never made eye contact.

"The boys are handling everything just fine at the ranch," she said after lunch. "Gracie is all shook up wondering when you're coming home." She looked out the window later. "Next time, we'll get a newer plane that will work better," she said as the sun set.

"I'm not getting another plane." Uttering the first words Jake spoke all day, his raspy voice sounded foreign to him, and even in his anger, he didn't intend to sound that mean.

Ellie never left his room. She was waiting for something Jake couldn't give her. Sometimes he would close his eyes and pretend to sleep so she would take a rest or leave the room.

At the end of the tenth day, Carl told the women to go home. "Y'all need to get a room in the house ready for Jake., I'll bring him home in the morning. The doctors already cleared it." Carl turned to Jake. "That sound good?"

Jake didn't respond.

Ellie approached Jake's bed. When her warm hand touched his, his insides cringed, the death in his body feeling at odds with the life in hers.

"I'm going home now to get the house ready, but I'll see you tomorrow." She waited for a response that didn't come. She gave up and squeezed his hand one last time. Reflected in the picture glass, she bit her lip as Rosalia put her arm around the girl's shoulder before they left the room.

And with the night came the solitude Jake had waited for.

The next morning, Carl carried his leg brace out to the truck while Jake rode behind in a wheel chair. Two hospital employees hoisted him into the pickup cab. He cringed with every motion as his burns still stung.

Jake was silent during the long ride home. Rosalia waited on the front porch with Gracie. The ranch hands helped Jake out of the truck. He tried to stand but couldn't. They helped him shuffle to the wheelchair. They rolled him up to the porch and stopped.

Jake instantly felt uncomfortable the moment he realized they didn't have a ramp and they would have to carry him up the stairs. Fearing the pity in their eyes, he looked down as they hoisted him like a sack of corn. Gracie reached for him, but Rosalia held her back.

Ellie gave up her first-floor lodging, trading rooms with Jake. Fresh linen covered the bed and a radio was set within reach of his left arm, also a lamp and bell he could ring, products of Ellie's thoughtful care. As soon as they got him into bed, Larry and Pete offered desperate condolences and got out quickly, uncomfortable looks on their faces.

"You're in my room for now because it's on the first floor. My things are in your room." Ellie led the procession inside. "I put the radio here so you can reach it. And here's a bell you can ring in case you need anything!" She bounced around the room.

Jake never met her gaze.

One by one, the family came to check on him at times throughout the day. Jake met every approach with silence. He spoke only when he had to urinate. "Make sure no one comes in," Jake said.

Carl nodded and stood outside the door. When he finished, Jake called Carl back into the room. Heat crept up his neck and face when Carl carried out the piss. Jake felt like a helpless puppy.

The hardest hours came when Ellie sat in the chair beside his bed to read aloud or ask questions. "Do you need anything?" Ellie fluffed his pillow.

"No."

"Would you like me to read some of this book to you?

"I don't care."

She tilted her head. "It's just the shock of pain that's making you hurt like this."

"I don't really want to talk right now."

When tears welled up in Ellie's eyes, Jake wished he'd kept silent. In the hallway, she whimpered to Rosalia.

Rosalia whispered loud enough for Jake to overhear. "He'll come around. He loves you."

When Mr. Weathers entered the room, Jake pretended to sleep, so he left. Later Jake couldn't avoid having the dressings on the wounds changed. Carl helped Jake scoot up into a sitting position and bend forward. Ellie cut away the worn and crusted wrappings. As they pulled away, the pain made Jake grind his teeth and start to sweat.

Sometime later Jake waited for his father and steeled himself to face the inevitable.

"How do you feel?" Mr. Weathers asked him.

"Fine."

"Okay, well…" His father looked down at him, "What were you doing trying to fly anyway, son?"

"I don't know."

"You've got no reason to, no need to. Planes are dangerous. What made you think you could be a pilot? And what made you trust that old heap?" His father made a fist in frustration. "What was so wrong with sticking to a horse and working the ranch?"

"It was stupid. I never should have done it."

"You're right, it was stupid. So you're done flying?"

"Yes."

"Well, okay then… I guess I'll let you get your rest." His father got up to leave.

"We're not getting anything for the shipment to Mexico… are we?" Jake said, knowing this conversation was unavoidable.

His father stopped and faced him. "No, we're not."

Jake cringed even though he had guessed his fate for a while.

"I don't know if this Gomez person intended to scam you from the beginning, or if he just realized he got a lot of free cattle after it was over. The entire company switched owners a few weeks ago. We tried to get something out of the courts down there but they weren't at all interested in an across-the-border civil suit. The hard truth is that you lost this one." His father looked at him.

"What kind of hit did the ranch take?" Jake said.

"I won't lie, it's a pretty sizable hit. We're not going to go belly up or anything, but I sold some old stock shares to ensure we can keep things at an even flow here." He nodded. "We'll be fine."

"I don't think I'm ready to be partner yet."

"Yeah... yeah, maybe not. We'll wait a couple of years and maybe start discussing it again later. Maybe when you're older."

Jake nodded and pulled the covers up over his chest.

"We're not bankrupt or anything." His father smiled. "Plus Aaron will be taking over for you while you're laid up. Don't worry, get some rest." He left the room.

So many thoughts flooded Jake's mind as he lay there that night and wondered why he had been such a moron. He found his place years ago and it worked just fine.

So why did I try to be more?

The embarrassment he caused the ranch with an absolute pathetic business decision disgusted him. What if he had sent off more cattle than he had? *I could have ruined the family.*

And trying to fly? His leg kept him out of the war and away from planes before. He would have stayed happy being "that other Weathers boy." The background was his place to dwell and he should have remained Aaron's quiet brother. He could be out there, pushing horns and playing the part that was his. *But I played the fool instead.*

His dark thoughts tore him down and broke him into pieces.

Jake stayed quiet most days. Over the next few weeks, Jake spurned Ellie's attempts to engage him. He wouldn't accept her help or let her change his mind. She never accused him of acting mean, but all the same he felt hollow, like a skeleton in body and soul.

On the fourth morning, Jake got in his wheelchair and rolled himself out on the porch. Ellie sat reading, but didn't try to talk.

Jake scanned the action near the ranchhouse. Larry worked on repainting the shed. No one had removed the charred skeleton of the wrecked plane yet. It sat exactly where it died a month before.

"Hey, hey!" Aaron's voice came from behind Jake. "Look who made it all the way to the porch today."

Jake cringed.

His brother slapped him on the shoulder as he invited himself to sit down next to Ellie. "Getting your casts off in three weeks. Think you'll be ready?"

"I'll do what the doctor wants."

"Good. 'Cause I am exhausted making up your slack out on the ranch." For one afternoon a week before, Aaron went out to help. "I'm only one man after all. We need to get gimpy back out there doing his job."

"I'll get there as soon as I can," Jake said.

"Please do." Aaron turned his attention to Ellie.

"Maybe then you won't have to keep playing nurse."

"I don't mind," Ellie said.

"All the same, it'll be good when things get back to normal," Aaron said. He blabbed on for a few more minutes and managed to make Ellie laugh. Then Aaron left and the awkward silence cast itself upon Jake and Ellie again.

Three weeks passed at a crawl. Jake let Carl drive him to the doctor in Odessa, because the old man hid his sympathy better than the others. If the doctor told Jake that his casts couldn't come off today, he didn't want any tears shed on his behalf. He just wanted to be invisible.

After the doctor examined him, he removed the casts. The scissors cut through as the mold crumbled. The flesh on his right arm had grown pasty and suffocated. The limb appeared puny and weak. It felt stiff and unsure in motions.

How would he ever toss a bale of hay again? After that, his right leg came free. Bending his knee took great intention on his part, only able to crook it forty-five degrees. The doctor assisted in swinging his legs over the side of the table. How would he ever climb on a horse?

And then Jake traded one shackle for another. As his right leg gained freedom, the doctor fit his old brace around his left. Before he stood, he leaned on the brace, but both legs felt too weak. While the brace absorbed much of his weight, he wedged the crutches under his arms and hobbled around the room.

The doctor told him how he should gradually add pressure to his right leg so it could regain its muscle. Jake would walk again, or at least walk in the way he once did.

Carl offered to pull the car up but Jake insisted on crutching through the parking lot. After all, the sooner he had his leg back, the sooner he could get in the saddle and be the ranch hand he was meant to be.

When he returned, the family and ranch hands at the house cheered. He tried not to wince at the pain. He wanted them to go about their business and not think about him. After a while he slipped away into his room, stopping at the mirror to take inventory. He looked at his arm and leg and tried to guess how long until he would heal. The tip of his burn scar crept above the collar of his shirt. The crinkled flesh would follow him to the grave.

Over the next few weeks, Jake worked himself reckless getting his strength back, walking as he used to walk. His hope was always that his every effort would one day make up for the money he lost. Four weeks later, he could more or less get around.

The first time Ellie saw him stride strong and well without his crutches, she lit up. She rushed out to him to give him a hug. "Jake!" She threw arms around him. "You're back!"

"No, I'm not." He held her with careless arms. "I have to go to work."

"I thought we might go for a ride." The hope in her eyes faded.

Jake still loved her but she distracted him from what he felt he should be doing. "I have to give all my energy to the ranch."

"But—"

"You want fairytales, I can't give them to you. You deserve someone better, someone able." He left her. She wanted bright colors from him. He was tinged with gray.

He once again hated being seen. Mr. Johnson came to visit and Jake stayed in the barn the whole time.

Days later, Jake saddled Rio and rode away as Puma stayed in the corral. He worked his tail off, morning, noon, and night. Often, when the others were at breakfast, he was already out pushing steer. He ate the cold remains of dinner.

And sometimes he would encounter Ellie during the in-betweens, and tried to be nice, but he would no longer play along with her charade that he would ever be anything except what he was meant to be.

One night Jake fell asleep on the couch. An hour later he woke up to voices in the kitchen.

"That boy is becoming a ghost, seems even more empty than before." Rosalia said. "*Dios Mio!* He never speaks, always in the shadows."

"I don't know, Rosalia. He was doing great, now he won't act without my word. And he's letting Aaron push him around again," Carl said.

Jake lay there, thinking it made sense for him not to act on his own since the last time he did, he nearly destroyed everything.

More than once, Jake caught Ellie with a bloody nose or pale complexion. Her eyes were sunken holes. The hazel stopped burning. In the moments Jake passed through the house, he knew she had retreated to her room and fallen into sick spells. She was using again.

But who was he to do something about it? He wasn't meant to say anything, not the man for the job and would never be. Even more hate for himself built up inside as he didn't say anything. She was killing herself and Jake didn't do a thing about it. There was nothing to say.

Then on a Friday, the two passed each other in the barn, like a wind through a graveyard. The sun crept through the cracks in the walls. The air hung thick with the scent of hay.

"What's wrong with you, Jake?" Ellie said.

"What do you mean?" Her abruptness caught him off guard. He tried to walk past her.

She grabbed his arm and spun him around. "Why are you still broken?"

"I've got work to do." He tried to pull away.

"No! You're going to talk to me! You're going to tell me! Right here! Right now!"

He faced her.

"I miss you, Jake. You never look at me anymore. I hoped that when your injuries healed, you'd come back to me, but now, you're letting yourself be injured."

She wiped tears from her eyes. "You were doing so well. So what if you messed up? You're still you!" She looked away. "It's not supposed to be like this. *You're* not supposed to be like this!" She pointed her finger at his chest. "You promised me a home, that I'd never be lonely again!"

Jake looked down at his boots. "I never should have

tried to be something else... I shouldn't have dragged you into it."

"What do you mean," Ellie raised her voice, "*something else?* You're not this! I know you're not this. I've seen what you can be! You don't have to be this just because you think everyone else sees you this way!"

"I'm not, I'm just being whom I'm meant to be. I should have been happy with what I am. I tried for more and I almost cost us the ranch and maybe I might have died in the plane."

"You did die in the plane!" Ellie yelled, "Jake, don't let them break you!"

"They just want me to be—"

She slapped him hard across his face. "No! You're the only one who has a say in what you are!"

"You don't understand. Sometimes people are just meant to be the way they are. You're a dreamer and always will be. I was confused at first. I let it distract me, but in this world, I have a role. I tried to break that."

He slumped his shoulders. "It wasn't worth the consequence. You deserve someone better, someone able. You belong somewhere else than with a cripple in west Texas. I'm sorry I deceived you into thinking you could be happy here.

Ellie's eyes poured the tears of a grieving widow. "Jake..." She looked up at him. "Don't you love me anymore?"

He sighed. He felt awful but owed her the truth. "I can't... love you anymore. You don't belong here. You deserve someone who can make you happy."

"But you! You can make me happy!" She wept as she pounded her fists against his chest.

"No." Jake grabbed her wrists and pushed her arms back. "I can't."

But in one last burst of fight she flared back and yelled, "No! No! I don't believe you, not when you say, 'I don't love you.'"

"It doesn't matter if I love you. I just can't. I'm not good enough!" he yelled back.

His words hung in the air. The pair was so small in the world, the broken cowboy and the lost gypsy. He finally realized the hidden truth that held him back for months; he really wasn't good enough. The phrase would become his anthem for life.

Ellie's nose poured blood. She looked at him with hurt eyes as she grabbed a rag from the tool shelf and held it to her face. Then the girl ran off to the house.

Jake didn't follow.

CHAPTER 22

Bleeding Gypsy

Driving Ellie to the train station was more punishment than either she or Jake deserved.

He looked at the sky. The rising sun had no business doing so. Today was a day for rain, for cold, for gray. Yet the celestial body dared to shine anyways. The hearts inside the truck cab were anything but ready for a sunny day.

Jake acted as if he didn't see the tears rolling down Ellie's face. After all, he didn't feel capable of drying her tears. She would go west the way she planned when she had first arrived. Jake knew she had to leave. She was meant for something bigger than this place.

Ellie had made no grand announcements or speeches when she told everyone she was leaving for San Francisco, where artists needed to be in this day and age. A detached Mr. Weathers and an ignorant Aaron bought her story. The rest acted so very sad. They witnessed the broken boy become a man because of her and their hopes were high. They had fallen in love with the girl, but the Jake she had created was dead.

In her final week, Ellie spent final moments with the family. She read countless stories to Gracie and held long conversations with Carl on the porch. Every meal Rosalia cooked, Ellie served as a kitchen aide.

On the way to the train station, Ellie cried endlessly; it was remarkable she had any tears left to bleed. She wiped them away with each passing mile. She gazed at every pasture and dirt road, soaking in what was once home before it faded away with the tracks. She coughed every few moments, as she sought comfort in her old demon.

Jake hurt through and through, powerless once again to his situation, to run the ranch or even run like a normal person. To be a plow was his existence. He would do the job he was given by the plow master. Then he'd get up the next day and do it again. He would be quiet. Laughing and caring weren't things he could do. She simply had to go. Ellie should understand she'd be better off without him.

He waited as she bought a ticket on the eight o'clock train for Albuquerque, her first stop on the way west. He kept his head down as he carried her bags to the platform, and couldn't help but think of when she had first stepped off that train and split his existence in two. He should have known then but he had not.

As the locomotive rolled into the station, smoke surrounded the broken cowboy and the aching gypsy, barricading them in the moment they couldn't escape.

The pair stood in the clouds. Jake handed her baggage to the porter. He intended to give Ellie her handbag, but her shaking fingers didn't seize it. The bag fell to the ground and, as it hit the platform, opened and two or three little brown bottles rolled out.

Jake bent to pick them up and put them in the bag. He made no protest, knowing he had no business telling her what to do.

She paused, as though waiting for him to say something, but only met his silence. Ellie took the bag.

"All aboard!" yelled the conductor, a voice coming from some distant place.

Ellie turned to board, paused, and then faced him. She came in close and touched his cheek, gently asking him to look into her eyes. Those hazel eyes that once burned like something out of a fairy tale.

She pulled him in and kissed him on the cheek. "You know Jake, I never saw you as broken..." Then she left him.

The wheels spun for a moment before they found traction. Then the steel beast made its way from the station. She looked out the window for him... he didn't come after her, and it wasn't the brace that held him back.

Jake watched the train meet the horizon and stared at the empty tracks for a long time after. He stood lost in thought, trying to convince himself that it would be for the best. She could find someone strong and able, someone to make her happy.

And so, one year to the day that she shook the earth with her arrival, she left. Ellie Peri was gone, leaving them as they always were... leaving him as he always was.

A young boy staring at his brace shook Jake from his

thoughts. He left the platform and got into the truck and headed back to Crane. And like that, Ellie's existence in his life seemed nothing more than a dream, a beginning and ending with a trip to the train station.

Over the weeks and months that followed, an old familiar shadow cast itself over the Weathers' ranch. The door to her dark room sat slightly ajar, a passage back into a dream.

Jake plunged into work on the ranch and nearly broke the legend horse with all his pushing. In the weeks ahead, he rode other horses to give Rio a chance to recuperate. He pushed on like a madman, now back in full strength and using every bit of it towards the ranch.

Jake moved like the devil chased him. He pulled ropes so hard his hands bled. His stomach would rumble as he often worked through meals. Some nights he wouldn't sleep. If he took enough lanterns with him, or if the moon was bright enough, he could mend fences through late hours.

He became more of the cattle herd than he was of the family, one of the animals out there on the pasture. And in the weeks and months that followed, he pushed hard and long enough that his lonely routine returned. He was again the quiet one. He did as he was told. And whenever he found himself thinking of Ellie or thinking about writing a letter, he would push ten times as hard. He had no time for regrets. The ranch needed him.

On one of his three day working binges, he even rode a horse to death, running it down. The horse had slowed to a limp stride, stopped, and then fell over. Jake climbed out from under the animal and looked it over. He couldn't do anything for the horse, so he pulled out his pistol and ended the pain.

"DAMN IT!" Jake hollered and hauled his saddle all the way back to the house, before throwing it on the next animal to keep going, but costing the ranch money forced him to slow down. He stopped pulling multiple day work binges.

And whenever he looked to the sky and remembered flying, he would touch the scar on his neck and remember that time was better spent working. Then he would bow his head and drive forward once again... pushing, pushing, always pushing.

One time, despite himself, he fell from his horse. He passed out right there on the pasture ground.

His one and only release was Gracie and he would read and play with her in every single moment that he wasn't working. Her warm, forgiving smile seemed to let him know he was still alive. They tore through volumes of books together and he carried her countless times around the barn on his back. She was the other half of his existence, always in contention with the ranch. At the end of every day, Jake looked forward to seeing Gracie, his one and only release.

She glowed a little less than when Ellie was there. When she finally seemed to realize that Ellie wasn't coming back, the little girl sat for days and days holding the silver brush Ellie left for her. She seemed to understand. The moments

Jake and Gracie spent together on the porch seemed to fill the void in their lives.

And he let himself be lost in Gracie's big eyes over and over again, eyes that also belonged to his mother. *If only she were here now,* ...but she never would be. So Jake accepted the way existence played out.

Months passed and the atmosphere around the house calmed. The family moved herds and conducted business. Days came and went. Along with those around him, Jake settled into who he would be for the rest of his life.

Jake felt perplexed at the way Mr. Weathers kept drifting into his spells. His father's aura at the ranch withered back to the time when Aaron was away at war. He locked himself in his study for hours on end.

Jake walked up on Gracie pulling at her father's locked door. "Don't bother him, Gracie, he's sad."

She looked up at him.

"I know, it used to not make sense to me either. Now, I understand."

She smiled.

"I'm just glad you'll never have to."

Four weeks later, Jake sat on the porch cleaning his gun and polishing his brace. When he finished, he found his way into the kitchen and asked Rosalia if she needed anything. Finally, he called to Gracie so he could read books with her. Maybe they could even play with her toys together. On the way to her room, Jake noticed an unusual level of quiet.

Gracie wasn't in his room, the guest room, or in their

father's office. He walked across the driveway and looked for her in the barn. Fear crept up his back. His steps grew more and more hurried.

"Have you seen Gracie?" he asked Carl in the workshop.

"No, I haven't. Is something wrong?"

Jake didn't stick around to answer. He found Rosalia and asked her if she knew.

"I thought she was with you." Rosalia put a hand to her cheek.

Jake tore through the house once again. Maybe she was hiding on purpose. In frustration he headed out onto the back porch, but he had not time to think. Way off, across one of the front pasture, her little figure ran about. Gracie wore one of her favorite dresses.

Jake breathed relief. *This isn't so bad*, he thought. She had just wandered off. He felt the slightest bit of happiness for the first time in a long time as he watched his sister enjoy herself.

"Gracie!" Jake called out.

She stopped and faced the house.

Good, he had her attention. "Come back!"

Then something happened that made no sense. Cattle grazed out where Gracie was, but one silhouette didn't belong. Its arched back and square shoulders didn't match the clumsy posture of the other animals. The lowered head and powerful posture seemed odd.

Jake noticed how far away Gracie really was, and how very much he didn't like that bull.

"Gracie!" he called again. "Come here!" He hoped that

the sweet child would escape the attention of the beast, but the animal's strides brought it closer to her.

"Gracie! Come on!" he yelled again and left the porch, running towards her. He finally pulled her attention away.

She looked around her and stiffened at the sight of the dark, ominous figure near her. She walked backwards, away from the animal. Then she spun around and moved in the fastest way her little body could.

Jake's chest froze as the bull lowered its head in Gracie's direction and trotted after her. GRACIE!" he screamed. He ran towards her. But she was still too far away and he was not fast enough. He ran and ran. The bull ran faster.

His heart broke as the terrible demon ran his little sister down, as one ton of muscle plowed her over.

"NOOOOOOO!" He screamed.

The bull tossed Gracie through the air like the soft floppy dolls she played with.

"GOD, NO!" Tears welled in Jake's eyes as he tried to cover the ground, but pain shot through his leg. He seized up and tumbled, all the while struggling to focus on Gracie's sprawled body.

"RIO, come here, boy!" he screamed through blood shot eyes. "RIO! RIO!" he sobbed over and over through a torn throat. Jake forced his way through the pain and stood up.

Somewhere in his mad confusion, hooves galloped behind him and he grabbed Rio's passing mane just in time to swing himself up on the horse's back. In seconds, Jake slid from his horse next to Gracie.

He was afraid to touch her. Blood pooled everywhere; her mouth, her nose, her face. With trembling hands, he rolled her over and lifted her head. "Gracie, no... please no," he whispered. Not her. Anyone, *anything* but her. "Please... please... Gracie."

As Pete reached Jake's side, the others came flying up behind him. Rosalia was hysterical, screaming. Aaron threw up. Their father fell to his knees and pulled at his hair. Carl knelt by Jake and placed his mouth over Gracie's and breathed into her lungs... nothing. He did it again... still nothing.

A small cough came over Gracie's lips, the slightest but loudest cough Jake had ever heard.

Carl yelled, "Pete, go get the truck!"

The ranchhand froze in shock.

"Pete, damn it!" Carl yelled again.

Pete shuddered and ran back to the house.

"Aaron! Go call Dr. Wilson and tell him what happened and that we're bringing her there," Carl said.

Aaron wasn't moving so Rosalia slapped him hard. He stumbled off towards the phone.

The moments felt surreal as Jake watched the truck drive off, carrying Gracie as she fought for her life. The vehicle powered across the pasture, straight for the gate. The family fell into their tears. Jake sat on his knees for a long time starring at the spot he last saw them driving away. He sat there as the warm wind brushed his neck.

The house fell silent. No one said a word for hours. They waited for the telephone to ring to tell them the best or worst news in the world. Rosalia held her rosary beads and went through her prayers over and over.

At three a.m. the phone rang. Their grief had entombed them in such an unearthly daze that the phone's ring seemed like a hallucination. But Rosalia picked up the phone.

Jake didn't move.

In the moments after, Rosalia's tears didn't answer anything. When she hung up, Rosalia told Jake and Aaron that Dr. Wilson did the best he could to stabilize her at his house. Then all three men took her to the hospital in Odessa where the surgeons went to work. Gracie had sustained a cracked rib, a broken finger, multiple cuts and bruises, and a black eye. That was all. In short, a miracle.

Jake received the news but spent no time in celebration. He made a stop at the gun closet and slipped away in the ruckus.

The cannon of a gun felt heavy as Jake rode across the ranch that night. Deep down, he knew it was stupid to ride around at dark, but he would be ready when morning came. In his pocket were five heavy rounds.

He didn't know where he was going and had no memory of where he had been. Jake had one focus and would ride to the death of him to make them pay. They would all pay for what happened to Gracie.

At mid-morning the next day Jake found the first bull grazing with a herd in the Back Forty. Jake rode up on his dark horse and loaded his weapon.

The creature never looked up as Jake pulled the gun into his shoulder. He slipped the hammer back and focused on the heart of the beast; his breath slowed. He waited for the perfect moment...

With a clap of thunder, the bullet ripped through the animal's side and destroyed its heart. And in a lifetime of invincibility, the demon met its end at the hand of a vengeful brother. The bull fell to the ground.

The recoil was so fierce it nearly knocked Jake off the saddle. His recent injury ached.

Jake never approached the body to inspect his kill. He had others to find.

For three days, he sought them out and brought them down. One by one, they all fell at his feet.

Larry passed Jake as he went about his lethal work. "Jake, you all right?"

Jake never responded.

Late in the afternoon came the moment Jake had been saving for last. He had found and killed all of the bulls, except the one that broke her. Jake guessed where he'd be.

The animal stood below as Jake and Rio waited on a ridge. The beast drank from a pond, taking big, deep mouthfuls.

Jake slipped off his horse. The shot had to be perfect. He couldn't rush it and steadied the long barrel over the stallion's saddle, waiting for Rio to stand still.

Jake watched the beast through iron sights and lined up on a spot that would kill the animal instantly, but Jake moved the iron. He aimed higher up the side of the bull. Then, boom.

The bullet snapped the bull's spine in two. The back

half of his body dropped. The beast crashed to the ground, screaming in agony. In a panic, it dragged its mass around with its front legs.

Jake rode up, grinning. The bull flared his nostrils in rage and crawled toward him, clumsy and broken. Jake drew his .45 and emptied a clip into the animal's face and chest. The bullets were far too small to kill a hulk of muscle like a bull, but they would start the bleeding and infuriate the animal. Jake wanted the beast to die in stages, in pain.

Gracie Ann Weathers lay in the hospital for six days before they brought her home. She got ice cream and had to be corrected whenever she tried to play too much, too soon. Jake never went to the range those first few days. He spent every possible second with her.

A month later his father summoned Carl, Rosalia, Aaron and Jake into his office. The man looked exhausted. "I've come to a decision," he said with a distraught face. "I should have done it years ago. It's been stupid and selfish to keep a child with Gracie's needs here. The hard reality of it is, a ranch is not a safe place for her to be." He paused in the heavy air. "I've decided to send her to the Whaley house."

"No, not that place! Not for Gracie!" Jake pounded his fist on the table.

"Jake, she'll be better off somewhere else," his father said.

"But I'll watch her more closely!" Jake said. "We all will!"

"Jake, she'll be much safer—"

"We can't ship her off to that prison!" Jake glared. "She's not some freak we need to send to the zoo! No!" Jake stood up from his seat, his eyes pleading. "We can't send her there! She'll be terrified and scared! She needs to be here, with us! With me!"

Carl straightened up. "Yeah, boss. This was the worst of things that happened to Gracie, but it might be just as bad or worse to send her off to a place so different from what she's used to."

"I've made my decision," Mr. Weathers rubbed his brow.

Remembering his place as an employee, Carl sat down in silence

"Please," Jake choked. "Don't do this…"

His father looked him square in the eyes. "She leaves on Thursday."

Jake stormed out of the room. He couldn't do anything. He was nothing and his father had all the say. Gracie didn't understand what all the yelling was about. Jake looked at her, feeling guilty he couldn't do anything to stop this. He couldn't even find anything to say to his sister.

And so he left the child there.

Jake didn't want to see them take her away, so he stayed out on the range when the car left, but it was in his head, over and over again. He could see it happening, as he pictured Gracie and how she wouldn't understand why her things were packed in a suitcase. She always smiled at car rides and she'd never know she wouldn't see the house again as it disappeared behind her.

After she left, the house grew silent as a grave.

Week after week, the hush in the house was deafening. Jake kept listening for her to charge into the room, wanting to play. He took a long walk by himself that evening. The house joined the list of places he hated to be. His leg started aching. *Why does my leg have to hurt?* He already had to live his whole life with the damn brace.

Jake felt beat to death. All the tragedy of his life caught up. First his mother, the anchor of their family. Ellie cast herself off to some dark fate, dying slowly in a place not her home. Sweet, innocent Gracie was condemned and cast away from everything she knew and loved.

And Jake, forced to walk the earth as half a man all his days… *Why God? Why? Why had this all happened?*

Jake looked at the sky in anger. "LEAVE MY FAMILY ALONE! DO YOU HEAR ME? LEAVE MY FAMILY ALONE!"

CHAPTER 23

A Hero's Encore

Might have been days, could have been years. Still, only months had passed since Gracie went away. Time became unreliable for Jake. Numb was how he felt about everything. He hardly noticed his own existence, never questioning if the new reality had settled or if things were the way he remembered.

Jake lost himself in the great dullness. For the first time in his life, he felt no excitement about the ranch. Pushing cattle didn't fulfill his dreams. He enjoyed little sense of purpose when he sat in the saddle and felt no magic in a hard day's work. He had no hope, no tomorrow, no later. With every blink, the date on the calendar would change. Nothing more.

Despite the calm waters after the storm passed, the Weathers' Ranch became a doomed ship, sinking slowly. The ship's crew stared at one another with eyes glazed over, no words spoken.

Jake surrendered to the brokenness. The water rising around him wasn't cold, it was not a shock. It was just there. But soon he wouldn't be able to breathe.

He had no fight or will left to tread water.

Jake felt broken to the core more than ever. Letting down the two people who meant most to him broke Jake to the core, but their absence forced him to mull over his crippled condition beyond skin deep. Without realizing it, Jake had made crutches out of the woman Ellie and the girl Gracie.

He had soaked up Ellie's encouragement and gone places he had never been before. Then he suffered consequences he wasn't ready to pay.

He had relied on Gracie's dim understanding as an escape. In her eyes he was everything and in no way broken. She thought of him as a superhero and saw him so much better than the world saw him, far better than he ever saw himself.

The challenge for him now was to figure out who he was without them. Cowboy? Second son? Cripple? Ranch partner? The answers eluded him.

Mr. Weathers disappeared for days and weeks inside the cave of darkness he always carried with him. When he emerged, the darkness followed him. He looked sick, like he was losing weight.

Jake would pass by his room and watch as his father stared at the wall and said, "I'm sorry, I'm sorry." Murmuring for hours.

Rosalia's eyes were constantly red, but she didn't cry in the kitchen. She stared down to her side where Gracie used to stand. Or she'd grab at the back of her apron as she did when Gracie tugged on it.

Carl often took long walks by himself. Or sometimes Jake passed him in the den as Carl studied photos of all the generations that had come and gone. And now more than ever, Carl sat on the porch, reading his Bible.

Even in his carefree existence, Aaron looked uneasy at the ranch. He spent more time away from the ranch. He rarely took the time to tease Jake anymore.

One day, a temporary reprieve from the stillness seemed to pass over the house when someone knocked on the front door. Jake peeked out the side window. A green military sedan sat parked out front, complete with a white star painted on the door.

He opened the front door. The visitors were fine specimens of the United State's military, with uniforms so neatly pressed, they could have been carved from stone. Standing at attention, their imposing presence filled the porch and followed them into the house.

"Mr. Samuel Weathers?" said the soldier in front of him.

"Yes?" His father answered over Jake's shoulder as he came into the entryway.

"Hello, sir." He extended a handshake so well executed it might as well have been a salute. "I am Lieutenant Rue Johnson." He stepped aside to make way for the other soldier. "This is Corporal Brian Cota."

Sam pulled back from the medal-clad heroes in front of him and showed them to the den. "Rosalia, won't you bring these gentlemen some iced tea? And tell Aaron to come here."

The soldiers sat down on the couch. Yet before they could settle, Rosalia reappeared with the beverages and they stood once again. After several minutes, a very tired-looking Aaron entered the room.

This was the first time that Jake or his father noticed Lt. Johnson was missing a left arm. It must have been some involuntary souvenir from some instinctual act of valor on the battlefield.

If Aaron expected some typical visitor or one of his father's business associates, the sight of these gladiators of modern day stole control of his face. Turning pale, he went weak at the knees and forced himself to grab the back of a chair.

Unsure what his brother would say or do next, Jake studied Aaron's face.

"Aaron? You're the Weathers son that served in the war, correct?" Their inquiry confirmed, the three saluted each other and announced their ranks. Finally, they all took their seats.

"Now we have in our records that you served with the 4th Infantry Division?" said Lt. Johnson.

"Yes, I did—"

"Oh, he did more than just serve," Mr. Weathers said. He hadn't had a chance to praise his son's military accomplishments in far too long. "He was a hero. Led the D-day charge on Utah Beach. Ran into a hail of bullets."

"Dad, please." Aaron frowned.

"Well, it's true." His father turned to their guests. "Everyone around here knows his story. He's the town hero."

"Oh, I'm sure it's well deserved," Lt. Johnson cleared his throat.

"There's really nothing to talk about," Aaron said.

"He's being modest," his father said. "And you, Lieutenant? What's your story?"

"Pretty basic, sir. I was a Ranger in the 2nd Battalion. We were sent to the old Omaha Beach, had a little trouble taking some fortified Nazi battery positions. They got a lot of us… they got a lot of me." He held up what was left of his arm. "But we took it eventually."

"You're a brave soldier," Mr. Weathers said.

"I try to be," Lt. Johnson said. "Anyways, sir, we don't want to take up too much of your time. We've driven all over West Texas locating servicemen. General Omar Bradley has traveled all over the country speaking in various states and cities on behalf of injured G.I.s. He's on a campaign to insure we're taken care of. In nine days, he'll be in Midland. The D.A.R. is sending us around to invite all the veterans in West Texas. Long story short, we'd love to have you and your family attend." He smiled.

Aaron squirmed in his seat. "Oh, well, that's very nice, but we're in the middle of the busy season right now. I don't think we'll be able to—"

"Nonsense!" Mr. Weathers said. "We'd love to come! There's no way we would miss this. Omar Bradley wants to see our Aaron!" He gathered himself. "Is there someplace or someone we need to R.S.V.P. to?"

Corporal Cota pulled out an envelope. "Here's your

invitation. Inside are instructions on what to do."

Mr. Weathers tried to convince the two messengers to stay for dinner, but they still had to visit a few homesteads before nightfall. He waved them all the way down the driveway, down the road, and until what Jake thought must've been the next county.

Mr. Weathers had forgotten how proud he was of Aaron. With something to channel his passion into, it was like a firework had gone off in a dark room. His enthusiasm became a harsh fluorescent light to Jake's dilated pupils.

That night at dinner, he made Aaron tell his war stories again. Aaron spoke of every charge into overwhelming numbers and the one that should have won him the Medal of Honor, but was classified. In his tales, he was always on a first name basis with the generals.

Jake wondered why Aaron now told them so half-heartedly. The same brother who wouldn't shut up a year ago lost so much interest in the stories. Most of the time his father would take over.

Aaron seemed very quiet over the next few days as the event drew closer. Every time Jake passed his father, he seemed to be staring wide-eyed into space.

The day of the event arrived. When Jake came off the range, his father said, "Get dressed, Jake. We don't want to be late."

"Where are we going?" Jake studied the suit his father wore.

"To see General Bradley speak for your brother, of course!" His tone bordered on annoyance.

"Oh, yeah." Jake climbed the stairs. Going to a crowded event an hour away seemed about as a miserable thing as he could be forced to do. But he always did as his father said.

He found a nicer shirt and put it on. It could probably use some ironing, but it wasn't worth the effort. He splashed some water on his face and went as far as to run his fingers through his hair, giving some shape to its workday mess.

Downstairs the family had gathered. He didn't let his mind think about a year ago when they had gone to the last military event for Aaron, trying to avoid thoughts about the individuals who weren't there now. Jake didn't want to notice the change in their demeanor. As he looked around, no one but Mr. Weathers looked like they wanted to go.

His father yelled up the stairs"Aaron! We have to go!"

When his brother came down the stairs, Jake stared at him. "What's that on your lip?"

Aaron looked around the room, stroking the wisp of facial hair. "It's... um, a mustache."

"It looks good, son." Mr. Weathers patted him on the back.

"You know, we really don't have to go tonight. We've already been to one of these things and it's so far—"

"Of course, we're going!" Mr. Weathers said. "Why don't you want to go?"

Aaron shuffled his feet. "It's just always the same people and same songs."

"You have to go. You're a hero."

Before Aaron could protest the trip again, his father swept them away to the vehicles.

The family arrived with the first wave of guests. All present seemed to share the Weathers' story--a young man in uniform, proud parents, and a few siblings or close friends. Many had girls hanging off their arms.

"Congratulations, Aaron!" The voice coming from behind the family sounded familiar. The Weathers turned around in unison

"Mr. Miller?" Aaron's face went flush when the wave of people trailed in his wake: Ricky, Mr. Bakke, Larry, Pete, Mary-Lou, and a sizable assortment of people they knew from back home.

Jake watched the exchange.

"What are you doing here?"Aaron rubbed the back of his neck.

"Your father invited us!" Mary-Lou said. "We all wanted to be here with our very own hero on this big night!"

"Look at him," Mr. Miller laughed. "He's speechless!"

Their father slapped Aaron on the back, giddy over the success of his surprise for his golden son. They laughed and made small talk for a few moments.

"Wait! Look at us gibbering away here," Mr. Weathers addressed them all. "We better get inside and find seats."

The procession of twenty or so people headed in together. Jake laughed at the signs for his brother the group brought.

They found their way to where tables were strewn across

a field that sloped gently downward to a makeshift stage, high with an archway of balloons crowning it. Aaron's entourage for the night found seats clustered together. Aaron sat with his head down, hiding his face.

All the local politicians tried to squeeze out some microphone time. Here and there some World War II heroes spoke about the situations they had gone through.

"Hey, Aaron," Mary-Lou whispered loud enough that the entire row turned their heads together. "They should have asked you to speak." A murmur of agreement rose up.

General Bradley took the stage to thunderous applause. His presence commanded the respect and attention of all. Yet he spoke in the most approachable and friendly way. He spoke of the duty and the bravery of the soldiers. He reminded everyone how they could all be heroes, even if they had not fought in the war. And when he finished speaking, the crowd sat ready to throw their money at these organizations.

"Aaron!" came a voice to the left of the visitors from Crane. "Aaron Weathers!"

Three soldiers, in dress uniforms decorated in medals, came up with grins on their faces. They paid no attention to anyone else, making their way to their buddy.

The blood drained from Aaron's face. In seconds sweat poured down his forehead.

"Aaron 'Encore' Weathers! How the heck are you?" One of them, a shorter soldier, stuck out his hand.

Aaron stared at the hand for an awkward amount of

time before he took it, holding it with a limp wrist.

"What's up with that ridiculous mustache, Encore? Still trying to suck up to General O'Hare?" another one of the soldiers said. "Trying to look like him now?"

Aaron sat there with a dumb look on his face and didn't say a thing. The aura of the table felt awkward.

"Hello there, I'm Sam Weathers, Aaron's father." He stood and shook each offered hand. "Did y'all fight with my boy here?"

"Fight with him?" The three of them laughed like they had heard a joke for the first time in their lives "Well, we sure fought, but I never saw this one near any German lead!" More laughter.

Puzzlement crossed Mr. Weathers' face. "What are you talking about?"

"Easy, sir, I didn't mean anything rough by it. I was just joking with Encore here about how he never had to carry a gun! Of course, on account that he was always waiting on the general and all. His favorite boy."

"Encore? Encore?" Their father's voice turned stern. "His name is Aaron. Why do you keep calling him 'Encore'?"

"Sorry, sir. Just an old joke we had back in the day. On account of how he always showed up when the fight was already over, like an encore."

"No... no... you have my son confused with someone else. My son is a hero. His place was on the front lines!"

The front soldier shook his head. "No... Aaron Weathers never saw a moment of action in his entire deployment. He was an aide." He nailed Aaron with his stern gaze. "Well, go on, tell them. Tell them!"

Through wet eyes, Aaron glanced up at his father standing over him. As his shoulders dropped, he sighed. "It's true."

Sam stared wide-eyed, rotating his head from side to side. Then his eyes narrowed and mouth closed tightly. He stormed off.

No one said anything.

The family were hurt, not just because they had bought a deception for so long, but also because Crane was a small town. They all had a stake in every individual who headed off to do something in the world and all had invested in this hero. He was theirs, an emblem of what could come out of a tiny corner in Texas. His adventures and heroism carried them.

Here it was, the fall of Aaron Weathers. Before the morning everyone in town, and beyond, would know.

As they made their way down dark country roads, Jake rode next to his brother in the bed of the pickup. The air was dry and the stars blazed in the sky above. Aaron hung his head low between his knees. The long road home was empty, there for them alone.

Jake watched his brother and felt sorry for him. The misery had touched the untouchable son, the golden one. Even Aaron couldn't escape.

It had been years since they were real friends, and ages since they truly got along.

"You don't have to say anything. I know I'm worthless."

Aaron looked up at the sky.

Jake stared at the road rolling away from them. "I wish you really were a hero. That way, people could believe in one of us."

CHAPTER 24

The Freedom Pistol

Carl stood from his seat by Jake. "I've watched that boy since the day he was born. Guess I never looked at him through the lens of infatuation, but I've always known he lacks the grit to be a hero. He doesn't have the heart."

"Why wouldn't you say anything?"

"People always need a hero, Jake." The old man walked away.

His brother loved and needed the praise. Aaron was capable of pretty rotten things, but Jake never suspected he would go to such lengths.

Jake was also sad. Their world could not handle this hit. Jake caused so much hurt and brokenness. He messed up so much. And now there was this.

Mr. Weathers stopped talking to his golden son and everyone else. His life descended into the darkest spell Jake ever witnessed. He drowned in liquid forgetfulness and was no longer a presence. He didn't run the business, he didn't emerge. He was lost, just where he wanted to be.

Aaron had floated on his hero status, but now he drifted,

living but useless. He no longer had a place or purpose. His throne of lies became his accuser.

The ranch began to die. The crew sat around with no orders to follow; the boss stopped writing paychecks. The cattle went unattended. And there was nothing Jake would do.

Carl and Jake watched Aaron start a fire in the pit behind the house. Then he went to his room and retrieved every uniform and military fatigue he owned. He threw the garments on the inferno and let the flames purge his lies. He took the medals and awards he conned and tossed them in the pyre. Even the banners made in his honor disappeared in ash. And later when he was by himself, Jake knew he would cry.

On Saturday, ranch hands, with nothing left to do, took a day off. Carl escorted Rosalia to the market. In the last few weeks, Aaron had made a habit of driving some place where no one knew his name. Jake figured the blank slate must have felt like a respite for him.

No one else but Jake was home, except their father who had barricaded himself in his office.

Jake wanted to be around someone unaffected by all this, so he took Rio for a ride. They headed down dirt roads and across pastures. The sky was somewhere between sun and clouds, dark clouds trimmed in white. The bright light of the sun made them glow, intermittently sending rays through. In the distance, sheets of rain fell to earth.

Jake sat on the horse gazing at the land. No matter how bad things were at the house, the rolling hills were unaffected. The ground remained the same on the family's best and worst days. It was bigger than any of them, there long before man arrived, and would be there long after they were gone. Consistent and unchanging, the land didn't need them and didn't care. Steers could roam the pastures or fire could leave the whole thing in ash. Through it all, the land would be there.

Jake rode back on Rio. He enjoyed the ride, his first tiny bit of peace in months. Some of the tightness left his shoulders.

In the distance, the house seemed dismal and gray. He lifted Rio's saddle off and put the horse out in the corral. Then he walked across the driveway and up the front steps of the porch. None of the vehicles had returned.

After passing through the door, he froze. An eerie feeling crept up his spine. He sighed, not wanting to deal with anything else, but something was definitely wrong. Even with the lights on, the place felt dark.

Jake saw it first as he walked down the hallway towards the office, a glimmer of crimson, caught in the light of the setting sun that poured through the windows. He pushed the door open and followed the trail of blood behind the desk.

"Figures." Jake's steps echoed as he crossed the room and looked down at the place his father lay. "You finally got what you wanted."

Samuel Weathers had shot a hole through the side of his head. The two-century-old pistol Jake thought only a decoration lay dormant.

Who would have thought it still fired?

After the years Jake and Carl spent keeping guns locked up, the one his father used was right in front of them, the word "freedom"carved on its stock.

Jake sat down in the chair and kicked his feet up on the desk. He rubbed his eyes long and deep. His father's suicide would be a new nightmare with no fix. So Jake stole a moment to himself to catch his breath one last time before the long struggle to come.

Jake opened the desk drawer and pulled the whiskey bottle from its place and poured the amber fluid into a crystal glass. He looked down at the corpse of his father and raised the glass to his lips. "Here's to how much you loved her."

A few minutes later, he reached for the office phone and called the police. Jake waited at the desk until cars came down the driveway. He opened the front door and showed them where his father lay. Jake thought it was unnecessary to send an ambulance for a dead man, but they wrapped him up and put him on the gurney, just in time to wheel him past Carl and Rosalia as they returned home.

Rosalia bit her lip and walked away. Carl listened to what happened. Jake accompanied the body into town and spent hours filling out paperwork and giving his statement. Later that night, a patrolman drove him home.

Up the driveway Jake thanked the officer and climbed out of the car. Aaron remained on the porch swing.

His brother's face was blank. Jake sat down next to him. In the silence, the two waited as they looked out at the stars.

"What's gonna happen now?" Aaron said.

"I don't know." And Jake didn't.

The burial of Samuel Weathers, cattle king, widower, and father of three was held on a Tuesday. Jake didn't feel disappointed or amazed by the masses that came. If anything, it was the exact number of mourners he expected. The ranch hands all came, except for the two men who resigned a few weeks before when they caught scent of the end.

The professional men Sam had relied on attended with their wives: his lawyers and bankers, his accountants, his estate managers.

Why did they come? They weren't his friends, just an annual appointment, seated on the other side of a desk. Maybe they wanted to witness for themselves if anything could be left of this place.

The Weathers didn't take the time to invite family. Jake was happy they wouldn't have to deal with houseguests.

Because the prosperity of the ranch gave Crane a leg up, the mayor and sheriff came around. A few teachers from the high school came as well.

As the memorial got under way, Aaron stood tucked behind Jake and Carl. Aaron, once their king, now was stripped of his crown. He huddled and hid and stared at the coffin, avoiding eye contact with anyone who might accuse him.

Jake and his family were never very involved in church since Maggie died. When the girl from New Orleans came to the ranch for a while, she took the Weathers men along with her to church. All in all, over the past decade, Jake was anything but regular.

The sermon given by Pastor Clancey and the words he spoke were impersonal. He had no vendetta against Sam Weathers. He just didn't know him. The clergyman spoke of forgiveness and, a savior, and the grave. Of three days later. Such beautiful hopes were hard for Jake to imagine these days.

Rosalia did the unthinkable and had no part in the meal's preparation. The good pastor's wife took care of it. The guests sat in the living room, den, and kitchen or trickled out to the front porch.

Laughter came from a corner of the room. It was odd to hear laughter at a funeral, but it made sense to Jake. That person probably had his own problems, his own hopes and dreams. He had his own loves and pains, own fears and victories. Whoever laughed had other things to do today. Coming to the funeral of someone they didn't care about was only a chore.

The visitors stayed behind as the others carried Sam Weathers' coffin away. Only Carl, Jake, Aaron, Pete, Larry and the minister took him to his final resting place.

At six o'clock, they buried Jake's father next to his mother. The two graves lay in the shadow of the old tree overlooking west Texas. The first shovel of dirt hit the coffin. Another one followed. Somewhere between the diggers' efforts, they entombed the man in dirt:

SAMUEL WILLIAM WEATHERS: 1896-1947. Beloved

Husband and Father, a Son of Texas.

Jake hadn't known what to write until the man who made gravestones suggested the epitaph.

Pastor Clancey signaled for everyone to prepare for a prayer. "Lord, thank You for offering salvation from the sting of death. We are not worthy that You, a hurricane, would acknowledge us, mere gnats. *He which testifieth these things saith, 'Surely I come quickly,' Amen. Even so, come, Lord Jesus.*"

Pastor Clancey lifted his head, touched Carl on the arm, and walked away.

They all left. All but Jake and Carl. The pair stood before the two graves, Jake's mother and father in the ground, a man and his wife. Sam, a man resigned to this world since the moment she left him, at last had gone after her. Maybe she would be waiting for him. Maybe he would find peace.

The worst part of the day was passing the time until the last of the guests left. Jake just wanted quiet. And when they lingered too long, Jake hiked up the ridge behind the house and sat under a tree. A light breeze swept up the rise at him. The sky was gray as it should be. He tried to think of something, of anything.

A few weeks later, Jake woke up, started to get out of bed but stopped himself. *Is there anything to be done today?* He always got out of bed to go work the cattle but this was only force of habit. *What are we going to do with the ranch anyway?*

He had spent his life getting up and moving. Now, Jake didn't know how to drop the habit. He wouldn't have gotten dressed, but his brace worked the best with jeans and boots. He meandered downstairs.

Rosalia hadn't fixed breakfast. The ranch hands weren't coming. His kind old friend Carl was nowhere to be found. Aaron… well, who knew?

Jake drifted outside and sat on the porch swing. The sunlight punished his eyes at first so he paused. Their dog Axle came up and waited. It had been a long time since Jake petted that dog, but today he had nothing except time. The fur was soft against his hand.

In the morning air, Jake caught a whiff of pipe tobacco. He stood up from the swing and followed the aroma to the bunkhouse. Carl lived in the rustic cabin as well, but half of the building belonged to him. The man had a house to himself.

Jake knocked on the screen door.

"Come in."

Jake headed inside. He could probably count on one hand the number of times he stepped into Carl's home. In his wisdom and ways, Carl seemed above the other men, his home a sacred place, the private quarters of a king or a great academic.

Carl sat in an overstuffed high back chair in the corner. A pipe smoldered in his mouth while his eyes locked on an old book. Around the room were a vast array of things, many of which came from Carl's days in Chicago.

"What brings you out here?" Carl said.

"I was wondering what you were doing."

"Just reading," Carl looked down at the text before

him. Then he grinned a little. "I used to say someday I'd have the time to catch up on all the reading I needed to do. Now that I have the time, I wish I didn't... such is life." He pointed to a kettle on the stove. "Would you like some tea?"

"No, thanks. I should probably go get the mail. I haven't picked it up in ages."

Jake left. He'd found himself at an awkward impasse. For some reason, he thought he'd get more out of the walk, but Carl gave him no wisdom.

But down the driveway, their mailbox stood guard at the other end. Jake looked over at the horse corral. It had been a few days since he had ridden, but it was only a mile and Jake's schedule was wide open.

As he walked, Jake appreciated the irony that he knew the land around the driveway the least. They didn't work the front pastures very often. The only time Jake encountered it was as he left the ranch. Most of the time he was in the truck with his eyes forward, going too fast to notice much. All the other parts of the ranch he worked on his horse and took the time to see every detail.

Before long he was at the mailbox. It didn't have much to do with business so it was the most dilapidated piece of equipment the Weathers owned. A once polished black mailbox now was tainted with rust. Their name was written on the side. The only problem was that the second "E" had fallen off.

Jake reached and pulled open the lid. Weeks worth of mail tumbled down. Jake bent on the dirt road to gather the envelopes. He shuffled through them. Some of them were informal letters, probably more condolences for his father's death. There were official looking mailings from different companies. A few lawyers' offices had written them, who knew what about.

Then Jake stopped. One letter stood out. Printed across its front were words in big type:

"NOTICE OF FORECLOSURE."

Jake went over to a tree at the end of their driveway and sat in its shade. He pulled out his knife and opened the envelope from the bank. As Jake read through it, he realized it wasn't truly foreclosure, rather a heavily-worded warning the bank's grace period with the Weathers was nearly through. The family had good credit so the bank extended them much more than the usual allotted time period, but here was the warning. Before long, the bank would seize assets in the amount they and the Weathers' other creditors were owed.

The family hadn't paid any sort of bill in a long time. In his father's last days, Sam didn't care too much for routine.

"Hmmm." Jake leaned back against the bark of the tree. He looked over the front pastures and down the highway. *So this is the end.* Gracie Weathers had been sent away. Maggie and Sam Weathers died long before they were old. And now the ranch, the reason they were all there in that time and place, would die. The thing their whole existence was built upon, here, now, was done.

The bank planned to seize the land, but maybe Jake

could keep one of the trucks. And if he kept a horse trailer, he could hire himself out as a ranch hand anywhere. He'd probably have to go to New Mexico or Arizona. Somewhere far enough away where no one had heard his name or knew the mistakes he'd made. It wouldn't be Texas, but at least he'd be in a saddle and he'd eat. What would Aaron do? He was resourceful. He had lied his way into a fake persona. He could probably figure out a way to make it.

The ranch hands were good men. It wouldn't be held against them that the family they worked for had fallen apart. They could find employment anywhere. Maybe Larry would even go work cattle in Nebraska with the cousin he didn't like. Gracie would be fine. Some state program that would take care of a girl with her condition who had no place to go.

Carl could... well, Carl knew machines. He could get a job working on engines anywhere. He might only have a few good years left, but that shouldn't stop anyone from hiring him... right? Maybe he had some money saved up so he could take care of himself in his old age. Jake always figured he'd stay here at home until he died, but Carl would have to leave like everyone else.

Rosalia could be a cook, or a housemaid anywhere. Too bad she never married. She would have children by now who could take care of her in her old age, but there were other ranches that needed someone who could cook. Surely there were...

But what if there isn't?

What would Rosalia do if she never found another

place around Crane to go? Was there someplace else she could live? Would she go back to Mexico? She never talked about relatives. Could she last on the money she had? What if she got old and needed someone to take care of her? What if there wasn't anyone there for her?

In the end, Jake didn't have enough good answers, and things didn't add up. Jake couldn't believe it would ever work out for the two of them. The image of Carl dying alone in some poor house with no one to remember him hit Jake in the gut. The thought of Rosalia sitting somewhere cold struck Jake in his soul.

The brand that hung over the driveway, the Weathers' "W," someday soon wouldn't be there. Someone else would come in and make it his own. What if he didn't like where Jake's mother was buried? What if he did something to her favorite spot? *What if none of them makes it?*

"I have to do something."

His own voice startled him. Jake's heart started racing. He couldn't let this happen. He *wouldn't* let this happen. Jake's story didn't deserve a happy ending, but he'd be damned if theirs didn't. He studied the foreclosure letter in his hand... *no.*

He made up his mind. "I have to move."

Jake stood up and walked back toward the house, but thoughts of urgency and his desperation made their way into his stride. He ran the whole way as best he could. No time to waste.

As he ran with everything his lame leg had to give, he looked at the sky and spoke to God. "Mend us, Lord...

mend us."

The house came into view, the house he needed to save. He ran up the stairs and into the office. Client contacts his father kept were next to the schedule of orders. He flipped back to the last delivery. Jake went forward and made a list of all the shipments they missed and the clients they let down... *Have there really been that many?* It finally clicked with Jake how long everything had been broken, much time passed since they functioned.

Starting with the first name, he called every customer they had failed. He left messages with some and got through to others. He needed to convince them that things were just fine at the ranch. Yes, Samuel Weathers had died. Grief over the loss of their father contributed to the missed orders and failed returns, but the company was ready and confident.

Jake needed to convince them all of this, to sound confident. But he knew he couldn't. So he lied.

Some former clients wanted nothing more to do with the Weathers' ranch. They couldn't trust them anymore, but some of them agreed. Jake offered them good faith reduced rates. He figured with the money left in the ranch's account and the profits to come from the reduced rates, they might survive, if absolutely nothing went wrong. Jake promised to get the clients the animals they needed immediately so he scheduled pick ups from dawn until dusk, every day over the next week.

After eight hours at the desk, Jake had made a good start. Next he needed to go plead to the bank for mercy and pay some of what they owed. Payments were due at many other businesses, but this was a good way to rebuild.

With two hours until the bank closed, Jake got in the truck and drove to town. He stumbled through the doors and sat down at the desk of one of the bankers he knew.

Jake showed up with the company checkbook and a hand ready to write checks. He pleaded and begged Mr. Wall, explained why they had been tardy, and said that things would be back to normal after this. He even pointed out to the man the tremendous business their ranch brought to the bank and why they should be helped.

At last the banker agreed and Jake wrote a check out in the amount they owed. But then he found out he was not allowed to write checks. His name wasn't on the company.

"… so, there's money in there, but I can't get access to it?"

"No, your name isn't primary. The only name on the accounts is Samuel Weathers."

"But if the money is in there, how is it supposed to get used?" Jake said.

"According to your father's will, the person he left the ranch to would have to bring the proper documentation before we could put his name on the accounts. Your father did have a will, didn't he?"

Jake was already out the door. He needed to see the estate lawyer before the office closed, but by the time he arrived, it was locked up. "Damn," Jake said under his breath in frustration.

Then a car pulled out from behind the building. "Mr.

Phenix!" Jake tried to flag the driver down.

"Jake Weathers," Mr. Phenix tilted his head. "What can I do for you?"

"Sir, I'm sorry to bother you, but we're very interested in taking care of my father's will. Our operations are at a standstill because my father's name is still primary on the business."

"Yes, I've telephoned the house a few times to try and arrange an appointment but haven't been able to get through."

"Sorry about that. Things have been kind of hectic."

"Not to worry. We just need all parties involved and a certificate of your father's death at my office. Then we can distribute everything as necessary," he said.

"All right." Jake nodded. "So who needs to be at your office? Who all did my father leave his estate to?"

Mr. Phenix's mouth drooped. "Why, your brother... he left everything to your brother."

Jake had trained himself to expect this, but hearing it still got him a little. *Wow.* He cringed and clenched his fist.

"I'll be at my office tomorrow morning at eight." The lawyer drove off.

The next morning, Jake woke Aaron at seven. "We're leaving in twenty minutes, Be ready."

Aaron rolled over and pulled the blanket over his face.

Jake tore the blanket away. "If you're not dressed when I come back, I'll drag you outside and tie you in the front seat of the car."

Three minutes early, Jake made good on his threat.

All the necessary paperwork from the house sat stacked between them.

When Mr. Phenix pulled up to his office, Jake and his brother were already waiting. They followed him inside and waited for him to get everything together. Then Jake watched his brother sign his name. Mr. Phenix notarized it and made it official. Aaron Weathers was the name on the ranch.

"Now I'll send these into the property registers office in Dallas," Mr. Phenix said. "Within a few days we should get the papers back making it all official."

"I'm sorry, Mr. Phenix, but did you say it takes a few days to get the paperwork back?" Jake said.

"Usually it does. Between the postal service and the line of paperwork to be filed in Dallas," Mr. Phenix explained.

"Could you give me the address of the office in Dallas?"

After they left the lawyer's office, Jake didn't drive Aaron up to the house. He stopped at the end of the driveway and let Aaron out of the car. His brother could walk the rest of the way. Jake had to get going.

In desperation, he drove by himself the eight hours to Dallas. He found the public office a half hour before it closed. Inside he begged and pleaded his way to the man who took care of the records. Fifteen minutes later, Jake drove away with the official filed and necessary documents.

He drove through the night, stopping at three a.m. beside the road to close his eyes for half an hour, and made it back to the Weathers' ranch at the crack of dawn. For the second morning in a row, he dragged Aaron into town at eight o'clock.

Jake showed Mr. Wall all he needed to see. The brothers paid what they owed and shuffled some of the funds around with Aaron present. At the end, they shook hands with the man and left Mr. Wall hopeful that he could continue to do business with the Weathers after so many years of success.

But Jake wasn't finished yet.

Larry looked surprised when he turned from where he sat at the bar to find Jake standing there.

"You ready to work?" Jake said.

"Yes?" Larry raised an eyebrow.

"We're rolling tomorrow morning like always."

Jake found some of the other ranch hands and told them when and where to be. He stopped at Carl's bunkhouse on the way to bed to inform him that tomorrow would be bright and early. Rosalia would have breakfast ready.

And that week was the single busiest week any of them had ever encountered while pushing horns. From sun up to sun down, they moved cattle. A rational boss would never layer so many shipments so close together, but this was not a rational time.

Once a day, Jake hauled Aaron somewhere to sign papers in order to fully gain control of the entire Weathers' empire. And at the end of the week, Jake rested.

CHAPTER 25

Birthright

J ake knew the ranch was a patched ship. It might make it to port or sink along the way, but for now, for this day, the wind filled the sails. Five weeks since the boss died, and steers came and went. The crew got up for breakfast everyday and Jake passed out orders with no time to spare. The ranch had to endure. He worked until his hands bled. Carl stood right there with him. The ranch hands remained.

Today was a sunny day.

Jake did some calculations. The ranch was close to regaining breathing room again.

"Aaron, we're going to the bank today." Jake leaned through Aaron's door.

"I don't think—"

"Be outside in a half hour." Jake left him.

When his brother came out of the house, he wore a large hat and high collar. Jake guessed it was a disguise. As the pair drove to town, Jake briefed Aaron on all that he had to accomplish once inside.

Jake pulled into the parking lot and threw the truck in

park. "Get going."

"Aren't you coming?" Aaron raised his eyebrows.

"No, I'm going over this paperwork. They don't need both of us. It's not hard, you can do it." Jake looked over the top of his sunglasses. "Go on."

Aaron sighed and got out of the car. He walked into the bank with his head down, then headed to Mr. Wall's desk.

Jake sat with the windows down reading the papers. Sometimes customers walked by his truck and he nodded at them.

When his brother exited the bank, Aaron's head hung so low and he moved so fast that he crashed into a passerby.

"I'm so sorry," Aaron stammered and looked up. He drew back. "Oh... hi, Jenny," he forced the words out.

She looked at him with hurt in her eyes. And Aaron seemed to finally realize how much pain he could cause another individual. Jenny had gotten the worst of it. She lowered her head and walked away.

"Wait..." Aaron begged. "I'm so sorry..."

The young woman turned back to him. But the pain Jake saw on her face seemed due to much more than Aaron's broken heroism. She looked into Aaron's weak eyes as tears slowly stole hers.

As she gently cradled her abdomen, years and years of regret painted her face. The secret that hurt the most was theirs together. "She might have been beautiful." She left him.

Aaron turned towards the truck, decades of regret on his face, and threw up in the gutter before climbing in.

"Please take me home."

All the way home, the brothers never spoke.

Jake looked at the clock. Two a.m. Since dinner, he'd been reading the books in the office, getting an idea of every little deal and detail related to the Weathers family. He couldn't believe how many investments they owned, ones his father never told him anything about it.

The family owned extensive elements of railroads, parts of banks. They rented out homes in Dallas, San Antonio, and Austin. Jake laughed at himself for panicking a month before when he thought the ranch was in an imminent shutdown and they would all be homeless.

He now saw that the ranch was by far their biggest source of revenue, but its collapse would be much more than survivable. He wanted to make sure that control of all their assets would be seamless. How dishonest people could be—so many strangers had a hand in their affairs.

Jake didn't trust anyone so he wrote down all the property managers' names and their contact numbers. He checked the names of each bank, then listed the names and contact information of the major railroad partners. Jake would force his brother to call them all the next day to make sure everything still ran smoothly

Jake pulled out the controlling deed from the safe. The single document listed everything from the ranch to railroads, properties to banks, even every vehicle and horse. His father had been very thorough. A few lines down, Mr. Weathers signed it over to Aaron. Aaron's shaky signature exposed the trembling hand which crafted it.

A noise that sounded like the front door came from the hall, interrupting Jake's work. *Who is up at this hour?*

He stood and walked from the office, taking quiet steps to the front of the house. He peered out the window just in time to see a figure disappear into the barn. Jake opened the door and crept outside without making any noise. Tracing the dark figure's steps, he approached the side of the barn. He still held a handful of papers and should have left them inside

Silent step by silent step he edged along the barn until he came to the open door. Someone rustled around inside. Jake peered into the darkness but couldn't see. He slipped through the door and found the barn's light switch. He flicked it on, sending a flood of dim illumination.

Aaron nearly keeled over in surprise. He clutched his chest and whipped around.

"Aaron?" Jake stepped into the barn. "What are you doing out here?"

Aaron was frozen, "...Uh, who, me?...nothing." The rise in his voice didn't sound convincing at all, like a little boy sneaking cookies before dinner.

Jake tilted his head.

Aaron clutched the keys to one of the trucks in his hand. In the passenger seat was a suitcase full of clothes, next to a wad of cash from the office safe and a bag of food from the kitchen.

"Aaron... you can't leave. What are you thinking?" Jake looked his brother in the eye.

Only a child glared back at him. Aaron ground his teeth in anger before the flood of emotions came pouring through. "YES, I CAN! I CAN LEAVE ANYTIME I WANT!"

"No, Aaron, you can't. The ranch can't do business if you're not here," Jake said. "Don't you understand?"

"WHY! I never even do anything anyways! You don't need my help! You've got this handled and always have!"

"Aaron, you're the owner. We can't even pay the electric bill without you here. Plus what? You can't outrun lawyers and the banks." Jake tried to speak calmly. "Everything will end."

"No it won't! You'll figure it out!"

"There is nothing to figure out," Jake said. "If you're not here, it all ends and this whole thing dies. Carl and Rosalia end up on the street. The street, Aaron! To die cold and alone. We're all they have. You gone means everything's gone. We'll lose all the hired hands. The cattle die where they are. Is that what you want? Is it? UNDERSTAND THIS!"

The air in the barn dripped thick with tension. It felt like the building would crumble.

"It's not my issue!" Aaron opened the truck's door. Jake kicked it shut before Aaron got in, denting the door. His brother looked over at him, shocked.

"Yes, Aaron, it is!" Jake's eyes flared.

"WHAT'S YOUR PROBLEM?" Aaron yelled.

Jake grabbed him by his collar and pinned him hard against the truck. Aaron went limp in his hands.

"My problem is that I'll be damned if I'm going to let

a selfish little prick like you bring all this down! Men far better than you built this!" Jake applied more pressure. "YOU will not be the end! You're staying here if I have to break both your damn legs and lock you in a room. You hear me? You're staying! I'll see this whole damn wreck go up in flames before I see you leave!"

Aaron's eyes flitted between the open door and his brother. His jaw sagged but no words came out as he gasped for air. He melted in his brother's hands. "But, Jake! I can't stay! I can't!" he yelled. "I CAN'T!"

"What the hell is this all about anyways?" Jake shoved him back against the truck.

His brother whimpered, his crying gave way to sobbing. "I can't be here anymore! This place hates me for what I've done! I'm not asking for forgiveness from anyone! I know I don't deserve it! But I can't... I CAN'T BE HERE!" Aaron shuddered.

"Well, that's tough! Deal with it! There's worse things than being hated!"

Aaron clawed at the front of Jake's shirt. "BUT I CAN'T!" he said, slurring his words. "NOW DAD'S DEAD!" He bent over heaving. "THERE'S NOTHING! I CAN'T! I CAN'T! I CAN'T!" He coughed through his sobs.

Jake jerked Aaron upright and punched him hard across the face, shutting him up and sending him to the barn floor. Aaron lay still, clutching his cheek.

Jake towered over his brother, looking down at the hysterical mess. Aaron's eyes were lost in despair, and Jake knew he wouldn't recover.

The papers still in his hand caught Jake's eye. On top was the most important, the deed and right to all things Weathers. Then Jake knew. He looked down Aaron squirming on the ground. "Give it to me."

"Huh?" Aaron wept.

Jake hoisted him from the floor with arms that had been tossing hay bales for years. "Give it to me."

"What do you mean?"

"Sign over the ranch."

"No—"

"You want to leave this place? Fine. Just as soon as you give me control." Jake laid the papers out on the hood of the truck.

"But..." Aaron sounded somewhere between desperation and hesitation.

Jake tightened his grip. "Sign it and I'll let you go. You can get your freedom. Escape all this."

Aaron eyed the pen, then his brother. He sighed and with a few strokes, he laid the ink down and signed over his birthright. In that instant, the older became servant to the younger.

As he finished the final page, Jake pulled the papers away. He let go of his brother. Aaron fell to the floor and leaned against the truck's wheel. Jake folded the deed and put it in his pocket. He looked at his brother again—his poor, scared, weak brother—and felt sorry for him. Aaron sat defeated with nothing left, like a varmint trapped in a cage.

Jake tossed Aaron the keys to the hot rod. Aaron stared

at them in his palm and looked up at his brother, confused.

"You can't take the truck. We need it here." He reached down and offered his hand to his brother.

Aaron gazed at it before he finally took it. Jake pulled him from the ground. Moments later, Aaron climbed inside the car. Jake shut the door to the hot rod. Disbelief crossed Aaron's face when he turned the key. The engine fired.

Jake leaned down to the window one last time. "And Aaron, we'll always be here when you need us." Jake gave his brother a smile.

Aaron nodded with a half smile before he headed down the driveway.

Jake couldn't guess where he would go or what he would do. It could be weeks, months, or never. Maybe he would see his brother again, maybe not. In his heart, he hoped his brother would settle someplace where he could make it.

As the taillights disappeared into the darkness, Jake stood in the driveway, the last of the Weathers.

All during the early morning hours, he walked through the dark house. Jake struggled to process what had happened and felt as though he had been watching someone else out there in the barn.

It was late, and he should have gone to his room. The door to his father's office clicked open ... to Aaron's office... to *his* office...

As Jake sat in the chair behind the desk something changed. It was *his* desk now. The walls, the floors, the big heavy desk became his. His fingertips went over papers strewn across the surface, each standing for something, some piece of land, some share of a business. They were *his*.

He wanted this for so long, before he had ever really realized it. This ranch was his blood. He was born here and he would die here. Every hill and fencepost, every tree and creek, every rock and all the dust... they were his now. He could protect it until the end of his days. He, the younger brother, that other Weathers boy, the one in the brace, was master.

He sat in the chair, king of anything, pondering his realm. *Where will I begin?* The Weathers were almost gone, but the ranch... the ranch would live on.

Dark skies gave way to hints of gray. Dawn crept over the horizon and cast hazy light through the windows, but Jake was miles away on Rio as the sun rose. They passed over the land he had seen a million times before. Today was as never before. Today was the beginning of the rest. His name, not just the Weathers, but Jacob Hebert Weathers would be engraved on everything.

He felt a little nervous, a little unsure, but enough like a tough cowboy who could make it happen for the sake of the acres he loved, and the people who loved him. Their futures were in his hands. He contented himself to get through this day, the first day, and then worry about tomorrow.

Jake came in firm and swift to breakfast. He looked them all in the eye as he gave them orders for that first day. When they finished their meal, one by one they passed through the front door and went to work.

Carl waited behind until only the two of them remained.

"I walked into the office this morning." He slid the signed deed across the table. "How very interesting." He grinned.

Jake nodded to him.

The day was good. Everything went well. Jake had an answer for every question. It was a new feeling, not having anyone to please, no respect to earn. He didn't have the weight of his unreliable brother on his shoulders nor the burden of his father. Jake took the freest breaths of his life.

Later, Jake drove to town and took the deed to the county office. He let them know he was now the owner of the Weathers' industry. And he didn't stop there. He spent a week driving around Texas checking in on all the family holdings and letting them know he was in charge. After all, if he didn't, everything would go under and he couldn't let it.

Mr. Phenix traveled with Jake as they barged into every bank and office that had even the most minute connection to the Weathers' holdings. After seven days, no one had any doubt that Jacob Herbert Weathers was the new chief and captain of everything.

Over the course of business, he wrote his name on every transaction. When the hands of the men they dealt with needing shaking, Jake did so. And he felt thankful that Carl stood next to him every day on the ranch.

A month went by. The ranch produced stronger than ever. Things operated perfectly and business went smoothly. The only difference? The Weathers' house remained a few residents short. It gave the structure a very hollow feeling.

Jake owned the ranch at last, the very future he loved more than any other in all the world. He had everything he ever wanted. He could lead the ranch for another hundred years.

The energy of running the ranch carried Jake for a while. When he rode the horse, he was on top of the world, but he couldn't spend every moment on the horse. Evenings and nights, the house felt so quiet.

Two days later during the afternoon, Jake stood in the barn beside Rio. He brushed the magnificent steed's coat as he started thinking.

From a legal standpoint, Jake now had money and leverage. And in that moment, one thing haunted him. He missed his sister.

Jake decided to change his environment in a way that would make him happy. He put down the horse's brush and led Rio into the corral. The thought got his blood pumping as he ripped the truck keys off the nail from which they hung in the barn.

Jake strode from the barn and climbed in the truck. Pulling the vehicle around in front of where Carl sat, he called through the window. "You coming?"

Carl grinned. "You look like a man that knows what he wants out of life."

"Let's go get it, then."

Carl didn't ask any questions and joined Jake in the truck. "I knew this day would come."

Jake floored toward the Odessa city line.

"Jake, are we going to get your sister?" Carl said.

"Not yet," was all Jake said. He turned right.

The sign out front read "Sweets." The people gathered at the outdoor ice cream parlor stared as the rusty pickup flew into a parking spot near the patio, its tires squealing and whining.

"Uh… sir? Can I help you?" the ice cream shop manager said.

Jake limped, grabbing his braced leg in pain. "Oh, it hurts! It hurts so bad!" Jake cried out to the crowd.

The manager shot a concerned look to his customers. "Uh…sir? Sir? How can I help you?"

"OW! It hurts! Help me! Help me! "Jake grabbed his leg and closed the distance between them.

A look of sincere consideration came across the manager's face. He stood there frozen as Jake limped closer.

"OW! Oh! The pain! The pain!" Jake cried out, as closer he came.

When he came close enough, he righted himself and struck the manager in the jaw with the force of thunder. The blow to his chin lifted the manager off the ground. He flew back—absent from gravity and absent from time— and fell through the air, slamming hard on a tabletop.

Not a sound hung in the air. No one reacted to the mad visitor who came out of nowhere and put an angry fist to the shop owner.

Jake was wild eyed but knew exactly what he was doing. He grabbed the man's collar sprawled on the table with solid fists and hoisted him close. "LOOK AT ME!"

The man forced himself to meet Jake's eyes.

"Do you see that man?" Jake pointed over to the truck in which wide-eyed Carl sat. Jake pulled him tighter. "Do YOU see *that* man?"

The manager offered a feeble nod.

"His name is Carl Jamison. Do you hear me? CARL JAMISON!! He is ten times the man you could ever hope to be! I've seen him calm the wildest of broncos and fix the most degraded trucks in the same afternoon! He can work a ranch better than any other Texan you've ever met! He'd be smarter than you if you studied a lifetime! You are not good enough to walk the same ground as him or breathe the same air! Go home and pray to God that one day you can make amends! You're not worthy to look into his eyes and you will never, EVER, refuse him service again! Do you hear ME?"

"Yes." The man whimpered.

He slammed the man once more. "Do you *hear* ME?"

This time the man yelled, "Yes...YES!" His eyes teared up.

Jake stared into his eyes, burning a path to his soul for a second longer. Then Jake dropped him back on the table.

Jake didn't say anything as he hopped back into the vehicle and fired up the V-8. He sought neither approval nor gratitude from Carl. He simply decided from now on, he would be a loyal friend.

Carl nodded. "Thank you, Jake."

"You don't have to thank me for what you deserve."

CHAPTER 26

Gracie's Brother

J ake didn't seek out a parking spot at the state children's home. Somewhere between the parking lot and the sidewalk, he stopped and nearly ripped the door off the hinges as he stepped out of the vehicle and his boots hit the pavement.

The Whaley House was a building, plain and simple. The state had built it for utility principles without pleasing any aesthetic principles.

It wasn't as cold a place as Jake envisioned. The staff must've done the best they could with the budget from the state. Plenty of kids surely benefited from the program they ran.

This place might be meant for other kids, but not his Gracie. He bore no ill will against this place. Jake didn't come to burn it down. He just came for her.

He paused for half a moment. "Okay, Jake. Go and get your sister back," he said under his breath and marched up the front walk with the determination of Napoleon. Carl followed a few steps behind.

Jake's plan was simply to explain who he was and why he had come. It would be best to remain calm, but his pumping adrenaline got the best of him. A loud clamor erupted in the wake of his vigor as the front doors crashed open.

All the people in the reception area snapped their heads in his direction. He wanted to give them angry looks for their stupidity in expecting him to be calm, but he knew it would be best to be cordial.

"Oops!" he smiled. "Doors are a little lighter than I imagined…"

They just stared at him. One little boy focused on his brace, but Jake didn't have time to worry about it.

"Ahhem…" Jake cleared his throat.

A woman about Jake's age rolled her chair over to the counter. "May I help you?"

"Yes. I'm Jake Weathers, Gracie Weathers' brother. I'm here to pick her up."

"Excuse me?" she said with confusion in her voice.

"I'm Jake Weathers. My sister is a resident here," Jake looked her in the eye, "I'm here to take her home."

"Uh, sir, taking a patient out is quite a process."

"Doesn't have to be, just bring her on out."

She stepped away. "Let me get the floor manager." Moments later she returned with another woman who had an air of being in charge.

"My name is Joy. How may I help you?" she stuck out a confident hand.

Jake looked at it before he took it, confused about why they were having such a hard time with his request. "Hi, Joy? My name is Jake. I'm here to take Gracie Weathers home."

"Gracie Weathers? Yes, she was only checked in here a couple of months ago." She tilted her head. "Now did any of the medical staff contact you about her case?"

"No, I'm just here to take her home. I really don't know how much clearer I can be. A mistake was made when she was brought here... a miscommunication if you will."

That sounds good enough. "Now I'm here pick her up. So... Joy? Just go ahead and bring her and her things out here and we'll get out of your hair."

"No medical staff contacted you about her condition?"

"No, we just want to take her home." Jake tapped his finger on the desk.

"I mean...well...we can't *just* let you take her home." She drew back.

"Um... okay. Is there anyone who can *just* let me take her home?" he said, annoyed.

"Well, it's up to the doctors when a patient is in a condition to go home."

"Then why don't you send that doctor out here so I can speak with him?"

"I'll... I'll try to find him." She turned away, looking hurt. She fumbled through a mess of keys before she found the one that opened the door leading back into the realms of the clinic. The door shut behind her.

Most of the people in the reception area were an audience to his interaction. When he looked back at them, they buried their faces in magazines and books. Fluorescent lamps above lit the tile floor. Almost all the chairs were empty.

Jake looked at Carl and rolled his eyes.

When another door leading off the reception room clicked open, Carl gave Jake a look that said, "Go to it."

A sweet-mannered nurse waited on the other side of that door. "Mr. Weathers?"

"Yes,."

"The doctor will see you now." She stepped aside to let Jake through. When she hesitated to include Carl, Jake said, "He's with me."

The nurse led them down a hallway lined with offices and took them to a door inscribed with "Dr. Charles Simms." She opened the door and led them inside. The room had a desk with chairs for the two of them. Only lamps lit the room, as there were no windows. Blue wallpaper covered the walls. The nurse informed them that the doctor would be right with them. They sat quietly as they waited.

After a while, the door opened as a red-haired doctor came through. "Sorry it took so long. I was dealing with patients, you see."

They shook his hand. The doctor settled into the chair behind the desk. He buried his nose in a file the nurse left on his desk, "Mr. Weathers, correct?"

"Yes." Jake hadn't quite grown used to being addressed by his father's title.

"But now... you're the son of Samuel Weathers, correct? You're Gracie's brother?"

"I am."

"How can I help you?" Dr. Simms said.

Jake was happy to answer. "You can bring my sister to me so I can take her home."

"Take her home?" Dr. Simms repeated.

"Yes. That's why I've come. She was brought here by mistake," Jake said.

The doctor buried his head in the file for another moment. "Now... it was your father, Samuel Weathers, who checked her in, correct?"

"Yes, that's correct."

He looked at the file again. "And he is since deceased?"

"Yes."

"Oh... I'm terribly sorry."

"That's fine, doctor. All men die," Jake said. "Now could you please go and get Gracie?"

"Well, now, that's just it." The doctor scratched his head. "Have you come here under the impression that Gracie is going home with you today?"

"Yes." Jake only had patience for bluntness.

The doctor looked him over. "I see... well, I'm afraid it is a bit more complicated than that."

Jake leaned back in his chair. "I don't see what's so complicated about it. You go and get Gracie. I take her home. End of story."

Dr. Simms laced his fingers together and sat his hands in his lap. "Well, you see, Gracie can't leave with you today as there are all sorts of issues. One, you're not registered as her legal guardian. Your father was. Now in the event of his death I'm not sure who has custody of her, but in the absence of your father, it's probably the state. Furthermore, I understand Gracie was brought here because of an incident that happened at your family's ranch, some sort of accident?" He waited for Jake's confirmation.

"Yeah, something happened, but that's been taken care of." Images of the bulls' carcasses paraded through Jake's mind.

"Really?" Dr. Simms shifted in his seat. "All the same. Gracie is a very special girl, with special needs. I'm not convinced Gracie is safe living in such an environment as a ranch."

"Oh, trust me doctor," Jake sat up straight. "It's exactly where she belongs."

"Well, I'm not so sure." Dr. Simms objected.

"I am."

Dr. Simms studied him. "You know, Mr. Weathers, I've worked with Gracie. She needs a lot of help. Frankly, even if you were her legal guardian, I find it hard to believe the state would agree with you. A girl like her needs to be here."

Jake looked back at the man. "That's how you feel, is it?"

"Actually, yes, that's how I feel."

"Even if you were to go to the state and apply for custody of the patient, I'm not so sure I would recommend letting her leave this facility. She may simply have to stay here."

Jake cocked his head, "Is that a fact?"

"Yes, that's a fact."

"So you're not going to let me take Gracie home today?"

"No, I'm afraid I'm not."

"Okay." Jake stood up. "That's fine." He left the doctor at his desk.

Dr. Simms stood.

"Okay," Jake said as he stepped into the hallway and looked around. A locked, caged door that led back to the residents of the facility loomed to his left. He headed towards it.

"Mr. Weathers? The door you're looking for is that way." The doctor pointed to the lobby.

"Okay, that's fine." Jake calmly pulled on the caged door. It was locked.

"Mr. Weathers!" Dr. Simms called out as he rushed over.

"Shhh... Calm down." Jake gave the doctor a look like he thought the doctor was the craziest person earth. The fluorescent lights flickered above.

"What are you doing, sir?" Dr. Simms raised his hands in disbelief.

"Hey, hey, it's okay. It's fine. Don't worry." Jake put his one hand up to calm the doctor down, while his other hand found the fire extinguisher hanging on the wall. Dr. Simms watched in bewilderment as Jake used the fire extinguisher to batter through the door. It crunched open. Jake passed through to the restricted area.

"STOP HIM!" Dr. Simms cried out.

Jake heard a thud and Dr. Simms fell quiet. Carl followed him.

Jake charged in. "Gracie!??" he called out, his voice boomed through the hallways.

"Sir! Sir! You can't be in here!" Joy came running from behind a desk.

"Sure I can." Jake looked at her like it was perfectly natural for him to be back there, trying to confuse her protests.

"But Mr. Weathers! Mr. Weathers!"

Jake's call down the hallways drowned out her voice. "Gracie? Gracie?" He ventured farther into the fortress, his boots colliding with the tile floor. "Gracie? Gracie?"

Doors slammed and trays dropped as staff swarmed him from all sides.

Among the orderlies that burst forward to control the intruder and the confused cries of the nurses came a giggle, a laugh in the distance. Jake paused and focused hard.

"HI!"

He rounded the corner. He couldn't care less for the crowd that bombarded him from every side. Everything stopped... there she was, ...down a long lonely hallway, waiting for him.

She looked happy and surprised to see him. And in that moment, she tore away from the nurse who held her and raced towards him.

Jake couldn't hear anything but the sound of her feet

running at him with everything she had. He came for her.

Everything may have collapsed. Thunder might shake the earth for all they knew. He didn't care. They could have been alone standing in that hallway. She jumped into him and Jake closed his arms around her and hoisted her into a warm embrace.

He took a moment to hold her, soaking in her unending, unconditional love. He had his sister back. And now it was time to leave. He turned to Carl. "Let's go."

With Gracie clinging to him, he and Carl marched through the crowd of protesters in a world shaken up. He didn't turn to the right or to the left as the staff screeched and hollered at him from every side. He only focused on the door that led out and walked through anyone who got in his way. Nurses and orderlies, trying to do their jobs, fell by the wayside.

The cries and pleas from the staff finally alerted the strongmen they kept on staff. Two tall and broad orderlies showed up at last and stood in the Weathers' way. "Sir! Please put the patient down and leave the premises."

A new obstacle stepped into his path. He stopped for a moment and shifted Gracie in his hold. He looked the two of them straight in their eyes until they drew back at his intensity and cringed in the aura of his energy.

"Listen to me." Jake glanced at their nametags, "Richard? Eric?" He waited for a dumb nod from them.

"This is my sister," he said in calm and slow tones. "I am taking her home today. And not you or the devil will stop me. If you get in my way, it'll be the worst mistake of your life. You will lie on the floor in desperate regret of the choice you made. This is my time to leave, and it's your time to get out of my way."

In speechless compliance they stepped aside.

Jake carried Gracie through the doors. Next came the reception room. Then Jake kicked the doors of the Whaley House open and led his little sister hand-in-hand into the sun.

When the truck pulled up in front of the house, Rosalia stepped out onto the front porch. She lifted her hand to her eyes, shielding them from the blazing sun.

The little girl raced towards her as the cook fell to her knees. She looked up with sweet tears rolling down her face, "But, Carl...how? What?"

The old man nodded at Jake. "Not me, that guy."

"She didn't belong there," Jake said.

Gracie glowed again, running around the house and sitting in every chair. His little sister found the most unusual things to inspect, making sure they had not changed too much in her absence. She stopped at her father's old office, as though she was looking for someone.

"Oh darlin'." Carl smiled at her. "He's not here right now." Maybe that answer would hold her for a night, maybe a week. Maybe she would never ask again.

No work was done the rest of the day. The remaining hours were devoted to piggyback rides around the house and laps on Rio with Jake. Rosalia resorted to her usual gift of love and baked an exceptionally large cake with pink frosting.

Gracie ate all the frosting by herself.

That night was the first time Jake Weathers looked down the road.

Carl joined him in the driveway. "They haven't come yet, but they will. Someday soon a car will come down the road and we'll have to answer for what we've done. They're not going to be happy with us. The question of her legal guardianship will be raised."

"Let them all come. She's not leaving."

The next day when Jake left to push horns, Gracie waved from her window. *Yeah, it was worth everything.* And later that morning when Pete rode up to tell Jake the sheriff came to talk to him, it was still worth it.

"I heard you paid a little visit to the Whaley house up in Odessa," Sheriff Thompson said.

"I had to check out a patient," Jake said.

The sheriff chuckled, a little uneasy. "Check out a patient, eh? Well I guess that's one way of putting it. The attendants of the Whaley House would put it 'kidknapping.' You two realize you can't just take patients out—"

"Sir, Carl had no part of this. This was all me. He was only there as my employee. I could have fired him if he didn't come with me."

"Either way, you can't go pulling her out like that when you're not her legal guardian."

"I'm sorry to say that my father is dead. I'm her only relative left. That makes me her legal guardian."

"That's not for me to decide. Just be in the courthouse at twelve on Wednesday. Now I'm already doing you favors.

Legally, I should take her back to the Whaley house until the judge figures this out, but Deputy Baker is apparently a fan of yours. He's convinced me she's better off here for now." The sheriff looked over at little Gracie smiling in the sun. She held something shiny.

"Look, just be there on time. Lawyer up if you want or if you don't." Sheriff Thompson climbed into his car and spoke through the window. "And wear a tie." He fired the engine up.

"I appreciate you, Sheriff." Jake waved him off.

The sheriff nodded and pulled away.

Jake looked at his happy sister and it was worth it all the more. He stood there in silence. *What to do?*

Then Jake smirked at their bewildered faces as he mounted up on Rio and went back to work. After all, it wasn't Wednesday yet.

The morning of the hearing, Jake gave Gracie the hug of her life. He headed out and got into the truck. He hated the tie and pressed pants, but if it helped, he would wear them.

Carl climbed into the passenger seat with him.

Jake wore a little smirk on his face.

"What's the joke?" Carl said.

"You'll see."

At noon, the county courtroom had a small but attentive crowd. Judge Bryan sat behind his bench. Dr. Simms from the Whaley house sat at the plaintiff's table. He was with a nurse and the home's legal council.

Jake sat behind the defendant's desk with Carl and

two other men. One man was the biggest name in law in
the entire city of Dallas. The other man was his primary
competition. They were the two best attorneys to be found.
Jake had hired them both. Carl finally got the joke.

The bailiff started to read the trial report but was
interrupted. The room looked up as Deputy Baker came
in, apologized, wished Jake luck, and sat down behind
Jake. The judge nodded for the bailiff to begin again but
was interrupted a second time. Mandy, who repeated what
her fiancé had done, sat down next to him and behind
Jake.

The judge tried to recommence a third time but the
tidal wave had broken. The room watched in astonishment
as Mr. Johnson and those crazy old men he passed his days
with entered in a ruckus and sat behind Jake. Soon, Mary-
Lou came in with her mother. Even Sheriff Thompson came
in. Later Mr. Longer who taught Jake to fly stumbled into
the courtroom, no need to dress up. A few others arrived
as well. Pete and Larry were the final two.

Jake knew he could never thank these people enough.
He would try, Not today, but someday.

Carl looked at Jake and those who stood behind him.
His eyes moistened.

The staff of the Whaley House, daunted by Jake's
corner, began feeble statements. They described Gracie
and claimed she wasn't able to live in safety on a dangerous
place like a ranch. They cited her diagnosis and demanded
that their facility could not be intruded upon.

Then it was the defendant's turn. The artful, logical

words of Dallas' best sent the plaintiffs for a spin. They started out lightly, but eventually the two attorneys started trying to outdo each other. Between them, they built a fortress around Jake's claim to Gracie. Needless to say, before the judge announced his ruling, he called Jake to the bench.

"Mr. Weathers..." he said so only Jake could hear. "One word: overkill."

Jake returned to his seat. Then the people of Crane erupted in victory as the judge declared that Gracie wasn't going anywhere. She wasn't leaving home.

CHAPTER 27

Good Enough

Late one night, Jake, the owner of Weathers' Ranch, got a call from a neighbor. The man reported that someone driving along the road outside the Back Forty lost control of his vehicle and plowed down a hundred yards of fencing. The driver was fine, so fine that he kept going and left without telling anyone about the damage. All they left behind was a bumper, some broken glass, and a side-view mirror.

This time of year the Back Forty was a high volume area for the steers. Whenever it got cold the animals headed there. And Jake wasn't going to lose any cattle. He had already dismissed the ranch hands for the night and given them the next day off. They were nowhere to be found.

He could have woken up Carl, but something in him, maybe the thrill of pushing himself, maybe vanity, sent him out to the Back Forty alone to handle the problem at this miserable hour. Another part of him just wanted to let an old man sleep. So he went to handle the problem at this miserable hour.

At eleven o'clock, Jake loaded a truck up with some

lumber and tools and headed into the night. Rio followed by rope from the driver's seat of the truck. He didn't need the horse but he knew he'd appreciate the animal's company.

All Jake could do was start at one end and work the other way. He worked by the light of lanterns and by the truck's headlights. Many pieces of the fence were left intact, only knocked out of the ground. He had to replace the timber here and there, cutting the new piece to fit the old location. This was the only part of the ranch that had wood fences.

Hours slipped away as he finished the fence. The electric light of one of the lanterns died. Later, the oil ran out in the other. And still more in divine timing, as he drove that last fence post back into the ground and rigged up the final cross pieces, the engine of the truck sputtered and died as the last of its fuel ran through the engine. He had idled the vehicle to empty.

But this was it, routine: wonderful, simple, routine. After what Jake went through, he would always appreciate routine, which meant nothing bad was happening. Jake had gone through enough terrible things to last him years and years. Everything had been brought to the brink. And now it was all back.

How distant those days seemed now. The ranch seemed just as good or better than ever. The way Jake ran things these days no one would guess all the tragedy that had befallen them. Clients were waiting in line to do business with the Weathers Ranch.

With the fence secure at least for now, he and his horse

headed home around 5:45 in the morning. Everyone else would be getting up soon, but Jake wouldn't sleep that night. He would just wash his face, eat a meal, and keep going. He wouldn't tell anyone, they didn't need to tell him to slow down.

Rio's steps met the ground, the only sound in the crisp pre-dawn air. Cold hung in the air, hinting at autumn's final days as winter approached. Jake's breaths mixed with Rio's as they made their way back to the house. They were tired.

He liked moments like this. It was just he and his ranch... *my ranch*. Whoever would have thought it would end up like this?

Rosalia wouldn't be cooking breakfast. On days that Jake gave the staff off, she gained some much-needed sleep.

Later he fired up the stove for himself. A pair of eyes that never stopped smiling came around the corner into the kitchen.

"Hello!" Gracie said.

"Well, hi there," Jake chuckled.

She was such a funny girl. Weeks had passed since he became her legal guardian, then weeks and months as well. She was home to stay.

"Are you hungry?" Jake said.

An exaggerated nod was her answer.

"Okay, let's do something about that," he said. He pulled some flank steak and eggs out of the icebox and threw them in the skillet and poured Gracie a glass of milk. After reaching to the back of the shelf, Jake found a bottle of coke. He put the plates in front of them and they sat down at the table.

Gracie looked at hers and shook her head.

"What?" Jake said. "Don't you want that?"

Gracie shook her head again.

Curiosity led Jake further. "Well then, what do you want?"

A mischievous grin came over Gracie's face. She stood from the table and went to the icebox. She pulled out half a leftover cake from the night before. She looked at him with big puppy dog eyes.

Maybe it was his tired state, maybe he just wanted to spoil his sister. He laughed to himself. Rosalia could make Gracie eat healthy later.

Gracie ate cake for breakfast next to her big brother. The dogs were excited because they got a plate of steak and eggs. Jake helped Gracie get dressed and ready for the day.

Rosalia and Carl came around later that morning. It was a leisurely day at the ranch, except for Jake who kept finding little things to do. He fed the horses and climbed to the roof of the barn to nail down some shingles, ready for winter. At last the final nail head sunk and he sat back on the roof to take a moment's rest. The sun fought its way in and out of clouds. The clouds were winning. A northern wind kept the temperature from climbing.

He pulled his coat in tight around him and breathed warm air onto his hands, then put them into his pockets. His left hand crunched something he didn't remember being in there. He closed his hand around it and pulled it out. The folded, worn piece of paper was familiar. *Have I not worn this coat in that long?*

He unfolded the charcoal sketch of a tired rider on a weathered horse. Ellie had said it was supposed to be him. *Ellie...* she had been gone so long. He missed her every day.

In the days of chaos and the routine that followed, it became easy to block out thoughts of her, but when he slowed, he caught the smell of her hair in the wind or the taste of her mouth on his lips. *Where is she now?* Oh God, please let her be happy wherever she is. And safe.

Jake hoped she found a place that was home for her. He wanted happiness for her badly, but he remembered the way she looked when she left. Some horrid voice in the back of his mind let him know she probably wasn't doing her best.

Had he ever really walked these halls and ridden these pastures with her? Had he ever spent hours lost in her, in her complexities and in her simple ways? Had he really lit up as he did for her and held her through the rain? Had she ever really come at all?

In the days after Gracie's return, she stopped asking where her father had gone, content to send him on an infinite trip. Jake found a peace that had escaped him for years. And still, the ranch continued. His void was filled.

Aaron had never seemed a real presence in the house. He was always on the outside of things, a shadow coming and going in the corners of Jake's days. He never took up space and so left no space, nothing empty to remember him by.

But Ellie left a huge hole. Not just in Jake but in all of them. They all loved her. She had made them laugh. Her eyes were warm. She was so lovely. She was like a sweet song to people who had never heard music before. Her void was nothing that could be filled, only walked around. And the hole was never to be stared into. Its depth would cast a spell on its witness and put them into a haze.

But oh, how Jake missed her. There were so many things he wished to have just one more time...

Folding that crumpled paper, he quieted the memories with it. He went to throw it off the roof and into the wind, but stopped his arm and looked once more at the picture. He put it back in his pocket.

Jake climbed down from the roof and crossed the driveway for the house. Carl sat on the porch swing smoking his pipe. The old man offered Jake the seat next to him... really not so much an offer but a request. It had been a long time since Jake sat with Carl there. Jake worked into the dark hours of night daily and missed Carl's evening meetings with his pipe.

And surely, Jake could do that for a friend. The still day's only disturbance was the wake of the motion of the swing.

He sat down next to his old companion. The aroma of the aged tobacco surrounded them.

A long time passed. Maybe Carl just wanted to get Jake to rest a moment, or maybe he didn't want to sit this day on the swing alone. After several more puffs, he said, "Jake,

I'm really proud of you."

"What do you mean?"

"You've really taken over here and done what needed doing." Carl drew on his pipe.

"Thanks," Jake shrugged.

"No, Jake, I mean it. You've been working your tail off. You brought this ranch back from the verge. You pushed until your hands bled."

"Thanks, Carl."

"Jake, think about how you went and got your sister back. She never belonged there and you knew it and did something about it. And I know why you push this ranch so hard. I know you want to take care of this old fool and that lady who does the cooking around here. You want your sister to have something that makes her happy. I know you'll do whatever you have to..."

Jake's mind blurted out, *I'd die for this if I have to.* All he said was, "Really, Carl, thanks."

Maybe Jake understood, so Carl left it alone, but it woke a stream of thought in Jake. He really would die for this if he had to, any part of it. For Carl, for Rosalia, for Gracie, for the ranch, for the continuation of the Weathers' legacy, to always have a piece of Texas. He'd die for it, just like that man Carl told him about so long ago. That man... the one in Chicago. *Who was he?*

"Carl?" Jake stared off the porch. "What was the name of that man you saw killed in Chicago? The man who had the bakery?"

For all the paths Carl had walked, he needed no

reminding as he pulled that one moment from the annals of his memory. "Marcin…" Carl saw the old baker's face. "Marcin Grabowski."

"Marcin Grabowski…," Jake nodded slowly. "He never flinched when they were going to kill him."

"No, he didn't," Carl said. "He wasn't afraid. Because you see, Jake, any fear is simply fear of the unknown. It is the unknown that makes people afraid of death, of losing everything. It is the unknown that brings fear of the future. Marcin wasn't scared. For him there was no unknown. He knew exactly what he was made of. He knew he'd get up every time because that's what it would take to make it. And because of that, Jake, he knew exactly who he was. And once you know who you are, you are free. You cannot love, you cannot win, you cannot lose, until you know who you are, at least not properly. Marcin had pushed his limits and been pushed back by them his whole life. He had always known— when his moment came—exactly what he would do. He knew he would stand there, between his life's work and the men with the gun. Maybe it was only a whisper all his days, only shouted loud in his final moments, but he knew, somewhere in his soul. Because he knew who he was and what he was made of. He could always look a man in the eye and shake his hand because he respected himself. Marcin knew Marcin…"

"Marcin knew Marcin," Jake let the phrase roll off his tongue.

They sat there for a while longer as Carl exhaled clouds

from his pipe. Then the fire went out. Carl knocked his pipe empty on the side of the swing.

"Well, that old tractor ain't going to fix itself." Carl stood and descended the porch steps.

"Hey, Carl?" Jake's voice stopped Carl where he stood.

"Yes, Jake?"

"Do you know who you are?"

"Yes, Jake, I do."

"Did you like what you've found?"

Carl got an honest grin on his face and turned back. "Most of it, Jake, most of it. But I *know*, and that's what matters." He turned to leave.

"What was her name?" Jake called out. "The girl in Chicago?"

Carl didn't break his stride. "Hannah." He continued into the barn.

"Hannah." Jake's thoughts were all over the place, but he didn't fight them. He let them go.

He got onto that old partner of his, Rio, and headed away from the house.

Who am I? Who is Jacob Herbert Weathers? The roads came and went.

"Who?" he was thrown by the sound of his own voice as he realized that he spoke out loud, waking him from his thoughts. He hadn't paid attention to it, but somehow he had come to the place where his parents lay. He sat atop the steed and took in endless colors of fire the low sun had thrown against the sky.

"Who is Jake?"

The breeze brushed his face. Out of habit he reached down and patted Rio's neck. Rio, the horse he never doubted would be magnificent when all others had dismissed him. The horse he taught to fly.

That was something he knew about himself, making horses good for the job out here. He might not be the best, but he had done well with this one. What about riding them? He could outrun the devil on a horse if he had to. He had seen his share of cowboys, and he knew he more than ordinary.

"I'm uncatchable."

His skills on a horse made him good for working a ranch in west Texas. This and he had absorbed a lot of knowledge over the years, on the cattle and business end of ranching. His wasn't the best—a load of ranches dwarfed the Weathers' place—but this ranch survived just fine. He grinned to himself. Despite some of his novice business decisions, he had also learned from those mistakes and he wouldn't be making them again. *Yeah, maybe not one of those huge ranches, but this one, here and now... yeah, I can do it.*

As his eyes moved up, a vein outlined on his forearm, the way veins do when muscles are worked. Oh, they were worked. He had been hauling hay bales and wrestling cattle his whole life. His muscles were there for him when he needed them. No, he wasn't the fastest or the strongest, but he was fast and strong enough for what his life asked of him.

That leg, the one in the brace, had slowed him down for

half his life. *What's someone with a brace doing working a ranch?*

Not letting a brace keep him from doing what he loved, that's exactly what that man with the brace was doing. He wasn't going to let that brace put him in a cage. Because Jake, the rest of him, was too strong for that brace to keep him off the range. So why had he let it make him so uncomfortable with people? Why had he let their looks shame him? If they knew anything, they'd applaud him. He did more with one leg then they did with two. Forget them.

With one leg? He shouldn't be walking around with one leg. Hell, he shouldn't be walking around at all! Who walks away from a car crash and a plane crash in one lifetime? Who walks away? Someone who doesn't give up.

Maybe he didn't die because of that same thing in him that pushed him to work until his hands bled. Maybe it was passion that drove him. When the ranch was on the verge, it was passion that replaced sleep. It was, passion that pushed every steer and worked every herd. He hadn't stopped... and he never would.

Just like he hadn't stopped when he rode through the rain, he wouldn't let the storm turn him back. He needed to save Ellie, and the storm was dangerous. He could have died in the flood, but she needed him.

He had conceded to death and rode after her into the darkness. *Why?* Because he loved her... he loved her... he loved Gracie, Carl, and Rosalia, too, and his brother. It didn't matter which one of them it could have been. He would have ridden into the dark. Every time.

He looked up from his thoughts. He took in his pastures and his hills. He breathed in the west Texas wind; this was his spot. He was a single word on a page in the stories of history. The world didn't know of him in all the eternity that existed before him, and they would soon forget him after he was gone. But in the moment, in this corner of the world, *he* was Jacob Herbert Weathers.

He hadn't always been loyal to his friends but from this day on he would die for them. He knew what fears he had and how to overcome them. How much he could love a woman and the faith he had. Hard work didn't scare him and he knew how long it took him to get up from being punched in the face. He knew enough about himself to look people in the eye... *really* look them in the eye. No walls, nothing to hide behind.

There was nothing in the world to him like waking up to a west Texas sunrise. There was something eternally pure about riding a horse over a ridge, something cleansing about seeing his own blood after a hard day's work.

He could have left when everything was on the edge, but he hadn't. Circumstances hadn't chosen him; he'd chosen them.

Who he was, was in the nights he went without sleep to work the ranch until it made it. He was in the saving of the sister he loved and in the standing up after he had fallen. He was in the brace and he was better than it. No storm existed that he wouldn't race into when he needed to. This was his existence. He knew what he would die for and what he would live for.

He would not be the best nor the strongest. He would not be the fastest or the most able. And he would not be the bravest, but he *was* strong enough and fast enough. He was able enough and brave enough. And he *was* good enough.

Jake Weathers knew he could ride with any cowboy of all time and work cattle like any ranch hand should. He might not be able to run a piece of land as large as a county, but he could run this piece just fine. He would work and when he was tired, he would look inside himself for the passion he had for this life and keep going. He would work this place until it made it or see the whole thing go up in smoke. When he needed to be brave, he would be.

Jake became all this and more. And then, in the dusty fields of west Texas, it finally came to the boy, to the man— the thought that would free him, the thought that would take away his fear. Jake finally realized it: he was some sort of real man, good enough for this place and now. And he always would be, despite all things. He didn't need to have Carl tell him or need to feel his sister's hugs. He didn't even need the love of Ellie to find his identity. He had become whole on his own. *He was* Jake Weathers.

No man deserves anything, but Jake had just as much right to ask God as the next man. He could look anyone in the eye.

So it was settled. Jake knew who he was. He was no longer afraid. He knew what he was made of. He knew it was good enough. He knew who he was and had his peace.

Now then, what do I want?

Jake caught the old man watching him from the porch as he crossed from the barn to the pickup. A single tear rolled down Carl's check past a wide smile.

"Just make sure the trucks get out this week and keep the boys pushing. I'll call and check in," Jake said as he climbed in the truck.

Carl walked over and leaned against the vehicle. "Where you going?"

Jake narrowed his eyes, and peered into the sunset. "San Francisco... she's there. I'm going to bring her home."

The old man smiled. "Sure are a lot of people there. What are you going to say to them?"

"I'm Jake Weathers. I'm looking for a girl."

Carl stepped away. "Yeah. That sounds about right... boss." He looked west. "He's coming, Miss Ellie."

And Jake Weathers drove off for Odessa to catch the last train west. Never to be the golden son, but the other son, the burning one.

ACKNOWLEDGEMENTS

I'd like to thank my parents for their endless support and encouragement. Also, the crew at Violet Crown Publishers, specifically Cynthia Stone, for all their hard work. Jesus, for more than words can say. The Kings of Leon for providing the soundtrack to which I wrote. And Mr. Daniels, my writing buddy.

ABOUT THE AUTHOR

Born in Flint, Michigan, Alex Reed always longed for Texas. Wranglers, saddles, boots, and brawlers, he first arrived upon attending Baylor University. Living in Waco, his love affair with the state grew. After college, he moved to Austin and then to Houston. While working in child-care as well as a private investigator, he crafted this novel, dreaming of hooves and chasing sunsets.